DEN OF SNAKES

AN ACTION THRILLER

DAMIAN VARGAS

Den Of Snakes

ISBN: 9798636575139

Published by Sierra Bermeja Fiction

www.sbfiction.com

First published June 2020

Copyright © 2020 Damian Vargas. The author has asserted his rights to be identified as the author of this Work in accordance with the Copyright, Designs and Patents Act 1988.

www.damianvargasfiction.com

This is a work of fiction. All of the characters, organisations, and events portrayed in this novel are either products of the author's imagination or are used fictitiously.

All rights reserved. No part of this book may be reproduced in any form or by any electronic or mechanical means, including information storage and retrieval systems, without written permission from the author, except for the use of brief quotations in a book review.

DEDICATIONS

I am grateful to everyone that has supported me in any way, be it big or small, in the creation of this novel.

As with any creative endeavour, producing a finished work of art is inevitably 20% inspiration and 80% perspiration, and the encouragement of others is often the difference between getting a project to fruition, or abandoning it.

In particular I must thank my beta readers whose early feedback brought benefit to both myself, as the author, and all subsequent readers of the book.

In no particular order they are; Igor Gakalo, Lisa Corti, Judy Corti, Kathy Bryan, Joe Towey, Andy Visser, Adam Brierley, Vlad Modorcea and Rob James.

Lastly, the culmination of this book happened in early 2020, a time in which the negative forces of uncertainty, divisiveness, anger and fear threaten to send societies back several generations.

This book is therefore dedicated to anyone that has worked at any level to heal, educate or support others, to bring people and communities together, and to make our planet a better place for everyone and everything that inhabits it.

Damian Vargas, June 2020.

*"Quaking boughs above my head,
In morning wind the sky was red.
I could have stayed at home today,*
But wisdom comes to those that stray."

Unknown poet

CHAPTER ONE
THE GYPSY WOMAN

Salamanca, Spain. July 1985.

The well-travelled Citroen 2CV van trundled to a temporary halt outside the roadside cafe. The old car would have been lost from sight to anyone nearby, hidden as it was amidst the cloud of yellow dust that it threw up as it left the tarmac road and encountered the strip of rough land that passed for a car park. There were, however, no observers. At least, none that Eddie Lawson could see.

He thanked the vehicle's driver - a spritely octogenarian who had been kind enough to give Eddie a lift for the last forty kilometres. The old man had talked at Eddie at a rapid pace, and in an impenetrable Spanish accent for the entire journey. The man had appeared grateful for company, even if that company had been unable to respond with much more than a smile or an embarrassed grunt.

Eddie opened up his beleaguered wallet and attempted to offer his talkative driver some recompense. 'For your troubles,' said Eddie, but the man dismissed the offer with a wave and a chuckle.

'*Bien viaje*,' the man cackled through the open passenger window as he pulled away. Eddie waved, then slung his khaki backpack over his left shoulder and made his way towards the cafe.

The building was more than a little ramshackle, but it was well-lit and inviting. The whiff of smoked meat and strong cheese entered his nostrils the moment that he walked in, making his stomach rumble. He had not eaten for many hours. He surveilled the interior, then selected a table in a shaded corner, grateful for the respite from the relentless sun outside. The only other people he could see were two male youths sitting at a table in the middle of the cafe. They were both dressed in a worn denim and a dirty tee-shirt combo.

'*Hola, qué quieres chico?*' Eddie looked towards the source of the female voice. A waitress was stood just three feet away. How had he not heard her approach? He rubbed his eyes. She seemed to be in her late-twenties like him. She wore tight stonewashed blue jeans and a sleeveless tee-shirt that was plain black except for a small smattering of little pink stars. She had long brown hair tied into a neat bunch, and a thin gold necklace adorned her perfect neck. She was beautiful.

'Sorry, luv,' Eddie mumbled. 'No *hablo* Spanish'.

The woman fought to control an involuntary laugh then repeated her question, this time in English. 'I said, what do you like?' Eddie felt as if he was being drawn up into her brown eyes. The waitress cleared her throat. 'We have good tortilla,' she said. His face must have shown some sign of confusion, as she followed up with, 'Is omelette in English, no?'

Eddie nodded. 'That would be spot on...I mean, that's perfect, thanks. And a black coffee. Please'.

The waitress smiled, spun around on one heel and headed off towards the counter. As she passed the young men, one of them sat back on his chair with his legs in a provocative pose, put one hand on his crotch and said something in Spanish. His friend snorted with laughter, spilling beer on the table. The woman retorted in an angry tone and with a vigorous shake of her hands, before striding away. The first Spaniard noticed Eddie's terse stare and muttered something to his compadre, who snorted once more. The uncomfortable exchange seemed to be over and, not wanting to attract attention, Eddie leaned against his rucksack and closed his eyes. He had been travelling for nearly two weeks now, and had not slept in a bed for several days.

The sound of a plate and cutlery being placed down shook him out of his sleep in, what seemed to Eddie, only a few seconds later. The waitress stood at his side, smiling. Before him, on his table, sat a plate loaded with tortilla, chips and salad.

'You were snoring, *Inglés*,' she said chuckling and walked away.

Eddie rubbed his eyes again and picked up his cutlery ready to tuck in, but then heard the waitress shouting from across the room. The taller of the two adolescents had trapped the woman up against the wall, pinning her hands above her head. His hand was making its way down from her face to her breast.

Eddie dropped his cutlery, rose and burst towards the man. His route, however, was blocked by the second man who stood facing him, holding a small rusty blade. The Spaniard barked something unintelligible in his mother tongue, phlegm emitting from his mouth as he shouted. The first man pushed the waitress down onto a seat and stood behind his friend, grinning.

'You leave, or Amos stick you with knife. Like pig,' he said in a sneering tone.

Amos, the man holding the knife, laughed, releasing yet more saliva. Eddie took a step back but glanced at the trembling waitress. She looked away, seemingly sure that the foreigner would not risk his own safety to come to the aid of a stranger. The Spanish men sneered as Eddie motioned to retreat, but as the blade-wielding Spaniard looked away towards his companion, Eddie saw his chance. Like a cat, he sprung forward, curled one hand around the blade, and side-clubbed the jaw of the man holding it with his other. As the Spaniard collapsed to the floor Eddie took another step, grabbed the tall goon by the neck and shoved him up against the wall. He leaned in, putting all of his weight against the Spaniard's throat and angled his elbows to prevent his opponent from escaping. Eddie stared deep into the man's reddening eyes as his face turned a pastel blue, but then he felt a gentle touch on his arm. It was the waitress.

'It's okay,' she said in a soothing voice. 'You can let him go'. Eddie relaxed, and the man slid to the floor, gulping for air like a freshly-landed salmon. Eddie pulled back. 'You are cut,' she said. She was pointing at Eddie's hand. He looked down and realised that it was bleeding from where he had grabbed the knife. Both his hands were shaking. She pulled a cloth out from her pocket, grasped him and dabbed at the wound.

'It's okay. It's not bad,' said Eddie.

'It could have been,' she said in the same way his mother used to speak to him whenever she found him doing something stupid. 'Thank you'. She turned towards the cowering man before her and screamed at him in Spanish then kicked him so hard on the shin that even Eddie cringed. The man lifted himself up and backed away, his hand on his Adam's apple. Amos too picked himself up from the floor and followed his friend's example. The waitress screamed at them both again, and they hobbled away towards the door. She turned back towards Eddie, who stood gawping at her, his mouth wide open. 'Your food is going cold,' she said, pointing to his table. She adjusted her hair then walked away, disappearing from view behind the counter.

Eddie devoured his meal, then sat back in the chair. The cafe was quiet, save for the intermittent humming sound coming from a tall drinks fridge. The two Spanish men had driven away in an old Renault. There had been no sign of the waitress for ten minutes.

He pulled his wallet from his pocket and took out the faded photo of Mary, his daughter, holding it before him with both hands. It was frayed at the edges, and the colours had worn in patches from frequent handling. Eddie had snapped the image on Mary's third birthday, two years ago. He had only seen her a handful of times since, the last over a year ago. How much, he wondered, had his little angel changed since then.

The sounds of light footsteps caught his attention. It was the waitress coming to collect his empty plate and cutlery. She glanced at the photo and smiled.

'*Ella es muy hermosa,*' she said, following up in English with, 'I said that she is very beautiful'.

'She is,' said Eddie.

'Your daughter?' He nodded.

'Her name is Mary'. He held up the photograph.

'That's a nice name. It was my grandmother's name, also. Well, *Maria*. The Spanish version'. She smiled at him. 'But she is no longer on this earth'.

'I'm sorry,' said Eddie, carefully tucking the photo back inside his wallet.

The waitress pointed at his empty plate. 'The tortilla. It was good?'

'It was, thank you'.

'You would like something else, maybe?'

Eddie was still hungry, but he had precious little money remaining, and he was still over four hundred miles from his destination. 'No, I'm good. Thanks'. He hoped that his stomach would not rumble at that precise moment to expose his lie.

'More coffee perhaps? Refills are free,' the waitress offered with a knowing look.

'Yes, please,' he said.

A large truck turned off from the road and into the empty

parking area outside the roadside cafe, its tyres throwing up a cloud of dust. The sound caught Eddie's attention, and he stared at it, forgetting for a moment that the woman was still standing next to him.

'You need to get somewhere?' she asked, following his gaze towards the lorry as it pulled to a halt outside.

'Yes, I need to get to the Costa del Sol. To Marbella'.

She nodded towards the white signage on the side of the truck. 'I think that truck goes to Málaga. I can ask the driver if you like?'

'I'd appreciate that,' Eddie replied.

'It is no problem,' said the waitress. She smiled again, picked up his empty plate, then headed back to the kitchen.

Eddie watched the driver as he clambered down from the dirty cockpit. He was a large bull of a man, dressed in dirty denim jeans, and a red and black chequered shirt. The man slammed the lorry door shut, then ambled towards the cafe door, pulled it open and came inside. He wiped his brow with a dirty-looking handkerchief, studied the building's interior and then sat down at the nearest of the red, faux leather-covered benches.

'*Buenas, chica*', he mumbled to the waitress in a gravelled voice. She hurried over and greeted the man in Spanish. After taking his order, she gestured over towards Eddie. Eddie nodded at the man and smiled, but it elicited no response from the big Spaniard who switched his attention back to the woman. A protracted conversation then ensued, with much waving of arms, after which the waitress came back over to Eddie.

'He says he can take you to Málaga, but he wants ten thousand pesetas for his troubles. He has a wife and four teenage daughters who spend his money quicker than he can earn it. Or so he says'.

Eddie opened his wallet and sighed. He had eight thousand pesetas left. 'Do you think he would accept five thousand? This is all I have, and I still need to pay for my food'.

She shot him another of her warm, reassuring smiles. 'I will see what I can do'. She touched his hand, then turned back towards the kitchen.

After another half an hour and, after finishing his tostada and coffee, the lorry driver rose from his chair - wincing as he did so - rubbed his back, muttered something to the waitress, and then wandered off towards the toilets. She came back over to Eddie's table.

'How much do I owe you for the food?'

The woman pulled the seat opposite him from under the table and sat down. 'There is no charge,' she said.

'But I must -'.

She stopped Eddie mid-sentence by clasping his hand. Her skin felt warm and smooth, her grip strong. 'I come from a line of *gitanos*. You say "gypsies" in English, no?' Eddie nodded, the energy in her hands preoccupying his immediate thoughts. 'I can tell if a person has a good heart'. She was examining his palms now. 'Why do you go to the south?' she asked. He looked up from his hands to her thin, lightly-tanned face and her penetrating brown eyes.

'A relative of mine lives down there. Somewhere near Marbella'.

'You have not seen him for some time?' she said, more like a statement of fact than a question.

'Not for a few years, no,' he replied. The waitress continued to hold his hand, pressing her thumbs into his palms. Eddie thought he detected a look of concern on her face. 'What is it?' he asked.

She lifted her gaze up to meet his. 'I do not know. Not for sure. But you must be careful when you get to Marbella. It is a town full of criminals'. She held his stare for a moment longer, then let go of his hands and glanced back towards the lorry driver who had just emerged from the toilets. 'His name is Gonzalo, and passes through here often. He has the look of a mean old bear, but I believe him to be a good person. I think he will look after you,' she told him.

'You know him?'

She laughed. 'Only as much as I know you'.

Eddie lifted himself up from the red bench, the plasticky material peeling of his sweating legs, and put his wallet back into his pocket. 'Can I ask your name?'

'You can, and it is Rosalita,' she said grinning. 'And before you ask, yes. You can come and visit me when you are next passing. I work here on most days'.

'I now go. You come?' said the barrel-chested lorry driver in pidgin English.

'Yes. I mean...*Sí*,' said Eddie.

The woman smiled again. 'And work on your Spanish before you see me again, Sergeant Eddie Lawson'.

His face betrayed his bewilderment. 'How do you -'.

She pointed towards the khaki green army backpack that he had just slung over his shoulder. 'Because it is written on your bag, soldier boy'.

The lorry driver was at the door holding it open. He said something in Spanish.

'He said that he can take you to Malaga,' said the waitress. 'Then you must find your own way to Marbella'.

'Ah, *gracias*,' said Eddie to the driver.

The woman stared at him for what felt like ten seconds, gave him one last smile then turned and walked back to the kitchen.

Eddie stood for a moment watching her as she disappeared from view. He longed to stay in the cafe, but he heard the lorry's engine start. He grabbed one of the small menus, checked that it had the cafe's address on it, then stuffed it into his pocket and darted for the door.

CHAPTER TWO
IMPRESSING THE LOCALS

The offices of Sinmorales Aseguró Partners, Marbella, Spain. July 1985.

Charlie Lawson stood peering through one of the toughened glass windows in the law firm's conference room, looking down at the entrance to the office building on the ground floor below. His guests were arriving. He downed the rest of the brandy he was holding, then hid the empty glass on the windowsill behind the green velvet curtain. He tightened his tie and patted his slicked-back hair once more, then turned to address his associates.

'They're here,' he announced. 'You ready Willy?'

Guillem Montcada, who Charlie had noted, was wearing his favourite Armani suit for the occasion, lifted himself up from his seat and stood upright. 'Of course,' he replied, smiling. Charlie knew that Guillem hated being called by that stupid nickname, but for one hundred pounds an hour, his lawyer would just have to suck it up. Charlie paid him twice what any local client would, and the additional - off-the-books - rewards meant that the Spaniard could look forward to an early and very comfortable retirement.

Charlie walked over to the other figure at the back of the room. Lucian Soparla was a thin, gaunt-looking fellow with oily black hair - the fringe of which dangled over the top of his face as he crouched over a teak cabinet upon which rested an open briefcase.

'Is that thing working?' said Charlie. He looked at the tape recorder inside the case.

Soparla pressed a button on the device. A small green light came on, and the two clear plastic spools of tape started turning. 'It's working'. Soparla closed the case and snapped the two metal latches into place.

'How many more are there?'

'Five. Between them they will pick up every conversation in the room'.

'Good. Better make yourself scarce,' said Charlie. 'They're on their way up'.

Soparla nodded. 'I'll be in the room next door,' he replied. 'Tell me when they have all left'.

Charlie waited until the Romanian was out of sight, then signalled to Guillem to accompany him to welcome the invited guests who he could hear were assembling in the office's reception area outside the wood and glass dividing doors.

'Let's fucking do this!' he said while cracking his knuckles.

The lawyer nodded and opened the door. '*Buenos dias, Señors*. Thank you for waiting. Please, come in'.

Charlie stood greeting each of the men with a firm handshake as they entered the room, with Guillem introducing each of them as they approached. One man, however, needed no introduction. Charlie knew who Juan Fernandez was. The tall man in his late fifties with a grey moustache and perfectly dyed, jet-black hair took Charlie's outstretched hand and shook it firmly.

'It's good to see you, Señor Fernandez,' said Charlie. 'I'm sure this will be well worth your time, sir'.

'Thank you, Mr Lawson. I've been looking forward to this. My advisors say that you have an exciting project here. I look forward to hearing more about it'. Fernandez stepped into the room.

Charlie looked at Guillem, smiled and winked. 'Please, gentlemen. Take a seat,' he said after the last of the guests had entered. He gestured towards the row of dark wood and green leather chairs that he had carefully laid out before the large wooden table upon which was located a handcrafted model of a white apartment complex. Sporadic trees made from sponge and wire, a few toy Matchbox cars and a smattering of small, plastic people gave the visitors a sense of the building's scale. Charlie stood waiting as the men took their seats. He was well-prepared and looking forward to this. Guillem closed the door, walked towards the rear of the seated guests, then signalled to Charlie that he could start.

'First, thank you very much for your time here today, gentlemen. I greatly appreciate it. I know that you are all very busy people'. He stepped slightly to one side and held out his arm to present the model behind him. 'This is Urbanizacion Majestico. A complex comprising one-hundred luxury, two and three-bedroom apartments that I will construct on a plot of land which I have acquired, a stone's throw away from Puerto Banús. You will each find a pack under your chairs that contains an overview of this investment opportunity and a draft of the marketing brochures that will go out to prospective purchasers. You are welcome to keep those, but I'd like to take a few minutes here to tell you about the highlights'.

Charlie was interrupted by the sound of the door creaking open which drew the attention of the audience. He followed their gazes towards the visitor who had stepped into the room. The man wore a tailored charcoal suit, and a white shirt unbuttoned at the collar. His dark brown hair was immaculately groomed. He closed the door firmly behind him, then strode over to join the group. The confident smile fell away from Charlie's face as he recognised the new arrival; Daniel Ortega, the head of one of Andalusia's wealthiest families, and a declared enemy of Charlie's.

'Good afternoon, gentlemen. Please excuse my tardiness,' said Ortega. Charlie shot Guillem an alarmed look.

His lawyer, who was clearly as surprised as Charlie, shrugged then rose from his chair behind the rest of the men. 'We were not expecting you here today, Señor Ortega,' he said. 'Can I offer you my seat?'

'No need. I can stand. I would not want to cause any more disruption'. He placed his hand on the shoulder of one of the seated men, shook his hand with the other while muttering something in Spanish to the man, who chuckled.

'If you don't mind, Señor Ortega?' said Charlie.

Ortega looked back at him with what Charlie knew to be a contrived look of surprise on his face. 'My apologies. Please continue,' he said. He half-smiled at Charlie, stood up straight and folded his arms. Guillem retreated to the back of the group once again.

Charlie took a handkerchief from his suit trouser pocket and wiped a trickle of sweat from his forehead, then stepped towards the overhead projector next to the model of the building. He flicked the power switch on, and an instant bright yellow-hued rectangle of light appeared on a screen hanging above the miniature apartment complex. Charlie took a transparent sheet from beside the projector and placed it down onto the machine's glass plate. Someone in the audience snorted, and Charlie looked up to see the slide was upside down. He reorientated the transparent plastic sheet, took a deep breath and stepped back in front of his guests.

'Urbanizacion Majestico will be a much sought-after complex of luxury holiday apartments, targeted at wealthy European and Middle-Eastern clients. With traditional

Andalusian styling, high-end north European construction materials and know-how, and a superb location very close to Puerto Banús, it will offer an unsurpassed living experience. This complex -'.

'You don't think our other developments in the region are well-constructed?' asked Ortega. Charlie grimaced at the interruption.

'I'm sorry, what?'

'You said "High-end north European construction materials and know-how". Do you mean to suggest that we cannot construct our own buildings here in Spain? Or that more established property developers, such as Mr Fernandez here, use sub-standard materials?' said Ortega.

Charlie looked at Fernandez, who appeared unfazed. 'No, I'm not saying that. I'm simply emphasising that this complex will combine the best possible combination of design, materials and construction expertise. After all, we should all be striving to ensure that each new development improves upon those that have come before them. I and Señor Fernandez, I am sure, feel a duty to maintain the wonderful legacy of the great Luis Banús'. Fernandez appeared satisfied with Charlie's answer and Guillam gave Charlie a covert 'thumbs up' sign from his vantage point at the rear of the room.

'So, as I was saying,' Charlie continued, 'this will be a world-class complex that will attract a new influx of wealthy and influential people and their families to the area. That will further bolster the local economy and create employment. Because gentlemen, while we do what we do as businessmen, we must also ensure that we can bring broader returns to this magnificent region in which we are so lucky to live'.

On a fucking roll now, Charlie.

'You will see the interior design, materials and other options in the brochure in your packs'.

The men opened the glossy document, and Charlie paused

to give them a little time to flick through the impressive-looking imagery.

'These do indeed look very good,' commented one of the attendees, a balding man in a light blue suit.

'How much will the units sell for, may I ask?' inquired another.

Charlie turned to face the man who's slender build and withdrawn posture gave him the appearance of a praying mantis. 'The provisional pricing is at one hundred and twenty thousand pounds for the two-bedroom properties, another thirty thousand for the three-bedroom ones'. The man seemed impressed.

'May we hear about the financing, Mr Lawson?' asked Fernandez who had already switched his attention to the financial document.

'Certainly,' said Charlie. 'The total project costs are estimated to be five million sterling. The building will take place over three phases, the first of which - comprising the forty, three-bedroom properties - will be completed within thirteen months of breaking ground. Phases two and three, the two-bedroom apartments, will follow and be ready in under two years'.

'And you are projecting total sales revenue at twelve and a half million pounds, I see,' said Fernandez.

'That is correct,' said Charlie, grinning. 'Which, will generate a profit of around seven and a half million pounds, a return on investment of one hundred and fifty percent'.

Heads nodded around the room except that of Daniel Ortega who, with his arms tightly crossed still, shook his head. 'That is very optimistic,' he said.

'I disagree,' said Charlie. 'The Spanish property market is booming and shows no sign of cooling down for the foreseeable future. If anything, I'd say that we will be able to charge higher prices by the time phases two and three are underway. As you know, the Costa del Sol is proving to be a huge attraction to affluent individuals from across Europe and beyond,' said Charlie.

'Yes, we are already attracting plenty of affluent individuals, but I'm not so sure that we want all of them here'. Ortega thumbed through the financial statements. 'I see you have already invested around nine-hundred thousand pounds into this project. That is a considerable sum of money'.

'Indeed it is,' said Charlie, wishing that one of the other guests would ask a question instead. 'And it should indicate the level of belief I have in this project'.

'As I understand it,' continued Ortega, 'your income here in Spain is derived from a tourist bar and a few other small investments'. He placed a particular emphasis on the word "small". 'As I'm sure you can appreciate, as potential investors, we must have reassurances as to the legitimacy of your funds. So, if you don't mind, would you share with us the source of your income? I, for one, would need to be certain it is, as you might say, kosher?'

Charlie looked around the room. A wall of expectant faces greeted him.

'Mr Lawson made his money in the scrap metal business in the United Kingdom,' Guillem interjected.

'Is that so?' said Ortega. 'We would need to see evidence of this should any of us wish to consider investing in your project'.

'Of course,' said Charlie, trying to hide his intensifying anger.

'Because, as I'm sure you are aware,' continued Ortega. 'There has been a worrying influx of compatriots of yours whose wealth is derived from…well, let me speak candidly here, illegal endeavours'. Ortega looked around the room. 'We've all heard of "Great Train Robbers" and the likes of Ronnie Knight, for example'. He gestured towards Fernandez. 'I feel I speak not just for myself but for the others in this room when I say that we could not possibly entertain an investment in your project until we had first received cast-iron assurances that there is no criminal involvement'.

'I assure you I am a legitimate businessman,' said Charlie.

'We do not doubt that,' said one of the other men. 'But I agree with Señor Ortega, here. For reasons of due-diligence, we would need to see guarantees as to the source of your funds'.

'Do you agree, Juan?' said Ortega to Fernandez.

'I would. Naturally, we all have both business and family reputations to uphold. But I assume this is not a problem for you, Mr Lawson?' said Fernandez.

Charlie did not answer. His stare was locked upon Daniel Ortega's.

'We can certainly assuage any concerns that any of you may have, Señor Fernandez,' said Guillem.

'Excellent,' said Fernandez as he rose from his chair. 'Then in the meantime, I shall study this information further, and we shall await an update from you regarding this issue'. He walked up to Charlie, the brochure rolled in his left hand. 'There is a lot of potential in this project, Charlie. I hope that we can work together on it. Good day to you'.

Charlie forced a smile and nodded as Fernandez and the other investors shuffled towards the open door. He heard Guillem force an artificial cough and turned to see that Ortega remained in the room, standing next to the architectural model.

'Couldn't keep your nose out of it, could you, Daniel?'

Ortega turned from the model to face Charlie. 'I told you before, Charlie. You and your associates are not welcome here in my town'.

'Your town?' Guillem tried to hold his arm, but Charlie brushed it aside and confronted Ortega. 'You know as well as I do where all those men get their money. Hell, Fernandez is a bent as a nine-bob note, you fuckin' hypocrite'.

Ortega leaned forward. He had two inches on Charlie and was in much better shape. 'The difference is, that Señor Fernandez and his family have lived here for generations'.

'You mean he isn't foreign like me'.

'I mean that he isn't a foreign *criminal*, like you'.

The two men stood glaring at each other until the lawyer interrupted.

'Gentlemen, please. There is nothing to gain for anyone from this. Charlie, I think we should leave now. I'll have the model brought to your house this evening'.

Ortega straightened his collar, grinned and turned his back on Charlie. 'The clock is ticking, Charlie. You can't hide here forever,' he said while striding towards the door. '*Adios, Guillem*'.

The lawyer watched him depart, then looked back at his client. 'Charlie?' he said.

Charlie looked past him to the office where Lucian Soparla remained ensconced. 'Lucian!' he shouted. The office door creaked open, and Soparla poked his head out. 'They've gone. Turn them things off and get over here'. He turned back to the lawyer. 'That wanker ain't gonna beat me'.

'You must be patient, Charlie,' Guillem advised.

'I have been,' Charlie snapped. 'But that bastard Ortega is testing my fucking patience to the limit'.

'I know, Charlie. He has influence but Fernandez and the others, they are their own men. We need to win them over. Don't let Ortega distract you. That is what he wants'.

'How did he even find out about the meeting?' asked Charlie while trying to pick up a small red toy Ferrari from the architectural model. It was glued to the wooden base.

Guillem shrugged once more. 'Marbella is not a big town. People talk'.

Charlie took a step towards him. 'Then we need to do more'. He turned to Soparla who stood nearby holding a box full of the tape recorders. 'Ortega does all his business from his office on Ricardo Soriano. I need you to get in there and bug it. Tap his line too. Can you do that?'

Soparla grinned. 'It will be easy'.

'Good. Bring anything you get to Guillem to sift through. Got it?' Soparla nodded, then walked out through the open entrance.

The lawyer closed the doors behind him, then cleared his throat. 'Charlie, I told you before, I am not comfortable dealing with Soparla'.

'I don't want to hear it, Guillem. Just get it done'.

'Charlie, I would really prefer -'.

'I pay you very fucking well, amigo. If you want a safe life, work for someone else. See how much they pay you'.

The lawyer rubbed his forehead. 'Fine, I'll do it, but there's no certainty he can get anything on Ortega. And you have little time left to get this project going. The town council will rescind the planning permission if you haven't got the funding in place soon'.

'Tell me what I don't already fuckin' know,' said Charlie.

CHAPTER THREE
LOS HERMANOS

Charlie pushed his way past a group of casually dressed ex-pats midway through the exterior doors of the offices of the law firm. He was carrying his suit jacket under his left arm, his tie hung loose around his neck.

'I say,' said one middle-aged English woman as Charlie barged past. He ignored her.

He fumbled around in his pocket for his cigarettes, then pulled open the packet of Benson and Hedges only to find it empty.

'Fuck's sake,' he shouted. He crushed, then tossed the golden container into a nearby shrub, then stomped down the yellow concrete stairs and along the busy pavement, weaving his way through the hoards of slow-moving tourists.

He had parked his car, a 1980-registered Porsche 928S, on the street a few hundred yards from the building where he had held the investment pitch. It was on a yellow line, but he had taken his chances earlier as he had been in a hurry. Besides, the traffic wardens around here never went on patrol in the midday heat. Or so he thought.

When he arrived at the big silver coupe, he was greeted by

the sight of a newly applied parking ticket under the right wiper.

'Poxy hell'. He ripped the plastic-covered document from the windscreen, crumpled it up and threw it to the passenger footwell as he got in. He thrust the keys into the ignition, revved the engine as soon as it started and, with barely a sideways glance, pulled away with a screech of tyres.

It took him twenty minutes to fight his way through the loathsome summer traffic to his beach bar on the far end of Marbella. When he had first bought the establishment just under five years ago, he had been lacking in creative juices, and opted to name it "Charlie's Bar". He had always intended to give it a more original signature title, but the name had stuck, so it had remained unchanged.

He pulled the Porsche into his private parking space next to the bar's entrance, slammed the door shut and clambered up the flight of wooden stairs to the glass door. The circulating air from the fan hit him in the face as he walked in and he stopped to wipe the sweat from his neck with his hanky again.

'Debs, get us a cold lager,' he barked at the petite blonde barmaid. He dropped the box of brochures down onto the wooden surface, slung his suit jacket on a nearby stool and removed his tie.

The woman placed a pint of beer down in front of him. 'There you go, Charlie. Nice and cold'.

He frowned. 'How many times do I need to tell yer, Debs? Beer mats. I only had the bloody thing re-varnished six months ago. Look at the bleeding state of it already'.

'Sorry, Charlie,' she said and reached for a green, circular Heineken beer mat for him. He raised the chilled glass to his lips, but before he had taken a sip, he heard his name being called. He placed the drink down, huffed and turned to see Barry his bar manager making his way towards him. The man seemed agitated.

'Wot is it, Baz?'

'Sorry boss, but there's a geezer outside in the garden. He showed up over an hour ago asking for you. Military type. Wouldn't give his name. He's only had a coke. Looks like a dodgy fucker if you ask me'.

Charlie took a step forward to get a better look at the stranger who was sitting hunched over a table, under a sunshade and facing in the opposite direction. Charlie clicked his fingers and, without turning to face his employee, said, 'Get us me shooter'.

Barry darted behind the bar, then returned with a silver revolver, which he handed to Charlie inside a rolled-up newspaper. 'You want back up?'

Charlie shook his head and walked towards the beer garden. He took a wide, circular route around the paved exterior, casually eyeing up the stranger who perched in the shade of one of the enormous umbrellas. The man was wearing a shabby black tee shirt and British army DPM combat trousers. His brown hair was curly and unkempt, and he sported a light beard. His skin was pale, except for the sunburnt patch on the back of his neck. He appeared to be dozing, his head resting in his hands. Charlie felt the reassuring weight of the silver Smith & Wesson in his hand and glanced around before coughing loudly. The man began to stir.

'I'm told you were asking for me,' said Charlie in a loud voice.

The stranger opened his eyes, lifted his head out of his hands and gazed up at him. 'Nice place you've got here, bruv,' he said.

'Fuck me,' said Charlie. The two men stared at each other in silence for several seconds, before Charlie placed the gun - still wrapped in the newspaper - down on a nearby chair. 'Eddie, what the bleeding hell are you doing here?'

'Nice to see you too, Charlie,' said Eddie. He remained sitting at the table.

Charlie approached his brother and held out his arms.

'Don't just sit there. Gimme a hug,' he said. Eddie wearily lifted himself up. Immediately, the smell of stale sweat hit Charlie. 'Fuckin' hell, you need a bath, bruv'.

Eddie let his hands drop to his side and pulled back. 'And you could do with losing fifty pounds'.

Charlie roared with laughter. 'Sign of good living, this is,' he said, patting his belly. He looked at Eddie's glass. 'You're empty'. He leaned over to the window. Barry stood observing from the doorway. Charlie mimicked sipping from a glass and held up two fingers. 'So?' asked Charlie.

'So what?'

'So why are you sitting here, in my bar? How did you even find me?'

'I ran into Steve Tucker in town a few months back. You remember him? His dad used to own the corner shop in Rayners Lane?' said Eddie.

'Yeah, course. Scrawny little sod. Used to sell us fags he'd nicked from his dad's store'.

'That's him,' said Eddie. 'Anyway, he'd been down here on holiday a few months back. He said he'd seen you here in this bar. He wasn't sure at first, but then he'd seen the name, so he knew it was you'.

'Why didn't the little bastard come in and say hello then?'

'Probably coz of that time you broke his nose in the playground after he called you an idiot'.

'Was that him? Fuck, yeah. It was weren't it,' said Charlie. He laughed. The barmaid stepped into the beer garden carrying two glasses of beer which she placed down in front of the two brothers.

'Thanks,' said Eddie, lifting the glass to his lips. He downed half of the drink before wiping his mouth with his hand, then leaned back in his chair.

'Needed that did you, little bruv?' said Charlie. 'You look like shit. Not in trouble, are yer?' He peered at his brother, who was fidgeting with a beer mat. 'C'mon, mate. What's up. I know we ain't seen each other for a while -'.

'A while? The last time I saw you was at my wedding. That was in 1977, Charlie. Eight years ago. Eight years!'

Charlie sighed. 'I know. I know. But it's complicated. You don't know -'.

'What was so complicated that you couldn't come and meet your new niece? Or to see me off before I left for that poxy war? Hey?' Eddie stared at his brother.

Charlie dropped his gaze to Eddie's midriff. 'I had stuff... things going on bruv. You don't know -'.

'What fuckin' things? You could have written letters. You could have come and visited us. I was only stationed in Colchester. It ain't that far away'.

'That's the thing, Ed, I weren't, was I?' said Charlie before taking a long swig of his beer.

'Weren't what?'

'I weren't in England, bruv. I came over here in 79.'

Eddie placed his drink down and lent forward. 'Shut the fuck up'.

Charlie shook his head. 'Honest. I've been here over six years now. I had to get out of Blighty, didn't I?'

'Had to leave?' said Eddie. 'Why?'

Charlie looked around. Three tourists were making their way into the patio area, one carrying a tray on which perched a trio of Piña Coladas. Inside the bar, he could see Barry stocking up a beer fridge and Debbie who was mopping the floor.

'Look bruv, there's a lot you don't know. I'll explain, but not here. Not right now. Look, I'm throwing a bit of a do up at my place tonight. There will be a few faces from when we were growing up. Why don't you come back with me? Get yourself cleaned up. Have some grub and a kip. You look like you need it'.

'I can't, Charlie. I'm just passing through. I'm on my way to Algeciras'.

'Alge-fucking-ciras? What do you want to go to that shithole for?'

Eddie took a long sip of his beer, placed the glass back down and looked his brother directly in the eye. 'I'm getting a ferry over to Morocco. Look, the past is the past. We can't change that. Neither of us. But listen, I really need some travel funds. I was hoping you could help me out'.

'Travel funds? Where are you going?

'Angola,' said Eddie.

'Angola? That's a fuckin' war zone init?'

'I've got work lined up down there'

'What work?' said Charlie.

'The kind of work ex-soldiers do'.

It took Charlie a few seconds to grasp what his brother was telling him. 'What, you're a fucking mercenary now?'

'It's the only stuff I'm any good at'.

'What about…your wife and -?'

Eddie rolled his eyes upwards. 'My wife's name was Hayley. And our daughter's name is Mary'. Eddie reached into his jacket pocket for his wallet and removed the photo from inside. 'That's her. About two years ago'.

Charlie picked up the photo and studied it for a moment. 'She's pretty'.

'She is. Smart too. I don't see her much these days. I split up from her mum a couple of years ago. After I got kicked out of the army'. His eyes dropped to the table, and he took another gulp of his beer. 'I was a bit of a mess after the war'.

'I'm sorry, that's tough bruv. But Angola? That's messed up too. If you need help to get back on your feet, I'm here for you. I've got a lot going on down here. Stuff you could get involved with'.

Eddie looked uncomfortable. 'People are expecting me. Besides, all I know is soldiering. I'm no good at…whatever it is you do down here.' He looked around at the bar. 'What is it you do? This?' He waved his hand around him.

Charlie grinned. 'This place? Nah, this is just a hobby. I'm in the property game now, mate. And other stuff. Listen, park those ideas about getting your head blown off in sodding Africa. Just for a day, alright? Come back to my gaff. I'll tell you what I've been up to on the way. How about it?' Eddie still seemed unconvinced. Charlie downed the last dregs of his beer and stood up. 'Just one day, okay? For old time's sake. And tomorrow I'll take you to fuckin' Algeciras myself. Deal?'

Eddie looked at his brother's outstretched hand, then shook it. 'Just one day, though. No more'.

'Deal', said Charlie. 'Come on then, we've got a lot to talk about'.

The newly reunited brothers walked down the wooden steps from Charlie's bar onto the street outside.

'That's my motor over here,' said Charlie, pointing at his dusty, silver Porsche.

Eddie let out a wolf-whistle.'Blimey, you're doing alright for yourself,' he said as he ran his hand over the wing of the German coupe.

Charlie laughed. 'I can't complain'. He inserted the key into the driver's door, and both it and the passenger door unlocked in unison. 'It's got central locking. And electric windows. Nice, huh?'

'My last motor was a knackered, old Vauxhall Chevette,' said Eddie. 'So yeah, anything's nice after that'. He sat down in the grey leather passenger seat. Charlie turned the keys in the ignition, and the big V8 under the bonnet growled into life. He dabbed the throttle a few times and grinned as the resulting guttural roar bounced off the surrounding apartment blocks. 'I bet your neighbours love you'.

They pulled out of the parking space and headed away

towards Avenida Ricardo Soriano, the main road that runs through the heart of Marbella.

'You into Phil Collins?' asked Charlie while inserting a CD into the car's stereo system. He pressed the play button on the device, and a few seconds later, "Sussudio" was playing from speakers in all four corners of the car's interior.

'I preferred Genesis,' said Eddie. 'He's gone all mainstream now'.

'Nuffin wrong with making some moolah, bruv,' said Charlie. 'If people want to buy what you have, then sell 'em it. That's my motto'.

Within a few minutes, they had left the apartment blocks and commercial buildings of central Marbella behind and were now proceeding along the wide boulevard in the direction of Puerto Banús. There was barely a cloud in the sky, and the sun's heat was intense. Eddie pushed the sun visor down. Charlie smiled.

'I reckon you could do with some sun, Ed. Get yourself some vitamin D and all that'. He noticed Eddie was gripping the passenger door handle as the car weaved rapidly in and out of the much slower-moving traffic around them. 'What's up, bruv? Am I going too fast for you?' he said, smiling.

'I'm just not used to being on this side of the car, that's all'.

Charlie let out a laugh, then pulled a packet of cigarettes out of his shirt pocket. 'Light one up for us. You want one?'

Eddie shook his head. 'I gave them up a few months back'. He lit one, then passed it to Charlie.

'Cheers,' said Charlie. He eyed up his sibling for a few seconds, then continued. 'So, must have been a rough deal? Leaving your wife and kid behind, I mean'. Eddie did not reply. 'Couldn't you find no work back home?'

'I had a few gigs. Nothing much, though. Nothing I could stick. It's pretty fucked up back home still. Maybe you don't know?'

'Yeah, I read the English papers?' said Charlie. 'The Tories are shaking things up a bit, aren't they?'

'Shaking things up? You have no idea. The miners, steelworkers, dock workers, factories shutting down and laying off staff everywhere - it's a fucking disaster. The only work I could get was cash-in-hand stuff. Labouring on building sites. Shit like that'.

'I thought they gave you ex-soldier boys retraining opportunities or whatever,' said Charlie. 'So you could train to be a stockbroker or something'.

'I went to a college for a bit, yeah. In Slough. It was fucking weird, though. Me, a few other ex-forces guys, and all these kids fresh from school. They looked at me like I was some kind of freak. The guy that ran the scheme there sat me down with this massive questionnaire and got me to fill out all these bullshit questions, like "Do you enjoy working with your hands?" and "Do you like working with people?" Utter bollocks, you know? Anyway, the end result was that they told me I should learn about computers. "It's the future," they said. I gave it a go. I really did. Went for about six weeks, but it did me head in. Couldn't make head nor tail of it. Weren't my thing at all. All I know is how to jump out of aeroplanes and shoot a gun'.

'So you jacked it in then?'

'Sort of,' said Eddie. Charlie gave his brother a suspicious look. Eddie sighed. 'Well, this lecturer guy…Geoffrey, his name was. He had some double-barrelled surname. A right posh twat he was. Drove a bright yellow Triumph Spitfire. Anyway, this one time we're in his office together and -'. Eddie paused. He looked embarrassed.

'What?' said Charlie, taking his eyes off the road for a moment. 'He never tried it on, did he?'

'What? Nah. Nuffin like that, no'.

'Well, what then?'

'He told me to sit down,' said Eddie. 'Like he was my bleeding C.O. or something. Then lectures me about not having the aptitude for computers and that I was wasting his and the college's time. He said he'd heard that there were jobs going at Woolworths. That I should apply there. I went ballistic. Told him I weren't no friggin' shop assistant. Do you know what he told me then?'

The Porsche lurched sideways as Charlie undertook an old blue Citröen.

'Go on,' said Charlie.

'He said that life is hard, and the world doesn't owe me a living just coz I was in the Falklands'. Charlie's mouth was wide open. 'And this is from a guy whose daddy probably bought him his house and car,' said Eddie.

'You're fucking having a laugh? What a prick. What did you do?'

'I smacked him one. Hey, watch the road bruv'. Charlie had just cut inside another slow-moving car.

'You punched your lecturer?' Charlie roared with laughter. 'Guessing you didn't get your qualification then?'

'As it happens, I did,' said Eddie. 'After that, he just left me alone. I got the certificate in the post a month later. It didn't help me none, though. I still haven't got a bleedin' clue about computer -'. Eddie's body suddenly tensed. 'Charlie! Red light!'

Charlie looked forward to see a stationary green Volkswagen Golf thirty feet ahead of the Porsche. He slammed his foot down hard onto the brake pedal, and the two brothers were forced forward by the sudden reduction in speed. Eddie, who was wearing his seatbelt, remained in his seat. Charlie, who never wore one, found his face propelled into the steering wheel, breaking his nose in an instant. The car lurched to a stop just inches behind the green hatchback, in a cloud of its own tire smoke.

'Fucking, poxy fuck,' screamed Charlie, blood dripping from

his damaged face. The blue Citröen saloon car pulled up next to them. The young Spanish driver and passengers were snickering and pointing at Charlie's freshly bloodied face. 'What the fuck are you laughing at you dago bastards?' He reached under his seat and started fumbling around.

'What are you doing?' said Eddie.

'Looking for my fuckin' gun,' Charlie shouted, blood dripping from his nostrils. He located the weapon and started opening the door, but his younger - and much stronger - sibling grabbed hold of the hand holding a black revolver.

'Don't be stupid. That was your fault, you fucking muppet'. Charlie continued to try to break free from Eddie's grip for a few seconds, his face red with rage. 'Charlie! Give it up'. The militaristic authority in his younger brother's voice jolted Charlie out of his red mist, and he relaxed.

'Okay. Okay. You're right. It's okay. You can let go now'. Eddie released his grip and Charlie placed the pistol back under the seat. He looked back at the blue car as it drove off. 'Wankers,' he shouted as he reached into the glove compartment to find a rag which he then held to his nose. 'Fuck, that hurt. Sorry, Eddie. I wasn't watching where I was going'.

'No kidding, you dozy twazzock. The lights are green. You alright to drive?'

'Yeah, no worries'. Charlie restarted the car, pushed it into first gear and pulled away.

Eddie wiped the sweat from his brow with his shirt sleeve. 'How's the nose?'

'It fucking hurts'.

'Uh-huh. And I guess the property business is quite competitive down here?'

Charlie glanced at his brother, then quickly returned to looking at the road ahead. 'What d'ya mean?' said Charlie.

'Don't play stupid. Why have you got a shooter?'

Charlie took a deep breath before answering. 'I told you, Ed. There's stuff you don't know'. He lifted the rag to his nose again.

'Then best you tell me,' said Eddie, looking at his brother.

'I will. Let's get to my place first. I need to sort my face out,' said Charlie.

They travelled for a mile before Charlie turned off the busy carriageway, and onto a smaller road that would take them up towards Nuevo Andalusia. It was a long twisting street lined with dozens of expensive-looking houses behind tall palm trees and imposing walls.

'Nice area. Don't tell me you have one of these gaffs?'

'Nah,' said Charlie. 'Mine's bigger'.

A few minutes later they pulled up outside a robust-looking metal gate inset into a ten-foot-high brick wall. The entrance was wide enough for two cars. Charlie reached for a plastic gadget in the glove box and pressed on one of the silver buttons. Eddie heard a whirring sound from behind the doors, which began to slide open to reveal a shallow driveway leading down to a big white villa. It was lined with small bushes of a uniform size and shape. Beyond it, there were lush green lawns and several towering palm trees.

As they pulled up outside the house, Eddie let out a whistle. 'Bloody hell. This is all yours?' His brother smiled as he opened the door.

'I told you, I'm doing alright. C'mon, I need a fucking drink'.

Charlie led his younger brother into the house. Eddie paused to take it all in. It was as impressive on the inside as it was outside - the entrance hall was spacious and well-lit, the ceiling was lined with cherry-red timber beams, and the floors were lined with grey and white marble tiles. Dark, wooden stairs clad in a cream carpet led upwards.

'The kitchen's that way,' said Charlie pointing towards an open door. 'There's a drinks cabinet at the far end. Fix us up a scotch. There's ice in the freezer. I'll be back in a sec. And check out the garden'. He turned and started up the stairs.

Eddie stepped into the kitchen which appeared to have been freshly installed; the smell of paint and tile grout still hung in the air. The kitchen work surfaces were fashioned from black granite, the units underneath it were a glossy black with brushed aluminium handles. He located the drinks cabinet and the freezer, made two drinks and then walked to the back of the house.

French windows opened up onto an expansive white-tiled patio and a sizeable swimming pool. Eddie guessed that it was about sixty feet long. A semi-transparent blue inflatable lilo floated on the still, dark blue water. A fat ginger cat lay in the shade under a portable barbecue. Such was the feline's lack of movement, Eddie wondered if maybe it was dead.

He placed the drinks down on a table underneath a sunshade and sat down on a white sun lounger. The vista beyond the garden was of a series of rolling green hills speckled with hundreds of villas of assorted shapes and sizes, that continued down until they met the sprawl of Marbella, below. The vast milky-blue expanse of the Mediterranean sparkled beyond.

'Quite some view, innit?' said Charlie as he stepped out onto the sun-drenched patio. He had changed into a pair of cream shorts and a black, short-sleeved shirt. A flesh-coloured plaster was covering the bridge of his nose.

'How's your face?' said Eddie.

'Ah, it's nuffin. Hungry?' He placed a porcelain mixing bowl full of potato crisps down in front of Eddie, picked up his glass and then slumped down onto the sun lounger next to him.

'So, are you going to tell me what it is you do down here?'

Charlie leaned forward as if mindful that others might be listening. 'Well, there's the bar. A few solid investments here and there - restaurants, a timeshare business and a car dealership. Oh, and a part-ownership in a men's clothing store over in Banús.'

'Investments?' said Eddie. 'And where'd the money come from to make these investments?'

'Here's the thing,' said Charlie before taking a large glug of the drink. 'Do you remember that big robbery on the Barclays depot in Chiswick a few years back?'

'Yeah, it was in the news when I was on my second tour in Northern Ireland. 1977, right?'

'1978. February the 12th. They said it was fifteen million pounds, but it was only about half that, really'.

'What are you telling me, Charlie?'

'You wanted to know what I did, bruv. Now you know. I ran a crew. We robbed banks. Now I live here'.

Eddie shook his head in disbelief. 'That Barclays job was you? Fuck,' he said. 'I mean, I knew you weren't no angel, not since you got sent to the Borstal when you was sixteen. But a bank robber?'

Charlie shrugged. 'It's in the past now. I don't do that no more. I don't need to. Not after that job. I've invested the money down here. Diversification and all that'.

Eddie reached forward and picked up his brother's packet of cigarettes, took one out of the pack and lit it. He took a deep intake, held it for a few seconds, shut his eyes and then let the smoke exit out through his nose.

'I thought you gave up the smokes?' said Charlie.

'I did,' said Eddie. He opened his eyes again and looked back at his brother. 'The last time I saw you, you were selling life insurance door to door. Now you're a gangster. So what? Are you hiding out down here then?'

'Thing is, there ain't no extradition treaty between Britain and the Spanish anymore,' said Charlie. 'That's why there're loads of us Brits down here. One of the Great Train Robbers lives just down the coast. I forget his name. Two of the guys what did the Brink's-Mat job too. And the crew what did that Security Express depot. They're knocking about here somewhere. Fuengirola, I think. Or maybe Benalmadena. Freddie Foreman, you've heard of him, right?' Eddie nodded. 'He's got a place a few miles away. I bumped into him in the supermarket a few months back. Looks like a bleeding' gorilla, but nice fella it turns out'. He took another swig of his whiskey.

'And the British police can't come after you?' Charlie shook his head. 'That's mental'.

'I know,' said Charlie. 'But as they say, "never look a gift horse in the mouth", right? As long as we don't put a foot wrong down here, then we're all as safe as houses. The Spanish love us spending our money here. They don't care where it came from. It's good for the economy. We have to grease a few palms here and there to keep people sweet. Local politicians. The police. A few local families. But that's alright'.

Eddie stood up and shook his head. He gazed at the enormous mountain to their left. A group of vultures were spiralling up into the sky above them. 'And you're not doing anything dodgy no more? Nuffin at all?'

'Nah, I'm retired'.

'Why the gun then?' said Eddie.

'Just a precaution. It's like the wild west down here. Lots of stuff going on. I'm sticking clear of all that business, don't you worry. But you've got to keep up appearances, don't you? You can't let anyone think you've gone soft.'

'It don't sound all that safe to me. Not if you have to carry a shooter around in your car'. Charlie waved away the question.

'It's all good here,' he said. Trust me. We've just got to keep our noses clean and look after a few locals, that's all. Now enough of this. I need to make a few calls now, but listen. I'm having a bit of a gathering here tonight. You look like shit, so why don't you have a kip then gets yourself cleaned up. I'll sort you out some clothes'. They both stood up and Charlie gave his sibling a bear hug. 'I know I've not been the best brother to you, Ed. Not since I left. But if you stick around for a bit, maybe I can make it up to you. Think about it, yeah?'

'I will,' said Eddie. 'Now, where can I get me head down? I'm dead on my feet'.

CHAPTER FOUR
FLASHBACKS

A flare lit up the dark, cloudless South Atlantic sky. Eddie Lawson stopped for a moment, mesmerised by the sparkling artificial star as it drifted back to earth down to the cold, wet hellhole he and his fellow Paras found themselves occupying.

A volley of yellow and red tracer fire emerged from a rocky outcrop a few hundred yards away in front of them. It tore into the column ahead of Eddie. The two dozen men were clad in numerous layers of jungle-patterned clothing to fend off the biting cold. They jettisoned their equipment and flung themselves to the floor, desperate to seek cover behind the irregular mounds of rocks and clumps of thick peaty earth.

Eddie saw the flashes of gunfire far off in the distance. A second later, bullets thudded into the ground around him and his comrades. They sizzled as they embedded themselves deep into the damp soil, causing slight puffs of steam to emerge from the holes they had made. A man screamed somewhere close by. It sounded like Jimmy Booth, the man-mountain from Nottingham. Eddie couldn't be sure, but he wondered if that was Big Jim that was now wailing like a tortured child. He wanted to roll over towards the source of the crying to help his comrade, but that wasn't what they had trained him to do.

Eddie's job was to fight, to kill the enemy - the injured would have to wait until the shooting was over before they could expect to receive attention.

He heard the barked commands of Colonel Hawkwood a short distance in front somewhere. Men around him were rising and propelling themselves forward. A chorus of sharp explosions of mortar rounds erupted amongst the black shapes from where the machine gun fire had originated. The hail of bullets slowed and became less accurate. His NCO stood up a few yards away bellowing orders.

'Get up. Move your 'effin backsides. Now'. Eddie forced himself up out of the wet gorse, freed himself from his eighty pound backpack, grabbed his self-loading rifle, and started moving as fast as he could. The horizon blazed with intermittent flashes; the Royal Artillery's hundred-and-fifty millimetre howitzers opened up a mile or so behind them, spitting out their high explosive shells towards the enemy positions. Several hundred Argentinian conscripts would now be burrowing themselves deep into their water-logged trenches.

Not all of them.

A bullet zipped past Eddie's ear and he stumbled, regained his balance and pushed onwards once more. Men were unleashing their battle cries; a screaming variety of accents from all across the British Isles. Men, who had previously had very little in common, were now melded by training, comradeship and a shared sense of urgency. They ran, a demanding task in the soggy, uneven ground. Eddie could see movement amongst the small outcrop fifty yards away. Tracers zipped towards the British soldiers once again. A man to his left cried, spun around and crumpled to the floor. Another para ahead of him shrieked as a bullet tore through his ankle, throwing the unfortunate man to the ground. Eddie's lungs were on fire. His heart was pounding. His mouth was dry and his thighs screamed at the exertion, but he kept pressing forward. Stride after stride, each a few feet closer to the hidden enemy up in those black rocks. Each a few seconds nearer to their objective.

And the world turned white.

The blinding flash was followed by a searing pain in his cranium. He dropped his rifle and fell to his knees. He lifted a hand to the source of his discomfort. There was a perfect hole the size of a penny drilled between his temple out of which came blood, as dark as old motor oil poured from the sump of a car engine, black as the night sky. Bright, white smoke enveloped him. He shut his eyes. The sound of his fellow paras and the surrounding battle faded away as swiftly as it had come. He could hear nothing but his own breathing, and the rattles and clinks from his uniform and equipment, as he swayed from side to side.

The pain diminished a little, and he opened his eyes. His hands were stained black, but the dark liquid from within his forehead was already dusty and cracked as if it had dried in the sun. He was on his knees, surrounded by swirling smoke illuminated as if by a bank of stadium floodlights somewhere beyond. There were bodies everywhere; big hardy paratroopers fanned out around him. They looked at peace, as if asleep.

Maybe they were?

He spotted what appeared to be his NCO walking towards him, a dark shape illuminated by the white backdrop behind him. 'Sergeant Burrows. It's me. Eddie. What happened?' he said, bewildered. The soldier's silhouette continued to approach, details becoming more apparent with each stride. 'Sergeant Burrows? Are you okay?' The man took a few more steps before collapsing into a heap close by. Eddie could see that the back of the man's head was missing, yet his NCO was still talking somehow, seemingly oblivious to the lethal damage his skull had sustained.

'You are not a man. You are not a father. She needed you. They both needed you'. Eddie stood up and edged towards the man.

'What are you saying?' Eddie yelled. 'Who needs me?'

'You left them. When they needed you the most'. Eddie tried to step clear of his NCO but struggled for traction in the heavy mud. He couldn't move. The man crawled forward and grabbed Eddie's legs. Eddie struck the injured soldier with the butt of his rifle, yanked his legs free and stumbled away. Behind him, the man started screaming. Eddie looked forward again. He glimpsed a little blonde-haired girl in a white nightgown. She was holding a bright orange teddy bear and glanced in his direction but disappeared into the swirling smoke. He ran after her, calling her name.

'Mary. I'm here. I'm here, baby. Where are you?' but from where she had gone into the fog, there emerged several soldiers wearing Argentinian uniforms. They looked to be but mere teenagers, not men of a regular fighting age. Their battledress was oversized and shredded trouser bottoms reaching down to the soles of their muddy black boots. They were straining to hold their heavy rifles.

He heard the girl again. She was shouting, 'Daddy, daddy, why did you leave?' He tried to back away, but his NCO was again gripping onto one of his boots. He fell over. The boy soldiers approached with weapons at the ready. Eddie raised his rifle and pointed it at the closest of the enemy combatants. He lined up the iron sights on the boy's centre mass and squeezed the trigger.

The sound of a glass smashing on the white-tiled floor next to him wrenched Eddie out of his tortured slumber. He woke up panting, his tee shirt soaked in sweat.

Just a dream, Ed. Just another bloody dream.

Eddie lay still for a few minutes, waiting for his heart rate to return to normal. The bedsheets were drenched with his sweat. He took a deep breath, flung his legs over the side of the bed and stood up. He picked up a shoe and used it to push the pieces of broken glass into a waste bin, then meandered off into the en-suite bathroom. He filled another glass with water, downing it in a few seconds but scrunched his face up as the water entered his mouth. It had an unpleasant metallic taste to it; his brother might live in a semi-palatial villa, but he still had to drink the same sub-par water as the Costa del Sol's package holidaymakers and its other, less-monied residents.

He stared into the mirror and at the weary human that looked back at him, its torso covered in an assortment of scars. There was a flat, smooth pink streak where an Argentinian bullet had grazed his left shoulder. A pair of stab wounds to his right pectoral, acquired during a drunken brawl in a Newcastle tavern - the mouthy sod who had wielded that blade had spent the next three months in hospital with a fractured skull. He also had a smattering of small scars across his stomach and arms. It had taken nearly a full day for the army surgeons to remove all the pieces of shrapnel from his torso and limbs after getting too close to that pipe bomb in Armagh. Eddie still could not decide whether his collection of wounds were all mementoes of good fortune or bad.

'Pull yourself together, soldier,' his former NCO's voice barked in his ear.

Will I ever escape that bastard? Eddie wondered. The man was shot in the head during the battle for Mount Tumbledown, yet his commanding voice still accompanied Eddie wherever he found himself, a full three years after the war.

He returned into the bedroom, and stepped out onto the balcony. It overlooked the impressive garden and pool area. People were milling around, drinks and smokes in hand, some in smart casual attire, others in swimming costumes on sun loungers or at the poolside.

Several expensive-looking cars lined up in the driveway. His brother's silver Porsche, a couple of Mercs, and a dark green Jaguar XJS among them. Charlie and his friends sure have a few bob between them, he thought.

His attention was caught by the bellowing wails of a high-performance engine coming from the main gate to his right. He leaned out over the balcony and saw a red Ferrari Boxer pulling up, sending driveway gravel in every direction. His brother greeted the driver as he struggled to clamber out of the low sports car. The man was tall, well-built, and looked to be in his forties. An attractive and much younger woman accompanied him. She had short black hair, in a style not unlike one of the girls in the Human League. She wore a white, low cut top and tight pink jeans. He gazed at her, captivated by her pale, slender body as she walked down the path and under his balcony. It had been months since he had been with a woman. His pulse increased, and his groin tightened.

'Eddie,' his brother shouted from below. 'Get yourself cleaned up. Ther's people here that I want you to meet'. The woman in the white top caught Eddie's stare before he had time to avert it. Embarrassed, he lifted the glass of water to his mouth to feign ambivalence. Only the glass was empty. The woman sniggered.

You idiot.

'Gimme ten minutes, bruv,' he replied and retreated into the bedroom. He shaved, took a shower, wrapped a white towel around his waist, and stepped into the bedroom's walk-in cupboard. There must have been a dozen jackets, twenty pairs of trousers and twice that many shirts. These were his brother's cast-offs.

'I've put on a bit of weight in the last few years,' Charlie had told him earlier. 'Seemed a waste to chuck 'em, though. Good job I didn't, right? Now you're here'. That Charlie was overweight had been plain to see the moment Eddie had encountered his sibling back at the bar.

'Flippin' heck,' Eddie had thought, but not voiced. *No surprise who ate all the Spanish pies.*

He picked out a pair of pale cream slacks and a dark blue, short-sleeved polo shirt. He looked at the label. It was a Ralph

Lauren. 'Makes a change from Debenhams,' he thought. He opened another cupboard. It harboured dozens of shoes. He wanted something lightweight and spotted a pair of light blue canvas Sperry Top-Siders. That would do. He carried the clothes back into the bedroom and hurried to get dressed, curious to see who that woman was.

CHAPTER FIVE
A NOT SO SMALL GATHERING

There were about thirty people outside by the time Eddie made his appearance, some well-attired in suits, others in casual shorts and shirts. Most of the men were in their forties or fifties, and well-tanned. He could only hear British accents, but presumed everyone present lived on the Costa now. There was an abundance of shaven heads, scars, tattoos and boxer's noses. Even those men with fuller heads of hair still carried themselves with that *"I'm somebody"* air about them. Almost all the men were accompanied by women, most of whom were significantly younger and prettier than their male partners.

Everybody appeared to treat Eddie with wariness as he stepped out onto the stone-tiled patio.

'Oi, Ed. Over here, bruv'. Eddie looked to his left and saw his brother sitting at a table under a sunshade. He was with a group of several people which included the Ferrari-owner, although the man's beautiful female companion was nowhere to be seen. Charlie clicked his fingers at a lanky ginger-haired man to beckon him over. 'Hey, Kieran, fetch my brother here a cocktail, will yer? I reckon he'll have a…Martini. Or maybe a Daiquiri. Yeah, Eddie?'

The waiter looked to Eddie for approval.

'A beer's fine, mate,' said Eddie to the waiter who then turned away and sauntered off towards a makeshift bar on the opposite side of the patio.

Charlie stood up and greeted his brother with a firm hug. 'Good kid that,' said Charlie. 'His Dad was in the IRA and is doin' time down here for gun-running'. Asked me to watch out for his boy while he was inside. Suits me, the kid makes the best cocktails anywhere on the Costa'. He lifted a conical glass up from the table and slurped at the bright red liquid.

'What? Are you friends with the bloody Provos, now?' said Eddie.

'Nah. Well, yeah. But it don't matter to me what he did before'.

'I did two tours in Northern Ireland,' said Eddie. 'I lost friends to those bastards'.

Charlie put the drink back down and raised his hands. 'I'm sorry, bruv. It's just that it's different down here. We don't do politics and religion and that crap. We left all that bollocks behind when we left England. Everyone's the same down here. Us Brits, the Micks, the Krauts, the Frenchies. Whatever. It don't matter none where you come from, or what you did back home. Down here on the Costa, it's just about doin' business and, well, enjoying life'. He put his hand on his brother's shoulder. 'Know what I mean?'

'Yeah, sure,' said Eddie. 'Fuck all that, right?'

Charlie smiled. 'That's the spirit, Ed,' he said, failing to pick up on the cynicism in his brother's voice. 'This is my life now. And this sorry bunch of people here…' he said, waving his hand in the general direction of the group, 'these are all what matters to me now'. He took another slug of the cocktail, then took a step back and eyed his sibling from head to toe. 'Fuck me, I'm glad I kept all them old clothes. You look like a right player'. He turned to face the group of men and women gathered around the table. 'What d'ya think, guys? This is my kid brother, Eddie. I've not seen him for a few years. He turned up at my bar this morning looking like a right down and out, he did. Now, look at him. Scrubs up well, don't he girls?'

'Cor. Not half, Charlie!' said one of the women, a bleach-blonde woman in her forties who had not taken her eyes of Eddie since he had stepped out of the villa. She was dressed in a tight black skirt and a flower-patterned blouse designed for a younger, slimmer body. 'He's in much better shape than you. You sure he's your brother?'

Another woman next to her, also of a similar age and dressed in a shiny gold blouse, almost spat out her drink laughing. She wiped her lips with the back of her hand. 'I think Judy's got a point, you know?' she said. 'This geezer's slim, right good-looking, and he's got all his hair still. I reckon one of you's adopted'.

The women looked at each other and cackled. One of the men next to them, a rugged-looking man in a blue pair of shorts and a white polo shirt, shuffled in his chair. He glanced up at Eddie and then at the woman at his side. The surrounding conversations paused.

'Shut it, Judy,' he said while grasping her arm.

The woman yelped in pain and yanked her arm free. 'Fuck off, Roger'. She rubbed her arm. 'That fucking' hurt,' she slapped the man on his arm.

'Nah, it's alright,' said Charlie. 'She don't mean it. She didn't know'.

'Didn't know what?' said Judy, still angry and oblivious to the changed mood.

'I was adopted,' said Eddie. He looked at the woman in the tight blouse. The group of people took a collective gulp. 'My mother gave me away in the hospital. She was a dancer in a club. That's right, weren't it Charlie?' He looked at his brother then back at the two women. 'I've no fucking idea who my father was. No idea at all. Don't want to neither. They didn't want me, so fuck them'. Charlie stood frozen to the spot, unable to speak. 'I got put with a couple, the Lawsons, in West London when I was still a baby. They already had Charlie'. Eddie looked at his brother. 'You were what, eight?'

'I was nine when mum brought you home,' said Charlie.

'Right. Nine,' said Eddie. 'Anyway, the Lawsons were planning to tell me this when I was in my teens. You know, when I'd be better able to handle it. But Charlie -'.

'Ed -,' said Charlie, trying to interject, but Eddie held up his finger and wagged it at his sibling.

'But Charlie here, my big brother…he told me when I was just four years old'.

'Shit,' said Judy. Roger looked at her with despair.

The ginger waiter was standing next to Eddie with a pint of beer on a tray.

Eddie took the drink. 'Cheers,' he said. He downed half of it then wiped his face. All eyes were on him still. He looked back at his brother. 'Oh, I'm sorry, Charlie. I just assumed that you'd have told all your close friends here about where I came from. No?' Charlie cast his eyes to the floor. 'Mrs Lawson, Mum, she treated us both decently'. He looked at Judy. 'Mr Lawson, not so much'. He pointed at an old circular scar on the back of his left hand. 'That's from a belt-buckle. The old bastard hit me with his belt one night coz I hadn't taken his mangy dog for a walk. I hadn't done it, coz I'd been doing my homework. Funny, huh?'

Judy glanced towards the sheepish-looking Charlie. Carol, standing next to her, stood motionless with her mouth wide open.

It took a few seconds of uncomfortable silence before one of the other men cleared his throat and stood up. It was the Ferrari owner. He was robustly built and taller than Eddie, with tight cropped blonde hair and bright blue eyes. An old scar ran from the lower part of his nose and across his right cheek.

He put one hand on Eddie's shoulder while gripping his hand with the other. 'Nice to meet you, son,' he said. The man relaxed his grip, looked at the two women, then back at Eddie. 'Pull yourself up a chair and get under this umbrella. You're lookin' a bit pink already. Gotta watch this flipping sun, it's hotter here than Southend'. He sat back down, chuckling.

'Sorry, Eddie. We didn't mean nuffin,' said Judy. She glanced at the woman next to her.

'Er, yeah. Sorry Eddie. Sorry Charlie. We were just havin' a laugh. Didn't mean nuffin by it.'

'It's alright girls,' said Charlie. 'Don't you worry your pretty faces over this'. He swivelled around to call the waiter over again. 'Hey, Kieran. Go fetch three bottles of Bolli from my private stash, alright? There's a good lad'.

'Ooooh, hark at you, Mr Flash,' said another of the men, a short, wiry-looking man in a yellow Fred Perry polo shirt and white cotton shorts. 'Gettin' the good stuff out now, are we?'

'Too right I am, Kenny. My kid brother's in town, ain't he? I think that's a cause for celebration'.

The ginger waiter arrived with the champagne and a box of plastic tumblers.

'Sorry Mr Lawson, I couldn't find no more clean glasses'.

'Don't you worry son, there ain't no airs and graces among this lot,' said Charlie. He handed a bottle each to Mike and Roger. 'Here, everyone take a glass and fill 'em up. This stuff's a hundred quid a bottle. Don't let it go to waste. He poured a glass and handed it to Eddie and one for himself then put his arm around his brother. 'Lets get formally introduced. That gorilla who just tried to crush your hand is big Mikey. He's from South Harrow'. Eddie nodded at the man with the scarred face who raised his glass in acknowledgment. 'This is Roger and his wife, Judy. Roger's from round our way, South Ruislip,' said Charlie while gesturing towards the man in the blue shorts and white shirt, and his recently chastened wife. 'That's Bill at the back there with the ridiculous comb over. And his wife, Carol. Bill used to drink in The Windmill in Ruislip Manor'. The man in the yellow polo shirt crossed his arms and nodded.

'Nice to meet you, Eddie'.

DEN OF SNAKES

'And this charmer here is Kenny. He spent a few years in the forces too, didn't yer Kenny?'

'Yeah, in West Germany. On the Rhine. A good couple of years it was too,' said Kenny.

'Yeah, till they caught him selling the supplies on the black market!' said Charlie, chuckling. 'He got eighteen months in the lockup for that'.

'And a good kicking from the bloody MPs,' said Kenny.

Eddie, who had several altercations with the military police himself, raised his glass towards Kenny. 'So how'd you lads all meet then?'

There was an uncomfortable silence for a few seconds. Eddie looked at his brother, an expectant look on his face.

'Well bruv,' said Charlie. 'Let's just say, we all worked together. If you know what I mean'.

Eddie wasn't sure how to take that answer at first. Then the penny dropped.

'Sorry, Dumb question. I'm a bit tired still'.

Charlie laughed.

'So are you stopping here for a bit then son?' asked Bill, clearly seeking to change the flow of the conversation.

Eddie shrugged. 'Nah, I'm just passing through'.

The conversation was abruptly interrupted by the sounds of an argument a few feet away. Eddie looked towards the raised voices. It was the woman he had seen earlier who had been wearing a white top and pink trousers, only now she was wearing a revealing scarlet swimsuit. From the shouting, Eddie deduced that the woman had been lying by the pool reading a paperback when a man had jumped in close by. A portly individual, he had soaked her and her novel. The woman was shouting at the rotund man who stood before her, dripping wet and wearing only a skimpy pair of swimming trunks.

'Get your gut and them ridiculous budgie smugglers out of my fucking face, you fat son of a bitch'. She started poking him with her finger.

'Watch your mouth, girl or -'.

'Or what, you fat fuck? What you gonna do? The man grabbed her wrist and looked like he would hit her, but checked himself when he heard glass breaking. Mike was standing behind the woman holding a broken beer bottle.

'Touch her again, and I'll gut that fucking whale belly of yours'.

The man in the swimming trunks let the woman go. 'Right. Yeah. Sorry, Mikey,' said the man. 'My mistake'.

'Don't apologise to me, you wanker. It's me missus what you need to be saying sorry to,' said Mike.

The man looked at the woman. 'Sorry lass. Maybe I've had a few too many. I wasn't gonna hit you. Honest'. The woman glared back at him, saying nothing.

Three large men had gathered close by, seemingly deciding whether to stand up for their mate. Mike took a step towards them, still wielding the broken bottle.

'Take that lump of lard away. He ain't welcome here,' he said.

'What if we don't?' said one of the men. A faint smile appeared on Mike's face, and he took another step towards the men.

But before events took a turn for the worse, Charlie arrived holding a bottle of champagne.

'S'alright boys, no need for any aggro. We're all friends here. Here, have this on me. It's Bollinger. It's the bee's knees, this stuff,' he said. 'Kieran over there, the ginger kid. He'll get you some glasses. Alright. Good. Nice one'. He turned back to face Mike. 'Mate, calm down. It's nuffin, alright. Nuffin,' he hissed.

'He had his paws on my Veronica, Charlie. He was gonna hit her. You saw it'.

'How many times have I told you, Mike? We need to think of the bigger picture here. We need allies. Not more enemies'. Veronica was standing close by listening to the engagement. Charlie shot her a look. 'Besides, you know as well as I do, she was winding them up. She was sitting right next to a swimming pool. Course she's gonna get wet. It's a pool party for Christ's sake'. Mike looked at his girlfriend who smiled cheekily back at the two men. 'Get her under control, mate. We can't afford no silly business here today. Okay?'

'Yeah, you're right Charlie'. Mike turned towards his girlfriend. 'Get yourself over here, girl. Stop causing trouble. You're upsetting Charlie'.

She shook her head. 'Wouldn't wanna do that, upset the mighty Charles Lawson, now would I?' She reached down and picked up her things. 'I'll be in the house,' she said as she strode away.

Both men watched her walk away. As she passed Eddie, she looked him over from top to bottom in the manner of a tradesman sizing up a potential job, before concluding that it would be lucrative. She licked her lips in a provocative motion, and winked at him. He watched her from behind as she walked away, her shoulders and hips swaying perfectly in rhythm to the Lionel Richie song playing from inside the villa.

'Sorry, Charlie. I know she's a pain sometimes,' said Mike as he walked past Eddie.

'But the crazy ones are the fun ones?' said Charlie. 'Yeah, I know mate'. Eddie watched as his brother gave his friend a playful punch.

The party carried on long after the sun had disappeared behind *La Concha*, Marbella's iconic, hulking mountain. Eddie sat watching, listening but keeping himself to himself as best as he could. He was warming to the group and, despite the initial resentment he had felt towards his erstwhile brother, he had to admit that it felt good to be in his company once more. His pint glass was empty, and he needed to take a leak.

'I'm going to the John'.

'There's a bog in the hallway, behind the kitchen,' Charlie informed him.

Eddie nodded, got up and made his way to the toilet.

Kenny was already in the large bathroom standing at the one and only toilet, one hand on his penis, the other patting down his hair.

'There you go, son,' he said whilst pushing the flush button. 'She's all yours'. Eddie stood at the pan, unzipped his fly and let out a sigh of relief as he started urinating. 'Sounds like you needed that,' said Kenny as he washed his hands. He reached for a towel. 'I don't want to speak out of turn here. But I think your brother's hoping you will stick around here for a bit. He could really do with your help, you know'.

'I don't think so,' said Eddie. 'He ain't got a clue what I've been through since we last saw each other'. He turned on the tap and ran the water over his hands.

Kenny handed him a fresh hand towel and fixed him with his stare. 'He's always talking about you, Ed. Told us all about what you've been up to'.

'He did, huh?' said Eddie, unsure whether to believe the man.

'In the paras wasn't yer? Served in the Falklands'.

'That's right,' said Eddie.

'You were at Mount Tumbledown. And Goose Green. Right shitty deal that must have been. You army boys did our country proud. You have my respect. You have all of our respect'.

'So, how long have you been down here, Ken?' said Eddie, keen to change the subject.

'Christ, over five years now. Yeah, I came down about six months after Charlie. I didn't plan to leave, truth be told, but I had no choice. The fuzz was all over us. Someone grassed on us. We never worked out who'.

'Do you miss it?' said Eddie.

'I miss me Mum, I guess. And the lads down the boozer. But other than that, nah'.

'And is it as safe as Charlie says? I mean with the "no extradition" thing?'

'Kind of'.

'What's that mean?' said Eddie.

'Well, officially the Spanish won't do nothing, as long as we keep our noses clean down here, but there was this one guy we all knew, Terry Gibson, he was wanted for a bunch of bank jobs back home. He refused to pay the locals, didn't he? Not a smart move, it turned out'.

'How so?'

'Gibbo ran a club down here, just up the coast. In Mijas. Raking it in, he was. But this one night, about a year ago it was, he vanished for a few days before turning up in England a few days later in the back of a bleeding Black Mariah'.

'He got deported?' asked Eddie.

'That's one way of saying it, I suppose. What we heard was that he was locking up his bar one night, when a group of men with ski masks jumped him. Some old granny who lived nearby saw it from her bedroom window. They hit him over the head with a cosh or something. When he woke up he was tied up and gagged in the boot of a car. When it eventually stopped, the occupants had left the scene, but he realised they had taken him to France when a local gendarmerie officer opened the boot. It's at least a twelve-hour drive. More, maybe. He was laying there, in the back of the car covered in his own piss and shit, so I heard. It must have been disgusting. Anyway, the French rustled him off to England and now he's doing a fifteen-year stretch. People say the Spanish, French and Brit police planned it all. He got off lucky, mind you.

'Lucky?' said Eddie. 'That don't sound very lucky to me'.

'Yeah, well, Gibbo was high profile. Had something to do with that Security Express job, I think. The Flying Squad wanted him bad. Others less well-known…well, they tend to just disappear. Especially if they've been up to their old tricks down here. The local families - the old money - they don't appreciate that. The hills around here are full of bodies'.

'Fuck me. How do you lot sleep?'

'Ah, it's not that bad. You just got to keep paying the right people. Money talks down here. They're all leeches, I tell you. Fuckin' leeches. I've spent over ten grand this year, trying to keep their noses away from my business. But you've just got to view it as a kind of tax. And just enjoy yourself'. The door opened, and another man entered. Kenny stood out of his way and beckoned Eddie to go through the door. 'Enough of this depressing talk. I need another drink'.

Over the following hours, there was much talking about the old days and frequent references to the "big job". Eddie had the distinct impression that this cabal of suntanned wide boys were living off their past glories, and doing all they could to convince those around them - and probably themselves - that they remained relevant.

Most of the guests had left by midnight, but Mike, Roger and Judy, Kenny, Bill and Carol were still going strong.

'Okay ladies and gents,' said Charlie. 'Now all them fuckers have gone, I want to show you all something. Follow me inside, I have a surprise for you'.

Charlie led the group inside the house to a sturdy wooden door while whistling "Gold" by Spandau Ballet. He inserted a key into the lock and then opened the door.

'Is this where you keep the bodies, Charlie?' said Carol. Her husband, Bill, shot her a look of amazement. 'What? It's a joke, innit,' said Carol.

Charlie flicked on the lights and walked around a large white table in the centre of the room. On top of the table sat the architect's model of a three-story apartment block. 'This, my friends, is Urbanizacion Majestico'.

'What? So you've been making models in your spare time, Charlie?' said Roger.

Bill snorted with laughter.

'You're kiddin' me? It's the property project I told you all about a couple of months ago. You remember Mike? Bill? You know…the investment opportunity'.

'Ah, right Yeah,' said Bill, none to convincingly.

'So you're doing it then?' said Roger.

'You better believe it, mate,' said Charlie. Mike reached over and picked up a mini apartment in his hand and examined it. 'Oi, put that back you fuckin' plonker. This model cost me a couple of grand'.

'You paid two thousand quid for a toy building?' said Judy. 'Fuckin' hell. You could have had a real house in south London for that a few years ago'.

'It's the way it's done, innit. You need to get the investors excited. Show 'em the possibilities,' said Charlie. 'So anyway, I had a good meeting with some important locals over in Banús this morning. It's looking good'.

'You went to the local families for funding? Bit risky, innit?' said Mike.

'Nah, mate. It's all cushty'.

'So they're in already?' said Mike.

'Not yet. But it won't be long, trust me. They know that they can make some easy dosh if they get in on this'. He cleared his throat. 'As can all of you. If you invest as well'.

Faces lifted up from looking at the miniature construction project.

'You're asking us to come in on it?' asked Bill.

Charlie nodded. 'Juan Fernandez and some other partners will stump up a million quid. If we get the project going first,' he said.

Mike stood, staring at the white building in his hand. Bill and Kenny looked to the floor.

'How much have you spent on it so far?' said Bill.

'About nine hundred grand,' said Charlie. 'To buy the land, pay the architect and get provisional planning permission and other stuff'.

'And how much more d'yer need to get it going?' asked Roger.

'About one and a half,' said Charlie.

'Million?' said Carol. Charlie rolled his eyes.

'Of course, million. That's for phase one. I need another three point five for the following phases'.

Mike whistled and put the building down. 'Now *that* is an expensive model,' he said.

'I can stump up another five hundred grand,' said Charlie.

'So you need another million to get the project underway?' said Bill.

'Exactly,' said Charlie, then lifted a cocktail glass to his lips.

'That's two hundred and fifty grand each,' said Bill. 'I dunno. What with the money I've got in other things, that would leave me pretty thin'. He looked at Kenny. 'What d'you think?'

Kenny took a cigarette out of the packet in his hands, lit it and took a long drag. 'Well, I don't know nuffin about property development,' he said, then took another drag. He looked across at Charlie. 'But if this geezer tells me it's a good idea, then I'm in. You just tell me what I need to do, mate. Okay?'

'Thanks, Kenny. I appreciate it'. He looked at the others who, Eddie thought, did not seem quite so convinced.

'So, what do the rest of you think?' Charlie asked.

'It's a lot of dough, Charlie. I've got the cash, just about. But like Bill said, it would leave me well exposed,' said Roger.

'I lent eighty grand to that Italian fucker, Fallaci, six months ago,' said Bill. 'You know, for that new trendy restaurant he opened on the beachfront in Benalmádena. He's supposed to have paid it all back by now. With an extra twenty for interest, but I've not seen a penny yet. I'd have gone round and shoved a shooter up his nose by now, but you told us all to keep a low profile. That and a few other things are givin' me sleepless nights'.

'I understand,' said Charlie. 'Tell you what. Me and Eddie will go pay that wop a visit in the morning for you. We'll make sure he pays up. How's that work for you?' said Charlie.

Eddie shot Charlie a look as if to say 'what the fuck?', but if his brother noticed, he ignored it.

Bill thought about it for a few seconds, then replied. 'Get him to pay up, and I'll think about it. Okay?'

'Good stuff,' said Charlie. He looked at Roger and Mike. 'Guys, I promise you, this is the opportunity we've been looking for. We put this cash in now and in less than a year we will be taking deposits on these flats. Anything you invest now, you double in less than a year'. He put his hands on Kenny's cheeks, looking for all the world as if he was about to kiss him. 'And the beautiful thing…it's clean money'.

'If it's like you say, guess it would be stupid not to,' said Mike.

'Good man' said Charlie. 'What about you, Rog?'

Roger glanced at his wife and scratched the back of his head. 'I'll talk to my accountant tomorrow. See what I can do. Alright?'

'Thanks, mate. You won't regret it'.

A little later, having seen Charlie wave off his mates and their female companions, Eddie approached his brother.

'Listen, what you said about visiting that bloke to get Bill's money -'.

'Don't worry about that, it'll be nothing,' said Charlie. He closed the front door and started towards the stairs, but Eddie continued.

'I ain't here to get involved in your business,' said Eddie.

Charlie put his arm over his brother's shoulder. 'We're just going have a chat with the geezer. But I can't do it by myself. I need you'.

Eddie sighed. 'And you'll front me the cash I need to get to Angola?'

'Of course,' said Charlie. 'It's the least I can do. That's what brothers are for, right?'

'Okay,' said Eddie.

Charlie gave him a friendly punch on the shoulder. 'Thanks, Ed. It's a big help'. He took a sip from the glass of scotch he was holding. 'Listen, Ed. I'm sorry. For what I did all them years ago'. Charlie put his hands on Eddie's cheeks. His breath was foul. 'I was a selfish git. I'm sorry, bruv'.

'Forget it,' said Eddie. 'I shouldn't have said what I did earlier. I don't know what came over me'.

Charlie stared into his younger brother's eyes. 'Things are different now. I'm here for yer. You know that, right?'

Eddie nodded. 'Sure, Charlie'. He extracted himself from his brother's grasp. 'I'm friggin' knackered. I'm going to bed'.

'Night bruv,' said Charlie.

CHAPTER SIX
BAD INVESTMENTS

Eddie woke up to the sharp morning sunlight. His skull was throbbing, and the roof of his mouth was as dry as blotting paper. He kicked the satin sheets off his legs, forced himself out of bed and made his way downstairs. He went to the kitchen, flicked the switch on the kettle and opened the cupboards in search of coffee.

It was only at that point that he realised that Charlie was standing in his office across the hall, engaged in what appeared to be an awkward telephone call.

His brother had the phone speaker on and had failed to notice Eddie, who could not help but overhear both sides of the conversation. A stern-voiced woman asserted that she could only give Charlie another four weeks to secure the investment he needed to start his construction project.

'Other parties are waiting to take over if you cannot get the financing closed,' she told him.

'And I bet one of them bleeding parties is Daniel-fucking-Ortega, right?' He plucked a tennis ball from off his desk and squeezed it in his right hand.

'I can't disclose that information, Mr Lawson'.

'Of course, you can't,' said Charlie, tossing the ball from hand to hand.

'Mr Lawson, my records show that you were told when you entered this process, that council bye-laws require that you can show that you have sufficient funding for the construction to begin, and -'.

'Yeah, yeah, yeah. They also advised me that we would get the planning permission in six months. It took two years, during which I've had nine hundred grand tied up in a plot of friggin' weeds'.

'Well, surely that gave you more time to secure investor interest?' the woman said.

Charlie took three rapid steps towards the desk and leaned into the speaker. 'I had investors. I had three of them lined up, but they all lost interest coz you lot took so fuckin' long'.

'Please do not curse at me, Mr Lawson. I am new into this role'.

'What happened to that last guy I was dealing with? Mr Cruz? Stick 'em on the phone, love'.

'Mr De La Cruz no longer works for Marbella town council,' said the woman. 'There were certain accusations made against him'.

Eddie saw Charlie look up to the ceiling, mouthing silent expletives.

'What accusations?' he said.

'That is a confidential matter, I'm afraid. But I am now the acting head of planning and development. I shall be your point of contact now'.

'Jesus Christ,' Charlie said. 'You're the fifth bloody person I've had to deal with. You lot are a friggin' shambles. For fuck's sake'. He spun around and threw the ball at the wall next to the open door, at which point he noticed Eddie standing in the kitchen and lifted the receiver off the phone. 'Hang on a sec,' he barked into the phone. He walked toward the door, handset to his ear. 'Won't be five mins, bruv. Chill in the garden for a bit, bruv,' he said while closing the door.

Eddie made himself a mug of black coffee before making his way out into the back garden. He squinted until his eyes adjusted to the sunlight. The sky was bright blue and cloudless. The view from the terrace looked out towards a set of slow rolling hills, crested with green trees and large white, pink, mustard and blue villas. He could see Marbella and Puerto Banús several miles below, the Mediterranean gleaming beyond. It was a stunning view.

He sat down on one of the several dozen white sun loungers, slung his legs up and laid back into the upright seat. The detritus from the previous night's party surrounded him. They must have got through a few thousand pound's worth of booze, he guessed.

'Easy to see the attraction of living here,' he thought. *Assuming you have the cash to do so.*

'Sorry about that,' said Charlie, who was ambling towards him with a glass in his hand containing an ample measure of what, Eddie presumed, was scotch.

'Spot of bother?' Eddie asked.

Charlie frowned. 'What? That?' he said, waving towards the house. 'Nah, that's just the normal way of doing business down here. You know, *mañana* this, *mañana* that. They're all just angling for a backhander to speed things up. The last geezer was helpful when he got money out of me. For a few months, anyway. That trollop will come round too, you'll see'. He pulled another sun lounger closer to where Eddie was laying. 'Sleep alright?'

'Not really. I'm not used to this heat. Or the friggin' mossies'.

Charlie laughed. 'Well, according to my Spanish cleaner, that means you eat too many candies. They like sweet blood, she reckons'.

Eddie forced a smile; his mind still on what his brother has asked him to do the previous evening. 'This business today, helping Bill get his money back from this Italian geezer,' he said. 'Is it likely to get feisty?'

'Nah, it's just a geezer taking the piss what needs a word in his wormhole, that's all. We're not gonna hurt him. I'm just going to appeal to his sense of social responsibility. We leave in an hour. Get yourself sorted, grab some brekky, Okay?' Charlie downed the drink and, without waiting for Eddie to reply, continued; 'I've got another couple of calls to make.' He pulled himself up off the lounger and strode back towards the house.

An hour later, Eddie sat in the passenger seat of Charlie's Porsche as his brother piloted it along the coastal road, towards Benelmádana. The traffic was heavy with coaches transporting tourists to or from their hotels, lorries belching black smoke and lackadaisical taxis.

Charlie had one hand on the steering wheel, the other on the car's horn, which he was using every few seconds.'For fuck's sake. Get out of the way, dickhead,' he bellowed at one taxi as they approached a stretch where the road opened up to two lanes.

'We in a rush?' said Eddie.

'These twerps wind me right up. They'd never pass the English driving test'. He pulled the car sideways to the right and motored past a slow-moving truck on the inside lane'.

'I reckon you need to relax, bruv. Don't want to bust that nose of yours again, do you?'

'We're almost there,' said Charlie while wiping the sweat off his forehead with a blue handkerchief.

Eddie was feeling the heat too. 'Mind if I stick the air con on?' he asked.

'It's up the swanny. Been that way for ages. Fuckin' kraut engineering'.

'Why don't you get it fixed?'

'Because the thieving fuckers wanted over a grand to mend it. Flipping ridiculous. The flipping thing's only five years old. I weren't paying that'.

'How much did you spend on booze last night?' said Eddie.

'That's different,' said Charlie. He looked over his shoulder and manoeuvred the car towards the approaching slip road, the large blue sign above it showing that it was the exit for Benalmádena.

'Got to impress the locals, right?' said Eddie.

'Exactly right, bruv. That was an investment in our futures. Havin' get-togethers like that is important for business,' said Charlie. 'You've got to bring people together. Find out what's happening. Oil a few deals and all that. Last night was putting cash to good use. Spending a grand on this piece of German crap? That's just burning money'.

'I thought money wasn't an issue?' said Eddie.

Charlie half glanced at him again, while wiping more sweat away. 'Yeah, it's just that this deal is taking up a lot of my liquid funds. That's my top priority. Fixing this bloody thing can wait'.

'How bad is it?' Charlie shook his head.

'It's just about investing wisely for a while. Until the property deal is underway. After that, once the cash is rollin' back in, I'll get rid of this jerry shitheap and get myself a Jag or something. One of them new XJS convertibles. They're right fuckin' sweet, they are'.

Charlie drove towards the seafront. It being the middle of July, the streets were awash with pink-skinned holidaymakers.

A group of Scandinavian-looking men in their twenties broke into a scamper as the Porsche approached, Charlie refusing to slow down as they crossed the road. 'Use the bleedin' zebra crossing,' he shouted as he sped past.

Eddie peered into the wing mirror to see one of the pale men trip over, before flipping a finger at the German car.

That's where we're going,' said Charlie, a couple of minutes later. He was pointing at a restaurant ahead of them, on their left; an Italian eatery called *Fallaci's*. Charlie continued driving, ignoring several empty parking spaces.

'You just passed two spaces,' Eddie said.

His brother was looking in his rearview mirror. 'I'm wanna stick it around the corner,' he said. 'Out of sight'. He turned left onto a side street, found a space and parked the silver car. 'Right. Let's do this,' he said as he got out of the vehicle. 'This Italian fucker is Gino Fallaci. Bill lent him eighty grand six months ago to get his place set up. He's not paid a penny back yet, even though I know he's rakin' it in'. Charlie thrust the key into the lock and twisted it, both doors locking and the indicators flashed twice in unison. 'The restaurant has been packed every night,' he said while he rolled up his sleeves. 'I reckon he's clearing four of five grand a night, easy'.

They started off around the street corner and marched up the pavement for a few hundred yards, before arriving at the restaurant.

Charlie tried the front door, but found it locked. 'We'll go round the back. I can hear someone inside'.

The brothers both clambered over a small row of shrubs and jogged towards an open door at the rear. A member of the kitchen staff, a short man in chequered blue and white trousers and a grubby yellow tee shirt, approached holding a bucket full of peeled potatoes. He attempted to block their passage, but Charlie shoved him and he fell backwards, the bucket and its contents emptying onto the white tiled floor. Eddie looked behind him to see the man clamber up, before running towards the exit.

Charlie stopped at a door marked "Prohibido" and took a deep breath. 'Just follow my lead, okay?' He pushed the door open and marched in.

A man in a cream flannel suit and a white shirt was leaning against a large wooden desk, smoking and studying a copy of *El Pais*. He looked up, a look of surprise clear on his face.

'Gino, how yer doin? You remember me, right? Charlie. A friend of Bill's'.

'H…h…hi. Yes, Charlie Lawson. Of course'. The man placed the newspaper on the desk and the half-finished cigarette down into a heavy-looking, chrome ashtray. 'How can I help you?' he said in a nervous tone. He looked towards the office door, but Eddie closed it.

'By paying Bill what you owe him. Today. Now'.

'The loan? Ah, but I need more time,' the man said, as he sat down on the leather chair behind the desk. He smiled at Eddie. 'I don't believe we've met. I'm Gino. And you are -'.

'Someone who's going to hurt you if you keep dishing out that bullshit,' said Charlie before his younger brother could reply.

'Charlie. Why the hostility? Bill will get his money. Business is a bit slower than -'.

'Shut the fuck up, you lying snake,' said Charlie, snarling. 'That's a brand new Beemer out the back there. A 635CSi, ain't it? What did that cost? Thirty grand? Thirty five?' He started moving the objects on Fallaci's messy desk. 'Where's the keys?'

The sound of several heavy footsteps moving on the wooden pathway outside interrupted them. Eddie stepped to the window and looked out.

'What is it?' said Charlie.

'Trouble,' said Eddie.

A group of men appeared at the door. One of them, a tall shaven-headed man with cauliflower ears and a flat nose, walked up to Charlie, fixing his stare into his eyes.

'What d'you want you ugly fucker?' said Charlie. 'A bleedin' kiss?' The man tightened his hands into fists and Eddie stepped closer.

'It's okay, boys,' said the restaurant owner. 'Mr Lawson and I were just having a friendly chat. Weren't we, Charlie?' Charlie did not answer as the Italian stood up and approached him. 'If I didn't know better, I'd say you were under a bit of pressure, Charlie'. He gave Charlie a knowing smile.

'You'll find out what bleedin' pressure is if you don't pay what you owe,' said Charlie. The Italian ignored the threat.

'I gather that things are getting difficult for you here in Spain. There are Scotland Yard detectives over here hunting wanted criminals, no?' He picked up the newspaper he had been reading, and held it up for both brothers to see. The headline was in Spanish.

'It says that the Spanish government wants to get rid of foreign criminals'.

'Then you should be worried, you Eyetie bastard,' said Charlie.

Fallaci laughed. 'Oh, but the Spanish like me. I'm just a hard-working restauranteur'.

'Who don't pay what he owes,' said Charlie.

Fallaci dismissed Charlie's statement with a wave of his hand. 'I understand there is also a famous TV reporter here looking for British who are, how you say…"on the run". Yes? If you ask me, I think you and your friends need to be keeping a low profile'.

'And I think you need to stick to the deals you make'.

'Or what?' said Fallaci, now with a grim look on his face.

'Or you will regret it,' said Charlie.

The enormous man with cauliflower ears took a step towards Charlie, but Fallaci signalled to him to stop. The Italian put his hands in his pocket and studied Charlie and Eddie.

'Listen, I will try to pay Bill some money later this week. Five thousand, maybe. As a sign of good faith. Some more next month, perhaps. We shall see'. He grinned again, revealing pearly white teeth, while glancing at the biggest of his employees, Mr Cauliflower Ears, who shuffled to one side, grunted and pointed towards the open doorway. Eddie could see the veins bulging on his brother's temple, but there was no point in resisting; the English brothers were outnumbered.

Charlie started towards the door and Eddie followed him, but Fallaci spoke again.

'You are the long-lost brother. Edward, yes?' Eddie halted, turning his head towards the Italian. 'You should caution your brother about coming here and trying to threaten me. I've been here much longer than he has and I've seen a lot of shit. I have connections to important people in the area. Charlie should remember that'. The Italian signalled to the big goon to escort the brothers away.

Eddie walked to the doorway where Charlie stood grimacing. 'Sounds like you need to tread carefully,' said Eddie. 'He seems to know people around here'.

'Everyone *knows people* down here. He's a nobody,' said Charlie as they made their way out of the building and onto the path to the paseo.

'What was all that stuff about Scotland Yard detectives and TV reporters?'

Charlie sighed as if he had had to field that question a hundred times before. He flicked the cigarette butt to the ground and motioned Eddie to walk. 'It's all bullshit. Some politicians back home pretending to be tough on crime and trying to distract attention from all the problems you were telling me about. The layoffs and factory closures. All that stuff you were telling me about'.

They were now at the Porsche. Charlie fumbled around in his pockets for the keys, then unlocked the car.

'And the TV reporter?' asked Eddie, as he pulled his door open.

'Jeremy Crampton. You must have heard of him?' Eddie's face must have shown that he had not. 'Don't you watch tele? No, matter. He's just some jumped-up media luvvie tryin' to make a name for himself at our expense. It's a pain in the arse right now, but it will soon blow over. Nuffin' to worry about, trust me'.

Eddie eyed up his brother as he piloted the big Porsche out

of the parking space and into the flow of traffic. 'And the Scotland Yard detective?'

'Detective Constable Philip Metcalf. Just some burnt out, old copper. He's no threat'.

'What's he doing in Spain?' said Eddie.

'Metcalf's just an old tosser who's got a bee in his bonnet about me and the lads. He wasted four years tryin' to nab us for an Abbey National job we did in '78. The old git never got close, even got himself suspended by the Met. He ain't got no power here. He's a joke. Nothing to worry about'.

Eddie frowned. 'If everything's golden, why do you need my help?'

Charlie gripped the steering wheel. 'Look, Crampton and Metcalf. They ain't the problem. But doing business down here is…well, it's different. It's all about getting the upper hand. It's about influence and who you know. Trouble is, the rest of the crew ain't cut out for that. They just wanna sit in their bars, swim in their pools and swan about town. But our money ain't gonna last forever. The lads only see the short-term, but we need to be smarter than that. We need to adapt to survive down here. That's why I need someone like you at my side. Someone with smarts'.

Eddie shook his head. 'This ain't my world, bruv. And people are expecting me down in Africa. The geezer that runs the company, Colonel Hawkwood, he stuck his neck out for me when I was in the army. More than once. I owe him'.

'I understand, but can't you put this Angola thing off for just a month, maybe? I could show you everything I've got goin' on down here'.

Eddie rubbed his eyes, then put his sunglasses back on. 'I'll think about it'.

'Sweet. Now, listen. I need to meet someone back at the bar. Why don't you have a little wander around town? Try some tapas. Have a nice cold beer? Then we can talk again later.'

'Sure,' said Eddie as the Porsche sped up back onto the dual carriageway.

Charlie cut across to the fast lane but found himself sitting behind a battered old Ford Transit minibus. He pressed his foot hard on the brakes, then sounded the horn for five seconds. 'Fuck's sake. I bleedin' hate this road,' he muttered.

CHAPTER SEVEN
THE COPPER WITH A SUNTAN

Charlie came to a halt at the side of the road on Avenida Ricardo Soriano in the centre of Marbella. It appeared to Eddie that practically every store was a clothing, fashion or jewellery outlet.

'There's money in this place,' he said.

'You better believe it - for those shrewd enough to make the most of it,' said Charlie, while removing his wallet from the storage space between the seats and pulling out a wad of Spanish pesetas. He counted out several large denominations before pressing the bills into Eddie's hands.

'That's about three hundred quid. Pick yourself up some decent clobber. We're going to a party tonight at the beach club'.

Eddie stared at the thick roll of pesetas and frowned. 'The stuff in your spare wardrobe is more than good enough'.

'No, it ain't. You can't be wandering around in my hand-me-downs. We're not kids anymore,' said Charlie. 'And when you're done, pop into Marlon's on the seafront. It's the best place for lunch in Marbella. Tell them I sent you there. I'll see you back at the bar in about three hours, yeah?' Charlie winked at his brother. 'Trust me, we're gonna have some proper fun tonight'.

Eddie watched as the Porsche pulled away, checked his surroundings and broke into a stride.

He ignored several clothes stores whose appearance he felt to be too upmarket for his down-to-earth sensibilities before forcing himself to go into one department store in a prominent position on the high street.

A well attired mannequin caught his attention the moment he stepped inside the airy interior, and he strode over to inspect the clothing. The trousers were a little too formal, but Eddie liked the jacket. He reached to examine the price tag, but dropped it as soon as he saw the number.

Christ on a bike, that's more than my last car.

A short walk later, Eddie stumbled upon a more modest store hidden away behind the Social Security agency. At first, he thought the shop was closed, so dim was its interior. He tried the door and to his surprise, it opened. He ventured inside.

A small brass bell chimed above the wooden door as he pushed it open and a thin, weasel-looking man poked his head up from behind an ancient metal cash register. The man appeared to be in his sixties and wore a grey blazer and a crisp white shirt.

'Good afternoon, sir. Can I help you?' the man said in a rather weary tone and without rising from his stool. He was Spanish, but spoke in perfect English. Eddie found himself again baffled about how the Spanish could determine he was British before he had so much as uttered a word.

'Yeah, please. I need a casual jacket and trousers for an event tonight. Do you have anything reasonably priced?'

The man groaned as he lifted himself up to his feet. He unfolded his arms, rubbed the small of his back inwards and gestured at Eddie to follow him towards a thin spiral stairwell. 'What is the occasion, may I ask?' he said, without making eye contact. 'A business event?'

'No. It's a party I've been invited to. I'm just passing through and travelling light so don't have anything appropriate,' said Eddie. 'It's at the Marbella Beach Club. Do you know it?'

The man raised an eyebrow. 'I am aware of it'.

'Not somewhere you'd recommend?'

The man scoffed at the notion. 'Far too many criminals,' he said. 'As there are everywhere in our province these days'.

Eddie sensed the opportunity to learn more about the town which is his brother inhabited. 'Criminals? Really?'.

'There are hundreds of them,' said the shop owner. 'They're all here on the run from the British police. They think they are untouchable. Well, those scoundrels are in for a nasty shock, I can tell you'. The man reached the top of the stairs and stepped into the first-floor room, a space with sizeable windows along the west-facing wall through which the sunlight illuminated the room. The store owner had stopped and was now regarding Eddie. He appeared a little less sure of himself.

Dust particles floated in the sunrays and Eddie could not help sneezing.

'Salud,' said the store owner.

'Thank you'. Eddie blew his nose while peering around. There were several wooden cabinets, each housing a dozen or more suits. 'Can you show me some casual jackets?'

'My pleasure,' the man answered, his tone somewhat nervous. 'I have some fine options, and I can offer you an excellent price, of course'.

Eddie nodded, but remained intrigued about the man's candid opinion. 'What did you mean, when you said "the scoundrels are in for a shock"?' he asked.

'Oh, nothing. Pay no attention'.

'No, really. I'm interested'.

The man cleared his throat. 'Well…well, the politicians here and in Britain intend to change things'.

'How so?' said Eddie.

'Your compatriots…or, at last, the criminal element among them that live over here - it will be much harder for them'. The man squinted at Eddie over the rim of his spectacles and dropped his voice. 'My cousin works for the federal government in Madrid. He tells me things'.

'You think they will start extraditions again?' said Eddie.

The man shrugged. 'It is inevitable. It's not that long since we got rid of the dictator and things are improving, but Spain has a long way to go. We must be part of the European Community. We need greater economic partnerships. And Allies. We cannot afford to upset the British government. And besides -'. The man paused.

'Go on,' said Eddie.

The storekeeper looked towards the stairs as if confirming that nobody else was listening. He moved a step closer to Eddie. 'The local families. They have tolerated the foreigners until now, but they don't like them, and they can see they are growing weaker'.

'What do they stand to gain? These families?' asked Eddie.

The man's eyebrows lifted. 'Do you know how much money flows around down here? Millions. Hundreds of millions. It's not just those bank robbers they show on the English papers and television. It's money laundering, financial fraud, illegal timeshares, drug smuggling and gun-running. The British have their fingers in all of it. Car thefts. Prostitution. Drugs. It is your countrymen who have run all of this. It's they who have been profiting from it. And they who have been corrupting local legislators and the police for years.'

The man's voice quivered as he turned away to look out of the shop window.

A gold-coloured convertible Rolls Royce sat parked on the opposite side of the road outside the branch of a foreign bank, its white-walled tyres astride a double yellow line. The British registration plate read; 'B4RRY 51'.

'They believe they are untouchable,' the man went on. 'But they are mistaken'. He remained, looking out of the window.

To break the uncomfortable silence, Eddie lifted a shiny, grey single-breasted jacket from where it had hung and examined the price tag. He decided that the price was acceptable and slipped it on over his tee-shirt. 'How does this look?' he said, breaking the shopkeeper out of his thoughts.

The Spaniard examined Eddie in the jacket and nodded his approval. 'Like it was made for you, sir'.

After making his purchase, Eddie stepped out onto the busy street outside, his purchase wrapped in a plastic cover under his arm. He looked at his watch. He still had ninety minutes to kill before meeting back up with Charlie; plenty of time to walk along the beachfront, and to find the restaurant his brother had recommended.

As he started walking, he noticed a sunburnt man in his late forties holding an expensive-looking camera. The man, who was sitting on a wooden bench and dressed in beige trousers and a bright yellow shirt, was pointing the camera in Eddie's direction.

Eddie pretended not to have noticed and sauntered past the man who turned his attention to the copy of Diario Sur that he had perched on his lap. Eddie noticed that the newspaper was upside down. He continued onwards for ten minutes until he saw the signage for Marlon's, the restaurant that Charlie had suggested, about fifty yards away. He paused at a souvenir shop and pretended to look at the cylindrical array of multi-coloured sunglasses, using one of the Ray-ban knock-offs to check the view of the street behind him.

The man in the yellow shirt was standing thirty feet behind him, half-concealed behind a palm tree. The man lifted the camera again.

Who are you then, buddy?

Eddie continued on his journey and headed towards the restaurant.

A waiter was standing at the open wooden door. '*Buenos dias, señor.* English, yes?'

Is it that obvious? Eddie shook his head in amazement. 'English, yes'.

'You want outside table? In sun?'

'No. I'd like to eat inside,' said Eddie. 'And my brother said to mention that he'd sent me here'.

The waiter regarded Eddie for a moment. 'Who is your brother, please?'

'Charlie Lawson,' said Eddie.

The waiter's face broke out into a broad grin. 'Charlie is your brother? Well, in this case, please. You come with me'.

The Spaniard directed Eddie to a large table at the back of the restaurant interior, past a dozen crowded tables occupied by tourists and beckoned at Eddie to follow him up a small set of steps that led up to a private area upon in which located a large circular table, surrounded by carved wooden panels and with a view out onto the beach. The man lifted a red rope away from a brass stand and waited for Eddie to pass through.

'I did say a table for one, yeah?' asked Eddie.

'Yes, sir. This is the area we reserve for special customers,' said the waiter, still holding the rope.

Eddie looked to his left, to an empty table with two chairs. 'That one will do,' he said, leaving the waiter standing with a look of confusion on his face. Eddie sat down, placed the bag with his jacket against the wall and chose the seat that afforded him a view of the building's entrance.

The confused waiter walked to his side. 'You said you are the brother of Charlie Lawson, no?'

'I did. And I am starving. Do you have spaghetti bolognese?'

'We do, sir,' said the waiter, still flustered. 'But maybe you would prefer something more…interesting, from our menu of the day? We have fresh monkfish and lemon sole. Or some veal, perhaps?' said the waiter.

'A spag bol is just fine, thanks. And a beer'.

'Uh, huh. Thank you,' said the waiter. He poured Eddie a glass of water, collected the menu that lay on the table, and removed unneeded cutlery. 'I'll instruct the kitchen staff to be quick'.

'No rush,' said Eddie. He watched the waiter stride away towards the kitchen, then fixed his eyes on the doorway at the front of the building. The man with the camera had entered and was being directed towards a little table near the toilets while scanning around the restaurant's interior.

Enough of these stupid games.

Eddie beckoned at a passing waiter to come over. 'There is a man over there in the yellow shirt,' said Eddie.

'Yes sir,' replied the puzzled waiter.

'Ask him to join me here, would you, please?'

'My pleasure, sir'.

The waiter walked across the room to the man in the yellow shirt who was still scanning the room. The waiter pointed over towards Eddie, who raised his glass of water and waved. They were fifty feet apart, but the man's disappointment at being rumbled was apparent. He rose to his feet, picked up his camera and ambled over to Eddie's table before halting in front of the table, a disgruntled look on his face.

Eddie pushed the seat opposite him away with his foot and beckoned at the man to sit. 'I figure you're either a stalker or a copper, and as I ain't famous I'm going for the latter,' said Eddie as the man sat down. 'I'm Eddie Lawson, but you already knew that. And you are?' He held out his hand, but the man ignored it.

'Detective Constable Philip Metcalf'.

'Nice to meet you, D.C. Metcalf'. Eddie noticed the sweat patches under the man's armpits. He turned to the waiter, who remained at the side of the table awaiting instructions. 'A cold beer for Mr Metcalf, here. And whatever he wants for lunch'.

'No food. Just a cola, thank you,' the man said to the waiter.

'So, I'm guessing you skipped the covert surveillance training at the Yard then, Philip?' He chuckled.

'What do you want Mr Lawson?' asked the man in an impatient tone.

'I'm just enjoying a lovely day here on holiday. I think it's you that wants something. Why are you following me?'

The waiter arrived with Eddie's beer and a glass of coke. Metcalf picked it up and took a long swig, his eyes flitting to the contents of the glass and then back on Eddie. He then placed his glass down and leaned back in his chair.

'So, is that what you're doing in Spain then? Having a holiday?'

'And why would that be any business of yours?'

'Because I think you are in Marbella is to join up with your brother's crew,' said Metcalf. 'I've got of pictures of you two together. And the rest of that bunch of crooks. I was watching at the party the other night'. The man smiled, then took another swig of his coke.

'Catching up with my brother ain't no crime,' said Eddie.

'Helping him with illegal activities is'.

'You are way off the mark, Metcalf,' said Eddie.

'I saw you earlier today. At Fallaci's place in Benalmadena. I'm guessing you went there with your brother to put pressure on its proprietor? He owes one of Charlie's crew, Bill Taylor, a lot of money I understand'. The English policeman was enjoying the exchange. 'Were you aware that Señor Fallaci has served time for property fraud and embezzlement? Four years, I believe'.

'I wasn't. But we can't hold that against the man, can we? He did his time, right?' said Eddie.

The policeman leaned forward. 'Let's cut to the chase, shall we?'

'Let's do that,' said Eddie while leaning forward himself.

The two men's faces were now just a foot apart.

'Time's almost up for your brother and his merry band of

villains,' said Metcalf. 'They've had their fun, but the winds are changing. Soon they'll be back in England staring through steel bars with nothing but memories of their fancy villas and fast cars'.

Eddie sat back, looked at the people around them and then back to the policeman sat opposite him. 'I don't see what that has to do with me'.

'Don't take me for an idiot. Your brother wants you to join him in whatever he's doing down here. I would advise you not to get involved'.

'Charlie's business is his business. I'm just passing through, so I'd appreciate it if you took that camera elsewhere. I ain't done nothing wrong'.

'Aside from some barroom brawls back in England, maybe not. Not yet. But if you stick around in Spain, you will. You all do your kind,' said the policeman.

The smile disappeared from Eddie's face. He placed his glass down. 'And what, exactly, are "my kind"?'

'Don't play innocent with me. Your brother and his mates are bank robbers, violent criminals and who knows what else? Drug smuggling? Fraud? Money laundering? They are all crooks, the lot of them. I don't know if you've crossed that line yet, Mr Lawson. But I'm warning you. If you stay here, you will. Mark my words. As sure as rain'.

'It doesn't look like it rains here much, detective constable'.

Metcalf placed his glass down. 'You aren't in their league. I don't care what you've done until now, but if you stay down here, you'll end up in the middle of their dirty business. Then I'll come after you too. And being a Falklands vet will not help you then'.

Eddie's face turned to stone. 'You done yet? My meal will be here in a minute'.

The policeman remained where he sat. 'You've got a wife and kid, right? Mary, isn't it?'

'I let that mention of the war go, Philip. But don't go

bringing up my family. We ain't in England now'. Eddie's clenched his fists under the table.

'I can help you,' said Metcalf. 'And I can help your family. If you just give me something to work with'.

Eddie stood up and leaned toward the policeman. 'You didn't do your research, detective. *My kind*, we look after each other'. He glared at Metcalf, before relaxing back on the wooden seat. 'Besides, there's no extradition treaty. A British cop can't arrest anybody down here'.

'Not yet. But it won't always be like that. Things are changing. Before too long the Spanish will step into line and then we'll be able to nab all the criminals hiding out down here. You need to decide before it's too late for you too'.

'Uh-huh,' muttered Eddie. He took a slow slurp from his beer. 'From what I heard, you ain't even a copper no more. What I heard was that you got yourself suspended. You lost your warrant card, didn't you? All over some crazy crusade to finger my brother and his friends, and with no evidence'.

Metcalf looked down at the table. He was making little circles on the table in the condensation that had formed where his glass had been. 'I got suspended, yes. But I'll prove the Force wrong. As soon as I've brought your brother and his criminal associates to justice. I'll get my job back, don't you worry'.

Eddie leaned forward again. 'I was told that your obsession with my brother cost you more than your job. You're divorced now, right?'

Their eyes locked for several seconds, but then Metcalf downed the rest of his drink, stood up and picked up his camera.

'Enjoy your spaghetti, Mr Lawson'.

Eddie watched Metcalf as he strode away. Charlie had seemed certain that the ex-policeman was of no concern, but something told Eddie he would be running into the man again very soon.

CHAPTER EIGHT
THE GENTLE ART OF PERSUASION

Eddie wolfed down his food, paid - even though the waiter declined to take his money at first - and made his way back to his brother's bar. When he went inside, he could see Charlie in the closed-off conservatory. He was in an animated state. The rest of the crew were all sitting at a table and there did not appear to be much eye contact between the men.

The door was locked. Eddie knocked and Roger strode across to open it.

'Alright, Eddie,' he whispered. 'I'm glad you're here. Maybe you can calm your brother down'. Roger ushered Eddie inside and closed the door behind him.

Kenny and Mike remained sitting with, what Eddie thought, were sheepish looks on their faces. Bill rose from his wooden chair and moved to the edge of the room where he stood, staring into a white teacup.

Roger coughed to gain Charlie's attention, then beckoned at Eddie to say something.

'What's up?' asked Eddie.

'It's Charlie's property project,' said Bill. 'Marbella council are threatening to cancel the planning permission if the financing isn't in place by the end of the month'.

'Ain't got a million quid in your pocket have you, son?' asked Mike.

'C'mon lads, we've been through this,' said Charlie. 'We put up the capital now, get phase one underway and then other investors will come on board. As soon as they see things progressing, they'll see the potential. It's all about confidence'.

'What if they don't though Charlie?' said Bill. 'What if something else happens? This is Spain, for fuck's sake. There's always something else that needs sorting. More money to shell out, councillors to pay off. Strikes. Stuff goes missing all the time. If we put this money in then, we'd all have fuck all left'.

'Bill's got a fair point,' said Roger. 'You know I believe in this project, mate. And in you. Christ, I've already sunk half my money into businesses with you'.

'And they was good investments, weren't they?' said Charlie.

'Mostly,' Roger replied. 'But this one's different. It's much bigger. It's a hell of a risk'.

'With a big fuckin' return,' said Charlie.

'Maybe,' said Bill. 'If it all goes like you say it will, Charlie. But who knows what can go wrong? And I don't trust them bloody people you've been pitching it to, especially that fuckin' Juan Fernandez. He's a weasel, parading around town like he's some kind of nobility'.

'He's as bent as us,' said Mike.

'It's true. People like him, they're like the flippin' Spanish mafia,' said Kenny. 'I don't trust 'em either, Charlie'.

'There's other sources of investment besides them lot,' said Charlie.

'Like what?' asked Bill. 'You said you didn't want no other Brits onboard. It's got to be clean money, you said'.

'And I meant it,' said Charlie. Look, I ain't proposing we go to Ronnie and John Knight, or any of the other crews. We just need to get the project going, that's all. Show some momentum. Then the banks will come in on it'.

'You really think so?' asked Roger. 'From what I've heard, the Ortega family control the local banks'.

'Then we don't go for local banks. We get our arses up to Madrid. That's where the real money is anyway,' said Charlie. He looked at Kenny. 'How about you, Ken?'

'Thing is, if I put this money in I'm pretty much broke'.

'Broke? What about the apartments you own?' said Charlie. 'And how many cars have you got? Four? Sell one of your Mercedes, for fuck's sake?' He put his hands on his hips and looked around the room. 'Boys, I've already put nine hundred grand into this. That's how confident I am. The plans are all in place. Construction would start almost straight away. We'd have phase one done inside a year'.

The crew exchanged uncertain glances between themselves.

Charlie turned his gaze towards Roger. 'Listen, I know it's a big ask. And, yes. The next year will be tough, but you all know we can't last forever here on the cash from the last job. We will have spent most of it within a few years, anyway. This is our chance to earn some decent money, and legally. We do this, we're set up for the next twenty years. No more paying off the local law. No more talk about doing another job. We could all sit back and relax in the sun and die of old age'.

'Or skin cancer,' said Roger.

'Your liver will give up before that, you bleedin' alkie,' said Mike.

'Better that than the clap,' said Roger. 'Which is how you'll go'.

Charlie sat down on an empty seat and lit up a cigarette.

'What do you reckon, Eddie?' asked Mike.

'Yeah, Eddie,' said Roger. 'You've got your head screwed on good. This is all fresh for you. Tell us what you think'.

'I know nothing about property development,' said Eddie.

'Don't think about it as money or property development. You're a soldier. You understand tactics and strategy,' said Roger. Eddie realised that they were all looking up at him at that point. Charlie placed a cigarette in his mouth and shot Eddie a pleading look, before dipping his head towards his zippo.

'Well, it all sounds great,' Eddie offered. 'I mean, if it comes off, you're all sorted. For a good few years, at least. Depends how many Ferraris you buy, I suppose'.

'Or women,' said Kenny. Bill and Roger laughed.

'But?' asked Mike, unsmiling.

'Well, it's this local family you all keep mentioning. I spoke to this guy today -'.

'What guy?' asked Charlie.

'Just a bloke in a clothes shop. He said something about how things are changing for the Brits down here. And how the locals would take advantage'.

Bill slapped his palms down onto the table. 'You see?' he said. 'It's not just us saying this. Everyone's thinking the same thing. That fuckin' Ortega is just waiting to stitch us up. You know it's the truth, Charlie. One of his cousins works at the town planning office, for fuck's sake. I reckon it's him that's holding up the project right now. They're just twisting the fucking knife'.

Charlie placed his cigarette down on a saucer and stood up. 'Look, boys. I own the land. I've got planning approval -'.

'Provisional approval,' said Bill.

'*Approval subject to demonstrating sufficient funding is in place,*' said Charlie. 'They've approved the architectural plans and all that stuff. Everything. It just all took longer than I thought, but -'.

'Like everything in this piggin' country,' said Bill.

'You can get on a plane back home if you want, Bill. See how that works out for you!' said Charlie. 'Can I continue? That okay with you?' Bill looked away like a chastised dog and nodded.

'So,' Charlie continued. 'I have all the permissions we need and the construction company can get going within a few weeks. Everything's lined up. I've got fixed prices, contracts agreed, timelines, everything. We've just got to have some balls. Go all in. If we fund phase one ourselves, I can't see how it can fail. Honestly, boys. I can't. Yes, it would be more comfortable to have additional partners on board, but that's not the case. We've just got to go for it. It'll be better in the long run. More profit for us. Them not backing us now…it's a flippin' opportunity for us. It really is'. Charlie looked around the room at each of the crew members, one by one. 'Mike's already told me I can count on him. What about the rest of you?'

Bill was the first to speak. He puffed out his cheeks and put his glass down on the floor. 'Okay, I'll have a talk with Carol this evening,' he said.

'Just fuckin' tell her, you wuss,' said Charlie. 'It's your bleeding dosh. I don't remember her being on the job with us'.

'She's my wife. I'll never hear the end of it if I do this without tellin' her,' said Bill.

'So we're looking at a quarter of a mill each?' asked Roger. 'So what d'ya reckon, Bill. You in?'

Bill ran his hands through his greying hair and looked up at the ceiling. 'I guess so. If I get that eighty grand back from Fallaci. Are you gonna go see him, like you said you would?'

Charlie glanced at Eddie. 'Yeah. Don't worry, me and Eddie went there this morning. It's sorted. He'll give you some this week, the rest next month'.

Bill relaxed in his chair. 'That's good. That's good. Thanks, Charlie. I was getting worried about that greasy wanker'.

'No worries, Bill. So, can we count on you, too?'

'Yeah, alright,' said Bill.

Charlie turned his attention to Roger next.

'Okay, yeah. Fuck it. I'm in too,' said Roger.

'Kenny?' asked Charlie.

'One for all, all for one, and all that'.

Charlie smiled. 'Sweet. Thanks, boys. I know this is a big

ask, but it's gonna be better for us all in the long run. This way, we're in control of the project. Fuck Ortega'.

'Yeah, fuck that wanker,' said Kenny.

'Right, I don't know about you fuckers,' said Charlie. 'But I need to go home and get ready for the party tonight. See you all there'.

Kenny, Bill and Roger got up and headed out of the room.

Charlie walked up to Mike, who remained leaning against the wall. 'Phew, that was a tough one, mate'.

'Yeah,' said Mike without making eye contact.

Charlie frowned. 'Don't tell me you're getting cold feet now'.

'It's not that Charlie. I'm behind you. Always. You know that'.

'Then what?'

Mike sighed and looked at Charlie. 'I'm not sure I can raise that much money'.

'What? But you said you had it last time we talked,' said Charlie.

'I know, I know. It's just -'.

'Just what?' said Charlie. Mike looked at him with the look of a guilty child. 'Veronica? It's Veronica, ain't it?'

Mike shook his head. 'Not Veronica, no'.

'Well what then?' said Charlie. Eddie could see the veins pulsing at the side of his head.

'It's another bird. Raquel. I just bought her an apartment in Estepona. And a motor'.

Charlie put both hands on his head and shut his eyes. 'For fuck's sake, Mikey. How many fuckin' tarts do you need? And why do you keep giving them all your poxy money? You're a fuckin' idiot.'

'I know, Charlie, I know. I am. But listen. I've got a plan. Raquel, she knows this Moroccan geezer. He's a big player over there. His family grow dope. Tonnes of it. They've got hillsides covered in the stuff, and -'.

'Stop. We're ain't getting involved in that bollocks. I told you before'.

'But Charlie, listen. This geezer. Omar, his name is, I met him a few days ago, and -'.

'You what? For fuck's sake. We agreed on this'.

'Wait, a second. Just hear me out. He's got bleedin' warehouses full of the stuff. His partners over here got nabbed a few months back. Since then, he couldn't move a thing. He said he'd sell it to us for a fraction of the going price -'.

'No,' said Charlie.

'But Charlie -'.

Charlie reached out and grabbed Mike by the collar and thrust him into the wall. 'I fuckin' told you, no'.

Mike shifted his balance, put a leg behind one of Charlie's and pushed him in the throat. In one swift movement, Charlie fell back towards the linoleum floor, but he was still holding onto Mike's shirt. His friend fell on top of him, at which point the pair started grappling. Mike clambered on top of Charlie and was about to punch him, but found Eddie's powerful arms around his neck.

'Calm the fuck down,' said Eddie. He had Mike in a neck lock.

'All right, all fuckin' right. Let go of me,' Mike shouted. Eddie looked at his brother who sat on the floor six feet away, with one hand on his stomach.

'S'alright, Eddie. Let him go'.

Eddie released Mike from his grip and stood back. Mike rubbed his throat.

Charlie forced himself up from the floor and walked over to Mike. 'You can't get us involved in that shit, mate. If you do, you'll risk everything we have, you know that. We gotta be squeaky fucking clean. You promised me, Mikey. You promised us all'. He held his hand out.

Mike grabbed it and pulled himself to his feet. 'I'm sorry, Charlie,' he said. He took a handkerchief out of his pocket and dabbed at his lip. It was bleeding. 'You're right. It's just that they're all fleecing us. The fuckin' cops and politicians. I pay them a few grand a month to keep them off my back. We all do. And you know the Irish are sniffing around. And the Dutch. I just figured we'd get all we need in one gig. Just one. It would see us through this property deal'.

Charlie stepped forward and put his arm around Mike. 'It's tough right now. I know. But we've got to stick together.'

'Yeah. Okay, okay. I'm sorry, Charlie'. The two men hugged. 'I'll be off. See you both tonight'.

Eddie watched Mike walk away, then turned to his brother. 'So, what's that all about?'

'When we first got here, we all agreed that we wouldn't do no dodgy business down here. If one of us breaks this agreement, does something and gets caught, the Spanish authorities will be all over us. Extradition treaty or not, they can make our lives miserable,' said Charlie. 'Mikey's my oldest mate, but he's an idiot sometimes. Especially with women'.

'Uh-huh. And what about Bill?' said Eddie.

'What about him?'

'You told him that Fallaci would pay up. That's not how it went down this morning'.

'Fuck that tosser,' said Charlie. 'He'll pay. He's just trying it on coz he's heard we're having some grief with this property deal. Like I said, we just need to get it going with our own cash, then we're back in control'.

'You really believe that?'

'It's how business gets done down here. You gotta stay strong, or people will try to take you on. We don't want no trouble, but we'll dish it out if we have to'.

Eddie shrugged. 'If you say so. This is your territory. I'm a stranger to this,' said Eddie.

'You don't have to be. We could use your help here. I could use your help'.

Eddie shook his head. 'I told you. I've got this gig in Africa. I gave them my word'. He looked Charlie in the eye. 'The bloke that runs it looked after me. When it mattered'.

Charlie put his hand on his brother's shoulder. 'Okay, okay. I get it,' he said. 'You made a promise. And you don't owe me nuffin. You're right. Just stick around for a few more days. Please? The boys are on edge here. We've always been tight, but we're fraying at the edges. I'm struggling to keep em all together. Just a while. Yeah?'

'I can stay for a few days. But no more. I'm serious, Charlie. All this gangster shit. It's not me'.

'I know. You were always a better man than me. That's why you are a soldier, and why I'm stuck here on the run from the law back home'.

'*Was* a soldier. Not any more, remember?' said Eddie.

The sound of raised voices outside caught their attention. Charlie made his way into the public area of the bar, but one of the staff stopped him in his tracks.

'It's that Inglés television reporter,' said the Spaniard.

Charlie peered out onto the street below. A camera crew were standing in the road surrounded by a small crowd of passersby. Eddie could see Mike and the others scrambling to get into their cars to make their escape.

'You can't run forever, Michael McNaughton,' shouted a portly man in a cream suit and a white shirt.

Kenny's silver Mercedes sped away, followed by Bill and Roger in a dark green Jaguar XJ6. Mike's Ferrari howled out of its parking space and onto the street, forcing the reporter and his colleagues to dive for cover, and leaving a cloud of white smoke in its wake.

'Jeremy fucking Crampton,' said Charlie.

'The TV reporter that's after you?' asked Eddie.

'Uh-huh'. Charlie gestured towards the scene below where Crampton was urging his crew towards the bar. He took a step forward, but Eddie stopped him, grabbing his arm.

'If you go down there, you'll be all over the British television tonight. Do you have another way out of here?'

Charlie, looking flustered, nodded. 'Yeah, this way. There's a door in the basement'.

A voice shouted from below, 'Charles Lawson, I know that's you. You cannot hide from the British law forever'.

Charlie shouted at the two men standing behind the bar. 'You two. Shut the bar for the night. And don't let that bastard in. Got it?'

The two men hurried down the stairs to the bar's entrance where another of their colleagues was trying to prevent Crampton from gaining access. 'This way,' Charlie shouted.

Eddie took one last glance at the scene below and spied several local policemen at the roadside. Next to them was a familiar face - the Detective Constable that Eddie had met at the restaurant, just an hour earlier. 'Fuck,' he thought as he picked up the bag containing his new jacket, before following his brother to a set of stairs that led down under the pub.

The basement comprised several rooms. One was full of boxes of crisps and crates of bottles. Another contained dozens of shiny steel beer barrels, their hoses snaking up to the bar above through a hole in the ceiling. A solid-looking metal door barred their access to a third room.

Charlie fumbled around in his pocket for a set of keys, before finding the one he was looking for and inserting it into the lock. He forced open the door and flicked on a light switch. 'Quick. Get in,' he said. Eddie snuck inside, crouching to avoid the low ceiling while Charlie closed the door behind him and locked it.

The room seemed to be old - much older than the bar upstairs. The walls were constructed from little weathered bricks. He guessed it dated back to the early twentieth at least, unlike the concrete-framed building above them. The air was crisp. Eddie could see three sizeable wooden work desks, one with an old vice. An assortment of modern tools lay on the surfaces, hanging from hooks on the walls and in metal boxes. There were several cameras and an expensive-looking camcorder on a white, fibreboard shelf. A large TV sat on one desk with a Sony Betamax video recorder next to it upon which rested a tower of videotapes. There were several boxes of various sizes containing a range of electronic components, including miniature microphones. On one wall was a cork board pinned to which were several sketches of architectural layouts, and what seemed to be covert photographs of people, cars and houses.

Charlie was standing in front of another sturdy metal door on the opposite side of the room. He stood still, listening for signs of movement on the other side. 'Okay, I think we're in the clear,' he declared. He inserted a key in the lock and twisted it, before he yanked three separate thick metal bolts open. The door opened and Charlie urged Eddie to go through, before locking the door. They were on the top of a small set of concrete steps leading down into an underground car park. The walls were white except for a single, horizontal red stripe painted on the walls and concrete columns. There were over fifty spaces. 'It's for the hotel above' said Charlie. 'This is my secret escape route, in case of moments like this one. None of the staff know about it' .

'And the workshop?' asked Eddie.

Charlie hesitated for a moment. 'That's where Lucian works'.

'Lucian?'

'The geezer who does the surveillance work for me. Gets me information. Stuff I can use to protect us all here'.

'You spy on people?'

'I gather information. I told you, we have to be clever down here'. He scanned the surrounding space. 'C'mon, we need to get out of here'.

'Who do you spy on?'

Charlie put his hands into his pockets. 'Politicians.

Businessmen. Civil servants. Bent cops. Some other Brits. Lucian used to work for the KGB or something. He knows his shit'.

'And how do you use this...information? Are you blackmailing people down here?'

Charlie started down the steps. 'Sometimes'.

'Jesus, Charlie,' said Eddie. 'That's not keeping things "squeaky clean", is it?'

Charlie snorted. 'And what would you have me do? The boys would all be penniless and stuck in a ten-by-six cell in Wormwood Scrubs by now if it weren't for what I do for them. Knowledge is power, bruv. It's how we move forward. The other lads are living in the past. I'm different. So are you. And if you were to stick around, we could -'.

Eddie held up both palms in a "please stop" pose. 'No,' he said. He took a few steps back and leaned against a black BMW. 'I told you, I ain't no gangster. I think I should -'.

The sound of a car starting up at the other end of the car park stopped him.

'Not now, bruv. C'mon, we ain't got time to natter. That bastard up there will figure out we've left soon. I'll leave the Porsche on the street. We can get a cab from the front of the hotel above'. He strode off towards a stairwell.

Eddie sighed. 'I need to get out of this mess,' he thought, then marched after him.

CHAPTER NINE
NO GANGSTER

The brothers made their way out of the hotel above the underground car park. Eddie watched as Charlie flagged down a cream-coloured Mercedes taxi.

'Nuevo Andalusia,' he said to the Spanish driver who replied with a lazy nod. 'And go the proper way. I'm not a tourist. *Comprende?*'

Charlie collapsed into his seat, wiped the sweat from his face with his shirtsleeve then wound down his window. His shirt was half untucked at the waist and his armpits were drenched with sweat. 'Fuck me, what a day. Do we need to get rat-arsed tonight, or what?' said Charlie, chuckling. He leaned towards the open window and into the passing air. 'There's a few people at the party at the party I want you to meet. I do a lot of business with them'.

'I told you, Charlie,' said Eddie. 'I ain't staying in Spain. I can catch a flight to Kinshasa from Morocco. I just need a couple of grand for the travel. Like you promised'.

'Whoa, bruv. You said you'd hang around for a bit. Don't make any snap decisions before you've had a chance to get the lay of the land'.

'Charlie, I told you. This ain't me. I'm sorry'.

The taxi slowed as it approached a pedestrian crossing and the driver shot his passengers a fervent look in the rearview mirror.

Charlie leaned towards his brother and lowered his voice. 'Ed. Look, these last few days…it ain't always like this. You've caught us at a bad time. Honest, all this business with the property project, that fuckin' reporter and all the other stuff. It ain't like that normally. Please, give it another week at least. You'll see'.

'I made a commitment to an army colleague,' Eddie said. 'End of story'.

Charlie sighed but was plainly not about to give up. 'I get it. I do. It's like you have this code of honour thing, right?' he said. 'But, Ed. That's just like the boys and me. Don't you see? It's the same'.

'It ain't the same,' said Eddie.

'It sort of is, Ed. We've had our battles too. Of a kind. We've had our victories, and we've had losses together. We've lost people. We've suffered. As a crew. As a family. But we stuck together through thick and thin and now look what we have'. He motioned at Eddie to look at the view out the window. The car was now making its way up a steep road lined with tall pine trees. Eddie looked at the big houses as they passed by with their large fences, walls and imposing gates, most of which were closed. 'I understand you want what you had in the army. That sense of togetherness, of purpose and camaraderie. That you were all in it together'.

'Charlie I can't-,' said Eddie.

'Just a sec, listen to me. I understand, I really do. And I know that what we have here ain't the same. Of course, it ain't. But neither is being a paid mercenary fighting in some godforsaken shithole in Timbuktu or wherever. They might give you a uniform and a gun, but it won't be like it was for you in the paras. It might feel like it is for a while, but before long, you will start to question what the hell you've got yourself into. Then what? Where do you go from that? Hey?'

'You don't know what you're talking about,' said Eddie. 'You've never served. All you've ever done is lie, cheat and steal from others. You don't know anything about duty and sacrifice. You're just a bloody criminal, Charlie'. He was shouting now.

Charlie tried to calm him, but Eddie's thoughts were being intruded upon by painful memories from that wet, cold island in the South Atlantic.

'I killed people, Charlie. I killed soldiers…kids. Kids who only were there because their government put them there. I did it because my government told me to. I did it. I came back, but others didn't. I saw good friends die in front of me, in my fuckin' arms. I was there, Charlie. I did that. For Queen and fuckin' country. And you try to compare that to what you lot do? You think shoving a shotgun in some security guard's face is like being in combat? Telling some poor old sod in a bank to hand over the keys to the safe or you'll top him and make his missus a widow? Make his kids fatherless? All for money? So you can have this?' He waved his hands at the scene outside. 'You think that's the fuckin' same as being a soldier?' His voice was shaking.

Charlie averted his brother's stare. 'I'm sorry. I didn't mean it like that, Ed. But this needs sayin'. Being a merc ain't the same either. Who the fuck d'yer think you'd be shooting kids for down there, then? Hey? Some oil baron or mining corporation. Or the CIA. That's who! You think there's fuckin' honour in that? Some higher cause? Fuck off is there!' Charlie noticed that the driver was watching intently. He leant forward, clamped his hand on the man's throat and pulled him back against the headrest. 'Keep your fuckin' ears shut and your eyes on the poxy road or I'll put you in hospital for six months. You hear me?'

'*Lo siento, señor*,' said the quivering driver. Charlie still had a firm hold of the man.

DEN OF SNAKES

'I think he's got the message, Charlie,' said Eddie. Charlie waited a few seconds then relaxed his grip. The driver coughed and quickly switched his attention back to the road ahead as Charlie sat back. 'I'll be going in a couple of days,' Eddie continued, puncturing the momentary silence. 'You gonna lend me that money?'

'If that's what you want,' said Charlie.

'It is'.

'Yeah then'.

'I'll pay you back,' said Eddie.

'I don't want it fuckin' back,' said Charlie as the taxi approached his villa. 'You can stop here,' he said, pointing. '*Aquí*. Stop *aquí*'. The driver nodded and pulled the car to a stop. Charlie pulled a wad of pesetas from his wallet and held them out to the driver. 'And next time mind your own friggin' business'. The brothers got out of the Mercedes. Eddie stood holding the bag that contained his newly purchased jacket. 'Listen, Ed -,' said Charlie.

'Forget it. I was out of order,' as he turned and walked towards the villa's entrance. Charlie entered a code into the door's security panel and Eddie heard the electronic buzz as it unlocked and slid open.

They walked down the driveway to the villa's massive wooden door, the gravel crunching under their shoes. Charlie fetched his keys from his pocket and unlocked it.

'I'm going to catch forty winks,' said Eddie.

'Hang on, bruv. We can't leave it like this,' said Charlie. 'Have a drink with me. Just a quick one, please?' He walked towards the kitchen. He reached for two glasses, picked up a bottle of Jameson whiskey then poured out two generous measures. 'Ice?' Eddie shrugged. Charlie fetched some ice from the nearby freezer and dropped two cubes in each glass. He handed one to Eddie.

'To Mum and Dad,' said Charlie and lifted the glass to his

mouth. They both downed their drinks. 'Look, Ed, about what you saw in the cellar -'.

'It doesn't matter what I saw'.

'What Lucian does -'.

'I said it don't matter,' said Eddie.

'But I need you to understand. I do it all for the boys,' said Charlie.

'Oh, come on, Charlie. All that 'all in it together' bullshit, you keep spouting. It's bollocks. They're all running out of money as far as I can see, but you seem to be doin' pretty nicely up here in this palace of yours'.

'It ain't like that,' said Charlie. Eddie shook his head and waved his hand around at the large room and shook his head.

'Keep telling yourself that if you want, but I think you're kidding yourself. You think you're living freely in a paradise, pulling all the strings, controlling everything. But you ain't. You may have escaped the law back home, for now. But you're a prisoner here instead. Alright, you've got a fancy house, flash cars and go to all these crazy parties every night, but you ain't free, Charlie. Not really. You're lying to your friends and doing whatever you're doing behind their backs'.

'You don't understand, Eddie'.

'I ain't stupid. You're using your friends. And I don't want none of it. I'm sorry, but this ain't for me. I told you. I gave my word to someone that I'd help him out. Someone that would do the same for me'.

Charlie stared at his brother, seemingly wrestling with inner thoughts before responding. 'But you won't do something for me?' he said. 'Fine. I get it. I weren't around for you, so why would I expect you to be there when I need help'. He slumped down into the couch and sighed.

'Why are you doing this?' said Eddie.

'I can't go back, Ed. To England. To prison. I can't. Maybe the others could take it, but I'd go fuckin' bananas. You don't know what it's like'.

Eddie placed the empty glass down and stepped towards his brother. 'What happened to "If you can't do the time, don't do the crime"?'

Charlie reached for the bottle and topped up his glass. 'I tried it. It didn't suit me. Besides, a man's got to tread his own path. That's what mum always told us, right?'

'Pretty sure she didn't have this in mind for you when she said that,' said Eddie. He turned and started walking towards the stairs. 'But anyway, my path is taking me to Angola'.

'You gotta do what you gotta do,' said Charlie. 'Come to the party, though, please? One last night together? For old time's sake. All on me, of course'.

'Too bloody right it will be,' said Eddie as he made his way up the stairs. He headed to his bedroom, pulled his damp shirt off and sat down on the bed. He thought back to when Charlie had left the family home, with the Lawson family. It had been the summer of 1967. Eddie had only been twelve at the time and his brother had promised to visit regularly. For the first few months he had kept his word, popping in once every week or so, but the attractions of the big city had quickly become a distraction and the visits became less and less frequent. By the time Eddie had reached his fifteenth birthday, he had not seen his older brother for nearly six months.

Charlie did not turn up for that birthday either. Instead, he had sent a scrawled note, which arrived a few days later with an apology. 'Something came up. Sorry. I'll make it up to you, little bruv. Happy birthday,' his older sibling had written, but even that had proven to be yet another promise that Charlie failed to keep.

It had been at that point that Eddie had realised that he was alone and that he had to take charge of his own destiny. Nobody else was going to help him. Mrs Lawson's health had been rapidly deteriorating. Mr Lawson, Eddie's adopted father, had become increasingly bitter, and sometimes violent. Eddie had joined a local boxing club in South Harrow, taking a bus there from school most afternoons. He would do his homework on the bus. One of the other regulars at the gym, a grey-haired Scotsman, was a former soldier who had served in Aden and Oman. The Scot had an endless repertoire of captivating stories and delighted in sharing them with his young protege. He often brought in extra sandwiches for the young Eddie.

'You need to put some meat on them bones, boy,' the old soldier would say.

Eddie had not been a high achiever at school but had nonetheless finished with a respectable set of four O-levels. On his sixteenth birthday, he took a train ride into central London and walked into the Army recruitment office in Westminster where he applied to join the parachute regiment. Nine weeks later Eddie left the Lawson household and joined the British Army. He had written to Charlie to tell him and asked if they could meet up beforehand but received no reply. His brother, he reluctantly concluded, cared only about himself.

Nothing's changed, he thought and reached for his wallet. He pulled out a business card and studied it for a few seconds. It had an expensive-feel. The paper was thick and a brilliant white, the ink a glossy black.

Col. John J Hawkwood (*ret.*)
Managing Director
Hawkwood International Limited, London.
01 434 7771

He picked up the telephone receiver on the bedside cabinet, dialled the number and waited for a reply.

'Hawkwood International, how can I help you?' said a female voice after a couple of rings.

'Hello. I'm calling with a message for the Colonel. My name is Eddie Lawson'.

'Hello, Mr Lawson. I can take your message'.

'Please tell the Colonel that I expect to be in Kinshasa within a week'.

'Understood. I will get your message relayed to Colonel Hawkwood right away'.

'Thank you,' said Eddie. He heard a couple of strange mechanical clicking sounds, but thought nothing of it as he placed the receiver down and laid back on the bed. 'Once a soldier, always a soldier,' he thought as he drifted off to sleep.

Eddie watched intently as his exhaled breath turned instantly into a misty, floating vapour in front of his position. It was the middle of the night. The moon and stars were hidden from view behind a thick layer of rain clouds. The only sounds he could hear came from the light drizzle dropping upon the dense clumps of upturned peat that had been thrown up by the British artillery several hours earlier. The sweet odour of cordite still hung in the air.

He took his hand off his rifle grip and slowly reached back to rub his lower back. He had been laying in the same shallow, damp depression for nearly three hours now, waiting for the expected counterattack from the Argentinian Marines that his patrol of paras had ousted earlier that day. The British had caught the South American troops by surprise and quickly forced them out of their forward position - an observation point located atop a rocky outcrop fifty yards from where Eddie presently lay. The paras had killed five of the enemy without suffering any losses. Not this time. One of the Brits had got shot in the arm, but the wound was not severe and the man, private Higgins, had been patched up and sent back out into the field. Higgins had made Monty Python 'flesh wound' jokes continually afterwards. Eddie chuckled. Moments like that were the glue that bonded the lads together when things got tough. He scanned the skyline again but saw nothing except blackness and drifting fog.

'Maybe they aren't coming back this time,' he thought.

His optimism vanished in an instant at the sight of an illumination flare which rapidly made its way up into the sky from behind a small hillock over to his left. It burst into life several hundred feet in the air, suspended under a small canopy, and then slowly drifted down towards the paras. The undulating topography of his surroundings offered little cover from its light.

'Here they come, boys,' the Colonel's voice bellowed from somewhere over to Eddie's right. 'Weapons at the ready.' His pulse quickened as he flicked off the safety catch, then peered through the iron sights of the black SLR. He scanned the horizon, searching for signs of oncoming Argentinian soldiers through the slow swirling mist. Nothing.

'Maybe they are just fucking with us,' he thought. Then came the now-familiar sound of bullets zipping through the air close by. He forced his chest and shoulders down further into the black soil.

'There they are,' shouted one of the other paras. 'Hundred yards ahead. About a dozen of the bastards'. The sky was suddenly full of bright tracer rounds, making their way back and forth between the two opposing forces. The disquieting silence of the previous hours was gone, replaced by a chaotic cacophony of small arms fire.

Eddie caught sight of a group of Argentinian soldiers crouching low as they made their way out of the cover of one of the low dips in the dark landscape. He took careful aim, squeezed the trigger and let off three shots. The targets merged into the darkness. He had no idea if he had hit any of them. A bullet smacked into the small wall of soil that he had pushed up in front of himself. He forced his face down into the dirt, laying still - waiting to be sure that no more rounds were coming his way. The smell of the peat was pungent. Images flashed by of a shopping excursion with his family to the local garden centre as a young boy.

Then he heard the roar of an aircraft overhead.

The jet flew over him in half of a second, then disappeared off over the horizon. He had not seen the plane, but he had recognised the sound. It was one of the Argentine Skyhawks.

He closed his eyes and braced for the inevitable explosion. The blast of the ordinance came a moment later and swept over him for what felt like forever. The hot air lifted the helmet off his head and pushed him several feet to his left. Pieces of steaming mud and grass rained down in every direction. He struggled for fresh air and rolled over onto one side. There was now screaming in all directions.

He forced himself up to his knees, picked up the rifle and lifted it to the horizon. At first, he saw nothing. Then, after a few seconds, men started standing up off in the distance. They were Argentinian Marines, each armed with a FN-FAL - a Belgium-designed weapon from which his British S1A1 self-loading rifle had also been derived. He took aim at one of the men and squeezed off a couple of rounds. The man started running towards him. Eddie fired again. Four shots in quick succession, but the man kept coming. More Argentinians started appearing from within the fog. Dozens of them, then hundreds. Eddie began to fire again, but none of the rifle rounds made their mark. He yanked the empty magazine from the weapon and glanced behind him, looking for support, but there was no sign of the rest of his patrol.

His comrades had vanished. They had deserted him. He was alone. He swivelled back towards the oncoming enemy. There were now thousands of them. He started firing, each shot surely landing plumb centre of the targets at which he aimed, yet none of them fell. They just kept coming. They were nearly upon him now, only thirty yards away. The entire horizon was full of camouflaged uniforms. His rifle fell silent, the magazine empty once again, and then it dawned upon him how each one of the soldiers running towards him had the exact same face. Horror gripped him as he realised it to be the face of the teenage Argentinian conscript he had killed among the slippery, black rocks of Goose Green just a day earlier. Bullets zipped past his ears. He stood up and let the rifle fall from his grasp. He closed his eyes.

His own yells brought him back into the present. They only stopped when he caught sight of the bright blue sky through the open window next to the bed. He was sitting up, his hands firmly gripping the bedsheets. He closed his eyes and attempted to regain control of his body.

One thousand, two thousand…just breathe. Calm. A dream, it's just a fuckin' dream. Calm. Eddie let the fresh oxygen flood through his body and then fell back onto the bed. The sheet was sodden, and he kicked it off. He wiped the dribbled saliva from his stubbled face, then reached over to the bedside table for a bottle of yellow pills and took two out. He put them in his mouth, picked up a plastic beaker and then washed the tablets down with a mouthful of lukewarm water.

When will this ever fucking stop?

At this point, he noticed that his new jacket which had previously been in the shopping bag now hung from the wardrobe door. A chair was positioned in front of it, with a piece of paper placed on it. He forced himself up and ambled over to the chair.

The note had his name written on it. It was from Charlie.

"I didn't want to disturb you. I have some business to deal with.
Thought I'd let you get some kip.
Kenny will pick you up at eight in a taxi.
See you at the party".

Eddie walked back towards his bed and picked up his watch. It was nearly half-past seven.

'Shit,' he said and marched towards the bathroom.

Kenny arrived a little after eight. 'Sorry I'm late,' he said over the intercom from where the taxi was waiting up at the front gate.

'No worries. I'll be right with you,' said Eddie. It was still uncomfortably warm, so Eddie carried the jacket over his shoulder as he made his way up the gravel path. He opened the side gate and was greeted by the smiling Kenny.

'How you doin' son?' said the older man. He was wearing a short-sleeved, light blue shirt and a pair of off-white cotton slacks.

'Good, yeah. Got some kip. Still hot though, innit?'

Kenny laughed. 'I guess so. You get used to it after a few years'. He ushered Eddie towards the taxi's open rear door. The driver, a skinny black man wearing a yellow tee-shirt and a red baseball cap, waited for both men to get comfortable then performed a slow u-turn to head down towards the coast.

'So, where's this party?' asked Eddie.

'Marbella Beach Club,' replied Kenny. 'It's our regular haunt. We've had some quality times there'. He leaned forward towards the driver. 'Mind if I smoke in your car, Mustapha?'

'No problem, Mister Kenny,' said the driver. Kenny held out the packet to Eddie who hesitated for a moment before declining.

'I keep tryin' to give 'em up'.

'Sensible man. Filthy habit,' said Kenny before putting a cigarette between his lips and lighting it. He inhaled, holding the smoke for a few seconds and then exhaled it out of the window. His fingers nails were stained a mustard colour. His skin was a leathery brown and freckled. Kenny appeared to be older than the rest of the crew.

'So, how d'you run into the rest of the guys,' asked Eddie.

'School. I was in the same year as Charlie,' said Kenny. He laughed. 'He was bleedin' sure of himself, even then. This one time, in a history lesson I think it was, the teacher caught him staring out the window when we were supposed to be doin' a test. On the industrial revolution, it was. I remember it clearly. The teacher started givin' Charlie a lecture about needing to knuckle down or he'd have no future and all that. Quite a big bloke, that teacher. Ex-soldier, like you. Only had one leg, though. Had it shot off in Korea, I think. Anyway, Charlie just kept looking out the window. The geezer starts screaming at him, all sergeant major-like. He was right losing his rag, he was'.

Kenny took another drag on his cigarette and laughed.

'But get this,' he continued. Charlie stands up, picks up his satchel and just walked out of the room. Didn't say a word. Just opened and shut the door behind him and left the building. The teacher was livid. Spittin' feathers he was'.

'What happened after that?' said Eddie.

'Oh, I think he got suspended for a few weeks. And the cane. But I just remember how the entire class was all mesmerised. We were all about thirteen'. He looked Eddie in the eye. 'You just didn't do that in them days. I remember seeing the faces of all the other kids, their mouths wide open. Bloody marvellous it was. He was never one for authority, was Charlie. None of us was. Still aren't'. He took one last drag of the cigarette, burning it down almost to the filter, then flicked the stub out of the open window. 'And I hear you're a bit of a rebel too'.

'What do you mean?' said Eddie. 'I was a soldier for over ten years. All I ever knew was taking orders'.

'But you got thrown out, right? Charlie told us you decked an officer. Got yourself locked up for a bit, didn't you?'

'That was at the end. After the war'.

'Yet you want to go back into that game. To be a merc?'

'That's right,' said Eddie. 'Once a soldier -'.

'Always a soldier?' said Kenny. 'As a hired grunt in some private army, fighting in some country nobody gives a shit about?'

Eddie shifted back in his seat. 'It's a job. It pays well'.

'I'm sure it does. But you can't do that forever. You're in good shape now, granted. But the years will catch up with you eventually. Trust me. And war's a young man's game'.

'You sound like my brother. Talkin' about something you ain't never experienced,' said Eddie.

'I did a couple of years'.

'No combat, though. A few cushty years in West Germany, weren't it? And, if I recall, you spent a lot of that locked up for nicking army supplies, didn't you?'

'Yeah, yeah. You're right, I never had anyone shootin' at me, nah. But I lost my old man in the war. Killed in France, he was. Shot by a sniper near Caen. My uncle Brian, too. He was in the far east. The family never knew what happened to him. I was brought up by a generation that went through that shit. We all were. Your old man was in the war, right?'

'My stepdad, yeah. He was in Africa, in the eighth army under Montgomery'.

'And he was pretty fucked up from it, weren't he?'

'This got a point, Kenny?

'Just that it seems to me like you should aim bigger, that's all'.

'You know, for a bunch of blokes what don't like authority, you all seem intent on telling me what to do,' said Eddie.

'We ain't trying to tell you what to do, Ed. We can see the potential in you and we'd hate to see it go to waste, that's all. You're big and strong, yes, but you're friggin' smart too, you're your own man. I think you could make something of yourself down here. More than gettin' your arse shot off in some bleedin' shithole nobody gives a flying fuck about'.

'What if that's what I want?' said Eddie.

'What? To die in Angola? Or Mozambique, or some other fucked-up country. Is that really what you want?' Eddie turned his face toward the window. Kenny put his hand on Eddie's shoulder. 'You've had a rough time. I get it. So does Charlie. You saw a lot of shit, did some things in the Falklands and it's affected you. But you are a strong fuckin' geezer, Ed. You and Charlie are very similar. That attitude. That determination. You can make a great life for yourself on the Costa. Make a lot of money. Money you could use to look after your family. But not if you throw your life away fighting somebody else's war for them'.

Eddie thought of his daughter back in England. Kenny had a point. After all, Eddie's plan to join the mercenary unit in Angola was all about making some money - money he could send to his ex-wife. Or so he told himself. And mercenary operations were not legal either. Even so, he thought, 'there's a big difference between that and what Charlie's crew did'.

'I ain't no gangster, Ken'.

'Nobody's suggesting that. Time's are changing. Just like your brother said. We need to adapt. Go legal. Be cleverer than we have been. Charlie's property project, bars, restaurants. Nightclubs. That sort of thing. There's money to be made here. Honest money. You've got an opportunity here, Ed. I think you should take it'.

'Thing is,' said Eddie. 'Me and Charlie, we've got…baggage'.

'Course you do. You're brothers,' said Kenny, laughing. 'I've got an older brother. He's a fuckin moron. Does me tits in, but I still love him coz he's my brother. He's family. Right?' Eddie smirked.

'I'm pretty sure if I stayed around here, we'd be at each

other's throats. Charlie is the main man. You all look up to him, I see that. It wouldn't be like that, him and me'.

'I'll level with you, Ed. Charlie ain't what he used to be. He's got less energy. He's not as healthy as he used to be'.

'He's got fuckin' fat, you mean?' said Eddie.

They both laughed.

'Charlie's enjoyed himself, yeah. And I want him to keep doin' that. That's why we need you. Why he needs you. I think you have what it takes to be the powering force to help us make the changes we need to. We've got cash and connections. We know how this place works. But we're all old-school, gangsters. You're not tarnished, like us. You could help us go legit. You could help your brother'.

A memory flashed back from one of the last conversations Eddie had had with his mother, a few weeks before the cancer had taken her. 'Promise me you will always look after your brother,' she had begged him.

'I'll think about it,' said Eddie.

'That's all I'm saying,' said Kenny.

They were approaching the beach club. Kenny leaned forward. 'Just here's fine, Mustapha. He placed several banknotes in the driver's hands then winked at Eddie. 'Right, let's do this'.

CHAPTER TEN
IT'S PARTY TIME

They arrived at the Marbella Beach Club at eight-thirty. A lengthy queue of expensively clad adolescent men and women blocked their passage. They were clothed, predominantly, in white.

Eddie examined his grey jacket and black shirt. 'I guess I didn't get the memo,' he thought while walking towards the back of the queue.

'Where are you going?' said Kenny. 'We don't queue'. He pointed to the entrance where a tanned man stood next to two well-proportioned security staff, waving at them to approach. Eddie followed Kenny, bypassing the waiting guests, and approached the man.

'This way, gentleman,' while lifting a red rope for them to enter. Jealous eyes drilled into the back of his head.

'How come they don't have to wait?' grumbled one of the queuing partygoers. Eddie eyed the man up. He was wearing a ruffled white blouse and tight black trousers. He wore black eyeliner, and his face was powdered white. His blonde hair would have graced George Michael.

'Coz we spend a fuck load of money here,' said Kenny to the startled man without stopping. He frowned at Eddie. 'Jesus, did you see that poof? Looks like a bleedin' bird'.

'Mr Lawson's group are in the far corner, on the other side of the pool,' said the doorman, a well-tanned man with spiky black hair and dark brown eyes.

'Is there some kind of dress code?' asked Eddie, nodding towards the column of white-clad guests standing behind him.

'Oh, it's the *Fiesta de la Luna Llena*...the new moon party. It's traditional to wear white'.

'Great,' muttered Eddie to Kenny, and pointing at his black shirt. 'I'm going to stand out like a sore thumb'. He nodded at the two doormen, and they made their way into the venue which was rammed with, Eddie guessed, over a thousand guests. An array of bright lights illuminated the artificial smoke that rose up into the warm evening sky, and the air throbbed to the sound of "When Doves Cry", by Prince.

'I need to take a leak,' said Kenny. 'Old man's bladder. The lads are over there'.

Eddie twisted his head to where Kenny was pointing and gave him a thumb's up sign. He negotiated his way between the swaying club-goers on the dance floor and the swimming pool. Cocktails were flowing. The pool was full of excited twenty-somethings in a variety of lurid-coloured swimwear. There were fine-looking men and beautiful women everywhere. He saw cocaine being openly consumed on several tables.

'Hey, Eddie'. He recognised the voice straight away, Mike's girlfriend Veronica. 'I hoped I'd see you here tonight'. She was wearing a figure-hugging, short white dress, a small black leather jacket and black fishnet tights.

Or stockings?

She was wearing hardly any makeup, but she didn't need to; she was amazing.

She is Mike's missus. Play it cool, he told himself. 'Hey. I'm looking for Charlie. Is he here already?' he said, trying to feign disinterest.

Veronica smiled and licked the inside of her top lip. 'Your big brother's over there with the rest of his boring friends'. She nodded towards the back of the venue. 'But you ain't boring, are you Eddie? I don't think so. I think you're very different'. She stepped to block his path and slid her body close to his, moving her hips in perfect rhythm to the music. 'Dance with me. Have some fun'.

He grabbed her by the waist and manoeuvred her to one side while looking over towards his brother's table. He could see Mike, but luckily the big man's back was facing away from the dance floor. 'Leave it out, Veronica. You'll get me in trouble'.

'Oh, don't be scared of Mikey. He's a big softy, really'.

'I doubt that, please. Get off. I ain't interested,' said Eddie with as much conviction as he could summon.

'That's not what little Eddie's telling me'. She grabbed hold of his crotch and giggled.

'Jesus…get off me. Seriously, this ain't funny,' he shouted. 'If you want to fuck around, knock yourself out. But leave me out of it'. He lifted her up and deposited her to one side, before he pushed a path through the crowd, striding away as fast as he could.

As Eddie approached the table, Mike swivelled around. 'Hey, Ed. Did you see my Veronica out there? She left to get a drink over forty minutes ago'.

'Yeah, she's just over there dancing'. Eddie pointed to where he had just been, but Veronica was nowhere to be seen. 'I guess she headed back to the bar'.

'No worries,' said Mike. 'I'll go take a look for her in a bit. She's like a flippin' whippet, that one'.

A wolf, more like.

'Eddie,' shouted Charlie. He was walking towards the table, a young blonde woman in his arms. 'Sleep alright, bruv?' His brother gave him a protracted bear hug. He wreaked of whiskey. 'This is Debbie. She works at the bar, but she's gonna be a singer'. Charlie pulled his brother towards the youthful woman.

'Hi,' said the woman and thrust out a hand.

'This is my younger brother, Eddie,' said Charlie. 'He's visiting for a few days. Say hello, bruv'.

Eddie shook the woman's hand. 'Nice to meet you. Sorry, I need to steal my brother away for a moment'. Eddie put his arm around his brother's shoulder and steered him away from the rest of the group. "The Cutter", by Echo and the Bunnymen, was playing on the sound system. 'Bit young for you, isn't she?' he said, glancing back at Debbie.

'Young is fun, bruv. Hey, this is that bunny man geezer, isn't it?' said Charlie.

'Listen, Charlie. I know you wanted one last night before I make off but -'.

'Woah, you're not going home already, are you, Ed? You just got here'.

Eddie paused. His brother seemed disappointed. 'It's just… look, I don't like crowds like this. Not since the war. The smoke and all the noise…it plays havoc with my head'.

'Stay for a couple, Ed. Please, I might not see you…for a while. If you go off to bleedin' Africa, I mean'. Charlie put his hands on Eddie's shoulders. His forehead rested on the bridge of Eddie's nose. 'C'mon bruv, have a drink with me. For old times sake. Please?'

Eddie took a deep breath and sighed. 'Of course'.

'Thanks, bruv' said Charlie.

A boyish man in a white vest top was lifting the chair that Charlie had been sitting on. He had blonde hair with a long floppy fringe and an undercut. 'Oh no you don't, you little tosser. That's my seat'.

The young man glanced at the swaying, overweight Englishman, paying him little attention. 'Naff off grandad,' he said and continued to move the chair.

In an instant, Mike leaped up, wrapped his right arm around the young man's neck, and forced him to the ground.

'You've got two seconds to start grovelling you little tosser,' he screamed in the man's ear.

Two of the man's friends appeared, both with well-groomed wedge haircuts. The first was wearing tight burgundy chinos and a white shirt, the second a white suit and a silvery-grey shirt. He was holding a beer bottle by the neck.

'Let go of him, you old bastard,' said the second man.

Mike glared up at the man who had spoken while squeezing his captive's neck a little harder. 'Or what? You gonna come at me with a hairdryer?'

Bill and Roger stood up and started walking towards the young man, both with fists clenched. Kenny approached from the other side, a knuckle duster in his right hand.

The man, realising he was surrounded, slammed the bottle against a metal column that supported the large sunshade above them. The bottle failed to break. Mike laughed, but the man tried again, this time successfully. The sound of breaking glass caught the attention of the surrounding people who had been unaware of the violence threatening to break out in their midst.

Charlie stepped into the middle of the group, in front of the man with the broken bottle. He had a silver pistol in his hand.

'What d'ya call me you little shit?' The man swallowed but kept waving the broken glass around him. Charlie lifted the gun. 'I'm gonna count to three. If you don't put that fuckin bottle down, I'm going to ruin the pretty white suit of yours forever'. The man kept waving the glass.

'One,' said Charlie.

'Put the flipping bottle down, Trev,' shouted a voice from behind.

'Two,' said Charlie. He sounded utterly calm.

'You won't shoot me here. Not in front of all these people,' said the man with the bottle.

'You're about to find out,' said Roger.

Eddie saw Charlie's finger curled around the trigger, ready

to squeeze. He leapt in between the man and his brother. 'Stop!' he shouted.

'Fuck!' shouted Charlie. 'Get out the way'.

'I won't. Put the friggin' gun down, Charlie. This little twat ain't worth it'. Eddie turned to face the man with the bottle. 'Give me that, get your friends and piss off. Or, if he doesn't shoot you, I fuckin' will'. Eddie held out his hand and snarled at the man who handed over the bottle.

'Steve. C'mon, we've got to get out of here,' the young man shouted at his friend, who was still being held on the floor.

Eddie nodded at Mike, who let go of the petrified man who quickly got to his feet. All three backed away and hurried off towards the exit. Eddie turned to his brother. 'Fucking hell, Charlie. What are you playing at?'

Charlie collapsed down into the vacant seat. 'I just wanted my chair, didn't I?' Eddie stared at his brother who, oblivious to the still assembled spectators, reached forward for his glass and started sipping the golden liquid inside it as if nothing had happened.

Mike starting cursing. 'Oh, for fuck's sake. The little bastard pissed himself. It's all over me shirt'. Bill burst out laughing. 'What are you laughing at, you sod? It ain't funny'.

Kenny and Roger started laughing, followed by Charlie. Eddie thought Mike was about to explode with rage, but his face broke into a grin and he too started to chuckle.

'Good job you weren't scarier, Mike. You might have actually scared the shit out of him,' said Roger before bursting into laughter.

'You boys are fuckin' mental,' said Eddie. Charlie stopped smiling. He lifted the silver pistol and cocked it. Eddie could see that it was an old second world war-era German Luger.

'For fuck's sake, Charlie. Stop waving that thing around'. Charlie, still unsmiling, pointed the gun at the back of a nearby dancer who was wearing a white and golden leather jacket, and oblivious to the apparent danger.

Charlie winked at his brother and took aim, his finger wrapping around the trigger.

Eddie's mouth dropped wide open. Time seemed to freeze. The music in the club muted in an instant. The smoke hung unmoving in the air. Everyone else in the club disappeared from his consciousness as he coiled to stop his brother. He made it only two feet before Charlie pulled the trigger.

And nothing happened.

Eddie fell at his brother's feet, panting. 'What the fuck?' he shouted.

'It's bleedin' deactivated innit?' said Charlie. 'I ain't gonna shoot nobody'. He roared with laughter, as did the rest of the crew.

Bill could well of been having an aneurysm, he was laughing so much. Kenny had tears rolling down his cheeks.

'Christ-a-fucking-live,' said Eddie. 'You idiot. You're fucking mad'.

'I'm sorry, I couldn't resist it,' said Charlie. Here, sit down and have a drink,' he gestured towards the empty seat Debbie had been occupying. She now sat perched on Charlie's lap.

Eddie sat down, still shaking his head, and Roger handed him a glass of whiskey. 'Here, get that down yer'.

Bill leaned towards Eddie from the seat next to him. 'Let me tell you our little secret,' he said. 'We ain't been no angels at times, but here's the thing. You don't normally have to hurt nobody to get your way, you just need the other guy to believe that you will. Nine out of ten times that works'.

'Not sure I believe that anymore,' said Mike. 'The world's changing. You've seen what the Irish have been like down here in the last year. And the eastern Europeans are making moves too. They can be right evil bastards. I'm telling you, we need to be ready to get our hands dirty if we want to keep what we have, let alone make more money'.

'And have the entire world focus on us?' said Charlie. 'How

many times do I need to tell you? It's time to get smart. Anyone can use a sawn-off, but them people always end up locked up. Or dead. If we want to keep all this, we need to play the long game. We need to make our money legally'. He nodded over toward another group of men nearby who, from their appearance, Eddie guessed were also British. 'Them wankers, and everyone like 'em, will fuck up. They'll all end up back in Blighty behind bars. I ain't gonna let that happen to me,' said Charlie, before adding, 'Or to you lot'.

Kenny was standing behind Eddie. He leaned down and whispered in Eddie's ear. 'See? Charlie needs you here to help pull things together'.

Eddie peered at his brother, who appeared confident and determined, but Eddie could tell that Charlie was frustrated. Eddie had seen it a thousand times in their childhood; if he didn't get his way, he would snap. He always did.

Maybe I could help him?' he thought. Maybe I should?

The rest of the crew pulled their seats nearer, drinks continued to flow, and soon Charlie's associates were regaling Eddie with stories about the 'old times'.

'There was this one time back in...when was it? Seventy-three?' said Mike.

'Nah, seventy-two,' said Charlie. 'I remember coz Chelsea had just lost in the League Cup final against friggin' Stoke. Remember? Ian-fucking-Porterfield scored. I still can't believe it'

'Seventy-two, yeah,' said Mike. 'Anyway, your brother and me had set out to steal a truck over near Slough. The coal came down on a train from up north and they filled these big lorries up at the rail yard. They had about two hundred quid's worth of coal in each truck. That was a couple of month's wages in them days. For plebs like us, at least'. He stopped to light a cigarette. 'Anyway, we climbed over the fence to get into the yard. No patrol guards or dogs, nothing. Except for this one geezer at the entrance. He opened the gate when they empty trucks arrived and again when they left, fully laden. That's it. Sounds piss easy, right?'

'I guess' said Eddie. He would not have admitted it, but he was intrigued about where this story was going.

'So, we'd been watching these trucks come and go for a few days. They would pull up next to the train. The drivers would nip out and go get themselves a cuppa from the cafe. When the trucks were full up with coal, they'd come back. The drivers never rushed, coz they were paid by the hour. They didn't give a shit about how long it took. They'd have their cuppa and read the paper. When they were good and ready, they'd get back in their trucks, drive up to the barrier and just wave at the guy at the gate. It couldn't be more simple. We could be in and out in less than five minutes'.

'So, how did you two fuck it up?' said Eddie. 'I mean, that's where this story has to be going, right?'

'All will become apparent, you impatient bastard. Anyway, so there we were, hiding behind the shed. The drivers climb out of the truck, but that was when we realised the flaw in our plan'.

'Which was?' asked Eddie.

'They were only both bleedin' Caribbean geezers, weren't they,' said Mike. 'And there was me and Charlie, as pale as ghosts. There was no way that the bloke on the gate wouldn't notice'.

'So what did you do, give it up?' asked Debbie. She had her arm around Charlie's shoulders.

'Did we, bollocks!' said Charlie. 'Go on, tell 'em, Mike'.

Mike took a long drag on his cigarette. 'Well, at first we thought we'd have to ram the gate or something, but Charlie had a lateral thought. We blacked up'.

'You did what?' asked Debbie.

'With the coal. We blacked up our hands and faces. Did a bleedin' good job 'n all. I hot-wired the truck. Charlie drove it up to the gate and waved. The guard glanced up at Charlie and me, presses the button to open the gate and off we drove. And get this. Not only that, but he even shouted "See you tomorrow, Delroy" '.

The entire group burst out laughing, except Charlie.'Yeah, ha fucking ha.' He said. 'But what Mike's not yet mentioned is what happened afterwards, when we dropped the stolen truck off'.

'Yeah. That bit didn't go so well,' said Mike. 'We didn't have time to stop anywhere to scrub up. We had to deliver the truck to this geezer who would take it off our hands. We'd get our seventy quid, catch the tube home. Cushty, yeah? Not quite'.

'So what happened?' asked Eddie.

Mike grinned. He was clearly enjoying building up the suspense. 'We had to meet this geezer, called 'Bob', in Camberwell which, as you know, is pretty close to Brixton. So off we went on the M4 to Hammersmith, down to Battersea, then Camberwell. It took about two hours. We pulled up under these railway arches as we'd been told to and sat there waiting till this bloke arrived'. Mike took another drag on his cigarette, finished it and stubbed it out in the ashtray. 'And then…"Bob" showed up'.

'And…?' said Eddie before taking a slurp of his pint.

'And, that was the point when Charlie and I who, you will recall were still as black as the ace of spades, realised that the bloke, and the half dozen blokes he had with him, were from Jamaica'.

Eddie spat out his beer. Kenny burst out laughing.

'They beat the shit out of us both and took the truck without paying us nuffin,' said Charlie. 'And I can't say I blame 'em'. He chuckled.

'I love that story,' said Roger. 'It never gets old'.

'You lot are crazy,' said Eddie. 'I need to take a leak, where's the John in this place?'

'It's inside the main building over there,' said Mike, pointing towards the black stone-clad building on the other side of the pool. Have a look for Veronica while you're in there, would you?'

Eddie made his way towards the building where he intended to do anything except to find Veronica. He did not have to. She spotted him as he made his way out of the bathroom.

'Want to go back in there with me, luvver?' she said.

Jesus Christ. This girl's a fruitcake. 'Leave it out, Veronica. This ain't funny,' he said, backing away. 'Seriously, fuckin' stop it'.

'Oh, don't be like that, Ed. I thought we were friends'.

'Friends don't try to get each other's head's kicked in,' said Eddie. She put her arms around him and gazed up at his face.

'Are you scared of my Mikey? Don't worry about him. He's off chasing tarts behind my back all the time'. Eddie attempted to peel her off him, but she clung on tight, twisting to her left and pulling him down towards an empty couch.

'Stop it. I mean it'. Eddie was getting angry, his eyes darting around the surrounding crowd, hoping he would not see Mike. Nobody was paying them any attention.

'I want you to screw me, Eddie'.

'Christ almighty, Veronica. Are you high?'

She giggled. 'Of course, aren't you?'

'No. I'm not into that shit. And I ain't into this either'. He applied pressure to her thumbs and broke free from her. He stood up and checked their surroundings once more. 'Your fella's out there. If he sees you like this, tryin' it on…well he ain't gonna be happy, is he?'

'Alright, I'll behave. If you stay for a bit and talk,' she said. She pulled a cigarette out of her purse and lit it. She patted the sofa next to her. 'C'mon, at least sit down and have a chat, Eddie'. Sensing that it was the best strategy in the scenario, Eddie lowered himself down on the red sofa. It smelled of stale beer.

'You're dangerous, you are,' said Eddie.

'Men like crazy girls'.

'Some men,' said Eddie. He watched her inhale on the cigarette. 'Gimme one of them'. She placed the packet of John Player Special and her lighter in his outstretched hand. 'So he cheats on you. You're pissed with him. I get it,' he said, before placing the cigarette in his mouth and lighting it.

'He screws around, yeah,' she said in a sarcastic tone. 'But I don't care about that. Not no more'.

'Why are you still with him? He's what…twenty years older than you?'

'For the money. That and he used to be an animal in bed. Now he's mostly drunk. Or angry.'

'Right now, I'd say he's worried about you. So why don't you stop all this business and go to him? It's obvious he cares for you,' said Eddie.

'He cares about your brother more'.

'Ah, I get it,' said Eddie and gave her a knowing smile.

'Do you?' said Veronica.

Eddie nodded, smiling. 'How long have you two been together?'

'About three years,' she said.

'And how long have Mike and Charlie been friends?'

'I dunno. Fifteen years or something?'

'More. About twenty,' said Eddie. 'That's a tight, fuckin' friendship. You know what I mean? They've been through some serious shit together. I bet you don't know the half of it'.

'I know I don't,' said Veronica.

'Then don't try and compete. That ain't gonna happen. Mike and Charlie are best friends. You won't change that. But it doesn't mean you can't have a good relationship with Mikey. He treats you okay, doesn't he?'

'If you mean, "he doesn't hit me", yeah. He treats me okay'.

'So, why are you acting like this? If he makes you happy, stick by him. If not, don't. It's pretty flippin' simple'.

Veronica gazed at him. He scrutinised her lips before realising that her hand was on his thigh. He left it there.

'I reckon you could make me happy', she said. She put her hand on his and leaned towards his mouth. He let her move forward, but only for a moment.

'Veronica, no!' he said, trying very hard to sound virtuous in his intentions. She let him get up, her hand brushing against his bulging groin as he did so. She could see right through him, and he knew it. Fuck. He stood over her. 'Get up. C'mon. I'm taking you back to your fella'. He held out his hand, but she did not move.

She smiled. It was a confident, "I'm-in-your-head" kind of smile. 'Did you know I was an actress,' she asked.

'No,' said Eddie, wondering where this would go.

'Yep. I was in Crossroads twice. And Dick Turpin on ITV, with Richard O'Sullivan. The Sweeney, too. I played a hooker from Glasgow for three episodes. Till I got murdered'. She laughed. 'And two other dramas. Did a bit of theatre too. I was good. Accents were my strong point. But I was young and stupid and got myself caught up in this whole Costa del Crime lifestyle'.

'You mean parties? Drugs?' said Eddie.

'That, and a penchant for moody tough guys,' she replied. 'Like you'.

Eddie rolled his eyes. 'So why don't you go back to England? Start again?'

'Ain't that simple'.

'It really is. You just pack up your stuff, get on a plane. You make it happen. If you really want to'.

'There are things you don't know about -'. She stopped herself.

'About what?' said Eddie. She smiled. It seemed forced.

'Don't matter. Ignore me. I've done too much blow. My head's all over the bloody place'. She giggled. It seemed forced. Eddie hesitated for a moment. He was curious, but alarm bells were ringing in his head.

She's trouble. Don't get involved. 'C'mon, let's get back to the others,' he said instead.

'Sure thing, lover'. Veronica grabbed his outstretched hand and lifted herself up like a creeping vine around an old tree trunk, flickering the tip of her tongue on the inside of her open lips. He grabbed her hand and pulled her into the dancing masses back towards Charlie and the rest of the British crew.

This girl will be the end of me.

When Eddie arrived back at the table with Veronica in tow, the topic of conversation was of a much more serious nature. The crew were huddled close and exchanging furtive glances around them. Eddie sat down and listened.

'It's safe, far away from Spanish authorities,' he heard Roger say. 'We just nip back, do the job, and come straight back to Spain. All in a few days'.

'I reckon it would be one of the easiest jobs we've pulled, Charlie,' said Mike, who was obviously keen on the idea.

Charlie, however, was staring at the ground and slowly shaking his head. 'Boys, I know things are a bit tight now,' he said, 'but we can't afford to draw any more attention on us. Besides, the property project will solve all our problems'.

'It ain't that we don't believe in your project, Charlie,' said Roger. 'But we all need cash now'.

'It ain't just the money. I'm getting fuckin' bored down here,' said Mike.' Look at em all…'. He waved his hand around, to direct Charlie's attention to a group of stern-faced, swarthy men at a nearby table. One of their number was eyeing the British group, unsmiling. He blew out a plume of cigar smoke. 'Everyone thinks we've gone soft,' Mike continued. 'They don't respect us. And throwing parties at your gaff ain't gonna change that'. Mike glared back at the tanned man with the cigar.

'Cut it out, Mike. They're some of Fernandez's boys. I need his support for the project,' said Charlie.

'I thought you said you weren't gonna go after the local Spanish money?' said Mike.

'No, but that bastard controls half the construction crews in the province. We can't burn bridges so just play fuckin' nice'.

'What d'you think, Kenny?' asked Mike.

'I'm with Charlie,' Kenny replied. 'It's too risky. You know I was lucky to get out of Blighty after the last job. I had to leave most of me bleedin' stuff behind. I'd like more dosh too, but I can't do another stretch. We'd get fifteen years if they caught us doin' this'.

'They wouldn't catch us, Ken, said Mike. 'Rog's got it all planned. Only an idiot could fuck this one up'. He nodded and gestured towards Bill. 'What are you thinking, mate?'

Bill put his hands in his pockets and glanced at Charlie. 'Well, to tell the truth, I am getting a bit grief off the missus at the moment. She knows the money ain't gonna last forever'.

'Enough,' said Charlie. 'Not here. Not now. We'll have a crew meeting tomorrow and discuss it properly like we always do'. He tossed an expired cigarette to the ground.

'Fair enough,' said Mike. 'I'll make the arrangements and let everyone know what time'.

'Fine,' said Charlie. He downed his whisky and lit up another cigarette.

Veronica slid over to behind Mike and put her arms around him.

'Hey you,' she said. 'Sure this idea ain't a bit risky?' She seemed to be genuinely concerned.

'Have you been listening in? I told you before, not to do that,' said Mike. She let her hands drop, shifted away and slumped into a chair, her arms crossed.

Eddie studied each of the group. Mike, Roger and Bill were sharing a joke and laughing. Kenny was looking towards the pool, seemingly hypnotised by the groups of young women in skimpy swimwear, Eddie decided. His other arm rested on his lap with an empty cocktail glass in his hand.

Charlie was cuddling the young blonde. *What was her name again*?

Eddie tried to make out what they were talking about, but "Girls Just Wanna Have Fun" by Cyndi Lauper, was blaring out of the club's music system. Veronica remained on her chair, her arms still resolutely folded. He leaned over and tapped her on the shoulder.

'You look like you need a refill. Martini, was it?' he asked. She nodded. He saw that she had tears in her eyes.

'Debs wants to dance,' shouted Charlie. 'Bring Veronica. Mike don't dance,' Eddie saw his brother being dragged towards the dance floor by the young blonde girl.

'Nah, I don't -'. He felt his hand being grasped.

'You've been given an order, soldier,' said Veronica. She was already standing up and looking into his eyes. He could not refuse her.

'Jesus, okay. One song though. I ain't no dancer'.

'I'll be the judge of that,' she whispered in his ear, before she backed into the crowd, beckoning at him to follow, swaying her shoulders to the music.

Christ, she's gorgeous.

Eddie walked towards her, noting the surrounding dancers. He had not been on a dance floor for several years, and the bizarre movements of the dancers were utterly alien to him.

'Don't worry what you look like,' said Veronica. 'Just let yourself go. Have some friggin' fun, you stiff'. She moved closer to him - so close he could smell her breath. As she wiped her forehead with her arm, Eddie's gaze inadvertently dropped to her cleavage. She noticed. 'You can have a better look later?' she said. Her tone sounded innocent but Eddie doubted that her intentions were. He averted his eyes. 'Don't think I haven't been watching you all night neither,' she said.

'Veronica -'.

She twisted one hundred and eighty degrees, swayed from one side to the other in perfect rhythm to the music, then arched her back, flung her arms in the air and fell back towards him. Eddie darted forward and grabbed her, dropping a cigarette to the floor in his panic. He found himself gazing down at her smiling, upside-down face and at her breasts again.

'My saviour,' she said, before twisting out of his grasp and resuming her dancing.

I think it's me that needs saving.

Eddie caught his brother looking at him from ten feet away, Debbie cavorting close by. Charlie mouthed something. Eddie was pretty sure it was, "Be careful". To Eddie's relief, the song ended and was replaced by "Rock of Ages", one of Eddie's favourite songs. He started nodding his head to the guitar riffs. Veronica grimaced.

'I bloody hate Def Leppard,' she muttered.

'Just when I was enjoying it,' he thought.

'Let's go get that drink'. She grabbed his hand and pulled him away but all of a sudden froze, her attention focused on something behind Eddie. He saw Mike standing a short distance away, repeatedly shoving Kenny who was back towards the pool.

'Here we fucking go again,' Veronica growled.

They pushed their way through the crowd towards the two men.

'I got a better fucking offer,' Eddie heard Kenny shout. Mike shoved the smaller man again, with more vigour than before. 'Leave it out, you wanker'.

Charlie made his way towards the pair who were now standing precariously close to the water. 'Pack it up, the pair of you,' he shouted. 'What do yer think you're playing at?'

'Daniel Ortega just walked up to me and said he'd bought Kenny's boat this morning,' said Mike, who was gripping Kenny's shirt in one hand, poised to deliver a punch.

'So what?' said Charlie.

'So he'd promised me I could have it,' said Mike.

'You only offered me eight grand,' said Kenny. Ortega offered me fifteen. And he had the cash there with him. I weren't gonna turn that down, was I?'

Eddie, who was now standing a few feet from Mike, glanced at his older brother to show that they were now the centre of attention for at least a hundred of the other party-goers. 'Do something,' he mouthed.

Charlie nodded and moved closer to Mike. 'Please, Mike. Everyone is watching. Calm down'.

Mike, still holding the shaking Kenny in a firm grip, peered around at the assembled audience then sighed and relaxed his grip. 'I ain't gonna forget this, Ken,' he said as he let go of his fellow Englishman.

'Good. Okay, let's all calm down, shall we?' said Charlie.

Kenny examined his shirt and noticed it was torn. 'You ripped my poxy shirt you thick fuckin bastard,' he shouted.

Mike twisted on the spot and, with the agility of someone half his age, punched Kenny full-force in the stomach with his left hand. His right followed half a second later, smashing into Kenny's nose.

Kenny, doubled up and with blood streaming from his face, took a step backwards, slipped and fell into the swimming pool.

'For fuck's sake,' screamed Charlie.

Eddie darted to the poolside. Kenny was floating upside down in the water, a small plume of water tinted pink by the infusion of blood. Eddie reacted without hesitation and leapt into the pool. He hit the water like an exploding mine, sending water over Mike and Charlie, swam to Kenny and lifted the unconscious man's head was out of the water. He pulled the bloodied Brit to the poolside. 'Quick, lift him out,' he barked.

Mike stood motionless, a sly smile on his face. 'Let the bastard drown,' he said.

Bill and Roger appeared at the side of the pool and reached down to grab their friend. They heaved him up and pulled him onto the white paving stones.

'Is he breathing?' said Veronica, her mouth obscured by her hand. Eddie lifted himself out of the water and up onto his knees. He remained there for a few moments, panting.

Charlie kneeled down next to Kenny's head. 'Ken? Can you hear me, mate?' he shouted. Kenny opened his eyes and nodded his head.

'Thank fuck for that,' said Bill.

'You fucking moron,' said Roger, and shoved Mike in the chest.

Charlie stood up. 'Enough, already,' he shouted before looking at Mike, and in a much quieter tone, muttered, 'Go home, now'. The two men stood staring each other out. Mike's teeth were clenched. 'I said go home, now,' Charlie repeated.

Eddie moved to stand next to his brother. 'You heard my brother,' he said.

Mike grinned. 'Wouldn't want to upset the Lawson brothers, would I now? C'mon Veronica, we're going home. Be a good girl, get my jacket, would you?' He pulled a packet of Rothmans out of his pocket.

'Get you own bloody' jacket,' she replied, before storming off towards the bar.

Mike shrugged. 'Maybe you was right about that one, Charlie,' he said. He put a cigarette in his mouth and turned towards Roger. 'Give us a light'.

Roger reached into his jacket pocket, found his lighter and stepped forward. 'You're bang out of order tonight, Mike,' he said while holding out the burning zippo.

'Always have been, always will'. Mike started walking towards the exit. 'See you all at the meeting'.

Charlie let out an anguished sigh. 'Why does he always have to make things so difficult?' He put his hand on Eddie's shoulder. 'Thank's, bruv'.

'Don't worry about it,' said Eddie, but he wasn't looking at Charlie. He was watching Veronica who stood thirty feet away, staring back at him, her arms crossed before her. She spun around and headed into the bar. Eddie was sure he saw her smiling.

Bill and Roger pulled Kenny to his feet.

'Get him cleaned up. We should get out of here before anything else goes down,' said Roger.

Charlie sighed again. 'Yeah, time to go. Just when I was enjoying myself, too. Are you two alright to get Ken home?' he said.

'Yeah, no worries,' said Bill.

'Good. I'm going back to Deb's place. You okay to get a cab back to the villa, Ed?' he held out a handful of banknotes.

'I'm good. See you in the morning,' said Eddie. Debbie was walking towards them. 'Have fun, bruv' he said.

Charlie smirked. 'I always do'. He walked off towards his girlfriend.

'Sure you're okay, Kenny?' said Eddie.

Kenny was holding a handkerchief to his nose. 'The fucker broke my bleedin' nose'.

'Don't go back on a deal with him next time, you plonker,' said Roger.

'I ain't gonna be doin' no deals with him ever again. Fuck that bastard,' said Kenny.

'You coming with us, Ed?' said Bill.

'Nah. I'll get another cab'.

'Uh huh,' said Bill, and gave him a knowing look. 'Steer clear of that one, son. She's poisonous,' he said before helping Kenny towards the exit.

Eddie waited until they had left before going off in search of Veronica.

He found her standing at the bar attempting to order another drink. She had been crying. Eddie shook his head at the bartender who got the message and moved to serve another customer instead.

'I think you've had enough already'.

'Not close,' Veronica said.

'You should go home'.

'I ain't being in the house with him when he's in that state'.

'Fine'. Eddie put his hand on her elbow and lifted her up from the barstool. 'Have you got a friend I can take you to?'

'Friends? Ha, you're kidding. He gets all jealous'. She pushed in front of him. 'Let me come back to Charlie's place. I won't be any trouble'.

Eddie frowned. 'That's not going to happen'.

'Please, Eddie. It's two o'clock in the morning. It's too late to find a hotel. Besides, it's the high season. They're all gonna be full, anyway'. Eddie gazed at her dark brown eyes. Her lips.

Those wonderful lips.

It was the early hours, but it was still uncomfortably hot. A strand of her hair was matted to the side of her face with sweat. That didn't matter to Eddie. He just wanted to kiss her. To undress her. Her hands were on his chest, exploring the contours of his pecs through his thin black shirt, her eyes fixed on his. He slid his hands down her side to the top of her hips. His fingers pressed on the edge of her firm backside.

'Take me back with you,' she said, her hands falling to his stomach and then to his belt.

'Sod it,' he thought. 'I'll be out of here in a few days, and her fella's an arsehole'.

'Let's go,' Eddie whispered and pulled her towards the door. 'Get us a taxi,' he said to one of the door staff, and placed a bunch of banknotes in the man's hand. The doorman signalled for a waiting cab which pulled up outside the entrance.

'Have a good night,' said the man winking at Eddie.

'Oh, he will,' said Veronica.

CHAPTER ELEVEN
THE MORNING AFTER

Eddie stirred from under his pillow, to the sounds of fat car tyres sending driveway gravel in all directions as Charlie's Porsche pulled up at the front of the villa. Fleeting images of the preceding evening flashed past his eyes; talk of a heist in England, Kenny floating unconscious in a pink pool, Eddie jumping in and lugging the comatose man out.

Eddie remembered sharing a taxi with Veronica. He lifted his head out from under the soft bedding, and the sunlight immediately penetrated into the back of his eye sockets. His head was thumping. The inside of his nose was burning. A peculiar, bitter taste lingered in the back of his throat.

Did I do cocaine?

The muted sounds of the Porsche's stereo system suddenly intensified as a car door opened. Eddie recognised the song immediately; Paul Weller singing "Eton Rifles". Charlie was attempting to sing along, but it was clear his brother only knew the song's chorus. Eddie shut his eyes again and rolled over, at which point he sensed the warmth of another body beside him.

Oh, shit!

He opened his eyes gradually, and as he feared, it was Veronica. She lay there fast asleep on her side, her bare backside facing him. New, more pleasant memories appeared and swirled around his brain alongside the images of the earlier events of that previous night. Paul Weller stopped singing and a car door slammed shut.

'Veronica. Wake up. Charlie's here,' he said while shaking her.

She moaned and opened her eyes. 'I don't wanna wake up yet'.

'We overslept. Charlie's here'. She stared at him blankly, evidently untroubled by the news. 'You need to go to another room before he sees us together'.

She pulled a bedsheet across her body and sat up. 'Eddie Lawson, are you ashamed of me?'

Christ, does she ever let up? 'Move. Now! The room across the hallway. Quickly'. He leapt out of bed, searched for his Y-fronts, pulled them on and marched to her side of the bed. 'Get up. Now, for fuck's sake!' He hauled her to her feet by her limp wrists, pushed her towards the open bedroom door, and pointed towards the bedroom across the corridor. 'Go in there and make it seem like you slept there last night. 'C'mon, hurry'.

Eddie glanced towards the sound of the front door being unlocked.

'My head hurts,' she moaned. She rubbed her head with both hands, and the sheet fell to the floor, revealing her toned, slender body once more.

Eddie felt his heart accelerate again. He lent down to pick up the sheet, at which point he realised that they both stunk of sex. 'Quickly,' he said. He wrapped the bedsheet around her, before he frog-marched her into the corridor. 'That door, there. Go,' he instructed. She took two steps but abruptly changed direction and headed up the hallway. 'What are you doing?' he said, totally exasperated.

'I need to pee,' she muttered and opened a bathroom door. Eddie darted out into the corridor, but she slipped inside the

DEN OF SNAKES

door and quickly shut it behind her. He tried the handle, but she had locked the door.

'You alright, bruv?' Eddie stood on the spot, slowly lifting his head to meet the gaze of his brother, who was now walking along the hallway towards him with an expression of confusion on his face. 'What are you doin?'

Eddie stood there in his blue and white underpants. He felt like a schoolboy who had just been caught by his headmaster, looking at girly mags. 'Listen, Charlie -'.

The sound of a toilet flushing stopped him, and his gaze fell to his feet. From inside the bathroom came the sound of Veronica humming as she washed her hands.

Charlie looked at his brother, a broad grin appeared on his face. 'Sounds like someone got lucky last night'. They heard the door unlocking from within. Charlie took a step backwards, a curious look on his face. Eddie sighed.

'Hi, Charlie. Splendid party last night,' said Veronica, smiling. 'I ain't had that much fun in ages'.

Charlie's jaw dropped. He snapped back to face his brother who, in a fraction of a second, burst at Eddie, forcing him up against the wall.

'You fucking idiot. What were you thinking?'

'I can't remember. I was drunk. I think we might have done coke. I fucked up, I'm sorry'.

'Sorry? That ain't gonna cut it if Mikey finds out'.

'Then don't tell him,' said Veronica. She closed the door behind her, one arm clasping the sheet to her body, and ambled off towards the bedroom. 'Just one more secret to keep, Charlie. Right?' She started humming again as she went back to Eddie's room.

Charlie still had his forearm across Eddie's chest.

'I'm sorry, bruv. Let go, please,' said Eddie. Charlie shifted his weight and released Eddie. He took a step back. 'Look, it doesn't matter. I'm booked on a boat to Morocco this afternoon, and a flight to Angola tomorrow. I'll be out of your hair, and you can pretend it never happened'.

'The two o'clock ferry from Algeciras?'

'Yeah,' said Eddie.

'That ain't happening,' said Charlie.

'What do you mean?'

'Algeciras is eighty miles away, and it's gone midday already. The coast road is shit after Estepona, and it will be rammed with tourists and other cars heading in the same direction. You ain't catching that boat today'. Eddie slumped against the wall. 'Another day won't kill you,' said Charlie. 'Mike might though'.

Eddie put his head in his hands. 'What was I thinking?'

Charlie leaned against the wall next to his brother. He pulled a cigarette packet out of his pocket, plucked one out and lit it. 'You were thinking, "She's a hot piece of ass and she's coming on to me," that's what,' said Charlie. Eddie gave his brother a sheepish grin. 'And I very much doubt you are the first or the last bloke to fall into that honey trap, bruv,' said Charlie. 'But listen, she needs to understand she can't say nuffin. She's had her fun, now she needs to keep schtum. Or we're all going to suffer, believe me'.

Eddie nodded and pushed himself off the wall. 'I'll talk to her,' said Eddie.

'Nah, I've got this. You get yourself cleaned up. You stink like a wet dog'.

'Alright. And I'm sorry, Charlie'.

'I know, mate. We all make mistakes, right?' Charlie winked at his brother, who sauntered back to the bedroom before closing the door behind him.

A taxi arrived twenty minutes later. Eddie, who stood freshly showered in his bedroom wearing a bathrobe, watched his brother emerge from the front door beneath his window. Veronica was at Charlie's side. She glanced back up at the bedroom window. Eddie thought she appeared sad. Charlie had his hand around her waist and was steering her up toward the main gate. They appeared to be having a heated discussion.

As they reached the gate, Eddie saw Veronica push his brother away, but he grabbed hold of her again. After another minute of animated talking, she departed through the gate. Shortly after he saw the car move off down the road.

Eddie dried himself and had started to get dressed when Charlie knocked on the door.

'Come in,' he responded.

'Hopefully, that's sorted. I frickin' hope that girl knows what's good for her,' said Charlie.

'It seemed like you were getting your message across alright. You didn't need to be so hard on her'.

'You don't know her like I do,' Charlie said. 'She's a snake'.

'I'm only sayin' you can't just blame her for what happened, it's my fault too'.

Charlie gave him a friendly punch on his shoulder. 'Just… you know, listen to what I'm telling yer next time. Alright?'

'It's for the best, me leaving. I ain't cut out for this life,' said Eddie. 'Stick me in the middle of machine-gun fire and artillery, that I can handle. But this place. And what you lot do…'. He shook his head.

'I get it,' said Charlie. 'And to tell you the truth, sometimes I wonder if it would be easier if I was back in London'.

Eddie shook his head. 'I don't buy that. I've seen you, you're in your element here. You, the crew, and the whole fraternity you have down here. You love it'.

'Yeah, I do,' said Charlie. He grinned. 'But it's like you said the other night, we're in prison here. We can't go home. We've all got friends back there. Family as well, in the case of the other fellas. People you can trust, not like here. But I can't go back. None of us can. We can't pop into our local boozers. Can't get on the tube and go up to the Bridge to watch the Blues'. He laughed. 'Mind you, that's probably for the best. Chelsea are still pretty shit these days, aren't they?'

'They're back in the first division,' said Eddie. 'They got promoted last year. They've got a good little team now. Jonny Hollins is back there as the coach'.

'Really? Well, that just goes to show how out of touch I am. Which is why you are right. You don't belong here. Not that I'm at all keen on you getting your ass shot off in Timbuktu or wherever you're going -'.

'Angola,' said Eddie.

'Yeah, right. Angola'. Charlie put his arm across Eddie's shoulders. 'And there's still no way I can talk you out of that?'

Eddie shook his head. 'I called the company - they're expecting me now. I don't want to mess those guys about'.

'Okay. Okay. Well, I promised I'd take you to the ferry port, so I will. We'll go tomorrow morning. Alright?'

'Thanks, Charlie. I know you'd like me to stick around, but -'.

'No. No need to say anymore. I get it'. Charlie glanced at his gold Rolex. Eddie could tell that his brother was attempting to hide his disappointment. 'We've got this crew meeting in two hours. We're voting on that job that Roger proposed last night'.

'Do you reckon they will go for it?' said Eddie.

'Nah, I've got a plan,' said Charlie. Eddie saw a malicious glint in his brother's eye. 'Tell you what, why don't you tag along?' his brother ventured. 'It won't take long, and I'll take you out for a decent meal afterwards. It can be your send-off. What d'ya reckon?'

'I dunno, Bruv' said Eddie. After all that had happened over the last few days, the last thing he wanted was to be around his brother's crew any more.

'S'alright, you can wait in the bar when I'm with the lads. Oh, I wanna check in on Kenny on the way there too. He spent the morning in the hospital. Only got a bleedin' broken cheek ain't he?'

'He was in a bad state,' said Eddie. 'Listen, Charlie, maybe it's best if I don't -'. The sound of the phone ringing interrupted him.

'Sorry, I need to grab that,' said Charlie, before jogging down the hallway to get to the phone.

Eddie sat down on the bed and was just about to pull his socks on when Charlie appeared back at the doorway. He was holding the portable handset, his hand covering the receiver and wearing a confused expression.

'Did you give somebody this number? It's some Scottish bird. She's asking for you'.

'For me? Did she say who she was?'

Charlie shrugged. 'She said it was a private matter'.

Eddie stood up and took the receiver from his brother. 'Hello. This is Eddie Lawson'.

'Mr Lawson,' said a woman in a Scottish accent. 'I'm calling from Hawkwood International. I have a message from the colonel for you'.

'Go on,' said Eddie, his pulse quickening.

'He said to tell you that the contract in Angola is no longer proceeding'.

Eddie could not believe what he was hearing. 'But that can't be right,' he said. 'It was going ahead just a couple of days ago'.

'The client cancelled. That's all I can tell you,' said the woman before adding, 'I'm sorry'.

Eddie's head was spinning. In just a few seconds, his world had turned upside down. The one thing he had clung onto that he knew could help him get his life back together, the mercenary job, had been snatched from him in an instant.

'Are you still there, Mr Lawson? Hello?' He stared at the receiver, then pressed the red button to end the call.

His brother was standing behind him. 'Problem?'

'The job I had in Angola. They called it off'.

'You are kidding me'. Charlie put his hand on Eddie shoulder. 'Did they say why?'

Eddie was still shaking his head in disbelief. 'She just said something about the client pulling the plug'.

'Mate, I'm sorry'. Charlie put his hands on his brother's cheeks. 'Look at me'. Eddie was slumped against the wall. 'Ed, look at me. This was your thing, I get it. But you'll find something else'. He put his arms around Eddie and hugged him.

'It don't make sense,' said Eddie, still grappling with the news.

'You'll find something else, bruv'. He held Eddie's head and forced him to make eye contact. 'I'm here for you this time, bruv. I've got your back. Okay?' Eddie nodded. 'That's the spirit. Now c'mon. Come with me now. I need to pop in to see Ken in Banús, then I have this meeting. After that, we will have a proper talk over dinner'.

Twenty minutes later they drew up outside a stylish apartment block on the main road that leads into Puerto Banús.

'Ken lives up there,' said Charlie, while pointing to the top floor. 'He's got a right nice penthouse'. They made their way into the building's lobby and approached the security patrol, a tough-looking man in his forties wearing a black suit, collar and tie. The man stood up and grinned as they approached.

'Alright Fletch, how's the family?' said Charlie.

'Very well, Mr Lawson. Thanks,' said the security guard with a northern English accent. 'Kenny said to go right up'. He nodded toward the open elevator door.

'Thanks. Say hi to the wife for me,' said Charlie as he walked past. He let Eddie enter, then pushed the button for the fifth floor and waited for the door to close. 'Poor sod. He used to be miner back in England, but they laid him off. He couldn't find no work. He works here in the day, then doing security in bars and nightclubs after. Does every hour under the sun but what he doesn't know is that meanwhile, his bird's out shagging everything in town. Right nymph, so I've been told'. He sniggered.

'Maybe someone should tell him then?' said Eddie.

'Best he don't find out if you ask me'. An electronic chime signalled their arrival at the fifth floor and the door opened. They were greeted by a dimly lit lobby and six dark blue wooden doors. 'Right, let's see what damage Mikey did,' said Charlie. He walked over to one of the doors and knocked on it three times.

'Who is it?' said a young woman's voice in a Mancunian accent.

Charlie had a perplexed look on his face. 'It's Charlie,' he said impatiently. They could hear a muffled conversation inside before the door opened partially. A short woman in her thirties stood glowering at them. Her bobbed hair was bleached blonde, but Eddie could see her brown roots. She was wearing an oversized Star Wars tee shirt featuring Han Solo and Chewbacca and pink flip-flops.

'You gonna let us in, luv?' said Charlie.

'Kenny needs to rest. He doesn't need any more trouble,' she said.

'We're just here to talk, that's all,' said Charlie and pushed the door open.

Kenny was lying on a black leather couch in the apartment's living room. He was wearing a white, short-sleeved shirt that was unbuttoned, and blue cotton Y-fronts. More apparent was the sizeable padded bandage around his head and his right cheek. It failed to conceal the extent of the bruising to his face, and Eddie could see traces of iodine yellow on his skin.

'Bloody hell, you look like you got hit by a train,' said Charlie. Kenny swung his legs down and sat up, then reached for a packet of Benson and Hedges. Kenny remained silent.

'Who's the tart?' said Charlie. He glanced over at that the woman who stood glaring back at him by the door with her arms crossed.

'Her name's Katie. She's looking after me,' said Kenny.

'I'm sure she is,' said Charlie. He nodded towards a black skirt and a pair of lacy red knickers that lay on the floor. He picked them up and held them out to the young woman. 'Make yourself scarce, girl. The boys here need to talk in private'.

She stomped towards him and seized her clothes out of his hand. 'Five minutes. He needs to rest. The doctor said so,' she said, then turned and walked to the bathroom.

'I've got to admire your stamina, Ken,' said Charlie. 'A busted face and you still wanna get your end away. So what did the doctor say?'

Kenny put his cigarette down into a silver-coloured ash tray. 'I've got a broken cheek, is what he said. I'm going back in tonight to have an operation. They're gonna put a metal plate in'.

'Fuckin' hell,' said Charlie. 'I didn't realise it was that bad. Sorry, mate. Let me know if I can do anything, alright?'

'You can get Mike to pay for the bastard operation, for one thing. It's gonna cost a few grand'.

'I'll have a word with him'.

'And I want a fuckin' apology too'.

Charlie's face made it clear that he did not think that was likely, and he sat back in the sofa. 'You did go back on a deal,' he said.

'What was I supposed to do? He was only gonna pay me eight grand for the boat. Ortega offered me fifteen,' said Kenny.

'Deals a deal, Ken,' said Charlie. 'But look, what happened, happened. We'll sort out the medical fees. You just need to rest and recover. I need you back up and on your feet'.

Kenny looked at him and Eddie. 'You goin' to the crew meeting?' he asked.

Charlie nodded. 'Yeah, gonna try to talk 'em out of this nonsense about doin' that job back in Blighty'.

Kenny looked across at Eddie, who stood with his hands in his jeans pockets. 'You going too, son?' said Kenny to Eddie.

'To the meeting? Nah,' said Eddie.

'I'm taking Eddie out after. He's gonna hang around in the bar till I'm done. Why?' said Charlie.

'Well, I can't go. And that's a problem for you'.

Charlie scratched his chin and looked at his brother. 'You do have a point,' he said.

Kenny shuffled forward on the couch. 'Can I ask a favour, Ed?' he said.

'What is it?' said Eddie.

'Go to the meeting. Be my proxy'.

Eddie took his hands out of his pocket. 'I dunno. I mean, I ain't a part of your crew. I don't think -'.

'Nah, it's easy. You just cast my vote. The boys will understand. We've done it before. Remember Charlie? When Roger had that funeral? Judy voted for him on that restaurant investment'.

'She did, that's right,' said Charlie. 'I'd forgotten about that'. He peered up at his brother. Kenny forced himself to his feet and walked over to a wooden bureau. He opened a drawer and took something out, then walked back over to Eddie. He held the item up for Eddie to see. It was an old brass bullet casing.

'It's how we vote,' said Kenny. 'We've got one each. We got our names engraved on them'.

'You're kidding me? You actually have bullet casings with your name on them?' said Eddie.

Charlie laughed. 'I guess it's a bit morbid when you put it that way,' he said.

'Take it,' said Kenny. 'Go to the meeting as my proxy. When they have the vote, just back your brother. That's what I would do. It's what I have always done'.

Eddie stared at the old cartridge case. Kenny had made it

sound easy, and he wanted to help his brother, but if Eddie had learned anything in the last few days, it was that being around this crew was rarely without drama. He could hear his mother's voice in his head asking him to look after Charlie, to keep him on the straight and narrow. 'I'd be betraying her if I didn't support him now,' he thought. All I have to do is drop a bullet case into a bag. Whatever happens is down to them. 'Okay, if it helps,' he said. He took the brass casing from Kenny's outstretched hand.

'Good lad,' said the older man, smiling. Kenny turned to look at Charlie. 'So, what d'ya reckon?' Charlie sighed and sat forward.

'Well it was Roger's cousin's idea, so he's dead keen. That and I think his Judy has spent most of his money already'.

'Robbing the bleeding bank of England wouldn't cover her trips to Banús,' said Kenny.

'And Mike's up for it clearly,' said Charlie.

'Look's like it all rests on Bill, then'.

'Looks that way,' said Charlie. 'But I had a word with him earlier, made him see sense. At least I think so'. He tapped Eddie on the arm. 'C'mon then, Ed. Let's get this over with. Take it easy, Ken'. He beckoned to Eddie to leave.

Kenny sat back down onto the sofa. 'Let me know how it goes'.

The brothers left Kenny's apartment and made their way back to Charlie's car.

'They're not really gonna go for it, are they? This job? They ain't that stupid, are they?' said Eddie. 'I mean, slipping back into England, hitting a bank or whatever it is, then getting back out again. That's pretty fuckin' nuts'.

'That it is,' said Charlie. 'Especially when we're so close to getting what we want here in Spain'.

'Then tell 'em they can't do it?'

'It's not that simple,' said Charlie.

'But you don't have to get involved, even if they want to do it, right?'

'I'd have to. We have this code. We discuss it, we vote. If the vote is to do it, we all do it.'

'Your havin' a laugh, right?' said Eddie.

Charlie shook his head. 'It's how we do things. Always have, always will. It's got us through some serious shit over the years. We stick together. The moment we don't, well, I hope that don't never happen'.

They arrived at the venue, the Hotel Fuerte, twenty minutes later. Charlie pulled the silver car into an empty parking space, turned off the ignition and looked up at the grandiose facade. He looked anxious.

'Just tell them how it is,' said Eddie. 'Make them see sense'.

Charlie looked at his brother. 'Will you tell 'em too?'

'Me?' said Eddie. 'Why would they listen to me? I'm not one of your crew'.

'No, but they all saw what you did for Kenny last night. And you was a soldier, too. They respect that. Maybe you can help dissuade them. Will you try?'

Eddie paused for a moment, his hand rubbing his temple. He puffed out his cheeks. 'Alright,' he responded finally. 'But I doubt you'll need my help. It's you they follow. Just listening to all those stories last night showed me how tight a unit you all are'.

'That was a long time ago. Things are different. We've all changed. It's different now'. They watched as a small group of tourists walked past, then Charlie opened the door and said, 'Let's do this'.

CHAPTER TWELVE
DEMOCRACY IN ACTION

Charlie and Eddie made their way under the lines of tall pine trees which concealed much of the hotel's light salmon-coloured facade from the road, then walked towards the gold and dark glass entrance. Charlie eyed the surroundings in the manner of a nervous game animal on an African savannah.

'So, have you booked a room for the meeting?' said Eddie.

'In a manner of speaking,' said Charlie. He pointed to the top of the building. 'We're going up there'. Eddie looked up to the hotel's roofline. Someone was looking down at him. It looked like Mike.

They entered into the lobby through the tinted glass doors. Eddie surveyed the interior. It was, without any doubt, a hotel for more discerning - and monied - guests than other nearby locations. There were no over-tanned British holidaymakers in replica football shirts and Hawaiian shorts to be seen in this establishment. A brass plaque on a column outside proclaimed that the Hotel Fuerte was first established in 1957 next to the ruins of an old fort from back when Marbella's tourist industry was in its infancy. Some framed black and white photographs hung on the wall depicting the original, smaller building which had since morphed into the much-larger, present-day version.

A grey-haired man in a sharp suit addressed them as they approached the reception desk. 'Señor Lawson, it is good to see you again,' he said.

'And you too, Felix. How's your family?' said Charlie.

'Very good, thank you. My grandson very much likes the Walkman you got him for his birthday. He is taking it everywhere he is going'.

'I'm glad to hear that,' said Charlie. 'Are my associates here?'

The man took a step nearer and quickly glanced around them. 'They are waiting for you'. The man handed Charlie a small set of keys with a quick, practised movement. 'Take all the time you need,' he said quietly.

'*Mucho gracias,*' said Charlie and turned to Eddie. 'The lift's this way'.

Eddie followed his brother to the elevators. Once inside, Charlie inserted a key into a hole in the lift's panel, turned it and then pushed on a button marked 'six'.

'You have the entire roof to yourselves?' asked Eddie.

'We do. It's safe from prying eyes and surveillance equipment up there. There's nothing taller around, and the sounds of the air con units and passing seagulls would mask any audio bugs'.

'Do you always meet here?'

'We've used it for the last three years'.

The lift came to a halt, and the doors opened. They found themselves in a small lobby area with a plain concrete floor, whitewashed cinderblock walls and two steel doors. One led to the elevator machinery room, the other to the large flat roof. Charlie opened the second and stepped out into the sunshine. Eddie saw Mike, Bill and Roger gathered around a table positioned between two sizeable air conditioning units. It was covered in a white tablecloth, and there was a plastic crate full of brown beer bottles. It looked like they were having a family picnic.

As they approached, Bill picked up two bottles, removed the caps and held them out. 'Afternoon gents'.

Mike was leaning against a large section of air conditioning ductwork. 'We don't usually invite guests to these meetings,' he said, staring at Eddie.

'Ed's standing in for Kenny who can't be here on account of him needing to get his bleedin' face fixed after last night'. Mike smirked. 'He's asked Eddie to be his proxy, just like that time when Roger couldn't make it. Remember?' He sat down at the table and addressed the rest of the group. 'Right gents, let's get this done'. The rest of the men pulled up a chair each and sat down.

Eddie remained standing, unsure if he was supposed to be joining the discussion or not.

'Sit down, son,' said Mike. 'You're making me nervous'.

'Right,' said Charlie. 'For Ed's benefit, I'll quickly explain the rules here'. He cleared his throat. 'Firstly, anyone can raise an agenda topic for the meeting. Unless something has changed, there is only one item from Roger, which is regarding a proposed job back in England. Is that right, or are there any other topics for discussion, gents?' He looked around the table and was greeted by a succession of shaking heads. 'Okay, so as per the process that we use for these meetings, Roger will pitch the idea he has. We will discuss it for a maximum of an hour. Then we will vote. A simple majority will carry the vote, no abstentions'. He looked at Eddie. 'Got all that, bruv?' Eddie nodded.

Charlie winked at him and smiled as he picked up two upturned glasses, placed them in the middle of the table, then reached for two paper napkins and a blue biro. He scribbled "YES" on one, and "NO" on the other, then placed one glass on top of each. 'When we're ready to vote, each man places his bullet case in the glass corresponding to their vote. Understood?' This time a succession of nodding heads greeted him. 'Alright Rog, the floor is yours'.

Roger took a deep breath and leaned forward in his chair. 'So, this comes from my cousin, Gary,' said Roger. 'He first told me about this about three months ago, but I didn't bring it up before coz he hadn't put enough work in at that point. I told him to come back to me when he had more to show. He's done that now, and I gotta say, it looks well sweet'.

'It fuckin' does,' said Mike, looking at Charlie.

'I want to hear it from Roger, alright?' said Charlie, his impatience clear to all. 'So, what's the target?'

'It's a United Security depot just outside Heathrow. This guy Gary knows has worked for them for ten years, but he's fucked off with them. The bloke was supposed to be in line for a promotion, but they gave it to some kid instead. Now this geezer - Angus his name is - he ain't a bad bloke, but he likes the pop a bit too much and he's always turning up for work late. I wouldn't give him a bloody promotion either, but that's beside the point. So anyway, he's drinking with Gary down the Windmill one night whinging about his job and starts talking about how easy it would be to rob the place. Says he's got some "insider information" - givin' it the big 'un, Gary said. Like he's a right proper villain. Gaz was humouring the bloke, but not really listening'.

Roger took a swig from his beer bottle.

'So there he is, waffling away,' Roger continued. 'Moaning how this depot is third rate and only handles small value stuff that wouldn't be worth thinking about. Ten grand of cash, gems or whatever. Gaz is getting proper bored at this point and is about to grab his coat. But then, get this. The bloke mentions he'd seen some documents he wasn't supposed to what said they are getting a shipment in that was much, much more valuable'. Roger looked around the table, making sure that he had a captive audience.

'What shipment?' asked Bill.

Roger gave him a cheeky smile. 'It's coming in on an overnight flight from South Africa,' he said. 'They're not supposed to handle this stuff'. He stopped to take another drink.

'What are we talking about? Foreign currency? Krugerrands?' asked Charlie.

Roger looked up. Eddie could see he was struggling to suppress a smile. 'Diamonds,' he replied. 'About a thousand carats each time'.

Bill wolf-whistled. Mike slammed his hand on the table. 'Now, that's what I'm talking about,' he said.

Charlie, however, sat back in his chair and shook his head. 'Ain't going to work, boys,' he said. 'It's almost impossible to shift precious gems, you know that. De Boars have the supply all sewn up. Each diamond is unique. Any trader worth his salt would recognise them. Even if we could get people to work with us, and they'd have to cut them up and rework them before they could sell them. And that amount of stones, well, it'd take years to introduce those back into the market without raising suspicions'.

'But that's the beauty of this, Charlie,' said Roger. 'This is De Boars, and these are uncut conflict stones. They're off the books. They are bringing them in all covert through some satellite company they control. De Boars import 'em as industrial stones because the customs authorities don't pay attention then but they find their way back into the jewellery market and they make a friggin' fortune doing it'.

'So how much would you be talking about?' asked Eddie. Charlie gave him a stern look as if to say, 'stop encouraging them'.

'Gaz reckons about ten mill,' said Roger.

'Woah,' said Bill. Eddie sat forward and put his forearms on the table.

'Ten million? Fuck me. Is it doable?' he said.

Roger nodded. 'I reckon it is,' he said. 'Gary's been watching the place for three months now. He knows the shift patterns. He knows their vehicles, their names, what they look like and where they drink. Christ, he knows when they take a bleedin' dump. Angus gave him the building layouts and walked him through the security protocols. You wouldn't believe how basic they are. This place is just asking to be hit'.

'And what does this Angus want?' said Bill.

'Ten percent,' said Roger.

'That's fair,' said Mike.

'I don't like it, Rog. The police could connect this Angus with your cousin, Gary,' said Charlie. Which means they could connect everything to you, and to us'.

'We thought about that, Charlie. Gary won't be on the team that goes into the depot either. He'll help beforehand and stuff, but then make sure he's seen somewhere else the day the job goes down'. Roger reached for a sheet of paper and started drawing the layout of the United Security depot. 'There are roads on three sides. The other backs onto an old, disused factory. Gary's been using it as an observation point'. He pointed to the drawing. 'The main entrance is here, there's another vehicular entrance on this side. There's two doors on the outside and two more inside the yard. There's four cameras covering the exterior and another three inside the loading area'.

'That don't sound like third-rate security,' said Charlie. Roger pointed to the secondary vehicle entrance.

'According to Gaz, we'd only need to keep to this path'. He drew a zigzag line across the inner yard area as he spoke. 'We'd be in blind spots. None of the internal cameras will pick us up'. The bloke who watches the screens is distracted easily, Gaz says. We only need thirty seconds, and we're at the back door'.

'Then what?' said Charlie.

'Here's the beauty. Almost all the guards smoke, but they aren't allowed to light up inside the premises, so they go out into the yard for their fag breaks. The guy on the CCTV smokes like a trooper. We'd just need to wait for Angus to signal that the geezer is away from his desk, and we move in'.

'What signal?' asked Eddie.

'Flash of a torch. They all carry 'em,' said Roger. 'The bog's next to the room with the screens. He can do it from there. It's easy to see from outside, they've checked already'.

'It can't be that simple,' said Charlie.

'How many guards in the building?' asked Eddie.

'Seven, tops,' said Roger. 'Less if someone's off sick or running an errand'.

'How do you figure on overpowering seven guards?' said Eddie.

'Exactly,' said Charlie.

Eddie pulled the sheet of paper nearer and studied it. 'I've done a lot of training for this stuff. If I were planning on taking this building, I'd want at least ten guys on my team. There's only four of you'.

'Mike's got an idea about that,' said Roger.

'Oh, really?' said Charlie.

'I know another crew,' said Mike. 'They are Millwall-based. A mate of mine worked with them in the past. They ain't the sharpest tools in the box, but they are right hard bastards'.

'This ain't a job for thugs. This needs finesse. It would have to go off with no trouble,' said Charlie. 'If a guard or passerby got hurt, we'd be in a world of shit'.

'Doesn't sound practical then, does it?' said Eddie. 'If you ain't got the manpower, I mean'.

Mike leaned forward. He was sitting opposite Eddie, a malevolent look in his eye. 'You still off to Africa to go play soldier, tomorrow?' Charlie raised an eyebrow. The question may have been innocuous, but something about the tone of Mike's voice was suspect.

'Why wouldn't I be?' said Eddie.

'Nothing. Just thought Charlie might have talked you out of it or something'.

Eddie stared at Mike. He looks like he knows, he thought. 'How could he?'

'Coz if you weren't, then I reckon you should tag along on

this job,' said Mike. 'Make some serious dough. You know, so you could look after that kid of yours'.

The group went silent. Mike kept his gaze trained on Eddie.

'Let's keep my brother out of this, boys,' said Charlie.

'He ain't said no yet,' said Roger, now also watching Eddie. 'It ain't a bad idea, you know'.

Mike leaned back in his chair, a cocky look on his face. 'So, how about it?' he said.

'One job, one big payoff,' said Roger.

It was tempting. The mercenary gig in Africa had been Eddie's one chance to earn the money that he needed to look after his estranged daughter and make things right again with her mother. But that trip would have paid thirty thousand pounds. It was not lost on him that if he did this one job, his cut would be many times that.

'You ain't scared, are you? You, a big tough soldier 'n all,' said Mike.

Charlie put his hand on Eddie's shoulder. 'Don't let 'em wind you up, Ed. I'd be very happy if you stuck around to help out'. He shot Roger and Mike a stern look. 'But only to help us build up the business. Not this'.

'Nah, you're right, bruv,' said Eddie. 'I'm just here to pass on Kenny's vote. Which, by the way, was a no'.

Charlie looked relieved. He gave his brother's shoulder a friendly squeeze then sat back, a content look on his hands.

'I am curious though,' he asked. How did you plan on getting in and out of Blighty? You can't jump on a plane to Gatwick, can you?'

Roger smiled. 'I've got a contact who works with this fishing trawler skipper up in Vigo. Normally, he does a bit of gun-running, but he would take us. For fifty grand. He goes up through the Channel every month on his way to the north sea fishing grounds. They would dock at Lowestoft for fuel and supplies. That's where we'd get off. Then, a few days later, we'd get back on when they come back to refuel before returning to Spain. That would give us plenty of time to get the job done'.

Charlie placed his bottle down and stood up. 'I've got to give you credit, Rog. You and Gary have put a lot of thought into this, and it is impressive I have to admit'.

'But?' said Roger.

'But it's a plan for where we was five years ago, not where we are now. It ain't a smart move, and as I keep on telling you lads, if we're gonna make this work down here, we need to be seriously fuckin' smart'.

'Ten million quid sounds pretty fucking smart to me,' said Mike.

'We could use it to fund your property deal,' said Roger. 'Not just phase one, but the whole bloody thing. You can't tell me that doesn't sound appealing, Charlie?'

'It's too bleedin' risky. There are a million things that can go wrong, any of which ends up with us all doing ten to fifteen in the Scrubs'.

'I need this,' said Mike. 'I need the money'.

'Coz you blew all yours on tarts,' said Charlie.

'Are you calling my Veronica a tart?'

Eddie kept his eyes on the piece of paper in front of him.

'No,' said Charlie. 'The others are tarts. Veronica's something else entirely'.

Eddie thought Mike would explode at Charlie, but Bill sought to defuse things.

'C'mon lads, no need to get personal. Let's focus on the matter at hand, yeah?'

Charlie broke away from Mike's angry gaze and looked at Bill. 'Is there anything else you wanna tell us, Rog? Or can we get on with the vote?' Roger shrugged. 'Sorted. Let's get this business over and done with'. Charlie pulled his bullet case out from his pocket and dropped into the glass that sat on the napkin marked "No" then signalled to his brother to do likewise. Eddie dropped Kenny's bullet into the same glass. 'That's two for no'.

Mike stood up and dropped his cartridge case in the other cup, then picked up a fresh beer bottle. Roger dropped his bullet case on top of Mike's, then leaned back on his chair's rear legs.

Charlie looked at Bill, who was staring at the bullet case in his hand. 'Remember what we talked about earlier, Bill,' said Charlie in a calm tone. 'We don't need this, remember?'

'Thing is, Bill's got a question. Ain't you, Bill?' said Mike in a manner that suggested he had been waiting to drop a bombshell.

'What question?' said Charlie.

Bill looked nervous. He was fidgeting with the brass casing, seemingly uncertain whether to say something. Mike flipped his bottle cap at him. It caught Bill on the forehead, and he winced with surprise. 'Leave it out, Mike'.

'C'mon you nonce,' said Mike. 'Ask him what you said to me earlier. About Fallaci'.

'What about him?' said Charlie, now sounding a lot less confident.

Bill swallowed and looked up at Charlie. 'I need that money, Charlie. Did he really promise to pay me back?'

'Yeah,' said Charlie unconvincingly. 'I told you. Ed and I paid him a visit. It's sorted'.

'Is that what happened, Eddie?' said Mike in an accusing tone.

'Is it, Ed?' said Bill.

Eddie could sense his brother urging him to lie.

One little lie. You don't know these blokes. What does it matter? But then he pictured his adopted mother in the cramped kitchen in the house in which she had raised him. Eddie had been about six-years-old. One of the freshly baked chocolate cookies she had left cooling in the kitchen had gone missing. Mrs Lawson had made the cookies for her colleagues at the library, where she worked part time. Eddie had denied taking it, even though Mrs Lawson had already pointed out the brown crumbs on his school jersey. 'The thing about liars, Eddie,' she had told him. 'Is that nobody believes them even when they tell the truth'. That guidance had remained with him to this day. He had done some awful things in his life, but there was no worse insult for Eddie than being called a liar. He looked at Bill and shook his head.

'I fuckin' knew it,' said Mike. Bill put his head in his hands, his fingers massaging his head as if this sudden revelation had caused the onset of a massive migraine.

'I always backed you, Charlie,' said Bill. 'Why d'you lie to me'.

'It ain't like that, mate,' Charlie pleaded.

'Did that wop fucker say he'd pay up or didn't he?' said Bill. Charlie did not answer. 'I was going' to borrow money against our fucking villa to raise some cash for your fantasy construction scheme. Carol flipped out, but I was going to do it still, coz I trusted you. Coz, I believed you were looking out for me. For all of us'.

'Bill, I'm sorry,' said Charlie. 'I'll make it up to you. I'll get you that money, I promise, but -'.

Bill dropped his bullet case in the "Yes" glass. 'Not this time, Charlie. I need this,' said Bill.

Mike punched the air. Charlie sat staring at the two glasses, as if unable to comprehend what had just happened.

'Get in. Right, we're doing this,' said Mike in an excited tone. 'Debate over. We all know the code. We've voted. Decision made'. He picked up his car keys. 'C'mon Rog, we're out of here. We've got a job to prepare for'. He walked around the table to where Eddie still sat, looking at his brother. 'If you want to help your brother, you join the crew and come on this job. We'd be better off with you onboard. Think about it, son,' he said, then turned to follow Roger who was waiting at the door, holding it open.

'Sorry, Charlie,' said Bill. 'But it had to be done'.

Charlie pushed back on his chair, rose up and walked away to the side of the building.

Bill nodded at Eddie. 'I've never gone up against him before. Not in fifteen years. I've always followed him, done what he said. But not this time'.

'I'm sure he'll get you that money back from that Italian,' said Eddie.

'Maybe, but that's not the point, Eddie. He tells us he's looking out for all the crew with all these ideas and schemes, but it's him what's doing best. Ask him about that slimy sod, Lucian. Ask him what he keeps locked away in that cellar under his bar'. Eddie's face must have betrayed his thoughts. 'Ah, so you've seen it?' said Bill. 'All that audio and camera equipment. They blackmail local politicians and businessmen, and not just the Spanish. Lucian collects dirt on the other Brits here too. Villains, but also their friends and families. I've never said it before, but it's like Charlie thinks he's the Godfather or something, trying to control people like puppets'.

'C'mon, Bill. I don't think it's quite like that'.

'Mate, I've run with Charlie since the early seventies. I'd take a bullet for him, he knows that. But the rest of the crew are bleeding dry here, and he's not seeing it. That's why Roger and Mike voted to do this job. That's why I supported them. That property deal, if it comes off, will be great, yeah. But the rest of us need cash now, not in a couple of years. That's why we're doing this job'. Bill looked over at Charlie, who stood with his back turned to them, staring out over Marbella below. 'And I hope you tag along. It would improve the odds'.

Eddie watched Bill leave through the door, then walked over to his brother.

'You alright?' he said. Charlie took a drag on the cigarette he had been smoking, then flicked the finished butt over the side.

'Just another setback. Not the first'.

'I gotta ask you something, Charlie'.

'You wanna know about Lucian'. Eddie nodded. 'The boys

can't see it, but it's for all our benefit. For our protection. We can't keep doing flipping bank jobs. Eventually, you get caught. Maybe not this time, maybe not the one after that. But you always get caught and then you lose everything. It's a mug's game'. He reached for another cigarette, but then decided against it. 'I've done time and I ain't never going back again. Never. We have to change. Smart people, the establishment, they make money from money. That's what we need to do. But that takes influence and access to the kinds of people what don't like to hang out with common old bank robbers'.

Eddie put his hands on the guard rail and looked out at the sprawling town around them. 'You really believe you can do that here?'

'One hundred percent,' said Charlie, but then paused. 'Look, Ed. What you said before about this life not being for you. Maybe you're right. Maybe you should walk away'.

'And go where? Do what? With that merc gig gone, I'm bang out of options. I've got nuffin'. Bollocks to it. I've decided. Mum told me to look after you, big bro. Count me in'.

Charlie looked surprised.'What? You wanna join the crew? And do this job with us?'

'Why the fuck not?' He grinned at his brother. 'I want to see what ten million quid's worth of diamonds looks like. And besides, who's gonna watch your back if I'm not there?'

The brothers took the elevator back to the ground floor where the sounds of a pianist performing an eclectic version of "Mad World" by Tears For Fears greeted them. They listened for a moment, but a shout from outside caught their attention. Eddie looked and saw Mike being assailed upon by a TV crew.

'Fuck,' said Charlie, and darted to the door. Eddie ran after him through the open door, but they were too late. The reporter was blocking Mike from getting into his Ferrari and thrusting a microphone into his face. The cameraman was filming everything.

'Michael John McNaughton, what do you say to the man you left crippled after your robbery at a Midland Bank branch in Shoreditch, in 1979?'

'Get out of my way,' said Mike in a calm but menacing tone.

'You shot the man in the knee with a shotgun,' said the reporter. 'He's crippled for life, now'. Mike stepped forward and knocked the microphone out of the reporter's hands, thrust his keys into the red sports car's lock and opened the door. Bill and Roger were already in their cars and heading towards the exit at speed.

'You can't run forever, McNaughton,' shouted the reporter. Mike spun around. He was holding a baseball bat. He lunged forward towards the cameraman and knocked the expensive-looking equipment out of the man's hands. It fell to the floor, several pieces breaking off as it landed on the road surface. Mike, however, was not yet satisfied. He waved the bat at the crew to force them back, then smashed the camera repeatedly. The videotape popped out. Mike smashed it several times with the bat, and reached down to collect the spool of black tape that had escaped from its plastic container. Crampton tried to make a grab for it too, but Mike punched him square in the face. The reporter collapsed backwards, holding his face. Mike returned to collect the bundle of black ribbon before getting into the car and starting the engine. He unwound the window and glared at the reporter who was now sitting on his backside on the floor.

'You keep this up Crampton, and you'll wake up one morning to find me standing over you with a gun pointed at your fuckin' head'. He pulled away and sped off down the driveway and onto the public road. Eddie could hear the wailing engine as the car disappeared out of view.

Charlie tugged on his arm. 'Quick, this way,' he said. They retreated into the hotel lobby and the doorman locked the door behind them. The hotel manager hurried over to them. 'Our driver will take you in the limousine. It has blacked-out windows. They won't see you,' he said.

'Thank you, Felix. I'll send someone to get the Porsche later,' said Charlie. He thrust some banknotes into the man's hand.

A few minutes later they pulled out of the hotel's underground car park, sitting in the rear of a long, black Mercedes. Eddie saw the reporter, Jeremy Crampton, holding a handkerchief to his bleeding nose. Crampton lowered the red-stained cloth and put both hands on his hips. 'That bastard ain't gonna let up,' said Charlie. 'I need to do something about him'.

Eddie sat back and let his head sink into the cream leather headrest. 'There's no going back now,' he thought to himself. As mum always said, 'you make your bed, you lie in it'.

CHAPTER THIRTEEN
TOOLING UP

A few days later, Charlie and Eddie met up with the crew. Kenny was the only omission. They had booked, at the very last moment, an upstairs function room above a grubby pub in Cancelada, ten miles down the coast from Marbella. The proprietor, a small nervous-looking Welshman in his sixties, had been glad to accept the last-minute request for a private function room for a children's birthday party, but equally confused when only five tough-looking men turned up.

'Will your other guests be arriving soon, Mr Smith?' he asked Charlie, who had given his name as Barry Smith.

'Nah, the rest decided not to come,' Charlie answered while stuffing a wad of banknotes into the man's shirt pocket. 'That's for the room hire. Be a good chap and make sure nobody comes up here until we're done'.

The publican appeared to be about to question the scenario in which he found himself until he saw Mike glaring at him. He checked himself and nodded. 'Absolutely, Mr…Smith. I'll let the bar staff know they're not needed'.

'Good man,' said Charlie and turned his back on the man.

'Not waiting for Ken?' said Roger, once the publican was out of earshot.

'He ain't coming. Nor is he coming to England'. A round of contemplative faces greeted him. 'He's in no fit state,' said Charlie. 'And we all know it'. The others nodded except for Mike.

'Bit harsh, ain't it, bruv?' said Eddie.

'He'd be a liability. Even without a broken face,' said Charlie. 'Truth be told, he's past it. He froze on the last job. Only I saw it, and I covered for him out of loyalty. I put the rest of the lads at risk. I was soppy. He's our mate, but he's in no shape to do this. It's like I said the other night, you can't be soft in this line of work'.

'You did the right thing,' said Bill.

'And we'll all do right by him when we get back,' said Roger. 'He gets a cut'. Bill and Mike seemed somewhat less amenable to that suggestion but said nothing.

Charlie cleared his throat. 'We can still do this without you, bruv,' said Charlie. 'No shame in pulling out now. Emotions were running high a few days ago. If you change your -'.

'I said I was in. I ain't changed my mind,' said Eddie.

Charlie grinned. 'Didn't think you would'. He lit up a cigarette. 'Right, let's go over the plan one more time. Mike, your turn'.

Mike rolled his eyes. 'Do I have to?' Charlie back slapped him on his shoulder. 'Yes, you bloody well do. And we will keep goin' through it until I decide otherwise, you lazy bastard'. Mike groaned but sat forward and addressed the rest of the crew.

'Alright. We're making our way up to…'.

'Vigo,' muttered Bill.

'Yeah, Vigo. I knew that. Anyway, we're making our way up in two cars. You and your brother in one, me and the boys here in the other'.

'What route are we taking?' said Charlie.

'We head to Algeciras, then make our way north up the A-whatever it is to Jerez'.

'It's the A381,' said Roger.

'It's the only fuckin' main road,' Mike snarled. 'What does it matter what it's called?' He made to pick up his pint glass, but Charlie stopped him.

'Concentrate. Who's driving the first leg?'

'Bill is'.

'Good, what then?' said Charlie. Mike sighed. 'C'mon, Mikey. I need to know you know this'.

'Jeez, okay. Then we go to Seville, on the A four…eighty, I think'.

'The A480, that's right'.

'Then up to Mérida, where we change drivers'.

'And who's the next driver?' said Charlie.

Mike looked uncertain. 'I am,' he said.

'Good guess. What next?'

'A straight run all the way to Famara'. Roger laughed out loud. 'What you laughin' at you wanker?'

'Famara? Where the fuck's Famara?' said Bill, sniggering.

'Zamora,' said Charlie in an impatient tone.

'Whatever, I'll recognise it when I see it on the soddin' road sign, won't I?' said Mike.

'I dunno, will yer? Rog and I better stay awake, or we'll end up in friggin' France with you drivin', you dyslexic prick,' said Bill who then threw a screwed up beermat at the increasingly vexed Mike.

'Leave it out,' Mike retorted.

Charlie smacked his palms down on the table. 'This ain't poxy playtime, you retards. This weren't my fuckin' idea, remember. You want to do this, you convince me I can trust you to do your jobs, or I walk. So will Eddie,' he snarled.

'Sorry, Charlie,' said Bill. Charlie scowled at Mike.

'Alright, you've made it as far Zamora, by some fuckin' miracle. Then what?'

'Erm, Roger takes over the driving. We head north for a bit, for about twenty miles or so, then we veer off to the west to…

erm...Oooren...Ourenser. Oorensey. Fuck it, I can never remember this one'.

'Ourense,' said Eddie. 'On the Rio Miño. Old Roman town'.

'Ooh, hark who's been studying. I reckon you was teacher's pet in school,' said Bill.

'Hardly,' said Eddie.

'Ourense, right,' said Charlie. 'Where after that, Mikey?'

Mike thought for a few seconds, then smiled. 'Vigo. On the coast where we get on the boat'.

'Finally, we got there. Thank fuck,' said Charlie. He switched his attention to Bill. 'What's the total distance?'

'Erm, about six hundred miles'.

'Bang on. We leave at six o'clock in the morning. What's the estimated time of arrival in Vigo, Roger?'

'Allowing for pit stops, about nine o'clock in the evening'.

'Correct. Now, remember. This geezer's planning to leave the port by midnight at the latest. Drive with care, don't be stupid, but make sure you get there on time. He's got a lockup for the cars. Understood?' They all nodded.

'And you're confident the car you've got is in good nick, Rog?'

'Yeah, it's a Ford Granada on French plates. It's the two-point-eight V6. She's only a couple of years old, and I had her serviced. She's right fuckin' luvly. It's gonna break my heart to get it crushed when we get back,' said Roger, shaking his head.

'You can buy flipping ten of them if this job goes to plan,' said Bill.

'Yeah, I know,' said Roger. 'Still a bleedin' shame though'.

'And you've all got your stuff packed?' said Charlie. 'Anyone need a shooter?'

'Nah, we sorted it all out this morning,' said Bill. 'In fact, we had to make Mikey take half an armoury out of his bag'. Roger chuckled. 'He had five shotguns, Charlie. Five'. Charlie gave Mike a disapproving look.

'I wasn't gonna take em all on the job. Just wanted the choice on the day, like. I get all superstitious, don't I?' said Mike.

'Alright, alright. Sounds like we're ready. Any questions?' Charlie gave each of the crew members a prolonged stare. They all shook their heads. 'Okay, then there's just one thing left'. He reached down to a sports holdall at his feet and unzipped it. He pulled out what was clearly a bottle wrapped in a brown paper bag.

'What's that?' asked Eddie.

'A tradition, that's what,' said Mike. Charlie opened the paper bag and pulled out a dusty, half-empty bottle of Ouzo. He placed it on the table, while Bill arranged five small glasses in a line.

'This goes back to the first proper job that the five of us did together as a crew. Seventy-four, weren't it, gents?'

'Yep, January the sixth,' said Roger.

'How the fuck do you remember that?' said Charlie.

'It was me mum's birthday. We all had a slice of her cake before we set out to the bank. You remember'.

'Yeah,' said Bill, chuckling. 'I was pukin' my guts up I was so soddin' nervous'.

'She was a good old girl, your mum,' said Charlie as he poured a generous measure in each glass, then pushed one towards each of his colleagues. He waited until they had each taken one, then picked up the last and held it up before him. 'To family and absent colleagues,' he said. They all downed their drinks. Bill coughed and spluttered. Each of them was struggling to suppress a look of disgust.

'I fuckin' hate that stuff,' said Bill.

'Yup, I really wish I'd pinched a decent bottle of brandy from the offy that day,' said Charlie. Right, I'll see you girls at the rendezvous site tomorrow morning. He shook Mike's hand, then Bill's and then Roger's, then turned to his brother, stood in front of him and placed his hands on Eddie's shoulders. Their eyes locked. 'No going back now, bruv. You're one of us. You're a fuckin' gangster now'.

The meeting ended, and the crew dispersed to make their last preparations for their lengthy journey up to the northwest of Spain the following day. Charlie drove back to his bar in Marbella with Eddie as a passenger. He pulled the Porsche up into his private parking spot.

'What are we doing now?' asked Eddie.

Charlie gave him a wry smile. 'I wanna show you something'. The brothers walked through the front entrance, and as they passed the bar, Charlie whistled to attract the bar manager's attention. 'I'll be downstairs with my brother. Don't let anyone come down'.

The bar manager nodded.

Eddie followed Charlie down into the cellar and to the door that led to the room through which they had escaped from the unwanted attention of the TV crew several days earlier. Charlie fumbled in his pocket for a bunch of keys, then inserted one into the door lock. Eddie could hear the metal door's interior workings moving. Charlie pulled out the key and pushed the heavy door open, then flicked on the light. 'C'mon,' he said, beckoning to his brother. Eddie stepped into the chilly room.

Charlie locked the door behind them, then walked over to the solid wooden bench that occupied the centre of the room. 'Here, give us a hand with this,' he said and leaned down towards a large, battered steel chest that sat under the bench. Eddie moved over, grabbed the handle on the left of the metal box. 'Careful. It's heavy'. They both puffed out their cheeks as they lifted the box out and up onto the surface of the bench. Charlie then opened it, to reveal a top shelf of spanners, sockets and other assorted automotive tools. He lifted the top tray of tools and placed them at the side of the box. The contents in the main compartment were covered by an old, oil-covered tee shirt. Charlie looked at his younger sibling, a dark excitement in his eyes. 'Open it,' he said. Eddie picked the rag up and peered inside. An assortment of firearms confronted him. There were two Browning 9mm High Powers, a Colt 1911, a Webley revolver, an old Spanish Civil war era Astra and a few more pistols he did not recognise. There were also two submachine guns; a German MP40 and a British Mark 1 Sten. The weapons all looked worn.

Eddie whistled. 'Quite the collection of antiques. Did you ever think about opening a museum?'

'They might be a little old, but they're all in good nick,' answered Charlie as he picked up the Sten and handed it to his brother. Eddie pulled back the bolt and examined the breach. It was immaculate. He tried the action a few times; it seemed in perfect working order.

'Do you service these yourself?'

'Nah, we've got a geezer over in Fuengirola who comes over and looks after them. Ex-world war two vet. He was in the Marines. Landed on Gold Beach on D-Day. Full of stories he is. Drinks like a fuckin' fish too'. He gestured toward the box. 'So, which one do you want, bruv'.

'If it gets to the point of having to use one of these, then we've already failed,' he said. He placed the Sten gun back into the toolbox. 'I ain't shootin' anyone'.

'I figured you might say that,' said Charlie. He pulled open one of the desk draws and pulled out another gun. It was the silver-plated German Luger that Charlie had used to scare the young men at the Marbella Beach club earlier in the week. He handed it to Eddie. 'Take this. You can't hurt nobody with it but stick it in someone's face, they won't argue with you'. Eddie took the pistol and examined it. The weapon was in perfect condition and he noticed the barrel had been inscribed in German with, "Nicht entgehet dem Tode, wer der Geburt nicht entgangen ist".

'It says something like "If you've been born, you can't escape death",' said Charlie. 'I got it off a Spanish kid who'd broken into this big, old villa over in Benalmádena a couple of years ago. The owner was some old kraut who had loads of old war mementoes. I reckon he was an old NAZI. There was quite a few of them here after the war. Anyway, the kid couldn't sell this flippin' thing on account that it's been deactivated. I gave him a tenner for it'.

'It's beautiful,' said Eddie, still studying the silver weapon.

'It's yours. I prefer shooters what put holes in stuff,' said Charlie, chuckling. 'Now, there's something else I want to show you'. He walked toward a corroded, old electrical panel that was embedded in the brick wall. The panel was about four feet tall and three feet wide. It looked unused for several decades. Charlie blew a layer of dust off it, then yanked out one of the archaic-looking ceramic fuses to reveal a keyhole behind the freshly exposed space. Charlie took out his key ring once again, selected a curious-looking key which he inserted into the lock, then turned it. 'This, Bruv, is where I keep all my secrets'. He pulled on one side of the panel which opened to reveal a series of metal shelves. They were packed with Betamax video cassettes, boxed audiotapes, 'black & red' notepads, piles of paper, and several thick photograph albums. The bottom shelf was occupied by a robust-looking metal travel case. Charlie held up a key.

'I got you a copy made,' he said. Eddie stared at the key.

'I don't understand,' he said. Charlie put the key into his brother's hand.

'Keep that on you at all times. If anything happens to me… if I get arrested or whatever. You come here and get all of this'.

'What's in it?' asked Eddie.

'A shit ton of leverage. You could probably bring down a government or two with this'.

Eddie examined the case, which had two wheeled-combination locks, each with four digits. 'Two-four-zero-four, and one-two-zero-six,' said Charlie. 'Our birthdays'.

'And what am I supposed to do with it?' said Eddie.

'You take it to my lawyer, Guillem Montcada. I'll give you his address and phone number. He'll know what to do with it'. Charlie placed the case back on its shelf, then closed the panel door. 'This is important, Ed. I told you, I ain't going back in the slammer. The information in that case is my protection. It's our protection. You understand?' Eddie nodded. 'And don't tell nobody. Not a fuckin' soul'. He turned and walked over to a wooden cupboard. 'Right, help me with this,' he said, opening the door to reveal shelves packed full of equipment. 'Tools, torches, gloves, rope, everything we need. C'mon. There's a duffel bag on the floor over there. Pack it in that. Then we will go get the car we're taking up to Vigo'.

The brothers filled the bag with tools and equipment, made their way upstairs, then went outside and down to Charlie's Porsche. As they put the bag into the car's boot, Eddie peered down the street towards the beachfront. He saw a man sitting in a light blue Renault looking straight back at him.

'Fuck,' he said. Charlie glanced at him from behind the car's elevated rear hatch.

'What is it?' he asked.

'It's that bleedin' copper,' said Eddie.

'Metcalf?' said Charlie.

'Yeah. Shit. He must be on to us. What are we going to do?'

Charlie grinned. 'Don't worry. I've got this covered. Get in.' They got into the car. Charlie started it up and blipped the throttle. 'We're gonna' drive nice and slow, like. Pretend we didn't see him, alright?' Eddie nodded.

'You know he will follow us, right?'

'Like I said, I got this,' said Charlie. They drove up the street for a hundred yards, made a right turn onto the main road and headed east. After a couple of miles, they pulled onto the A7 and headed towards Málaga. Charlie glanced at his gold Rolex and smiled. 'I reckon my motor needs a bit of a clean, don't you bruv?' he said. He indicated right and pulled onto a slip road towards a service station.

'Ain't we got other priorities right now?' said Eddie. Charlie winked at him as he drove towards the rear of the cafe building towards an automatic car wash. The enormous machine had three separate lanes, the middle of which was blocked off with two orange traffic cones. He pulled the car to a stop in front of the cones and pressed the horn. A man in jeans and a red tee-shirt stepped out of a Portakabin next to the car wash, gave Charlie a wave, ran over and picked up the cones.

Eddie peeked into the passenger's side mirror. The Renault was pulling to a halt thirty feet away, and he saw Metcalf peering at them from behind the steering wheel.

'Undo your seat belt,' said Charlie. 'Once we're inside, get out, grab the bag and run to the front. We've got about fifteen seconds until the machine starts. Got it?'

'Uh-huh,' said Eddie. The man in the red tee shirt gave them a thumb's up sign, walked up to the car wash control panel and pushed a green button. Eddie heard the machine's inner workings whirring into life and a red light started flashing above the entrance.

'Right, we're on,' said Charlie. He lifted the handbrake and manoeuvred the big car into the interior of the car wash. A curtain of water appeared in front of them before moving back over the roof and towards the car's rear. 'Now. Get the bag. Go'. They leapt out of the vehicle. Charlie lifted the rear hatch and Eddie heaved the heavy sports bag out. 'To the front, quickly,' said Charlie. The machine's operator was getting into the driver's seat. 'Good man, Miguel. I'll sort you out later'.

'Key's in the ignition, Charlie,' the man responded. The brothers rushed to the front of the car wash.

'This way,' Charlie shouted. A gold-coloured Vauxhall Victor sat hidden from view behind the Portakabin. 'That's our ride. Get in the back and duck down'. Charlie jumped into the driver's seat and waited for his brother to get in, before slowly pulling away; the Porsche still obscured by the two large cleaning rollers that were making their way down the front windscreen and bonnet.

Charlie slammed his hands down on the top of the dashboard. 'Now, that's how it's fuckin' done,' he shouted. He pulled out onto the A7. 'You can sit up now, bruv. That dumb fuck's still sitting there staring at the Porsche. Miguel will take him on a wild goose chase for an hour'. He laughed.

'That was impressive,' said Eddie, as he buckled himself in.

'Told you, bruv. You have to be smart in this game'.

Charlie came off at the next junction, drove down to the underpass beneath and crossed under the dual carriageway before rejoining it in the opposite direction.

They drove westward for about thirty minutes before pulling over once more to a petrol station near Estepona. Charlie gave Eddie some money to pay for the fuel, while he filled the car up. 'Get us plenty of fags. It's gonna be a long journey'.

Another hour later, they pulled over at a roadside hotel near Algeciras. Charlie selected a secluded parking spot to the building's rear. Eddie glanced at the clock on the dashboard - it was nearing nine o'clock in the evening. The sun was setting far off to their West.

'Right,' said Charlie, as he got out of the car. 'We're stopping here tonight'. Eddie closed the passenger door behind him and stretched his back. 'We'll get a decent meal down us and try to get as much kip as we can. We set off again at six'.

They strolled around to the entrance at the front of the building. An old man sat in a wooden rocking chair, watching the traffic go by. He was wearing a pair of old grey trousers and a stained chequered shirt with braces. His skin was dark and wrinkled, and he appeared to be blind. Several empty brown beer bottles lay on the ground next to him. He started to laugh maniacally as Charlie and Eddie walked past, holding up a chipped, metal cup.

'Wonder what that old sod's laughin' at?' said Charlie as he walked into the hotel.

Eddie fetched a few coins out of his jeans pockets and dropped them into the cup. The man continued to laugh. 'Perhaps he knows something we don't,' he wondered.

CHAPTER FOURTEEN
THE ROAD TO MÉRIDA

The brothers set an alarm for 5:30 am and were on the road half an hour later. Eddie took the first driving stint, the four and half hour leg up to Mérida, where they pulled over at a roadside cafe for some much-needed coffee and food. They sat outside on a wooden picnic table, basking in the glorious sunshine.

'What do you think mum would say about this?' asked Eddie as the waitress arrived with their order.

'About what?' muttered Charlie, who sat sprawled on the opposite bench, his eyes shut.

'You and me, doing this job together'.

Charlie yawned. 'I reckon you know the answer to that one,' he replied. Eddie stared into his mug of coffee.

'Thing is,' he said. 'She made me promise to stick clear of trouble, but she also told me to look out for you'.

'So you're damned if you do, damned if you don't,' said Charlie. He still had his eyes closed and looked like he was about to drift off.

'Drink your coffee, I don't want you falling asleep at the wheel. You're doin' the next two hundred miles'. Charlie groaned, opened his eyes and sat up. Eddie pushed the bowl of sugar cubes toward him.

Charlie waved them away. 'I'm sweet enough already,' he said loud enough for the waitress to hear. She rolled her eyes upwards and walked away, Charlie staring at her backside.

'I thought we were on a tight schedule?' said Eddie. Charlie lifted the mug to his mouth and blew on the hot liquid. Eddie looked up to the sky. There was a trio of eagles overhead. They looked magnificent, drifting in the warm wind, their heads darting from left-to-right searching for a target.

'What was it like down there?' said Charlie, interrupting his thoughts.

'Down where?' Eddie asked, although he knew what his brother was referring to.

'The Falklands'.

Eddie sighed. 'It was cold. Cold and wet,' he said.

'Did you see much action?' asked Charlie.

Eddie put his cup down. 'What do you want to ask me, Charlie? If I shot anyone. If I killed any *Argies*?' Intense memories flashed before Eddie's eyes. He shrugged them away.

'Rough, huh?'

'Not so much at the time. The training kicks in. You're not thinking about what you're doing. It just…happens. Like you're watching a film or something'.

'And afterwards?' said Charlie.

Eddie pulled a packet of Marlboro Reds out of his pocket, put one in his mouth and lit it. 'The army doesn't do much to prepare you for that part. They only teach you how to do the killing stuff. You're supposed to handle what happens afterwards, yourself. Coz that's what proper men do, right?'

'I heard Dad talking about it once,' said Charlie.

His brother's statement surprised Eddie, who had never heard his step-father talk about his wartime experiences. 'He never said nuffin to me. Or mum. At least, not as far as I know. When was this?'

Charlie's face screwed up as he struggled to recall the moment. 'It was in the working men's club in South Harrow.

You was a baby, so early sixties. It was a New Year's Eve, I remember that. He was properly tanked up. They all was, the blokes. Us kids was supposed to be in the family room, but I'd gone in to scrounge for a glass of squash or something. He didn't know I was standing there. He was at a table with about five other fellas, talking about one of his friends gettin' killed in a tank. Dad had tried to get the poor bastard out, to save him. But it was all on fire. He said he could hear his mate screaming as he burned inside'.

Charlie took a sip of the coffee. His eyes were watering up.

'Dad was crying. In a right mess, he was. And this was like twenty years later and he still hadn't got over it. At first, I didn't get it. I…we only knew him as that mean bastard, right?' He sipped his coffee, then continued. 'You know what he was like with us. No affection. But there he was, a total mess. And all his pals were consoling him'. Charlie looked up at Eddie. 'And that's when I understood'.

'Understood what?' said Eddie.

'Why he was like he was. Why he was always angry. Why he screamed at us for no reason and lashed out at mum. Why he hit us. And why he drank. I ain't making excuses for him. He was a bastard at times, there ain't no denying that. But he never got past it, Ed. The war, I mean. What he did, what he saw. It stayed with him all his life. It destroyed him. The bloke that mum married in the late thirties. He went off to war, and he never came back. Not really'. He placed the mug down.

'Is that why you never came to see me off?' said Eddie. 'Before I joined up, I mean? Did you think I'd come back like him?' Charlie shrugged. 'I wrote to you. Several times'.

Charlie averted his gaze. His fingers were scratching at his stubble. 'I thought you were throwing your life away,' he said. 'You always had so much more going for you than me, because you're smart. You could have done anything'.

'Plenty of people would say serving your country was doing something'.

'And where's it got you, bruv?' He leaned forward, but Eddie pulled away from him. 'I heard you when you were sleeping. Shouting. Moaning'. You sounded just like Dad used to. Maybe you ain't as bad as he was, I dunno. You tell me. But either way, being a para ain't exactly set you up for life has it?'

Eddie exhaled a cloud of smoke. 'Maybe you're right. The old man was how he was and I fucked up my marriage, coz I went to war. So what's your excuse? For being a villain?' said Eddie.

'Coz that moment, seeing him like that, that's when I knew I weren't gonna let that happen to me. I was going to get what I wanted from the world'.

Eddie shook his head. 'Other people get what they want from this life without holding up banks, Charlie'.

'Not people like us. We're just cattle. Cannon fodder. Nobody gives a monkey's about the likes of you and me, Ed. That's why I did what I did. Same for the other lads. We would not be told what to do, how to live our lives. We wanted our fair share. So we took it'.

Eddie stubbed out his cigarette in a white ashtray on the table. 'Why are we talking about this now?'

Charlie looked up at the eagles as they drifted above them once more. 'Dunno. Seemed like an opportune time'. He looked at his watch. 'Guess we should get back on the road'. He pulled some money out of his wallet and placed it under his mug.

They both stood up and started walking towards the gold Vauxhall saloon. 'Right,' said Charlie. 'You're in charge of the music. But none of that "tears for queers" crap though'.

The rest of the trip was uneventful, and they arrived at the port at Vigo just before nine o'clock that evening.

One of the trawler's crew, a tall, gangly man in a yellow rain mac, guided them in with a torch and they parked the

Vauxhall inside an old wooden boathouse. The rest of the crew turned up half an hour later in the black and grey Ford Granada.

'Good trip?' asked Charlie. 'Did Mike get lost?'

'Nah, but we've had to keep the windows open the last two hours on account of Roger's arse,' said Bill.

'I can't help it,' said Roger, one hand rubbing his stomach. 'Them bleedin' tapas dishes are playin' havoc with my gut'.

'Great,' said Charlie. 'We're gonna be stuck in a bleedin' fishing boat with you for the next thirty-six hours. He turned toward the cars. 'Get the kit onboard and stowed sharpish. We don't want nobody seeing us if we can help it'. They each grabbed a bag out of the car boots.

'*Ha terminado*?' asked the fisherman, pointing at the cars. Charlie nodded, and the Spaniard pulled a large tarpaulin over each of the vehicles. Mike was standing outside, scanning their surroundings.

'All clear?' asked Charlie.

'Seems so'. The crew made their way through a series of narrow passages between the workshops, garages and lockups that stood between them and the waterfront.

'So, what's the boat skipper get out of this gig?' asked Eddie.

'Fifty grand,' said Bill. 'Twenty now, thirty when he drops us back'.

Eddie whistled. 'Well, I hope the onboard cafeteria service is up to scratch,' he replied.

'Beans on toast. A lot of it,' said Bill.

'Just what Roger's guts need,' said Mike in disgust.

The trawler's skipper was pacing alongside his boat when they arrived. 'I am Xavier, the captain of this ship. We must be quick. The Guardia Civil patrol here often'. He gestured towards the gangway that led from the quayside up into the boat. The pungent stench of fish was all around them.

'Flippin' heck. It ain't gonna pong like this the whole bleedin' way, is it Charlie?' said Roger.

'Retribution for the car ride,' said Bill. 'You sure you didn't shit yourself'. Eddie could not help laughing out loud.

'Shhhh!' said Charlie.

'I told you I didn't want that tapas,' said Roger.

'Christ all fuckin' mighty. Call yourself professional villains?' said Charlie. 'It's like being in a bleedin' Carry On film with you lot. Shut the fuck up and get in the boat'. The skipper signalled to two of his crew to pull up the gangplank and told the Englishmen to follow him.

'I'll take you to your bunks'. He moved to pick up Mike's bags but was rewarded with a short growl.

'Just show us the way,' said Charlie.

The boat appeared to be in perfect condition, Eddie observed. 'How big is she?' he asked the skipper.

'Forty metres,' the Spaniard replied. 'She's only one-year-old'. He pulled open a hatch and waved at the crew to go in. 'It is the room at the end. There is clean bedding, and the heaters have been on for an hour. It should be…how you say…"toasty", in there'. He laughed. 'We leave in twenty minutes. Keep away from the windows and don't come up to the top deck until we're at sea'.

Charlie stopped as he reached the open hatch and held out a brown package. 'Twenty grand. Like you and Roger agreed'.

'A pleasure doing business with you, Señor Lawson'. They made their way along the corridor towards the cabin. As the captain had promised, the heating was on and each bed had been made. Eddie took off his jacket and stuffed his things into a tall metal cabinet.

'I'll take the bottom bunk,' said Charlie. 'It'll be like when we was kids'.

Eddie stepped onto the short ladder at the side of the bed and hauled himself up, then sank into the mattress.

'Anyone up for a spot of poker,' said Mike, waving a set of playing cards in the air.

'Nah, I'm flippin' knackered,' said Roger.

'Me too,' said Bill. Mike tutted in disappointment.

'Boring bastards,' said Mike.

'Nobody wants to play, coz you always take their money you cheatin' bastard,' said Charlie.

'It ain't cheatin' if you don't get caught,' replied Mike as he clambered into his bunk.

'Wise words, Michael,' said Bill.

'They was, weren't they?' Mike said as he pulled his blanket over him. 'Might be my next tattoo. If we get away with this job'. Deep below them, the trawler's engines started up. The cabin walls hummed from the vibrations.

'Sleep well, gents,' said Charlie as he flicked the light switch off. Eddie closed his eyes but could not suppress fleeting memories of the arduous journey he had made down to the South Atlantic in a very similar cabin. A journey from which several of his fellow paras had not returned.

A long, squelchy fart erupted from where Roger lay, already fast asleep.

'For fuck's sake,' muttered Mike, and buried his head under his pillow.

It's gonna be a long trip, thought Eddie, with a smile on his face as he drifted off to sleep.

CHAPTER FIFTEEN
BACK IN BLIGHTY

The trawler docked at Lowestoft late in the afternoon, two days later. Eddie listened as Charlie spoke with the skipper, making sure that the man understood the schedule, as the crew made their way down the gangway. Roger's cousin, Gary, was waiting for them on the dock next to a well-used, blue and cream-coloured Commer camper van.

Mike kicked one of the van's rear tyres and gave Gary a disapproving look. 'You tellin' me this wreck's getting us to Kilburn?' he said.

'The limo's in for a service, Michael,' said Gary, laughing. 'It'll get us there, don't worry. I've been all over the country in this beauty. She won't let us down'.

'I won't be frickin' laughing if the fuzz pull us over when a bleedin' wheel falls off'.

'Stop fucking kickin' it then,' said Charlie. 'It's fine. Get in'.

It took three hours to get to the temporary digs, a semi-derelict maisonette in Kilburn. Gary parked the van on a nearby street.

'It's through there,' he said while pointing towards the entrance to an alleyway. 'Five minutes walk. I don't wanna park too close'. The crew clambered out from the van, its hot engine ticking in the chilly evening air, and stretched weary arms and legs.

'Next time, find something a bit newer,' said Mike, still unimpressed.

'Ain't gonna be a next time,' said Charlie. 'This was one last job, remember?' The crew made their way through the dark alleys until Gary stopped at the back entrance to one of the terraced houses. He fetched a key from out of his pocket and unlocked the wooden gate.

'C'mon, get in. We've got the upstairs maisonette'.

'No neighbours?' said Eddie.

'Nah. Downstairs was a squat for a bit. Right bleedin' mess it is. Ain't nobody gonna want to live in there till it's fixed up, and the geezer what owns the place ain't, shall we say, at *liberty* to do that just yet'.

'Mate of yours?' asked Roger.

Gary nodded. 'He got sent down for shifting stolen motors about a year ago. He's not out for another six months. I gave his missus three hundred quid to use it'.

Eddie saw a flicker of a smile on Gary's face. 'Grateful was she?' he asked.

'In many ways,' said Gary. He was smirking as he opened the back door.

They made their way up the outside staircase to the upper floor. Gary flicked on the hallway light. 'Living room's straight through. You can dump all the kit in there. There's two bedrooms, both with mattresses on the floor, and two sofas. I brought plenty of blankets'.

Roger picked up one blanket, which was cream-coloured with two blue stripes. 'Hang on. These are from the bleedin' war,' he said. He ran his hand over the blanket's material. 'They're itchy as fuck'.

Gary shrugged and walked into the kitchen. Eddie peered into one bedroom and was hit straight away by the damp, musty smell. The wallpaper was peeling off the wall in places.

A single light bulb hung from the ceiling, bereft of a lampshade.

Mike stood next to him, distinctly unimpressed. 'I've stayed in better prisons'.

'What was you expecting, the fuckin' Hilton?' said Charlie.

'It'll do just fine,' said Bill. 'It's only for a few days. We'll be back in Spain before you know it'.

'If everything goes to plan,' said Roger.

'If everyone does their bleedin' jobs,' said Charlie.

Eddie felt the compulsion to touch the wooden door frame for luck, before walking into the room and dropping his heavy rucksack down onto one of the single mattresses. The crew unpacked their kit while Gary went out to pick up some takeaway food. He arrived back half an hour later, carrying two bags laden with food.

'What d'ya get?' asked Roger.

'Hopefully, something that ain't gonna make your arse any worse,' said Mike.

Gary lifted the bags up to reveal the writing on them. 'Indian'.

'Christ all fuckin' mighty,' muttered Mike. 'Get the windows open'.

Gary and Bill distributed the tin foil cartons between the crew. Eddie's stomach was rumbling. He had eaten nothing since breakfast. He ripped the lid off his main dish and was rewarded with a rich waft of chicken vindaloo. The food was only lukewarm at that point, but it bothered him not.

Charlie checked his watch. 'Eat up fellas. The main man from the East End crew will be here in half an hour'. Eddie swallowed a chunk of chicken and wiped the sauce from the side of his mouth.

'They're coming here? Bit risky ain't it'

'They know the score,' said Gary. 'They'll come in the back entrance'.

'Oh err,' said Roger, laughing. Bill sniggered.

Charlie rolled his eyes. 'Yeah, yeah. Laugh it up,' he said. 'Just remember, if we fuck this up, a bit of backdoor action is all you'll have to look forward to for the next fifteen years'. He collected the empty food packaging and put it into a bin bag. 'All rubbish goes into these sacks. Gary's gonna take it away and burn it all when we're done. Don't leave nuffin' behind. Not so much as a fag butt or a sweet wrapper. Got it?' He kicked Mike's booted right foot.

'I got it,' Mike replied.

The sound of the back gate opening caught Charlie's attention. Mike jumped up and peered through the gap between the curtains. He smiled. 'It's them,' he said.

'Right boys,' said Charlie. 'We need these blokes if we're gonna get this job done, so play nice and get to know them'. They all rose to their feet. Charlie walked over to where Mike was still looking out the window. 'You better be right about this lot. I ain't never liked cockneys'.

'I thought you had family in Peckham? Uncle, weren't it?'

'Yeah,' said Charlie. 'And he was a right bastard'. There was a light knock on the back door and Bill darted down the hallway to unlock the door and returned a moment later followed by two men.

The first, a tall man with greasy brown hair and wearing a black donkey jacket, grinned as soon as he saw Mike. The second, a wiry-looking man with a Harrington and tight jeans, hung back near the door with his hands in his pockets.

'Mikey, how the devil are yer, son?' said the first man in a strong East London accent. He appeared to be in his late thirties, Eddie decided.

Mike took a few steps towards him and thrust out his right hand. 'Doin' just fine, Bobby. Good to see you again. How are you doing?'

'Never better'.

'And the old man?' asked Mike.

'Cancer got him last year,' he replied.

'Shit, sorry about that, mate'.

The East Ender shrugged. 'Don't be. It was the old fucker's time. To tell the truth, he was doin' me tits in by the end. I was tempted to put a pillow over his head and finish him off myself'. He laughed and glanced around the room. 'So, you gonna make the introductions, Mikey?'

Mike pointed at Charlie, who stepped forward. 'This is Charlie,' said Mike. 'Charlie, this is Bobby Pickering. Me and him did a few jobs together in the mid-seventies. When you was doing your stretch in the Scrubs'.

Charlie shook the East Londoner's outstretched hand and gave it a firm handshake. 'Good to have you and your lads on this job, Bobby'.

'The pleasure's all ours. I appreciate you lads puttin' your trust in us, Mr Lawson. To tell the truth, my boys are all a bit in awe of you and your crew. But we won't let you down, that you can count on'.

'I don't doubt it. And none of that "Mr Lawson". It's just Charlie'. He gestured towards the sofas as he sat himself down on a wooden chair. The East Ender sat down on the couch, followed by Mike. 'So, I take it Gary's gone through the plan with you?'

'Of course. And I made sure it's ingrained in my boys' heads,' said Pickering.

Charlie nodded at the lad in the Harrington, who returned the silent greeting with a nod of his own. 'So, where's the rest of your crew?'

'I thought it best not to bring everyone. Might attract attention'.

Charlie smiled. 'Good thinking,' he said.

'Told you these geezers was sharp,' said Mike.

'Well, let me introduce this lot,' said Charlie. He pointed at Roger, who was standing talking to his cousin, Gary. 'This is Roger, Gary's cousin, and this is Bill'. He gave Bill a slap on the thigh.

DEN OF SNAKES

'Good to meet you,' said Bill. Pickering gave him a cordial smiled.

'And this is me brother, Eddie'.

Pickering leaned over to where Eddie had plonked himself down next to Mike and shook his hand. 'A genuine pleasure, Eddie. Fought in the Falklands, didn't yer? Para, right?'

Eddie let his hand drop. 'I was,' he said while giving his brother a questioning stare.

'Well I hope you got your share of Argies,' said Pickering. 'Fuckin' dagos. We gave em' a right good hiding, didn't we?'

'Did we?' said Eddie. 'If you had been there you'd know just how close they came to kickin' us back into the sea'.

The East Londoner smiled wryly. 'I meant no offence'.

'S'alright,' said Mike. 'The kid's just a bit tired, ain't you, son?' said Mike.

'Tired of people that weren't there tellin' me what it was like,' said Eddie.

'Alright boys,' said Charlie. 'Bobby didn't mean nuffin' by it. Let's focus on why we're all here, why don't we?' Charlie gestured towards the young-looking skinhead in the Harrington. 'So, what's your name son?'

The man looked to Pickering, who answered on his behalf. 'This is my young lieutenant, Gerry Lannigan. His old man's a Paddy, but we don't hold that against him'. He laughed. 'One hundred percent reliable, he is. Never let me down'. The East Ender shifted his stare at Eddie. 'Just like the rest of my boys. Solid fighters, the lot of them. They do what they're told'.

'It ain't fighters we need,' said Eddie.

'Nah, you need blokes who you can trust to follow orders and stick to the plan. My boys will do that,' said Pickering. Gary approached carrying a six-pack of Castlemaine XXXX cans. He offered one to the East Ender. 'But if it comes to it, they'll get stuck in too. They're proper friggin' warriors. Trust me'. He opened the yellow and red can and took a long swig.

'Well, let's hope it don't come to that,' said Charlie, taking a can from Gary.

'So, out of curiosity,' said Pickering. 'What are you after in the depot?' He got no reply. 'Or, shouldn't I be asking that?' he said, looking around the room.

'Trade secret, I'm afraid,' said Charlie. 'But you'll get your hundred grand if it goes to plan. That's all you need to know'.

Pickering chuckled. 'Figured you'd say something like that'. The East Ender took another swig of the beer. 'Furry muff, as they say. So, we meet up tomorrow at seven?'

'That's right', said Gary. 'The Wheatsheaf in Harlington. The car park's round the back. Nice and quiet'.

Pickering placed the can down on the threadbare carpet and stood up. He held out his hand to Charlie. 'Good to meet you. All of you. I'm lookin' forward to this. The start of a beautiful friendship, I reckon'. He smiled at Eddie. 'See you at the pub, lads'.

Eddie watched as Pickering walked towards the rear door, followed closely by his quiet lieutenant. He waited until he heard the door shut.

'I don't trust him,' he said.

'No?' said Mike. 'Well, I do. And they're in on it now, so pucker up and get your head in the game'.

Eddie stood up to face Mike. 'Ain't me that needs to step up,' he said.

'Calm it, ladies,' said Bill, pushing himself between the two men.

'Bill's right. It's been a tiring trip. We're all friggin' cream crackered,' said Charlie. 'Go lock up, Roger. Bill, start collecting the trash. After that, it's time to get some shut eye'. He watched as the crew made their way out of the living room, before shifting towards his brother. Eddie was shaking his head. 'What's the problem, bruv?'

'I told you, I don't like them'. Charlie dismissed his brother's assertion with a wave of his hand.

'Look, you don't have to like them. But Mike vouches for them, and I back his judgement. He's known Bobby Pickering for over a decade. When you've done a few jobs with someone, you get to know them trust me. Get yourself some kip, you look knackered'.

Eddie glanced at his watch. It was only just past nine o'clock. 'I need to unwind first'. He walked over to the old TV that sat on an upturned Britvic crate, switched it on, and sat back down on the sofa and lit a cigarette. The nine o'clock news was on BBC One. Bill walked across the room and punched on the third button to turn the channel over to ITV.

'What the fuck?' said Eddie, glaring at Bill.

'The Crampton Report is on,' said Bill. 'You know? That wanker who's been following us around in Spain'. Eddie sighed, but he could not be bothered to argue. Bill picked up two unopened cans of lager and sat down next to Eddie. 'He's after some timeshare sellers on the Costa Brava in this one. That's what it says in this'. He held up a copy of the Radio Times. A smug-looking Noel Edmonds stood, arms folded on the front cover above the headline, "Telly Addict".

Eddie sat back on the sofa. He realised that it was the source of the room's musty atmosphere but was too weary to care. The show was already several minutes old when the presenter, Jeremy Crampton, could be seen being manhandled by two enormous men, one of whom was threatening to hit him with a cricket bat.

'Fuck off, or I'll bloody smack you with this,' said the rotund man in a Birmingham accent. Bill laughed out loud, attracting Roger and Gary back into the room.

'What are you watching?' said Roger.

'It's that Jeremy Crampton show, innit?' said Bill.

'I hope they give him a good kicking,' said Mike from the kitchen doorway. He walked back in and picked up the last remaining can of beer.

'I thought I told you lot to get some kip,' said Charlie, also now in the room.

'It's that wanker TV reporter,' said Roger. 'The one Mikey lamped in Marbella'.

'I barely touched him, the bleedin' faggot,' said Mike.

They sat in silence watching the proceedings for the next twenty minutes, routing for the shifty fraudsters who had, Crampton stated, tricked dozens of naive Brits out of over a million pounds for timeshares that did not even exist.

'That's the way to make some dosh,' said Roger. Bill looked towards Charlie and said,' Maybe we should get in contact with them, Charlie. They might want to invest in the property deal'.

Charlie shook his head. 'Not on your nelly. Friggin' cheats, the lot of them. I wouldn't trust them further than I could throw them'.

The programme finished and cut to the closing credits. The crew pushed themselves up from the sofas, but their attention was suddenly caught by the channel announcer.

'Next week, join Jeremy Crampton as he investigates the seedy British criminals living in the south of Spain in the next episode, Gangsters on the Costa del Crime,' said the voice from the television. A short video clip showed.

'Hang on,' said Roger. 'That's Marbella, ain't it?' Charlie stood motionless, the cigarette in his hand burning perilously close to his fingers. The clip continued and, to the group's collective discomfort, cut to a scene that they all knew only too well; the moment just a few days earlier outside Hotel Fuerte when Mike had accosted Crampton and his crew before driving off in his Ferrari.

'Shit,' said Bill. 'They must have had another camera'.

'Fuck,' said Mike. Eddie stared at the screen. Grainy police profile photos of Mike, Charlie, Kenny, Roger and Bill were being displayed under the title, "Gangsters in Paradise". Charlie sat down on the wooden seat and dropped his cigarette butt into the beer can. Eddie heard the short sizzle as it made contact with the dregs inside.

'What do we do now, Charlie?' asked Bill.

Charlie sat staring at the top of the beer can, saying nothing.

'Charlie?' said Roger.

Charlie pointed at the television. 'Turn that fucking thing off,' he said.

'What about the job? We still doin' it?' asked Bill'.

'Too late to stop now,' said Mike. 'We're at least a hundred grand in the hole, what with the fishing boat captain, vehicles and everything else'.

Charlie nodded. 'Exactly,' said Charlie. 'We're gonna have to be even more careful. But we're here now. It's too late to pull out now'. He crushed the can and dropped it into a black bin liner that Gary had been using to collect the rubbish. 'We'll meet up with Pickering's crew in the morning and do our recce. If all looks good, we hit the depot the day after, as planned'. He stood up. 'I'm going to bed'. With that, he walked off to the nearest bedroom.

The crew glanced at each other for a few seconds before following Charlie's lead. Eddie was the last to get up. He finished his lager and tossed the empty can into the refuse sack.

'What else can go wrong?' he thought as he ambled to the bedroom door.

CHAPTER SIXTEEN
SCOPING OUT THE JOINT

Eddie opened his eyes. It was dark, save for a sliver of artificial light from a lamppost breaking its way through the crack in the curtain. He could hear footsteps in a nearby room. He lay still, waiting for his senses to resume normal functioning.

Where the fuck am I?

He recognised Charlie talking in the living room outside the door, and it brought him back into the present. His breathing slowed, and he unzipped the sleeping bag he had brought from England to Spain and, now, back again. He was thankful he had not had to use the ancient army-surplus blankets that Gary had provided to the other members of the crew.

He pressed the tiny button on the side of his LCD wristwatch to illuminate the display. It had just passed five o'clock in the morning. In twenty-four hours they would set off to rob the United Security depot near Heathrow, at which point he would become that which he had promised his mother he would never be - a criminal.

He got up, found his jeans and the tee-shirt from the previous day, and dressed, trying not to wake Mike who was snoring gently on another mattress a few feet away. The wooden door lacked a lock, and he had propped his backpack against it to keep it shut the previous evening. He pushed the bag aside with his foot and opened the door.

Charlie stood at the doorway to the narrow kitchen, talking to Bill and Roger, who were both holding small white teacups.

'Alright, bruv. Sleep okay?' said Charlie.

'I did,' said Eddie, reflecting on the fact that he had slept for seven hours solid free from nightmares.

'Beat's that friggin' boat,' said Bill.

'Does it half,' said Roger. 'I hate boats. The booze ferry to Calais used to be bad enough. At least that didn't smell of flippin' fish'.

'Brew?' asked Charlie.

Eddie nodded and slipped into the kitchen. 'Tell me the plan again,' he asked.

Charlie handed him a cup of tea. It was piping hot. Eddie blew on the liquid's surface before taking a careful sip. 'We're meeting up with the East End crew in Harlington to do a recce for ourselves. We need to make sure Gary's intel is kosher'.

Eddie's stomach rumbled.

'There's a greasy spoon around the corner,' said Charlie, smiling. 'Gary has nipped out for some bacon sarnies before we set off'. Charlie placed his empty mug into the ceramic sink. 'I'll go wake the sleeping beauty. You lot drink up. We're setting off in twenty minutes'.

Gary arrived back a few minutes later with a bag full of tepid bacon sandwiches. The crew devoured them before then setting off out of the maisonette's rear door, through the alleyway to Gary's camper van.

The drive to their rendezvous at the pub in Harlington took forty minutes, and as they pulled up behind the building's rear, they found the East End crew already waiting for them stood smoking around a blue Volvo estate. Bobby Pickering stood with one hand in his jeans pocket, scrutinising the Commer van as it pulled up. He had a wry smile on his face.

'Let's keep this professional, boys,' said Charlie, his eyes fixed on Eddie. 'We need 'em, remember?' he reached into his pocket and pulled out a small torch.

'I'll play nice,' said Eddie as he pulled the side door open.

Pickering walked over to the van and held out his hand. Eddie gave it a firm shake. 'Good morning, Edward,' he said.

'Only me mum called me "Eddie". He was still holding the East Ender's hand.

'Right you are,' said Pickering. 'Listen, I hope there ain't no hard feelings about last night. Me going on about the Falklands and all that. Didn't mean nuffin by it, you understand?'

'He understands,' said Charlie. 'Don't you, bruv?'

'Of course,' Eddie replied. 'I was just knackered after that boat trip'. He relaxed his grip and Pickering withdrew his hand. Eddie felt sure he had made the man wince.

'West London, East London, it don't matter. We're all on the same team,' said Charlie. 'If we stick together and do our jobs, we make a lot of money. If we fuck it up, we're each looking at a long stretch inside'.

The two sets of men introduced themselves before Charlie interrupted them by turning on his torch. He was holding a large paper envelope out of which he removed several pieces of notepaper. He held the light above the top sheet. 'These are layouts of the depot and the surrounding areas'. He held one of the photocopied sheets up and pointed at the map sketched on it. 'There's four vantage points marked. Get familiar with the layout. Also, there's four escape routes marked. If the shit hits the fan, make your way out on foot down one of these'. He checked the faces of the surrounding men. 'Not that the shit will hit the fan, coz everything will go just like we planned it. Like clockwork, right Mikey?'

Mike shuffled his feet and mumbled something in Roger's ear.

'What was that?' said Charlie.

'I said yes, Charlie. Like clockwork'.

'Good. Now let's get this show on the road'.

The crews returned to their vehicles and set off, the light blue Commer taking the lead with the Volvo following. The United Security depot was just twenty minutes away in Hatton, to the south-east of Heathrow Airport. It was still dark when they pulled up outside a disused brick building. Eddie peered up at the two-story structure as Bill jumped out of the van, a pair of bolt cutters in his hand.

'It's an old Lucas factory,' said Gary. 'They used to make car alternators here. It's been like this since it closed down in the late seventies when they started importing them from Japan. Bill cut through the rusty chain that had secured the factory's gate, pulled it open, and waved at his brother and the East Londoners to drive in. Eddie observed in the van's side mirror as Bill pulled the gate shut again. The building was C-shaped, with a small courtyard in the middle that was just big enough to keep both vehicles out of sight from the service road on which they had arrived.

Eddie opened the door and climbed out of the van. His boots crunched on the broken concrete surface underneath. The sun was up now, and it tinged the top of the building in a yellow-orange.

'Over here,' said Charlie, waving his torch. 'Gary will run through things'. He laid one of his photocopied maps on the Commer van's dented bonnet, and the two crews gathered around.

'The depot's one hundred yards over there to the north,' said Gary. He gestured past the facade of the building behind Eddie, before handing out the sheets to the waiting men. 'There's a cafe here'. He pointed at a rectangle on the map. 'It's well busy up to mid-afternoon. There can be up to fifty punters in there. If you get a window seat, you have an unobstructed view of the east side of the depot'.

'So we want to have eyes there for a start,' said Charlie. 'Two or three men, revolving for an hour at a time. Send two your boys with Roger, okay Bobby?'

Pickering nodded then addressed two of his crew. 'Dave, Gerry. You go first. Watch your manners and don't engage in no conversations with the locals. Keep to yourselves'. He poked the boyish man in the Harrington jacket. 'That means no chattin' up the waitress, Gerry. No matter how good-looking she is!'

The ginger-haired man nodded obediently.

'Next up, on the opposite side of the depot, on the north side,' Gary continued. 'There's a construction site. It is going to be an MFI, but it's just a concrete shell at present. We can see the activity in the yard from there. Me and Bill will head over there for the first shift'.

'Good,' said Charlie. 'Mike, you take Bobby and his other two lads for a long walk. Get to know the entire area. Watch out for coppers, security guards, CCTV. You know the drill. Got it?'

'Where will you and Ed be?' asked Mike.

Charlie pointed to the upper floor of the building to their left. 'Up there. We're gonna check out all the comings and goings'. He swung towards Gary. 'So, when's the special delivery arriving?'

'Around midday, according to Angus'.

'And what time does his shift start?'

Gary glanced at his watch. 'He should be here in about ten minutes. He's got a brown Hillman Avenger. You'll be able to hear it a mile off, the exhaust is fucked'.

'Okay, everyone clear what they're doing?' asked Charlie. A round of nods and grunted confirmations greeted him. 'Right, how do we get into this place, Gazza?'

Gary pointed towards a set of old, wooden double doors. 'Just shove 'em open. Staircase is to the right. There are a few old chairs scattered up there'.

'Good stuff. Okay gents, we all meet back here at two o'clock. Keep your eyes peeled'. He pulled a torch out of his pocket. 'C'mon Eddie,' he started towards the doors.

They made their way to the top floor and towards the side of the building that overlooked the United Security depot. Eddie approached a window he gauged would afford his brother and him a suitable vantage point. A grimy film covered the inside of the glass, so he rubbed it with his sleeve in a circular motion to clear a section he could look through.

Charlie arrived at this side, carrying two old wooden chairs. 'Here you go,' he said. 'You stay here, I'm just gonna check the rest of the building'.

Eddie lifted a small pair of binoculars from his coat pocket and peered through them at the security depot opposite his position. The building looked to be pre war, most likely constructed in the twenties or thirties. It had been extended several times by the look of it. One section seemed to have received a substantial repair - a large V-shaped section of bricks was newer than their neighbours. It was probably bomb damage from the war, thought Eddie, who could remember plenty of similar scarred buildings in his youth.

The painful sound of a faulty car exhaust caught his attention. He pressed his face to the glass and saw a brown saloon approaching from his left. It was Angus's brown Avenger. He watched as the car pulled over to the side of the street. A man in a security guard's uniform got out of the vehicle. He locked the car door, glanced up towards the top floor of the disused factory where Eddie was sitting, then walked towards a service door. He waited for about twenty seconds before the door opened, then went in.

'Was that Angus?' said Charlie, who had finished his rounds and was walking back towards his brother. He reached into his bag and lifted out a battered silver Thermos flask and two white teacups.

'Yep'.

'Cuppa?' asked Charlie.

'Cor, not half'.

'Ain't got no biscuits though,' said Charlie.

Eddie smiled. 'Remember how Dad used to dunk his digestives in his tea?'

'Course I do,' said Charlie. 'He'd swear like a trooper if a bit of the biscuit fell off into his cup. You'd have thought he'd just stood in dog shit or something'. Charlie laughed. 'I couldn't stop giggling. Not till he clipped me round me head, that was'.

Eddie took his eyes away from his portal in the window to look at his older brother. Charlie was staring at the teacup in his hand, lost in his memories. 'You miss him?' he asked. Charlie looked up, surprised.

'Course I do. He was my old man,' he said, his tone somewhat accusatory. Don't you?'

'I weren't close to him. Not like you was,' said Eddie, knowing that this was not the moment to express how he really felt. 'To tell the truth, I never felt that he wanted me around'.

'You what? Dad treated you just like you was his own'. Eddie dropped his gaze and peered back through the glass. Charlie was not about to let the topic lie, however. 'I reckon you was his favourite'.

'You're kidding me,' said Eddie.

Charlie shook his head. 'Remember that bike he got you for your birthday,' he said. 'When you was what…eight? Just after I got back from the Borstal. A Raleigh, weren't it?'

'A secondhand Raleigh Sport, yeah'.

'He saved up for months for that flippin' bike for you. And he spent ages scouring through the classifieds till he found one he thought you'd want'. Eddie thought back to the moment he'd first cast his eyes over the bicycle standing in the kitchen room against the table. Mrs Lawson had got him out of bed that day and taken him downstairs for his present. Mr Lawson had gone to work already.

'I loved that bike,' he said.

'Did you ever tell him?' said Charlie.

'Probably not'.

'The only decent bike I ever got was from uncle Bob when I

was about twelve. He'd nicked it from some posh kid in Pinner. When mum found out, she took it away and handed it in at the local nick. She told them she'd found it in the park'.

Charlie unscrewed the Thermos and poured tea into one cup, then held out the steaming drink to Eddie.

'Thanks,' said Eddie as he took the cup. He watched as Charlie poured the hot liquid into the second teacup. 'I always figured they only took me in for the extra benefit money'. Charlie looked up, an incredulous look on his face.

'You ain't serious?' he said. Eddie shrugged.

'Well, they got extra dosh, right?'

His brother shook his head. 'They adopted you coz mum couldn't have no more kids'.

'You what?' asked Eddie.

Charlie sighed. 'She couldn't have no more. Not after me'. Eddie gawped at his brother. 'Wait,' said Charlie. 'You didn't know? She almost died'.

Eddie did not know how to respond to this revelation. Charlie put the cup down, fetched a cigarette from its packet and placed it between his lips. Eddie could see his brother's fingers trembling as he lifted the lighter to the tip. 'What are you tellin' me, Charlie?

His brother inhaled on the cigarette and let the smoke linger in his lungs before releasing it out and upwards. 'After she had me, she was in the hospital for a month. Her insides were all fucked up. They had to operate. Took out her womb, didn't they?'

'What? How…how d'you know that?' said Eddie, putting down his drink.

'Mrs Green told me. Remember her? We used to call her "Auntie Green" '.

'I thought she was our auntie,' said Eddie,

'Nah, you stupid sod. She was a neighbour. Lived up the road. She looked after us when Mum and Dad was both working. I thought she was pretty hot, except for the big mole on her chin. She told me all about it one evening when she was babysitting for you when you was a nipper. I think she had a thing for the old man. She said it almost destroyed him, he was so worried'. Charlie took another long drag on the cigarette.

'I had no idea,' said Eddie.

'Course you didn't. They protected you'.

'So, why are you telling me now?'

Charlie did not answer. He stood looking down at the concrete floor, the burning cigarette in his right hand. A lorry had pulled up down on the road beneath them. Charlie swivelled around and pushed the window open a few inches. Eddie could hear a metallic scraping. He guessed it was from the security depot's rear gates being opened, but continued looking at his brother. And then it dawned on him.

'You blame yourself, don't you?'

Charlie remained staring through the window. He cleared his throat. 'I wasn't the only one,' he said. 'It's probably why I never got a nice bike for my birthday'.

Eddie sat back in his chair, unsure how to respond. 'Bruv… listen, I -'.

'Forget it. Ancient history'. Charlie's face gave no hint of how he was feeling, his eyes fixed on the scene outside. He pointed to the depot. Eddie looked out and saw Angus standing at the gate as the orange lorry made its way into the yard. He was holding a torch in one hand as he dragged one of the big, black doors closed. He pointed it up towards the old Lucas factory where Charlie and Eddie were watching from, flashed the light on and off several times, then turned and closed the gate behind him. 'That's them, bruv. That's the diamonds'.

The following hours passed by, Charlie and Eddie waiting until it was two o'clock before they made their way down to the two vehicles to wait for the rest of the two crews. Roger and Gary arrived first, then two of the East Enders. Mike and Bill turned up a few minutes later, followed by Bobby Pickering along with Gerry and the last member of the East End crew.

'Load up, gentleman. I'll be with you in a sec,' said Charlie while strolling over towards Pickering. Eddie watched from the back of the van as the two men conversed for a few minutes before Charlie returned and clambered into the van's passenger seat. Pickering and his crew got into their Volvo.

'What was that about?' asked Eddie as the Volvo pulled away.

'Just going over a few details,' said Charlie. He banged his hand on the outside of the door. 'Let's get going, I'm fucking starving'.

Gary dropped the Lawson brothers, Roger and Mike off around the corner from their digs in Kilburn, then he and Bill headed off in search of takeaway food and beer.

Mike made himself comfortable in front of the TV set with Charlie watching an old Western, while Roger occupied himself with a crossword puzzle he had found on an old copy of The Sun he had found lying on the floor of the squalid flat. Eddie used the opportunity to grab some sleep and took himself off to the makeshift bedroom.

He awoke an hour later to a commotion in the living room. He could hear Charlie's raised voice. Something was up. He pulled his jeans on and opened the door to see Gary astride a wooden chair with his head in his hands. Charlie was shouting at him. Mike sat on the old sofa, a cigarette in one hand and a can of Heineken in the other. Roger stood peering out of the window between the swanky old curtains.

'What's going on?' asked Eddie.

Mike answered him. 'It's Bill. The rozzers got him'.

'When? How?' said Eddie.

Gary lifted his head. 'We was in the chippy. Bill wanted chicken. The geezer behind the till said it would be twenty minutes or so. I mean, that's pretty normal, right? Thing is, I thought he was looking at Bill a bit funny-like. Bill didn't notice, so I told him when the geezer had his back turned, but Bill said it was nuffin. He said I was being paranoid. I figured he was right, so I popped to the offy next door'. He paused for a moment and ran his fingers through his hair, then continued. 'Couldn't have been five minutes later when two jam sandwiches pull up outside and suddenly there's six or seven uniforms running into the chippy. They had Bill out in seconds. Pushed him to the floor, cuffed him and took him away'.

'Jesus Christ,' said Eddie. 'How come they didn't nab you?' Gary shrugged.

'I guess no one clocked I was with him. I heard the chip shop owner talking to one of the coppers. He said he'd seen Bill's face on that TV show. The Crampton Report'.

'Mother fucker,' said Mike. He crunched the metal can in his hand and lugged it across the room. 'We should have shot that fucker in Marbella when we had the chance'.

'Like that would have helped us,' said Charlie as he stubbed out a cigarette into an empty beer can.

'So now what?' said Eddie.

Charlie's eyes darted between his brother, Roger, Mike and Gary. He reached for a can of beer, opened it, then took a slurp. 'Gary will have to take Bill's place,' he said.

Gary swivelled around on his chair to look up at Charlie, clearly surprised at the development. 'But, I need an alibi. We agreed I'd be in my local when -'.

'The rest of us ain't got alibis,' said Charlie. 'If you want your cut, you take the same risks we do'.

Gary looked to his cousin, Roger, who had pulled the curtains closed and was now leaning against the wall. 'But I set this up. That was my job. Rog, tell him. I weren't gonna be on the crew'. Roger stared at the floor, offering no response. Gary looked back at Charlie. 'That weren't the plan'.

'Plan's changed,' said Charlie. 'Deal with it'.

CHAPTER SEVENTEEN
THE BIG DAY

The crew got up at five o'clock again the next day, but there was none of the banter of the previous day. They checked then rechecked their equipment in silence as if they were veteran soldiers preparing to go into battle. It triggered half-forgotten memories in Eddie's mind of preparations for early morning border area patrols in Northern Ireland. Roger was the last to step into the living room, where he dropped his rucksack to the floor.

Charlie stood, holding a brown and orange sports bag. He looked at his watch. 'Good. Now, before we go, I want everyone to have one last check to see if we've left anything. I don't want no sign we were ever here, got it?' The crew nodded. 'We're meeting Pickering and his boys at the Wheatsheaf. Gary will be here any minute now. He's got a Transit van that he borrowed a few weeks back. He's had it resprayed and fitted with fake plates.'

'We ain't in that bleedin' Commer van then? Thank the Lord,' said Mike, smirking.

'He still ain't happy about being the driver,' said Roger.

'We're a man down. It has to be that way,' said Charlie. 'And it ain't the only change'. All eyes turned to him. He cleared his throat. 'It will be Mike, Roger and me that go into the depot with Pickering's crew'.

Eddie shot his brother a confused look, thinking that perhaps he had misheard him.

'But, what about Ed?' said Roger.

'Eddie's goin' to be looking out for us,' said Charlie while he reached into the holdall at his feet and lifted out a black walkie-talkie. He held it out to Eddie. 'Take this. I want you up in the factory watching for the signal. I was going to use one of Pickering's boys, but better they're all in the depot with us'.

Eddie refused to take the radio. 'You're kidding me, right?' said Eddie, but Charlie ignored the question.

'Radio me a report every sixty seconds. Use channel twenty-seven. I want to know if you see so much as a paperboy move on that street. You got that?'

'What the fuck? You got me all the way here just to be a friggin' lookout?' said Eddie.

Charlie looked at Roger and Mike and gestured to them to leave.

'You two get yourself downstairs and look out for Gary'. The two men picked up their gear and walked towards the rear door, avoiding eye contact with Eddie.

'I don't understand. What did I do?' said Eddie.

'You didn't do nothing, bruv'.

'What then?'

Charlie hesitated for a moment, struggling, it seemed, to find the right words to say, then looked straight into his brother's eyes. 'This might not go to plan'.

'Which is why you need me in there with you,' growled Eddie.

'Ed, you've got a fuckin' toy gun in your pocket'.

'Which you said is enough to scare the guards'.

'Listen, that depot's full of experienced security guards. They might not be easily intimidated. Maybe this is one time when scaring them ain't enough'.

DEN OF SNAKES

'That's bullshit. I'm coming with you'.

Charlie thrust the radio into his brother's chest. 'I said no,' he shouted, then turned and strode towards the back door. 'This is my crew. Take the radio and do what I fuckin' tell you. End of discussion'.

Charlie, Mike and Roger were already sitting inside the Transit van by the time Eddie made his way down.

Gary stood outside smoking. 'Hurry kiddo,' he said in a hushed tone, then dropped the cigarette butt and ground it into the dirt with his boot. He waited for Eddie to climb into the van, then closed the door behind him. There were no seats in the van, so the crew sat on the ribbed, metal floor with their legs outstretched for balance.

Eddie lowered himself down opposite Roger, who was working his way through a packet of Wine Gums. He held up the bag to Eddie.

'Want one?' he said. Eddie shook his head and looked at Charlie, who was sitting up against the bulkhead behind the driver's compartment. He had his eyes closed.

'It's for the best,' said Roger. 'You being up in that factory, watchin' out for us. And if it does go up shit creek, at least you won't get caught'.

Eddie did not reply. Somehow, he doubted that Charlie's last-minute change of plans had been driven by a desire to protect his brother.

They arrived at the Wheatsheaf just over thirty minutes later. It was still dark, and one of the East End crew guided them in with a small torch. Gary got down from the driver's seat and walked around to the van's rear door, which he opened to let Pickering and his crew in.

'Morning, ladies,' said Pickering as he clambered in. 'What, no, cushions?' He sniggered. He sat down next to Roger, then pulled his pistol out of his shoulder holster. It was a Browning High Power, the standard-issue sidearm that Eddie had carried when he was in the army. Pickering pulled the magazine out, examined it and pushed it back in, then put the gun back in the holster. He looked at Eddie and winked at him.

'All set?' said Gary.

'All good,' said Charlie.

'Right, let's get this show on the road,' said Mike then banged on the van's inner wall. They set off once again, Gary driving more cautiously than before as they made their way towards Heathrow. They pulled up to the rear of the old Lucas factory after ten minutes.

'This is your stop, Ed,' said Charlie. 'We will wait here until you are in position. Give me a squawk when you're at the window'. Gary opened the rear doors, and Eddie pushed himself up to his feet, then clambered out of the van.

'Channel twenty-seven, remember?' said Charlie.

Eddie nodded and looked into the van full of men. 'Good luck,' he said.

'See you later, soldier boy. Enjoy the show,' said Pickering as Gary closed the doors. The van pulled away as Eddie pushed the rusty metal gates open, then jogged towards the factory building. He made his way up to the top floor, to the same position where he and Charlie had sat the previous day, and opened one window a few inches. The road was deathly quiet, save for the mechanical whirring of a ventilation fan in the depot opposite. He depressed the button on the radio for a second.

'All clear?' replied Charlie in a whispered tone.

'Roger that,' replied Eddie.

'We're moving in now'.

Eddie shifted his position to get a more unobstructed view of the scene outside. A minute later, he saw the van appear at the end of the road. It continued to trundle towards him for a few seconds, then pulled over to park a hundred yards from the depot. He depressed the radio's send button. 'I see you. Sit tight'.

Eddie looked at his watch. It was approaching seven o'clock.

Angus was on an early shift that day and would send his signal - several flashes from his torch - from the guard's first-floor toilet window as soon as it was clear for them to move in. He put his hands into his jacket pocket and fixed his eyes upon the depot.

Except for an Express Dairy milk float that trundled by, there were no signs of activity in or around the depot for over three-quarters of an hour. Eddie had to fight off the desire to doze off. The morning sun had risen high enough now to illuminate most of the interior of the depot when one guard emerged from inside the depot building and sauntered around to one of the parked vans. He leaned against a wall and lit up a cigarette.

'I have movement. One guard is having a smoke,' Eddie whispered on the radio. 'Might be the CCTV operator'.

'Is he a fat fucker?' said Charlie.

Eddie looked at the guard, who was certainly not a skinny man. 'Well, he's quite big. But he ain't what I'd call porky, no'.

'Angus said the CCTV guy is proper huge'.

'It's not him then,' said Eddie.

'Roger that,' said Charlie.

Eddie peered at the second-floor toilet window above the man, waiting for the signal. Nothing. The man in the yard finished his cigarette and let himself back into the brick building, closing the door behind him. 'The smoker's gone back inside,' said Eddie.

He placed the walkie-talkie down onto the window ledge but then caught sight of the first of several bright torch flashes coming from the toilet window. He reached into his parka pocket and pulled his own torch, a chrome-plated Maglite, and sent several flashes back to acknowledge the message. This is it, he thought, then grabbed the radio. 'Contact made, repeat contact made. Acknowledge'. He poked his head out and looked towards the van.

'Did you get the signal?' said Charlie over the radio.

'Confirmed. It's on. Move in'.

'Roger that. We're moving in'. The Transit van pulled away from the kerb and crept towards the depot. It stopped next to the building's rear entrance, and the radio squawked. 'Clear to go?' said Charlie.

Eddie scrutinised the depot, then pressed the transmit button once again. 'Clear to go. Repeat, clear to go, over'.

Almost immediately Eddie heard a brief tire squeal as the van drove up onto the kerb and mounted the pavement, stopping inches from the brick wall of the depot yard. The side and rear doors opened in unison, and Mike, Roger, Charlie, Pickering, and his four men burst out from inside the van. Mike and Roger both carried a ladder. Roger placed his one next to the van. Mike then scrambled up it, clambered across the roof and onto the depot's surrounding wall. Roger passed him up a pair of bolt cutters which Mike used to make quick work of the barbed wire on top of the wall. Roger and Charlie then passed up the second ladder. At the same time, Pickering and his crew members made their way up to accompany Mike. They stooped low to keep out of sight from those inside the depot. In a few seconds, Mike hauled the ladder over the wall and down into the yard. One by one, the eight men made their way over the wall and out of Eddie's sight.

Gary drove away from the pavement and back onto the roadside. He looked up at Eddie from inside the van. Even from this distance, Eddie could tell that Gary was nervous. Eddie refocused his attention back onto the depot yard. He could see Charlie leading the line of men towards the back door of the main building. Mike was brandishing a sawn-off shotgun, Charlie and the other men all had pistols in hand.

Eddie watched, his heart beating in his ears as the crew stood, waiting for the large CCTV operator - who would have told his colleagues he was popping outside to smoke - to open the door.

'Christ sake, come on,' he said. At that moment, the door opened, and the man appeared. He was, indeed, a substantial figure and Eddie could not help wondering how his employer had found a uniform to fit him.

Mike grabbed the guard and pushed him back into the building. Charlie and the others then followed. They were in.

This is happening.

Eddie glanced at his watch, made a mental note of the exact time, then looked back at the building across the road. There were no signs of activity. The street remained quiet too, except for Gary who sat in the driver's seat, tapping his fingers on top of the steering wheel. Eddie picked up the walkie talkie.

'All clear. I say again, all clear'. He got no response, save for some white noise. He sat still, radio in hand, listening and scanning the depot until less than a minute later, Charlie's voice barked out from the radio.

'Area secured. How are we lookin' outside?'

'Nothing to report out here,' Eddie replied.

'Keep your eyes open, we -'. Charlie stopped mid-sentence. Another voice was shouting. It was Pickering, but Eddie could not make out what he was saying. The transmission cut out. Eddie stared at the radio, then at the depot. Then, just a moment later, he heard a muffled bang from inside the depot.

Eddie knew a gunshot when he heard one. He got up and looked up and down the street, then pressed on the radio's transmit button. 'What the fuck was that? What's going on in there?' There was no reply. He tried again. 'What's going on in there? Do you need back up?' he shouted.

The radio crackled. Eddie could hear shouting and then a man crying. Whoever he was, it was obvious he was in agony. 'Do you need backup?'

A voice barked out from the radio, but this time it was not Charlie. 'Stay where you are,' shouted Mike. 'We're coming out now'.

Eddie checked the street again. Gary was looking up at him. Eddie signalled to him to get ready with a frantic wave of his hands. He heard the van's engine splutter into life and a slight cloud of blue smoke coughed out of the vehicle's exhaust.

Eddie's mouth was bone dry. He swallowed to stimulate some saliva.

For fuck's sake, get out of there.

The radio crackled into life once more just as the first of the crew emerged from the open door. It was Roger and Mike. Roger was carrying what appeared to be two black briefcases. Mike was holding his shotgun. They both sprinted in the direction in which they had left the ladder. Pickering's crew hurried out, pistols in hand, and a few seconds later, Charlie and Pickering also came into view. Charlie pushed the younger man towards the rest of the crew, turned to check behind him, before he too broke into a run.

Eddie heard Mike's voice again from the walkie talkie, 'Get yourself downstairs. We're coming for you'.

'On my way,' replied Eddie. He picked up the torch and crammed it into his pocket, then sprinted towards the staircase. He could hear the loud squeal of tyres from outside as the van accelerated away from the crime scene.

Eddie was panting hard by the time he arrived at the factory gates, just as the Transit van slowed to collect him. The door flew open and Mike flung out his hand, which Eddie grabbed and hauled himself inside. Charlie thumped on the back of the bulkhead behind the driver's compartment and shouted.

'Go go go'. Eddie pulled the side door shut and squatted down in the corner of the van interior, bracing himself with his feet and elbows as it sped up. He looked at his brother.

'What happened? I heard a gunshot.' He scanned the occupants of the vehicle. All were present and with no apparent signs of injury. Nobody answered.

Roger was scowling at Bobby Pickering. 'He shot one of the guards,' he said.

'You what?' shouted Eddie.

'The geezer was making a run for it,' said Pickering

'He was our insider, you dumb fuck,' shouted Roger.

'How was I supposed to know that? He moved, I shot him. It was instinct'.

'Shit,' said Eddie. 'How bad?'

'Bad,' said Roger.

'He got it in the stomach,' said Mike, who was also glaring at Pickering.

Pickering shrugged, then turned his head to look out of the rear windows.

Twenty minutes later the van pulled up outside a lockup under an old railway bridge in Hayes, on the north-western outskirts of London.

'How's it look?' asked Charlie.

'Can't see nobody,' replied Gary, from the driver's compartment. 'Stick tight, I'll check'. Eddie heard the driver's door open as Gary got out.

Pickering rose and put his hand on the rear door handle. 'Sit the fuck down,' barked Mike, brandishing his sawn-off shotgun.

Pickering snorted and looked towards Mike. 'Do we have a problem, ladies?' he replied.

'Too right we fuckin' do,' said Roger, also now pointing a gun at the East Londoner. Pickering's crew reached for their pistols.

'Everybody calm down,' said Charlie. 'We will all get inside, and then we can have a civilised discussion'.

Gary got back into the van, having opened the double doors of the garage and reversed the Transit inside. As soon as he turned off the ignition, the crews clambered out. Gary's Commer van was parked inside, ready for Charlie and the rest of the team to leave.

'So, like I said,' said Pickering. 'Do we have a problem?'

'You shot our inside guy,' Mike snarled. He raised the shotgun.

Pickering slipped his right hand towards his pistol in its shoulder holster. 'I told you,' he said, 'I thought the geezer was gonna make a move. How was I supposed to know he was your man?'

Pickering's men stood nearby. The one nearest to Eddie had his jacket open. Eddie could see the butt of a revolver stuffed in the young man's belt. This could go south quickly, Eddie thought, now wishing he had something more potent than the deactivated Luger.

'Way I see it, this it was your fault,' said the East Ender.

'How d'yer figure that?' said Mike.

'Coz you didn't see fit to sharing all the details,' said Pickering. He gestured to the two briefcases that lay on the floor of the van. 'Like what's in them two little cases. It ain't banknotes now, is it?'

'We ain't got time for this,' said Gary. He was standing by the open doors. 'Charlie, we need to split'.

'He's right, Mikey,' said Charlie. 'Let it go. We can't change nuffin' now'.

Mike remained glaring at Pickering, his finger quivering on the trigger guard.

'Mike, enough,' said Roger. 'Charlie's right. What's done is done'.

'So that's it? We just shrug our shoulders and forget what happened?' said Eddie.

'Yes. That's exactly what we do,' said Charlie. He walked over to the Commer van, opened the passenger door and lifted out a blue and white Slazenger bag. 'Seventy five grand'.

The smirk disappeared from Pickering's face. 'We said one hundred'.

'We said a hundred, if it all goes to plan,' Charlie snarled. 'You shot one of the guards. That weren't in the fucking plan'. He dropped the bag at the East Ender's feet.

Pickering bent down and unzipped it to reveal the contents.

'And under the circumstance, excuse us if we don't give you a lift back to your car,' Charlie added. Pickering smiled, then looked at his companions.

'Looks like we're getting the train home, boys'. He zipped up the bag and started towards the door, brushing past Eddie as he walked.

The Lawson brothers looked at each other. Eddie resisted the temptation to utter the words, 'I told you so'. After all, he thought, what would have been the point?

The journey to Lowestoft took nearly four hours. An overturned truck on the A12 had caused a long tailback near Chelmsford. There had been little conversation along the way and the van pulled into an industrial unit close to the port at close to two o'clock. Eddie could see several dozen boats on the water, but not the trawler in which they would escape.

Gary turned off the ignition. 'Right gents. This is where we part company'. He pointed towards an alleyway between two of the units. 'That'll take you down to the water. It's about five minutes to the docks'.

'Let's hope our ride is still waiting,' said Roger.

'They don't get the other thirty grand otherwise'. He shook Gary's hand. 'I'll be in touch as soon we've sold the stones'.

'I'm counting on it,' said Gary.

'Then you can get yourself a proper van,' said Mike as he walked past.

Eddie was scanning the road outside. There was a group of men in blue boiler suits standing outside a nearby building, smoking. One of them was staring at Gary's van, which sat parked on a double yellow line. 'We're attracting attention,' he said.

The crew gathered their things and climbed out from the

van, then scurried towards the alleyway, avoiding eye contact with the nearby workers. Much to the group's collective relief, they spotted the Spanish fishing trawler moored at the dockside as they rounded the corner at the end of the alley. They stopped thirty yards away from the boat, waiting until one of the Spanish sailors spotted them and signalled at them to approach. The Englishmen jogged across and made their way into the trawler as quick as they could, where they were greeted by Xavier, the boat's captain.

'A profitable trip?' he asked, a wry smile clear to see.

'It was,' said Charlie. 'How long till we can get going?'

'We are ready now. Just the matter of the remaining money'.

'When we get back to Spain, Xavier,' said Charlie. 'That was what we agreed'.

The Spanish captain scratched the bristle on his chin. 'The thing is, Charlie. We saw the television. The police are looking for an armed gang. They say they shot a security man'.

'And what of it?' grunted Mike.

'My men and me, we are taking a bigger risk now. This was unexpected. We would be happier if we can see our money. You understand, I think'. A group of three sailors stood along in the corridor. They looked tense.

Charlie reached down, unzipped his sports bag. He pulled out a wad of banknotes and split them in half. 'Half now, half when we dock in Vigo. No discussion.' He held out the money. The captain smiled and reached for it, but Charlie withdrew it. 'But, if you fuck us over, Xavier. It would be bad for you and your crew. Very bad. *Comprende*?

'I would never do that, Charlie. You can trust me'.

'What about them?' said Charlie, pointing at the sailors.

'All of us, Charlie. *Tranquilla, por favor*'.

Charlie handed over the money, which the captain took and began to count.

'Check it later,' said Charlie. We need to get going now'.

The captain stuffed the cash into his coat pocket and barked orders in Spanish at his crewmen. 'We will be on the water in ten minutes. Please make yourselves comfortable'. The Spaniard ushered the crew towards their accommodation. 'We will eat together later. Paella. I have excellent wine, also'.

Eddie heard the low rumble of the boat's engines starting up and looked back towards the external door behind him as one sailor closed it.

'How long until I see England again?' he wondered.

CHAPTER EIGHTEEN
THE VICTORS RETURN

It took over two full days before the boat arrived back in its home harbour of Vigo at three o'clock in the morning. Xavier, the captain, received the rest of his money and another stern reminder as to the necessity to keep quiet.

'I provide many things to many people, gentlemen,' said the Spaniard. 'But in my world, discretion is the most valuable commodity of all. You need have no concerns about me or my crew,' the man had told them. 'Hasta proxima, Charlie'.

'Next time, we're gettin' on a plane,' said Mike as walked down the gangway. 'I'm goin' to stink of poxy fish for a month'.

'I told you before, there ain't going to be a next time,' Charlie had replied.

The crew returned to their vehicles, where Charlie handed Mike one of the cases of diamonds.

'Best we split them up. Just in case we get stopped,' said Charlie. 'Stick it under a seat or something'.

'Don't worry. I ain't lettin' this beauty outta my sight,' said Mike.

'We meet back up at the bar tonight. Let's say, ten o'clock, okay? Drinks are all on me'.

'You might regret sayin' that, Charlie,' said Roger.

Charlie grinned. 'Oh, I intend to hide the quality stuff first'. He shifted to face Roger and in a stern tone said, 'Now, don't be getting all sentimental about that motor. Take it to the yard and get it crushed'.

Roger glanced towards the Ford Granada and sighed. 'That's gonna kill me, Charlie. But yeah'.

'You make sure you see it done. Don't trust them gypo fuckers. You got it?'

'Yeah, Charlie. I got it,' said Roger.

'See you in Marbella,' said Charlie as he walked over to the Vauxhall, climbed into the passenger seat and lit up a cigarette.

Eddie turned back to Roger and Mike. 'Guess I'm driving first then'.

The brothers made the long drive south to the Costa del Sol, taking turns with the driving. The temperature had peaked in the mid-thirties at six o'clock, and they were both exhausted by the time they arrived back at the roadside service station near Marbella to collect Charlie's Porsche.

They retrieved their bags from the boot of the Vauxhall - it's weary engine still ticking from the lengthy journey - and wandered into the cafe where they found the carwash owner propped up on the bar, fast asleep. Charlie kicked his stool, and he jolted awake.

'Hard day?'

The man rubbed his eyes and swivelled towards Charlie. 'I hooked up with one of my ex's in a bar in Banús. I'd have been happy with a quick shag, but she wanted to go all bleeding' night. I'm knackered'.

Charlie laughed and slapped the man on his back. 'You're getting too old to party all night, mate,' said Charlie as he placed the keys to the gold Vauxhall on the bar. 'What are you goin' to do with it?' he asked the man who was still rubbing his weary eyes.

'I'll take it up into the hills. There's an old quarry up there. Nobody has used it for decades and the water is very deep. Nobody will find it there'.

'Perfect,' said Charlie as he cast his eyes around the bar. He reached into his pocket for his wallet and pulled out a wad of banknotes. 'Here you are. Don't suppose you gave me motor a wash, did you?'

'Of course, I did it myself'. He handed Charlie the keys to his Porsche. 'She is around the back, out of sight'.

'Good man,' said Charlie. 'Pop into the bar some time and say hello. Bring your ex as well. She sounds fun'.

The man waved, before resting his head back down on the bar.

The Lawsons made their way back to Marbella and to Charlie's bar, where he parked the German car in his private space. Eddie glanced at his watch. It was a quarter to nine. The last vestiges of the day were disappearing over the horizon to the west.

As he got out of the car, Eddie noticed a familiar red Ferrari lower down the hill. He nudged Charlie on his arm.

'That's Mike's motor. He's here early'.

Charlie peered at the red car. 'Yeah,' said Charlie. 'And that's Roger's Jag just behind it'. He scratched at his several-days-old stubble.

'Do you think something's up?' said Eddie.

Charlie looked up at the bar entrance. 'Let's find out'. Charlie locked the Porsche before striding up the steps to the entrance to the bar.

The bar manager approached Charlie as he entered. 'Nice to see you back, boss,' he said.

'Nice to be back, Barry. Are the lads here already?'

'Yeah. They've been waiting for a while now'.

Charlie scratched at his chin again. 'Bring me and Ed a cold one, would you?'

The bar manager nodded and walked back to the bar.

'Let's see what's up,' said Charlie.

They made their way into the glazed room where Mike and Roger sat amidst several empty pint glasses. Roger's head was in his hands. Mike was leaning back on a chair, gazing at the floor with a smouldering cigarette between his fingers.

'Wasn't expecting you boys already,' said Charlie as he opened the door. Mike twisted his head to face Charlie and Eddie.

'Show 'em, Rog,' he said. Roger puffed out his cheeks and stood up. He was holding a newspaper, the News Of The World, which he opened and laid down on the table.

'We've got a fuckin' problem,' said Roger.

The statement was unnecessary, the newspaper's headline said it all; "Murdered at dawn". An aerial photograph of the United Security depot sat underneath the large, bold type.

Eddie stepped forward to read the article which reported that armed robbers had shot a security guard at a security depot near London's Heathrow Airport. He read the next line aloud. 'It says, "Doctors battled for several hours to save the man's life but to no avail". Shit. Angus died'.

'We'll be wanted for murder now,' said Roger. He sighed and sat back down.

'Fucking Pickering,' said Mike. 'He's dropped us all in it'.

'Hold your horses there, boys,' said Charlie. 'Does the paper say anything about who they think did it'. Roger and Mike remained quiet. 'Well, does it or doesn't it?' said Charlie. He reached across and picked up the paper. He examined the story for a few moments before flinging the newspaper back onto the wooden surface. 'No, it don't. It just says "masked assailants". They ain't got nuffin' on us'.

'The fuzz ain't gonna let this lie, Charlie,' said Roger.

'We was careful. They don't know we even in the country. There ain't no way they can link this to us'.

'What about Metcalf? He knows we were up to something,' said Eddie.

'Metcalf ain't even a copper no more. He ain't got a fuckin' clue. No bugger's gonna listen to him at Scotland Yard'.

'I dunno, bruv. He seemed very intent on putting you lot behind bars when I spoke to him'.

'Maybe we should do him in as well?' said Mike.

'What? You wanna stiff a bleeding copper now?' said Eddie.

'But he ain't a copper no more, is he?' said Mike.

'Are you hearing yourself, Mikey?' said Roger.

Charlie slammed his fist on the table. 'For fuck's sake, boys. Put a lid on it,' he said, glancing at the crowded patio area outside. 'There ain't no crew better at this caper than us lot. We left no evidence, we was all masked, we all had gloves, and we burned everything afterwards. Pickering and his crew know they need to keep schtum. Especially now'. He pulled up a chair and sat down next to Roger. 'Besides, and believe me I don't take no pleasure in sayin' this, but Angus croaking…it's kind of done us a favour, ain't it?'

'How do you figure that?' said Eddie, hardly believing what he had just heard.

'Coz, he was the inside man, weren't he? The fuzz will be tryin' to work out which of the guards was in on it. They always do, coz there always is an insider, ain't there? Except they can't find ours now'. Charlie put his hand on Roger's shoulder. 'The fuzz are gonna spend days…weeks, even, questioning the rest of them poor bastards that was there that morning, trying to make one of them crack. But we know that can't happen'.

'Coz our bloke's dead,' said Roger.

'Sad, but true,' said Charlie.

'Seems Pickering did us a favour,' said Mike.

How very convenient, thought Eddie. 'I think you're forgetting about Bill, though,' he said.

Charlie removed his arm from Roger's shoulder and sat back. 'What about him?'

'Well it ain't rocket science, is it? Him getting nabbed the day before the job. That's not good, is it? I mean, he turns up in London after several years hiding out down here. Him, a core member of the infamous Five Bullet crew, and the next day there's a bleedin' big robbery where some poor sod ends up with a bullet in his gut. It ain't gonna take Sherlock flippin' Holmes to join the dots up, is it?

Mike shifted in his chair, hands stuffed into the pockets of his cut-off jeans shorts. 'The kid's got a point,' he said.

Charlie shook his head. 'They ain't got nuffin' on Bill. Him getting nabbed could be a blessing as well'.

'How's that exactly?' said Eddie.

'Well, there ain't no better alibi than being cooped up in a police cell at the time of the robbery, is there?' He stood up. 'Think about it. He's only nipped back home to Blighty, to see his old dear. She's been ill for a while now, ain't she Mikey?' He glanced at Mike, who nodded.

'Yeah. Throat cancer, I think'.

'There you go. Throat cancer. Old Mrs Taylor is poorly and wants to see her son before she carks it. She lives in Shepherd's Bush, which ain't that far from where we stopped over. Bill made his way to London to see her. He's stopped to pick up a battered sausage and chips on his way, got recognised and ends up in the back of a jam sandwich'. He pointed to the newspaper. 'The next day, a bunch of unknown assailants do a job over near Heathrow'. He took a swig from a half-empty glass of beer on the table.

'But he's still in the nick, ain't he?' said Roger.

'If they have anything on him from the previous jobs, it's circumstantial. They might try to get him to incriminate himself, but Bill ain't daft. You know him as well as I do, he's been in this situation a dozen times. He won't give them nuffin. They've got no evidence to link him to the crime. Not this job, nor none of the others. He knows it'. He picked up the newspaper and crumpled it up in his hands. 'We did it, boys. We got the job done, we got the stones and now we're back in the sun. So relax'. He patted Roger on the back and stood up. 'Now, where's my sodding beer?'

Just at that moment, Barry arrived at the glass door, a tray with four fresh pints of beer on it. Charlie beckoned him to enter.

'About flippin' time. I'm dying of thirst here, Baz'.

'Sorry, boss. I had to change the barrel. We've been rushed off our feet all week. We'll need to get an extra order in or we're going to run out'.

'Well, in that case, stop serving these freeloaders and go make me some money'.

'Yes boss,' said the barman as he placed the glasses down and walked back out of the room, closing the door behind him.

Charlie picked up his pint glass and signalled to the others to do likewise. 'We got the job done. Business is going well, and pretty soon we'll have the cash to make all our problems go away'. He took a slow drink of the beer, downing half of the pint. 'Trust me, fellas, this time next year, you'll have forgotten about all of this,' he said as he wiped his mouth with his arm. 'You'll be in fancy new villas, counting your Ferraris and wondering what all the fuss was about'.

'I'll drink to that,' said Mike, holding up his glass.

'Which means…,' said Charlie before taking another swig of beer, 'that I can count on you all to chip in to the property project, right?'

'How much did you need from us, Charlie?' said Roger.

'Two hundred and fifty thousand,' said Charlie.

Roger peered at Mike, seemingly seeking his friend's direction. Mike stood up and raised his glass in a salute to Charlie. 'I'm in'.

'Me too,' said Roger.

Charlie grinned and raised his glass in response. 'Good stuff, lads. You won't regret it. I promise'. Roger and Mike lifted their glasses to their mouths and started to drink. 'But, there's just one more thing,' said Charlie. 'We need to sort out Kenny too. He needs to get his cut on the job'.

Eddie saw Mike's eyes bulge. The big man had clearly not been expecting to hear that. He lowered his pint glass and stared at Charlie in disbelief.

Roger, seemingly sensing an imminent confrontation, attempted to interject. 'But Kenny wasn't there, Charlie,' he said.

'He wasn't there because Mikey messed him up,' said Charlie, looking directly at Mike. 'And over an argument over a poxy dinghy'.

'It was a yacht,' snarled Mike.

'It don't matter what kind of boat it was. You fucked him up for no good reason'.

'He broke our agreement'.

'Someone else offered him a lot more,' said Charlie.

'That ain't the point'.

'No, it ain't. The point is that for us all to survive down here, we need to stick together. Not fall out over a bleeding' row boat'.

'It was a yacht,' repeated Mike. Charlie walked towards Mike and placed his pint glass on the table.

'Listen, Kenny wanted to come on this job, but it was me what wouldn't let him. He wanted to do his bit, but he couldn't even see properly. His face was a mess, and he needed to stay behind. You fucked him up, Mikey. Badly. Maybe he should have stuck to your deal, I get it. But you overreacted, admit it'. Mike still was not meeting Charlie's stare. 'Look at me you ugly old fucker,' said Charlie, laughing. He put his hands on Mike's cheeks and moved even closer. Their faces were barely an inch apart now. 'We're a team, we look after each other. We've been through far too much shit to lose it over a...yacht, ain't we?'

Mike nodded. 'I suppose,' he muttered.

'Good. So c'mon, we share it out equally,' said Charlie. 'Like we've always done'. He picked up his pint glass and finished the remaining lager. 'Right, I'm dead on me feet. I'm going home. But tomorrow, we celebrate. I'll get us a table at Da Vinci's in Puente Romano. Let's show all them fuckers out there what we're about'. Charlie took a step back and, to everyone's amusement, attempted a John Travolta dance move. They all laughed. 'I've still got it,' said Charlie.

'In your dreams,' said Roger.

CHAPTER NINETEEN
KEEPING UP APPEARANCES

Eddie awoke. His throat was parched and the roof of his mouth felt as if covered with a slippery plastic sheen. He swallowed several times to stimulate some saliva and reached over to pick up his wristwatch he had left on the bedside cabinet the previous night. He rubbed his eyes in disbelief when he saw the time - it was three o'clock in the afternoon. A collage of strange memories collided in his head - the fishing trawler, the skanky digs that the crew had used in Kilburn, and the dilapidated factory where he had been hiding as the robbery had taken place. He remembered the meeting at Charlie's bar the previous evening, and the unwelcome news that the security guard had died.

He rubbed his eyes and sat up. Music was emanating from downstairs. He clambered out of bed, picked up the crumpled tee-shirt from the floor, put it on and made his way downstairs.

He found Charlie reclined on a sun lounger near the pool, a large glass and a bottle of Gordon's Gin on the floor next to him. His brother was fast asleep despite a large silver portable stereo on the floor next to him which was playing a Neil Diamond song. He was snoring. He was also completely naked.

'Ahem,' said Eddie, but his brother remained comatose.

Eddie tried again, 'Oi, bruv. You look like a sleeping walrus. Wake up'. Still nothing. Eddie picked up the pint glass at Charlie's side. 'Jesus, who drinks gin by the pint?' he thought. The glass was half full and contained the shrunken remnants of several ice cubes. Eddie chuckled as he poured the cold liquid over his brother's midriff, an action which worked precisely as Eddie had expected; Charlie shrieking like an angry choir boy who had been bitten by a small dog.

He jolted himself up into a sitting position while simultaneously throwing his hands upon his manhood. It was the funniest thing Eddie had seen for months, and he roared with laughter.

'What the…fucking fuck?' Charlie yelped. He glared up at his younger sibling with extreme annoyance. 'You wanker. What did yer do that for?'

Eddie struggled to respond. He was bent double with laughter, tears in his eyes. 'Coz…it…was…funny,' he replied. 'Very…fucking funny'.

Charlie leapt up. He appeared about ready to charge at Eddie but then relaxed, a broad grin breaking out across his unshaven face before he too laughed. 'Yeah, I suppose it was,' he said. 'You're still a wanker though'. He picked up a pair of swimming trunks from the floor, stepped into them and yanked them up. 'Had a good kip, did yer? You was gone with the fairies when I checked on you earlier'.

Eddie wiped the tears from his eyes and stood up straight. 'Yeah, I ain't never slept like that before. I must have needed it,' he said.

'We both did,' said Charlie.

'Is it always like this?' asked Eddie.

'What do you mean?'

'You know, after a job'.

Charlie grinned and rubbed his eyes. 'Ah, the "come down". Yeah, mostly. You plan these things for weeks, months. The tension builds and builds, ties your gut into knots'. He turned away, looking towards Marbella at the foot of the hills a few miles below. 'After that, if you've prepared well, the big day comes and you're like a machine. Like a robot. It goes down. Things go to plan, or they don't. Next thing you're back home watchin' Crossroads on the tele with a bag of swag hidden in your loft, unable to muster the energy to even get up and make a cuppa'. He cleared his throat. 'Assuming you didn't get caught. That's a whole different feeling, trust me'.

'How many jobs do you reckon you've done?' said Eddie.

Charlie shrugged. 'Dunno. Depends what you count as a "job". Banks, Securicor vans, post offices, pubs, newsagents… lorries full of washing machines'. He smirked. 'All a bit of a blur, to tell the truth, bruv. The first ones you remember. And the big ones, them you don't forget. But the others? I don't know. A few hundred? We was all young, dumb and quite often drunk in the beginning. That's why we got caught. After a stint in the Scrubs, you either stop doing it or you learn from your mistakes and get your act together. That's what we did. And we got pretty flipping' good at it'.

'I noticed,' said Eddie. 'It was impressive'.

Charlie shot him a wry smile. 'You weren't expecting that, was yer? The lads being so professional? Go on, say it'.

'I didn't know what to expect,' said Eddie.

'There are only a few crews that can do the jobs we did. Most of them are either banged up now, retired down here in the sun or six-foot under'. Charlie picked up the bottle of gin and the glass and started walking back to the house.

'What you said. Were you serious?' said Eddie. 'That was the last job?'

Charlie nodded and gestured towards the surrounding countryside.

'Too right. Look at where we are, Ed. And what we've got. It was always about getting this. For me, at least'. He waved his hands towards the house, and then towards the coastline in the distance. 'Why on earth would I want to risk losing this, now I've got it, hey?'

'And the rest of the lads?' said Eddie.

'What about them?'

'From what I saw, they enjoyed being on the job. Like they were all in their element. I noticed it too, the buzz'.

'And that's what gets geezers like us locked up. Or dead. You gotta know when to get out. You've gotta have an endgame. Other people I know, people what was as good as us, they lost sight of that. They got it into their heads they was all tough guys. Villains. They want to maintain a certain image. Fuck all that. It ain't about havin' strangers nod at you as you walk by coz they're in awe of you, or scared of you. That's a bunch of bollocks'.

'So what is it about?' said Eddie. 'For you, I mean?'

'Freedom. That's all what matters. But I told you before, you gotta be clever. Things ain't always gone to plan. I didn't want to do this last job, but I did it. We got there. There's a shitload of diamonds locked up in my safe. We will fund the property project and make a shed load more cash, and we get to enjoy the rest of our lives. If others want to dick about giving it the big 'un, that's up to them. Life's too short, bruv. You gotta grab it by the bollocks and enjoy it. Now get dressed. I'm taking you and the rest of the lads out for a slap-up meal'.

Eddie watched as Charlie shuffled back into the villa through the French windows. The sun was beating down on his exposed neck. He stared back behind him, at the sparkling blue water in the pool, at the distant sprawl of Marbella and up at the towering mass of *La Concha* above them. The despair that had hit him when the mercenary gig was called off now seemed like a hazy memory. How had he built it up to be the only option open to him? Had he been blinkered all along, just like Charlie had kept telling him? Even the risky trip back to England just a few days earlier felt like ancient history now. The south of Spain was undeniably stunning.

Maybe, he thought. 'Just maybe this is where it all gets better. And I can put that sodding war and all the other fuckups behind me and get myself sorted out'. He took a deep breath, closed his eyes and let the sun warm his face. He held out his arms and whirled around, a broad grin on his face.

'Oi! What are you doing, you pillock?' Charlie shouted from an open window above. 'Hurry and get ready'.

The brothers arrived an hour later at Da Vinci's, a restaurant on the western outskirts of Marbella, having collected Kenny from his apartment on the journey there.

The swelling on his face had diminished somewhat, but the effects of Mike's punch and the subsequent surgery were still plain to see. It appeared as if someone has sprayed him with purple and yellow paint while he wore a badly fitting balaclava. He was wearing a white Trilby, no doubt in an attempt to hide under it. Eddie thought it made him appear even more conspicuous.

Charlie tossed his car keys at a parking valet. 'Do not put it under a tree. I don't want to come out and find it covered in parakeet shit,' he warned the young Spaniard before making his way up into the restaurant.

The building was dimly lit and surrounded by a dozen short, plump palm trees. Eddie peered up at the red, gold and white signage above the door which displayed a single Michelin star. The dark wooden entrance porch was draped in a thick covering of artificial vines from which hung a multitude of small, multicoloured Christmas tree lights. At least half of the bulbs were inactive, Eddie noted.

Kenny stopped at his side and poked a finger at the sign. 'Shit, ain't it? The bloke what owns it bribed the inspectors fifty grand for that star,' he said. 'Food's good though so who gives a monkey's?' He walked up the wooden steps towards the open entrance. Eddie followed, ducking to avoid a trailing plastic creeper.

They were greeted by a waiter who directed them towards a large rectangular table at the rear of the restaurant. Mike and Veronica were already waiting; he was drinking from a pint glass, she was staring into space with a smouldering cigarette between two fingers. Charlie plonked himself down at the head of the table. Eddie waited for Kenny to get himself comfortable before he sat down opposite Veronica. She seemed oblivious to his presence.

'What's with the hat?' said Mike to Kenny.

'It's a trilby,' replied Kenny, making only the slightest of eye contact.

'You look like a cock,' said Mike. He nodded towards Eddie. 'And how are you, son? Good?'

'I'm good,' said Eddie.

The waiter walked to the table and started passing out menus.

'Vodka tonic,' said Veronica, pushing an empty glass towards the man.

'Whoa, slow down, love,' said Mike, touching her on the arm. 'We've only been here ten minutes'.

She pushed his hand away. 'If I want another drink, I'll bloody well have one,' she said. Mike sat back, folded his arms and stared out of the window to his right. Veronica shot Eddie a furtive glance while fidgeting with her silver necklace.

'What are you having, bruv?' said Charlie. Eddie broke his gaze away from Veronica and cleared his throat. Charlie stared at him, waiting for an answer. 'Something celebratory, maybe?'

'A beer's fine,' Eddie said to the waiter.

'I'll have a Martini,' said Kenny.

Charlie stared at his table companions and shook his head. 'Well I am having something decent. A whisky. Single malt, something expensive. And make it a large one, 'n all'.

The uneasy atmosphere was interrupted when Roger and

Judy arrived. She was wearing a skimpy, low-cut black and silver-striped dress. He was sporting a white polo shirt tucked into a tight pair of shiny grey trousers.

'Evening, all,' said Roger in an upbeat tone and took a chair. 'Sorry, we're late'.

Judy put her arms around Charlie and gave him a kiss on the cheek. 'Hey Charlie, how are you?' she said.

'I'm alright, girl. All the better for seeing you, but put them boobs away. You're gonna get me all worked up'. He chuckled.

Roger sat down next to Eddie. 'You good, Ed? Get a good night's sleep?'

Eddie could see a white powder substance on Roger's moustache. 'Yeah, not bad,' he replied. He leaned forward and, in a lowered voice, said, 'You've got a bit of something on your tache, Rog'.

Roger shuffled towards Eddie and rubbed at his facial hair. 'Did I get it all?' he whispered. Eddie nodded. 'Thanks, mate. I'm not usually into that stuff, but we thought we'd just have a bit. You know, to celebrate gettin' the job done. That and it gets Jude in the mood if you know what I mean?'

Eddie eyed Judy, who was sitting on the other side of her husband. She glanced back at him, her cheeks a little reddened.

The waiter returned with the group's drinks order. After he left, Charlie tapped a spoon against his glass. He gave the table nearby a furtive glance and, satisfied that they were not being spied upon, leaned forward and addressed his crew and their partners.

'Gents. Ladies. I just wanna say a few words,' he began. He checked the neighbouring table once more before he continued. 'I know things ain't been perfect between us all over the last few months. He was looking at Mike. 'But we've gone through much worse in the past. Some of us have done time. Some of us have lost a lot. Money, houses. Friends. Family. But that's all in the past now'.

He was looking at Eddie now.

'You all know that I weren't in favour of doing that job last week,' Charlie continued, 'And to tell the truth, in the same situation, I'd still argue against it. It didn't all go to plan, what with Bill gettin' pinched and all, but we did what we always do. We adapted. We rolled with the punches, we worked together as a unit and we got the job done'. Charlie pushed back his chair and stood up. 'It was an honour working with you fellas again. We're all fatter and greyer these days, and we've all got a lot more lines on our foreheads, but we're still the best fuckin' crew in England. I'm proud of what we've done'.

He raised his glass and waited while the rest of the crew got to their feet and did likewise. 'To the Five Bullet Crew,' he said and took a swig from his glass.

'To the crew,' said Mike before downing his drink.

'To us,' said Roger.

'And Eddie,' said Kenny. 'Our newest recruit'.

'But now,' said Charlie, as he sat back down. 'I'm disbanding it'. He shuffled in his chair.

'You what?' asked Mike, who froze midway through sitting back down. Everyone was now looking at Charlie.

'We're done. That was the last job. We agreed,' said Charlie. He reached into his trouser pocket and pulled out his personalised bullet casing. Roger glanced at Kenny, then at Mike. Judy's stare dropped to her glass. Veronica smirked at Eddie.

'Well, we said we'd stop, Charlie. Yeah. But who knows what the future will hold?' said Roger.

'There ain't gonna be no more jobs,' said Charlie. He placed the brass cartridge case down onto the table. 'So, there's no need for a crew'.

After a lengthy silence, Mike spoke up. 'So, what now?' he asked.

'We put our money to good use. We use our smarts, not our fists, and we make our money work for us. It's nineteen eighty fuckin' five. It ain't the seventies no more. We're all getting' too old for this, and the world is catching up. Bank jobs and all that is for mugs nowadays. Let someone else do that from now on. Idiots like Bobby Pickering'.

'It was Pickering what helped us pinch them diamonds,' said Mike.

Charlie leaned low towards his friend. 'It was him what almost fucking dropped us in it. Or have you forgotten what happened already, Mike?'

'Are you ready to order?' asked the waiter.

Charlie sat back. 'Give us a few more minutes, mate'. The waiter nodded, and Charlie watched as he walked away. 'From now on we meet at the bar. No need for secrecy coz we've got nuffin' to hide. From now on, we're businessmen. We're gonna get the apartments built, make a ton of dosh and see where that takes us. No more of the old work. We're going straight'. He paused to study at each of the crew members, one by one. 'Are we in agreement?'

Roger and Kenny both nodded.

Mike simply shrugged. 'You're the boss,' he said before lighting up a cigarette.

The meal came and went. Kenny, who had ordered a lasagne, had struggled to eat and left half of his food untouched. Mike, who had polished off his rump steak as if he had not eaten for a week, had jabbed his fork into Kenny's meal and finished that off too. Charlie, Roger and Jude had worked their way through two bottles of wine and several other drinks and had spent the evening reminiscing over memories of earlier times in West London. Veronica had sat silent, picking at her spaghetti carbonara and watching the other Brits with what, Eddie determined, to be an air of disinterest.

Or was it disgust?

A Spanish waitress, no older than twenty and very pretty, arrived at the table to collect the empty glasses.

'You like more drinks?' she asked, smiling.

'Nah, I think we're done, luv,' said Charlie. 'Just *la cuenta, por favor*'. She nodded, smiled and walked away to get the bill. Charlie watched her for several seconds, transfixed. 'I wouldn't mind gettin' on that,' he muttered.

'Charlie Lawson. She's half your age!' said Judy.

'And?' said Charlie. Roger laughed, wine spilling from his glass. Judy crossed her arms and rolled her eyes. Charlie scrunched up a napkin and tossed it at Eddie. 'C'mon. Support me here, bruv. Am I wrong?' he said, but Eddie did not get the chance to respond.

'I waz told youz was all…ere'.

It took Eddie a moment to recognise that it was Bill's wife, Carol. Her eyes were bloodshot, her mascara smeared across her cheeks. She was wearing jeans, dirty trainers and a faded Queen tee-shirt. 'Bill's locked up in a friggin' prishun shell, and yous lot are owt havin' a…a fuckin' parrrty'.

She put her hand out to steady herself on a wooden column, but missed and toppled forward. Her flailing arms sent Judy's dinner plate to the floor, where it smashed into several pieces. Her face planted straight into Charlie's lap.

'For Christ's sake, Carol. What are you playing at, girl?' he said, while trying to manoeuvre himself away from the mass of crimped blonde hair on his groin. Eddie stood up and gently lifted the dishevelled woman. She threw her arms over his shoulder and buried her face in his chest.

'Here, sit her down,' said Roger, who was also now at her side. He pushed his chair forward so that Eddie could lower Carol down, and bent down next to hold her hands. The commotion had attracted the attention of nearby diners, and Eddie could see seven olive brown faces at the table next to them staring at the scene next to them. Mike snarled at them.

'Mind your own fuckin' business'. The people appeared to

be of a Middle Eastern origin and may not have spoken any English, but they recognised the threat and quickly turned away.

'Bill's locked up. Yuuuv…got to 'elp him, Charlie,' Carol pleaded. She wiped her nose on her sleeve.

'We will, Carol. We will. But you can't be out talkin' about it like this. Not in this state, neither,' said Charlie in a lowered tone.

'Wot about hiz share, Charlie?' she asked.

Mike grunted. 'Oh, here we go,' he said. 'Worried you ain't gonna get your hands on the dough are you, Carol?'

'It ain't like that,' shouted Carol.

'Course it ain't,' said Judy. 'Leave her alone'. She put her arms around her sobbing friend and peered up at Charlie, who was attempting to wipe a splash of gravy from his trousers. 'You just want Bill back. That's all. And Charlie and the boys are gonna help, ain't you Charlie'.

'Course we will, girl. I've already got an English solicitor on it, ain't I?' said Charlie. He lowered himself down so that his face was close to Carol's and gently lifted her chin. 'Look at me, Carol'. He pulled out his handkerchief and dabbed at the tears streaming down her face. 'I'm gonna sort it'.

'Really?' asked Carol.

'Absolutely,' said Charlie. 'He knows what to do. And don't you worry none, neither. Bill's got nabbed by the filth before. Plenty of times. He won't be fretting none. Before you know it, he'll be outta that cell and on his way back here'.

'D'yer promise, Charlie?'

'I promise. And don't you worry about Bill's cut, neither'. He signalled to Eddie to help him lift Carol up. 'Listen, Jude. Maybe you two should take her back to your place, yeah? I'll call her tomorrow, when she's sobered up'.

'Yeah. You come back with me and Rog, alright?' said Judy. She glared at her husband. 'Go get the car'.

Roger glanced at Eddie and tutted. 'So much for gettin' my end away tonight,' he whispered.

'I heard that,' said Judy. 'Get the flippin' car, or you won't be gettin' none ever again. Roger gave a sheepish wave towards Mike and Kenny, before wandering away to fetch his car from the valet. Charlie and Eddie stepped forward, each taking one of Carol's arms and lifting her to her feet. Her eyes were closed now, and she was mumbling something incomprehensible. Saliva hung from her lower lip.

'Jesus Christ,' said Charlie. 'C'mon, Ed. Help me get her out of here'.

They walked Carol out of the restaurant, Charlie grimacing at anyone that looked their way. The parking valet pulled up in Roger's silver Mercedes.

'Is the lady okay?' the concerned man asked, as Eddie laid her down on the back seat.

'She's just had a long day that's all,' Charlie replied, and placed some money in the man's hand.

They watched as Roger's Mercedes pulled away. 'Suppose I'd better give that solicitor a call,' said Charlie.

'You what?' said Eddie. He swung around to confront his brother. 'You just told her you'd already got someone on it'.

'Well, I had given the bloke a head's up, yeah,' said Charlie. He started walking back towards the restaurant entrance.

Eddie grabbed his arm. 'But you ain't given him the go-ahead? Why not?'

'Coz, he charges a hundred quid an hour'. Eddie could not believe what he was hearing.

'Are you fucking having' me on? You've got ten million quid's worth of diamonds in a briefcase'. Charlie shrugged his shoulders.

'I told you already. Bill will be alright. But cash is still tight. More than ever after cash-flowing the job we just did. I need to shift them stones'. He started towards the door again, but Eddie grabbed him again.

'One of your crew…one of your best friends, is in a police cell, and you don't want to spend a few hundred quid to help him?' Eddie was almost shouting.

'Shhhh,' said Charlie. He glanced at a young couple who were approaching them. They were not paying any attention to the two brothers, but Charlie put his arm over Eddie's shoulder and steered him away. Then, in a hushed tone, said, 'You're right. I should have done it already'.

'Tell Carol, not me'.

'I will, I promise. I'll give the geezer a call first thing in the morning'.

'You better had,' said Eddie.

'Good man. Right, c'mon. Let's see the others off'.

They strolled back into the restaurant, but as they approached the table, Charlie halted. Several of the staff and about a dozen of the guests were standing between them and their table.

'Oh, fuck,' Charlie said.

Eddie followed his brother's stare to their table where the investigative TV reporter, James Crampton, stood with a microphone in his hand. Behind him stood two men, one with a camera, the other holding a bright light. Crampton positioned himself between the camera and the table, before pointing the microphone at Mike.

'Michael McNaughton. Did you pull the trigger that ended that man's life? He was a father of two. Did you know that?'

Charlie and Eddie pushed between the onlookers.

'Please don't do nuffin', Mike,' whispered Charlie.

Crampton noticed Charlie approaching, gave a sly smile, then continued his speech. 'The British public demand answers. How do you and your villainous friends have the audacity to sit here in full public view celebrating your latest criminal exploits when back home a family is without a father, a husband, a son?'

Mike leapt up and, in one fluid movement that would have graced an athlete half his age, flew at Crampton, sending the reporter backwards and to the floor. In a second Mike was on top of him, one hand around the man's throat, the other raised behind ready to strike.

'Mike, no!' shouted Charlie, but if Mike heard him, it had no effect. His giant fist crashed down onto Crampton's face. Eddie heard a crunching sound as the stricken man's nose flattened, followed by a spray of rouge upon the restaurant's white marble tiles.

'Shit,' says Charlie.

The cameraman moved forward and pointed the lens at Mike. He must be a consummate professional, thought Eddie. Or just stupid.

Mike glared up at the onlookers, and grunted at the cameraman. 'Get that fuckin' thing outta my face, or I'll shove it up your fuckin' arse'. The camera and light operators both took a few steps back, but Eddie could see that they were still filming. Crampton, meanwhile, was rolling around on the floor, his hands covered in blood.

Eddie pushed a waiter aside, and strode to Mike, who was now on his feet. 'Time to leave!' he said.

'Bit late for that,' said Mike, directing him to turn around.

Eddie peered over his shoulder to see a group of four Police officers marching towards them. 'Where the hell did they come from?' he thought.

The policemen pushed their way through the small crowd, batons drawn. Mike put his hands together, held them out, and was swiftly rewarded with a pair of handcuffs around his wrists.

'Michael McNaughton, you are under arrest for assault and for causing a public disturbance,' barked the more senior-looking of the Spaniards who wore a commander's insignia. The other policemen surrounded Mike and pushed him towards the door through which Eddie could see a flashing blue light.

As the police manoeuvred Mike away, Charlie tapped the

commander on the shoulder. 'You'd better treat him well, Paco,' said Charlie.

The man spun on his heels, one hand on the pistol in its holster. He took a step towards Charlie. 'What did you call me?' said the officer.

'I was just reminding you, officer. That the boys here and me have supported our local police officers over the years and -'.

'You think because you have bribed the local police that you can tell me what to do, Mr Lawson?' said the man. 'They sent here me from Madrid to deal with scum like you British. You think you can bribe me? Think again!'

'I was just pointing out -'.

'That man assaulted that reporter in full view of the public,' said the officer. 'There are a dozen witnesses. And a video recording. Walk away, or I will arrest you for obstructing justice.' He still had his hand on the pistol butt.

Veronica slipped past, brushing against Eddie as she did so. Their hands made contact for a fraction of a second.

Kenny stood next to Charlie, who was still locking eyes with the Spanish policeman. 'C'mon, Charlie. We need to go,' said Eddie. Charlie followed him out of the front entrance, cursing under his breath, to where Mike was being pushed into the back of a police van. Two police cars were parked behind it. Jeremy Crampton stood holding a blood-soaked handkerchief to his nose, his cameraman capturing the scene.

'This was a setup,' said Kenny.

'What do you mean?' asked Eddie. Kenny nodded to one of the on-watchers. It was Philip Metcalfe, the former British policeman.

'Bastard,' snarled Charlie, and started towards the man who was holding a rolled-up newspaper. Eddie put his arm across Charlie's chest to stop him. Metcalf grinned and advanced towards the brothers.

'You won't be able to keep him locked up here. He'll get out. You know that, right?' said Kenny.

'Your crooked lawyer might get him out in a few days, yes. No doubt some local judge will be a few quid better off. But it won't matter.'

'I think you'd better fuck off now, you pretend peeler,' said Kenny.

Metcalf remained still. He locked eyes on Charlie. 'You will pay for your crimes, Lawson. I will put you behind bars'.

Charlie snorted and pushed past his brother. Two of the Spanish policeman approached.

'Charlie, don't -,' said Eddie.

'S'alright, bruv. I ain't gonna do nuffin'. Not here'. He stood in front of Metcalf, looking him over. 'You ain't got shit on me. Never did. Never will'.

'Don't I?' said Metcalf. He leaned forward and, in a hushed voice, replied, 'I know you did it'.

'Did what?' said Charlie.

'The United Security job. I know it was you lot'.

Charlie shook his head. 'We ain't been back in England for years. You're pissing up the wrong tree'.

Metcalf grinned again, and shifted to face Eddie. 'You should have taken my advice and got out of here, Edward. You're one of them now'. He handed Eddie the Spanish newspaper. 'This hits the streets in the morning'.

Eddie unfurled the paper and held it open.

'Now I don't speak much of the local lingo,' Metcalf continued, 'but I'm told that what this says is "Government orders crackdown on foreign criminals", or something like that'. He peered back at Charlie, a wry smile on his face. 'The Spanish government will sign a new extradition treaty with Britain. Make the most of this time, Charlie. It won't be long before you're back in England, doing a fifteen-year sentence'. He backed away and strode off.

'Give us that,' said Kenny, and took the newspaper from Eddie. He studied the print, then sighed.

'Well?' said Charlie.

'They reckon there will be a new treaty in place by the autumn'.

Charlie snatched the paper out of Kenny's hands and scanned the article.

'So, what now?' said Eddie.

'We'll worry about it another day,' said Charlie. 'First things first. We need to get out of here'. He glanced over to where a medic was treating the still-bloodied TV reporter. 'Come on, before that wanker starts filming again. He signalled at the parking valet. 'Give me my keys'.

'I can get your car, sir,' the man replied.

'Just give me my fucking keys,' shouted Charlie. The valet plucked the keys from the wooden stand and held them out. Charlie snatched the keys from out of his hands.

'And if it's covered in bird shit, I'm coming back to find you'.

CHAPTER TWENTY
SOMEONE'S OUT TO GET US

The next morning Charlie and Eddie drove down to meet Charlie's lawyer, Guillem Montacada, at the Policía Nacional station just outside Marbella.

As they approached the building's entrance, Eddie spotted Philip Metcalf. He was leaning against a yellow postbox with a large camera in hand and began snapping photos of the Lawsons as they approached.

Eddie tapped his brother on the elbow. 'Metcalf's over there,' he said.

'Ignore the tosser,' said Charlie.

'Good luck keeping that mad bastard on the straight and narrow,' shouted Metcalf.

'He's really enjoying this,' said Eddie.

'Yeah. Trouble is, he's right'.

Guillem was beckoning at them from inside the door of the grey edifice. As they entered, he motioned at Charlie and Eddie to follow him to a secluded corner of the building's sizeable entrance hall.

'So?' asked Charlie.

'They want to charge him with aggravated assault and

affray. That could mean up to two years in prison,' said the lawyer.

'Two years? Fuck me. Are they serious?'

'I think not. Probably they want you to know they are watching'.

'So, what now?' asked Charlie.

'The hearing is in one hour. Bail will most likely be set at around fifty thousand pounds,' said Guillem.

Charlie puffed out his cheeks and put his hands on his hips. 'Fifty grand?'

The lawyer nodded. 'Mr McNaughton asked if the crew will put up the money,' said Guillem. 'He said that he has no liquid funds. He intended to surrender his sports car, a Ferrari, as collateral but…well, there was a problem'.

'A problem?' said Charlie.

Guillem's eyes dropped to the floor. 'It seems the car was not…legally registered'.

Charlie scrunched his face. 'It was stolen?'

The lawyer nodded. 'It appears so,' he replied. 'The authorities have confiscated the vehicle'.

'For f -'. Charlie motioned as if to punch the wall, but remembered where he was. 'That moron will be the end of me'.

'What shall I tell him?' asked the lawyer.

Charlie hesitated for a few seconds, his hands working his car keys in his jeans pocket. 'We'll try to get the money together,' he replied. 'It's gonna take a day or two, though. So that idiot's gonna have to suck it up in here until then'.

Guillem nodded. 'I will let him know. I'll call you later'. He shook Charlie's hand, before heading back to meet Mike in his cell.

Charlie leaned towards Eddie, who was propped up against a window, listening to the conversation. 'I was tryin' to hold off shifting the stones for a few more days. While the heat's on, like. But I ain't got the cash to deal with shit like this. We've gotta get rid of them and quick,' said Charlie, scratching his stubble.

'How you gonna do that? Have you got someone who can take 'em?' said Eddie.

'I know this local guy. Jewish geezer'.

'You trust him?' said Eddie. Charlie smirked. Eddie shot his brother the same face he had used a thousand times before - care to explain yourself?

Charlie started towards the doorway. 'Well, he's a respectable, married man with five kids and a fine reputation to uphold…and a weakness for rent boys'. Charlie held the door open for his younger sibling. 'Lucian caught him on camera. So yeah, we can trust him!'

The brothers made their way back to Charlie's Porsche, all the time wary of Philip Metcalf and his telephoto lens. The former policeman was, however, nowhere to be seen.

'He's probably gone home to wank over the photos he took this morning,' said Charlie, as they reached the car.

'Where to now?' asked Eddie.

'Kenny's. I need him to chip in for Mikey's bail'.

'You think he will do that?' said Eddie.

'Yeah, I'll talk him around. No worries,' said Charlie as he got into the car.

Half an hour later, Eddie and Charlie were standing in Kenny's living room where Charlie's attempt to persuade Kenny to chip in to cover Mike's bail money had fallen on deaf ears.

Eddie stood leaning against the bar, maintaining a respectable distance from the two older men.

'The quack said my eyesight is damaged, Charlie. Possibly forever,' said Kenny, stubbing out a cigarette into an ashtray on his mantlepiece. 'So, no. Fuck him. He can rot in that fuckin' cell for all I care'. He sat down on his couch, crossing his arms, his eyes fixed on Charlie.

Charlie lowered himself down next to Kenny. 'I know how you feel, mate, but -'.

'I said no, Charlie. And I mean it'. Kenny crossed his arms.

'Mate, we got to stick together,' said Charlie.

'We? What "We" ?' said Kenny.

Charlie seemed hesitant. 'Us. The crew,' he replied.

'There ain't no crew. You disbanded it last night,' said Kenny. 'Or have you changed your mind already?'

Eddie could see that Kenny's answer had thrown his brother into a quandary.

'Yeah, well…what I meant was no more jobs. We've still gotta stick together'.

'He punched me in the face and knocked me into the fucking pool, Charlie. In front of everyone'.

'I know, but -'.

'And don't think I don't know about him not wanting me to get a cut on the job, neither,' said Kenny. 'Rog told me'.

Charlie rolled his eyes. 'You'll get your cut, mate,' said Charlie.

'I better bleedin' do. Coz until that happens, I ain't got the cash to invest in no property projects neither. So, end of conversation. I ain't helping that cunt'. Kenny pushed himself up from the red leather couch. 'Now, if you don't mind, young Katie will be here in a minute. She's bringing me my lunch'. He strode to the apartment door and held it open. Charlie shook his head, sighed, stood up.

'Enjoy your lunch,' he said as he walked to the door. Eddie nodded at Kenny and followed his brother. The siblings entered the elevator. Charlie punched the button for level one.

'So, now what?' asked Eddie.

'Time you met Lucian,' said Charlie.

Charlie's Porsche pulled to an abrupt halt on the street outside his pub, taking Eddie, who had been gazing at the surroundings from the passenger seat, by surprise. He followed his brother's stare towards a blue Policía Nacional van parked in Charlie's private space. Two policemen stood at the foot of the stairs. Two more were escorting the bar staff from the building.

'What the fuck?' said Charlie. Philip Metcalf stood on the street nearby, taking photos. He appeared not to have noticed Charlie's car pull up. Lucian Soparla, Charlie's private snoop, as he stepped out from the bar's entrance and began to shuffle up the hill. The Romanian glanced down the street towards the silver Porsche and gestured at Charlie to keep on moving.

Charlie put the car into gear and drove forward, before pulling over a hundred yards up the road. Soparla walked to the car, glancing behind him to see if he was being followed.

'Quick, let him in,' said Charlie. Eddie opened his door, got out, and lifted his seat forward. Soparla slumped down into one of the rear bucket seats, and Eddie climbed back in. Charlie pulled away from the kerb and shot Lucian an expectant look in the rearview mirror.

'Well?'

'They arrived thirty minutes ago. They informed your bar manager that the bar must be closed,' said Soparla. Charlie slapped the steering wheel.

'Did they give a reason?' asked Eddie.

'They said it was because of "Financial irregularities". The local magistrate has suspended the license as well'.

'Wankers,' said Charlie.

'Was Metcalf there when the coppers turned up?' asked Eddie.

'He was,' said Soparla. 'The bastard Spanish forced everyone to leave. I saw the English policeman at the bottom of the stairs with his camera as I left the building'.

'Tell me everything's locked-up downstairs, Lucian,' said Charlie, staring at the thin man in the mirror.

'They will find nothing'.

'So what's going on? Are they coming after you?' said Eddie to his brother.

'Not just me,' said Charlie. He was pointing at a cafe outside which was another police vehicle, blue lights flashing. 'That's Carol's place. Looks like they're hitting all of us'. He drove past, shielding his face with one hand. 'Lucian, where've you got the photos of that Jewish bastard?'

'I have them in my apartment'.

'Good. That's good,' replied Charlie. He glanced at Soparla in the mirror again. 'Call him. Tell him what we've got on him. Tell him I'm coming for a visit in the morning'. The Romanian nodded. Charlie pulled over at the side of the road below a white apartment block and swivelled around to face Soparla. 'This one yours?' The thin man nodded and Charlie beckoned at his brother to let Soparla out. Eddie opened the door and climbed out, alert for any signs of trouble. Soparla moved to climb out of the back seat, but Charlie grasped his arm.

'Make sure he understands his predicament,' said Charlie. 'Tell him what will happen if he fucks me over'.

'He will understand,' said Lucian, grinning and clearly unconcerned at the prospect of threatening the jeweller. 'I'll call you later'. Lucian winked at Eddie, then sauntered away as Eddie got back into the car.

'Where did you find that slimy git?'

Charlie sniggered. 'Someone made me an introduction. He's not so bad. He's also flippin' invaluable to us, so don't go antagonising him'.

'If you say so'.

'I do. That bloke has a unique set of skills I need. What we all need, if we're gonna shift them stones and get this heat off our back'.

Charlie pulled out into the traffic and put his foot down. The Porsche's exhaust barked, the noise bouncing off the surrounding buildings.

Eddie could see his brother's forehead was speckled with fresh sweat. 'Don't you ever think maybe it's time to move on?' he said.

'What do you mean?'

'Sell up. Sell the bar, the house, and whatever else you have here. Take the money and start again somewhere else'.

'Why would I do that?' asked Charlie, agitated.

'Bruv, it doesn't seem like things will get better for you here,' Eddie said. 'This extradition treaty sounds like it's gonna happen. So what then?' Charlie looked at his brother. Eddie could tell he was not in agreement, but he pushed the point further. 'And you said it yourself, the crew ain't united anymore. I can't see Kenny and Mike reconciling soon, and -'.

'They've always been at each other's throats. Nuffin's changed there'.

'And the others? They went against you to go do that last job. It doesn't look to me like your crew is a tight unit any more. And obviously the Spanish authorities are on your case now'.

'And where would I go?'

Eddie shrugged. 'South Africa? Thailand? South America, maybe?'

Charlie shook his head, eyes on the road ahead. 'I'm too old to up sticks and start again,' he said. 'And besides, I've got too much riding on things down here now. He put his hand on Eddie's shoulder. 'I've got it all planned'.

'Yeah?' said Eddie. 'But things don't always go to plan, do they?'

CHAPTER TWENTY-ONE
STONES

Early the next morning Eddie stood outside a low-rent jewellery store in Marbella with Charlie, Roger and Kenny.

Charlie, who was carrying the diamonds from the United Security robbery in a black, leather briefcase, seemed to be readying himself for a confrontation. 'How long's it take to open an effin door?' he cursed.

'What are we doing here?' asked Eddie.

'We are going to cash in our chips, bruv,' said Charlie, before pressing on the doorbell for the third time.

They heard multiple locks being turned one by one, before the door opened outwards to reveal an obese man in a white shirt and black trousers. His hair was shaven, except for two long orange plaits that hung from the side, and was topped by a black skullcap.

'Shalom, Avram. How the fuck are yer?' said Charlie.

'I've had better days'. The man peered up and down the street while the group entered, before closing the door. 'This way,' he said and descended a flight of concrete stairs.

The Englishmen followed him down into the jeweller's subterranean workshop. Eddie saw two lines of stainless steel desks upon which were an array of well-worn machine tools, surrounded by empty fast food packets and soda cans. He ran his fingers over one of the work surfaces. It was coated in a film of fine dust.

'So, you gonna do this for us?' said Charlie as he surveyed the room.

'Do I have a choice?'

'Not if you don't want them photos finding their way to your father, your mother, your wife, your kids, and your fucking rabbi,' snarled Charlie.

'Okay. Let me see them,' said the fat man.

Charlie placed the brief cases down on one of the few available spaces on the tabletops and thumbed at the combination locks. He opened it to reveal several polythene bags full of what appeared to be small chunks of dirty, rock salt. It occurred to Eddie that this was the first time he had laid eyes on the diamonds. There were a lot of them.

'Christ almighty,' he said.

'His lot don't believe in that fella,' said Kenny.

'They believe in anything if there's a profit in it for 'em, though,' said Charlie. 'Ain't that so, Avram?'

The jeweller closed his eyes and took a resigned breath. 'Can we just do this?' he asked.

'Be my guest,' said Charlie, stepping back from the case.

The fat man pulled a set of black-rimmed spectacles from his inside pocket, put them on. He lifted one bag from the case, thumbed at the contents and held the bag up to a desk light. He frowned. 'I need to examine them properly,' he said to Charlie.

'Of course,' said Charlie. The fat man was emptying the bag out into a stainless steel tray.

'What are they worth?' asked Kenny.

The jeweller answered without looking away from the diamonds. 'On the open market? Ten, maybe twelve thousand a carat'. He picked one stone up with a pair of tweezers and scrutinised it. 'I don't understand,' he said. 'Is this some kind of test?'

'What you talking about?' said Charlie. The man discarded the first stone and examined another before peering back at Charlie, evidently bewildered.

'But these are no good,' he said.

'What do you mean "no good"?' said Kenny.

'They…they -'.

'They what?' demanded Charlie.

'They're not diamonds. They're just quartz, basically'. Charlie grabbed the now very-frightened jeweller by the throat, pulled a pistol from his belt and pushed it to the man's temple.

'Are you trying' to cheat me, you Jewish cunt?'

'No, Mr Lawson. I swear'. The jeweller pointed towards a small hammer. 'Pass me that. I can show you'. Charlie gestured at Eddie to pass the silver tool across, took a step back, his pistol still pointing at the petrified man.

'Show me,' demanded Charlie.

The jeweller took the hammer from Eddie, placed one stone on a nearby vice and hit it. The stone disintegrated into dozens of small shards. 'You see? Diamonds don't break,' he said.

Charlie's eyes were bulging, his jaw wide open. He grabbed another stone from the case, wrenched the hammer out of the jeweller's hand and brought it down hard on the second stone. It too shattered into multiple pieces. He grabbed another stone and hit that with the same result. Then another and another before dropping the hammer to the floor.

'What the fuck is happening?' said Eddie.

Charlie grabbed a handful of the stones from the case and held them out in front of the petrified jeweller. 'Are you telling me -?' He stared at the bags of worthless rocks in the case. 'Are you telling me we stole a case full of fuckin' glass?'

The jeweller's lips quivered, but he could not muster a reply.

'Someone must have switched them,' said Kenny.

'How?' said Roger. 'We had them the whole way'.

Charlie dropped the remaining stones onto the floor, sat down on a red plastic chair, and placed both hands on his head, one still holding the black pistol. 'It must have been a setup,' he said, staring at the floor.

'What do you mean?' said Kenny.

'Right from the start. The entire job. We got played'.

'Played? By who?' said Roger.

Charlie looked up at his fellow crew-member. 'Angus. It must have been Angus all along'.

'Angus is dead,' said Eddie.

'That was an accident,' said Charlie.

'Pretty fuckin' convenient, don't yer think?' said Roger.

'Not for him it wasn't,' said Eddie.

'You reckon Gary was in on it?' said Kenny. 'And Bill? Getting himself pinched like that'.

'You fuckin' what?' shouted Roger.

'No? The timing stinks, don't you think?' said Kenny.

Roger shook his head. 'Not Gary and not Bill'.

'Well someone fucking fucked us,' said Kenny.

Roger sat down on one of the metal seats. 'Charlie, do you think it was De Boars all along?' Charlie did not respond.

'So, what the hell do we do now?' said Kenny. They all looked at Charlie who sat motionless, eyes fixed on the floor still.

'Bruv?' asked Eddie.

Charlie looked up at him. He was holding his chest, and his bottom lip was quivering. 'I've got to pay the first instalment on the apartments this week'. He pushed himself up from the chair. 'I've got to pay that money, or I'm fucked'. He put his pistol back in his belt, and ambled to the stairs, his shoes crunching on the broken quartz. The others followed him towards the door.

'What about the photos?' said the fat jeweller.

He got no reply.

CHAPTER TWENTY-TWO
WE NEED TO TALK

Eddie stood on the street outside the jewellers as Roger and Kenny drove away. Charlie was ripping open a fresh pack of Benson & Hedges.

'What are you gonna do?' said Eddie.

'Find whoever stitched us up and shoot 'em in the fuckin' head, that's what!' Charlie put the cigarette between his lips and thrust a gold Zippo in front of it.

'How are you going to do that?' asked Eddie. Charlie was thumbing repeatedly at the lighter's flint wheel, but it refused to ignite. 'I think you're out of gas' Eddie said.

Charlie tried several more times before throwing the lighter to the floor. 'Piece of shit!' he shouted. He was attracting attention from several passersby.

'Calm down,' said Eddie. Charlie was shaking, his face red and his fists tight, fit to explode. Eddie put his arm around his brother's shoulders and attempted to manoeuvre him towards the silver Porsche. 'Want me to drive?'

'No, I don't want you to drive. I'm fuckin' angry, not fuckin' disabled,' Charlie snapped.

Eddie nodded towards a group of nearby tourists who had

stopped. They were all now staring at the angry Englishman. 'We're causing a scene'.

Charlie stood poised like he would storm towards the group but, much to Eddie's relief, checked himself and instead unlocked the Porsche and slumped down onto the driver's seat. He slammed the door shut. Eddie climbed into the passenger's seat and closed his door. The potential drama over, the onlookers walked away.

'I'm fucked, bruv,' said Charlie.

'You'll think of something'.

'No. You don't understand, Ed. I have got to make the first payment to the construction firm by next week'.

'How much?'

'Five hundred grand'.

Eddie sat back. 'Five hundred. Fuck'.

'I'll lose everything I put into this if I don't find that money'. Charlie had a tight grip on the wheel with both hands. 'Ain't no way I can find that kinda cash'.

'Get the crew together. Talk it over'.

Charlie shook his head. 'I don't know if I can trust them'.

'What are you talking about?' said Eddie.

'We was stiffed on them diamonds. Maybe it was Angus? He could have been working with someone at De Boars. Gary could have been in on it as well? He brought us the job. Or maybe it was Bill? Or Mike, even? They both pushed us to do it. They made it happen. Fuck, it could be any of them'.

'You ain't thinking straight,' said Eddie, shaking his head.

Charlie paused for a moment, staring into space. 'Or, maybe I'm seeing things clearly for the first time?' he said as he placed one hand behind his younger's sibling's head. 'But, I need to know I can rely on you, Ed. No matter what happens next. I need to know you've got my back'.

'Sounds like we're going into battle' said Eddie.

Charlie nodded. 'We are,' he said.

The next morning Charlie and Eddie drove to a run-down beach bar near Cancelada, ten miles west along the coast from Marbella.

As he clambered out of Charlie's Porsche, Eddie paused for a moment to regard the ageing structure.

'This…is a restaurant?' he said. 'It looks more like a shipwreck'.

'I like it. It's private'.

The brothers entered the ramshackle building where they found Roger, Kenny and Carol sitting around a wooden table, looking glum. Charlie placed some money on the bar and, without checking to see if the elderly waiter was even aware of his presence, ordered two coffees before then walking over to the rest of the group. Eddie followed.

'Tell men,' said Charlie. 'What's happened?' He stared at Carol who gulped at her drink - which, despite the earliness of the hour, Eddie guessed was a Gin and Tonic - wiped her mouth on the back of her hand, and responded.

'They said my restaurant had cockroaches,' she said.

'It does,' said Roger.

'Every bloody bar and restaurant on the Costa has cockroaches. But they chose *mine* to close down,' said Carol.

'What about you, Rog?' said Charlie.

'Some asshole from the council came to my showroom. He had a copper with him. He demanded the registration documents, purchase invoices, MOTs, records of previous owners and a shitload more paperwork for every bleedin' car I have in stock. I've got over forty here, twenty more in Estepona'.

'Are some of them hot?' said Eddie.

Roger glanced back at him indignantly. 'Nah, they're all legit, but the fucker took everything and said I was prohibited from trading until he'd checked every document'.

'How long will that take?' asked Kenny.

'No idea. Weeks, probably. This is Spain, it could be months. I can't afford that, Charlie'.

'Ain't just us,' said Kenny. 'I heard they've been leaning on other Brit crews up and down the coast'.

'That's good,' said Charlie.

Carol eyed him like he had just broken wind. 'How's that good, Charlie?'

'Coz, it means they aren't just picking on us, don't it?'

'We've still got to do something,' said Roger. 'I'm pissing cash away if I can't shift no motors'.

'Same here,' said Carol. 'I had to throw away two fridge loads of food that had gone off'.

'They're putting' the squeeze on us, but it won't last. It never does'.

'It might be different, this time,' came a Spanish accent from behind them. Eddie shifted around to the source of the voice to see Charlie's lawyer, Guillem Montcada.

The barman approached with the coffees Charlie had ordered and asked Guillem if he wanted anything. If the lawyer heard the man, he chose to ignore him.

'This comes right from Madrid,' Montcada said, while pulling a chair towards the round table. He checked his surroundings before continuing. 'Spain needs to get into the EEC. The government applied in seventy-seven. It has taken much time, but now it is happening'.

'What's that got to do with us?' asked Carol.

Guillem puffed out his cheeks and snorted. 'Mrs Taylor, this is worth billions to Spain. They will do anything to make it happen now. And that includes agreeing to renew the extradition treaty with Britain'.

'For definite?' asked Roger while fidgeting with his lighter.

Montcada nodded, a stern expression on his face. 'We must assume so'.

'What will that mean for us?' asked Roger. 'Do we have to leave Spain?'

'The new treaty will not be retrospective, so it won't apply to…past indiscretions'. Roger seemed relieved. 'But it also means that you won't be able to leave the country. Not even for one day. If you leave and then return, they will arrest you, and they will put you on a plane to England'.

'So? Who we gotta bribe?' asked Kenny.

'You can bribe individuals,' said Guillem. 'But you cannot bribe the Spanish government. And besides, the local politicians will not want a fight with Madrid. They dependent on federal funding'.

Charlie had sparked up a cigarette, which he sucked on and released the resultant smoke upwards. 'So it's just like I've been sayin' all along. We have to keep our noses clean'.

Guillem nodded vigorously. 'Yes. The footage of Mr McNaughton hitting that reporter is all over Spanish and British television,' the lawyer said. He reached into his leather case, pulled out several British newspapers and laid them on the table. Eddie picked up a copy of the TODAY paper. The headline on page three was entitled, "COSTA DEL CRIME". He scanned the article.

'What's it say, Eddie?' asked Carol.

He stopped at one sentence and read it out aloud. 'It says that Parliament had a debate about the "Escaped British criminals living with impunity in Spain" '.

'Your newspapers and television stations are all covering the story,' said Guillem.

'Like flies on shit,' said Kenny.

'And Mikey locked in the slammer ain't helping none, is it?' asked Charlie. His question was directed at Guillem and seemed, to Eddie, to be more than a little rehearsed.

The lawyer uncrossed his legs and shifted to face Kenny and Roger, who were sitting to the right of him. 'It would be most advisable to post Mr McNaughton's bail so that the journalists focus on one of the other crews'.

Kenny sighed. 'Remind me how much that's gonna cost us'.

Guillem glanced at Charlie before he answered. 'In British Pounds, about fifty thousand'. Kenny shook his head, eyes to the ceiling.

Charlie leaned towards Roger. 'We got to club together and get him out,' he said. 'Mikey would do the same for us'.

'You sure about that?' said Kenny.

'You know he would, Ken'. Charlie's tone was terse. Eddie had flashbacks of a drill sergeant back at Colchester that had spoken to the soldiers in the same commanding manner.

Kenny thrust his hands into his pockets. 'If I do this, that flipping' gorilla has to pay me back,' he muttered.

'We'll work everything out at the end,' said Charlie. He glanced at Guillem as if to say 'now tell them the rest'.

The lawyer obliged. 'The bail is high because Mr McNaughton is considered a flight risk.

Carol snorted with laughter. 'How can any of these lads be a flight risk? You just said they can't go nowhere else,' she said.

'I am simply telling you what the magistrate told me, Mrs Taylor'. The lawyer seemed resentful, thought Eddie. Guillem turned towards Kenny. 'Now, even if you do post bail and Mr McNaughton is released, the light is still on you. All of you'. He studied at the men one by one. 'Therefore, you must all behave like angels now. You cannot afford any more incidents. You are walking on eggshells. You understand?'

Roger nodded, Kenny too.

'And there's something more,' said Guillem. 'I had a call this morning, just before I left my office to come here. Actually, it was more of a warning'.

'A warning? From who?' said Charlie.

'He was English. He did not give a name, but he made it clear he was representing one of the other groups'.

'Ronnie and Charlie's crew?' said Roger.

'Or them Brink Mat geezers?' said Kenny. 'We don't want to get on the wrong side of them fuckers'.

Guillem shook his head. 'I do not know'.

'What did he say?' asked Roger.

The lawyer took a deep breath, his eyes glancing at Charlie for the slightest of moments. 'He said that they were not pleased that there are many journalists in Spain. And he said the British newspapers and television knew where his clients lived and they knew things. Private things. He said that was…surprising'.

Eddie glared at his brother, who seemed distinctly unfazed by this revelation. 'Sounds like they think somebody slipped some information to the press?' he said.

Charlie shrugged, avoiding his brother's gaze. 'Better for us if we're not the centre of attention. Don't worry about that. Just keep your heads down'. He picked his car keys off the table. 'C'mon bruv. We're going to Mijas,' he said as he strode towards the door.

'What's in Mijas?' said Eddie.

'Not *what*, bruv. Who!'

CHAPTER TWENTY-THREE
TWIST SOME THUMBS

Sophia de Rodríguez Velázquez sat sipping from a porcelain espresso cup in La Cacharrería, an upmarket cafe in which she had a commercial interest, on the outskirts of Mijas's old town. Ernesto, her bodyguard and occasional lover, stood in the old building's entrance porch observing the street outside. A sign on the door informed passers-by that the establishment was closed for the day for "staff training".

Known by the local press as 'Doña Sophia', she was an influential figure in the regional Andalusian junta where she held the role of Minister of Finance, Industry and Energy. One day, most journalists were sure, she would become the region's president. To the outside world, she had been a devoted servant of the Socialist party since entering into politics in the late seventies after concluding a prominent, twenty-year career as a government prosecutor.

Her decision to join the socialists had been a surprise for many a political commentator, given her well-known uncle's long and fruitful role at the heart of Franco's rather more right-leaning regime. For the opportunistic Doña Sophia, however, politics was less about traditional policy positions, a deep-held aspiration to give back to society or, well, public service. She had very much adopted her uncle's sage advice to her to "make sure you always back the winner". Pinning her badge in 1977 to the revitalised, and quickly dominant, Socialist party's flag had presented no significant pangs of the soul for the ambitious Velázquez. Her calculated choice had paid off in abundance.

The country's rushed transition to democracy, post-Franco, had created a uniquely oblique period in Spain's recent history during which the nation was striving to rebuild the socio-political structures and institutions of federal, regional and local government. This period of flux generated many opportunities for those with what one might term 'a fluid moral compass'. Doña Sophia was such a person, and she had embraced the uncertainty that such a dynamic time offered to gain significant influence, power and wealth in a short space of time.

Ernesto waved to gain her attention. The *Inglés* were approaching. She reached for her packet of Sobranie Black Russians, extracted one of the gold and black cigarettes, placed it between her lips and lit it with a small silver lighter, then sat up straight and straightened her blouse and jacket. Her bodyguard had advised against meeting the Englishman. Ernesto was not, however, well appraised of certain prior business dealings that she had had with Charles Lawson.

The Lawson brothers approached La Cacharrería where Doña Sophia had insisted they meet after Charlie had called her secretary less than two hours earlier.

'Keep your eyes open,' said Charlie.

'For what?' said Eddie. 'You still haven't told me what we're doing here'. He grabbed his brother's forearm. 'Who are we meeting?'

'A woman called Doña Sophia. She works for the regional government. She's a minister'.

'A government minister?' 'How is that keeping a low profile?'

Charlie waved away the question. 'She's bent, bruv. And she owes me, big time'.

Charlie tried the front door but found it locked. He rapped on the solid oak and attempted to peer in through the small, tinted window. A few seconds later they heard a bolt being slid across. The door creaked open, and Charlie found himself confronted by a burly Spaniard in a sharp suit.

'Ernesto. How are you, mate?'

The man did not respond, merely stepping back to pull the inner door open for Charlie while gesturing towards Sophia Velázquez who sat facing them at a table towards the rear of the darkened space.

Eddie closed the front door behind him then followed, but the big Spaniard moved to obstruct his path further. 'Not you,' said Ernesto, eye to eye with Eddie.

Charlie turned back. 'He's with me. He's me brother'.

Sophia Velázquez spoke from the back of the room. 'Your brother will wait for you there'.

Charlie glanced back at Eddie, who stood facing the bodyguard. To any observers, they would have resembled two boxers at a weigh-in. 'You alright there, Ed?'

'I'm fine. Go do your thing'.

'You sit there,' said the Spaniard nodding towards a small bench seat behind Eddie. Eddie sat down and crossed his arms. The Spaniard did likewise, lowering himself onto a metal stool behind him.

Charlie strode towards the small table at the back of the restaurant where Sophia Velázquez sat facing him.

'Sophia, my darling. How the devil are you?'

She exhaled her cigarette smoke, her face stern and cold. Charlie pulled out a chair and sat down. The odour of her cigarette was intense, almost caramel sweet. He pointed at the packet of Sobranies. 'Blimey, they're a bit pungent. What are they?'

'What do you want, Charlie?'

He grinned. Sophia Velázquez had always been direct. Charlie had first met her four years earlier when she had sought his help to take down an internal party rival, Albert Betancourt - a rising star in the party and who had been a shoo-in for the role as the Socialist party's Minister for Agriculture, a position that Velázquez had also coveted. Betancourt would almost certainly have secured the position had certain information about his apparent use of recreational Class-A drugs not come to light. The revelation had come a few days before the regional president was expected to announce his cabinet choices. Instead, Betancourt, who denied the accusations most vociferously, found himself forced to stand down, and history took a different course; Doña Sophia dutifully stepping up to serve her party, and to take her first senior role.

'I need your help,' said Charlie.

'What help?' said Velázquez, her eyes trained upon Charlie's.

'A friend of ours is currently in police custody'.

'Michael McNaughton?' said Velázquez, before inhaling on the Sobranie again. 'This is not a matter I can help you with'.

Charlie reached over to the black cigarette packet, opened it and examined one of the cigarettes. 'How much do these flippin' things cost? Bleedin' expensive, I reckon'. He pushed the gold and black tube back into the packet and slid it back towards the woman.

Velázquez was shaking her head.'I am the minister of finance, industry and energy,' she said in a slow, assertive tone. 'The police, the criminal courts…these things I have no influence over'. She blew out a thin plume of smoke from the side of her mouth. 'Like I said. I cannot help you. You are wasting your time'.

'Actually, I was thinking you could have a word with Mr

Velázquez,' said Charlie. 'He's still the regional state prosecutor, ain't he?' He sat back, hands on his lap.

'My husband cannot help you,' she said.

'Can't or won't?'

'Cannot and would not,' said Velázquez.

Charlie chuckled and glanced back towards Eddie and the bodyguard. 'Does Mr Velázquez know you're shagging Ernesto over there?'

Sophia Velázquez laughed. 'Is that really the best you can do?'

'What?' said Charlie sarcastically. 'You'd rather break your devoted hubby's heart than to persuade him to help me out with one little problem?'

Sophia Velázquez leaned towards Charlie, an assured expression on her face. 'I can't believe I let you into my bed,' she said, shaking her head again.

'You didn't complain at the time,' he replied.

Velázquez sat back in her chair, straightening her blouse again. 'I am sorry to disappoint you, Charlie, but my husband and I have an open relationship. You will not get what you want with that squalid tidbit'. She reached for her cigarette packet and lighter, placed it into her red leather handbag and started to stand up. 'I suggest that you let the legal process take its course. Who knows? Perhaps Mr McNaughton will be released?' She laughed, clearly aware that this was unlikely. 'So, as I said. You are wasting your time. And also mine'.

Charlie remained still, unfazed. He reached into his jacket and pulled a brown envelope from the inside pocket. He placed it down on the table.

'How's young Alfredo getting on at university? Studying in Paris, ain't he?' He scrutinised her face.

For the first time, Sophia Velázquez seemed less assured. She shot Charlie a hostile glance. Her bodyguard, detecting that his charge was in some way uncomfortable, started to rise from where he sat opposite Eddie in the porch. Sophia Velázquez signalled at him to remain where he was and sat back down herself.

'What…is that?' she demanded, with obvious trepidation in her voice. Charlie slowly pushed the envelope towards her, but kept his forefinger firmly on it.

'Did you and Mr Velázquez know that little Alfy was…well, how should I put it?' he whispered. 'Oh, yeah. A dirty little scag-head queer?'

'You dare bring my son into this?' she said, her eyes rapidly reddening.

'I do what I have to, Sophia'. He lifted the hand from the envelope. Velázquez remained glaring at it. 'Open the fucking envelope,' he snarled.

She reached for the envelope, her hand trembling, and pulled out the contents, several black and white photos.

'That was in his boyfriend's flat,' said Charlie. 'They were at it for an hour or so, and after that, they shot up. My man thought they'd OD'd for a while. Not a pretty sight. Imagine if the papers got hold of these?' He shook his head with feigned sympathy.

Velázquez wiped a tear from her left eye and placed the photographs back in the envelope. 'I wonder, Charlie. I wonder if your brother over there knows what a monster you really are?'

Charlie smiled ruefully, glanced over towards Eddie, then fixed his gaze back on Doña Sophia. 'If Mikey ain't released within twenty-four hours,' he stabbed at the envelope, '…these will be on the desk of every newspaper editor across Spain before the end of the week'.

Velázquez, her eyes watering and her bottom lip quivering, fumbled around in her handbag for her silver lighter. 'You really are a piece of shit, Lawson. Your time will come. Mark my words'. She reached for her cigarettes, but Charlie snatched them away.

'You toffs. You all make the same mistake,' he said, peering into the packet. 'Do you know what that is?'

Velázquez looked up at him, pure venom in her eyes. 'Illuminate me,' she hissed.

'You underestimate me. When you look at me, and all you see is some low-life street hustler'. He pulled one of her cigarettes from the packet. 'But, you're going to look at me differently soon'. He snapped the cigarette into two pieces, crushed them between his fingers, and dropped the remnants onto the table. 'Good seeing you again, Sophia'. He pushed his chair back, stood up and walked towards the door.

Eddie and the Spanish bodyguard stood up in unison as Charlie approached.

'What was that about? Said Eddie.

Charlie winked at Ernesto and pulled the front door open and beckoned to his brother to leave.

'That,' said Charlie, '…was how you get things done on the Costa del Sol'.

CHAPTER TWENTY-FOUR
WALKING ON EGG SHELLS

Guillem Montcada, Charlie's lawyer, arrived at the villa that evening to deliver the news that the state prosecutor had decided, unusually, to drop the charges against Mike.

The lawyer accepted a glass of white wine from Charlie and sat down on one of the big cream couches. 'I do not know what you did, Charlie, nor who you spoke to and I have no wish to, but whatever it was, it seems to have been effective'.

Charlie lifted his wine glass towards Eddie, who sat perched on a barstool, and winked at him. 'So,' he said, 'What time should I get him?'

Guillem shook his head. 'You cannot. There will be paparazzi at the police station. And your stalker, that former English policeman, might be there with his camera. I will collect Mr McNaughton and take him home. Remember what I said. You are all walking on eggshells, yes?'

'Furry muff,' said Charlie. He lit a cigar and sat down opposite the lawyer. 'That's one problem sorted, what else do you have for me?'

Guillem cleared his throat. 'I made some enquiries with a contact at Scotland Yard,' he said.

'And?'

'I am told that Mr Pickering and his associates have…gone to ground'.

Eddie, who had been paying scant attention up to that point, now took a sudden interest. 'You think it was Pickering?' he asked, replaying the day of the robbery in his head. 'You think they were somehow involved?' He glanced at Charlie.

'Who knows? They could have been working with Angus all along? Or with De Boars? Maybe there weren't no diamonds from the start?' Charlie stood up, wineglass in one hand, cigar in the other. 'It would explain why Pickering shot the poor sod, don't you think?'

'But it was Mikey what suggested bringing Pickering's crew in on the job,' said Eddie.

Charlie pondered on Eddie's assertion for a moment. 'Maybe he was in on it as well?'

'Who?' said Eddie, confused. Charlie looked at him, one eyebrow raised. 'Wait, you can't be serious?'

'What are you saying, Charlie?' said Guillem.

'I'm just sayin' that it was Mikey what pushed that job on us, said Charlie, waving his cigar in the air. 'And Bill voted for it after promising he'd support me. You was there at the meeting when it happened, Ed. And Gaz…well, to be truthful, I ain't never trusted that bloke'.

'Charlie, you've run with these boys for years, now you're suggesting that they've all stitched you up,' said Eddie.

'What about Roger?' said Eddie.

Charlie pondered for a moment before responding. 'Nah, Rog doesn't have the brains for something like that'.

'Well, it all still sounds more than a little paranoid, don't you think?' said Eddie. Charlie exhaled a cloud of cigar smoke, eyes darting left and right, his mind considering the possibilities.

'I have to say that I agree with Eddie,' said Guillem.

'Perhaps you are right,' said Charlie after several seconds, in an unconvincing tone. 'But someone fucked us over, and that has caused me serious problems'. He took a gulp of his wine before continuing. 'Which is why I had to borrow five hundred grand from Juan Fernandez'.

'You did what?' said Guillem, aghast.

Charlie sat back down. 'I had to this place and the bar up as collateral. And my share in Roger's car dealership'.

The lawyer lifted one of his thin hands to his forehead as if Charlie's revelation had triggered an instant migraine.

'Who's Juan Fernandez?' asked Eddie, trying to keep up with each new revelation.

'Señor Fernandez is a prominent local businessman. Someone with much influence,' Guillem told him, before swivelling back to face Charlie. 'He has leverage over you now, Charlie. Why did you not tell me before?'

'I'm telling you now,' said Charlie. 'But I had no choice. Without that money, I would have lost the project'.

Eddie rose to his feet, the potential consequences of this development forming in his head. 'So, where do we go from here?'

Charlie peered at his lawyer for an answer.

'I have some better news,' said Montcada. 'You need Mr Taylor released in the UK, so you can establish if he remains loyal to you and your crew, yes?' He was holding his wineglass in front of him, twisting it back and forth between thumb and forefinger.

'Go on,' said Charlie.

'I spoke to the solicitor in England about the case and he told me the British police are on thin ice, and they know it. It would not take much to force their hand and ensure his release'.

'How are we supposed to do that?' said Charlie

'I think there is a way. Do you remember when you told Soparla to bug Ortega's office?' said the lawyer. 'After the investment pitch you did'.

Charlie raised an eyebrow. 'Of course'.

'Well, we didn't get much that I felt would be of use at the time but I went through them again yesterday. Does the name, "Sir Godfrey McCallister" mean anything to you?'

Charlie's eyes narrowed. 'Yes, he was the judge that sent me down in '72. Why?'

Montcada smiled and refilled his wine glass. It was almost as if he was delaying his answer to build suspense. He sipped from the glass.

'It seems,' he said, 'that Sir Godfrey is now the Director of Public Prosecutions for England and Wales'.

'So?' said Charlie.

Montcada reached into his jacket pocket and extracted an audio cassette. He held it out for Charlie to take. 'A call, two weeks ago between Daniel Ortega and the aforementioned Knight of the Realm'.

Charlie took the tape and examined it as if, by doing so, he would somehow understand the significance of the recording. 'What did they talk about?' he said.

'Nothing much at first. Sir Godfrey has property down here and is a keen golfer. It seems Ortega and he play golf often'.

'Guillem, you're killing me here,' said Charlie. 'Get to the point, for fuck's sake'.

Montcada chuckled. 'Just towards the end of the call. They mention a gathering that they had both attended some months previous. A party that they had both very much enjoyed. A special kind of party'.

Charlie's jaw dropped open. 'You're not talking about one of Madam Gigi's exclusive shindigs?'

'I am,' the lawyer replied, evidently very satisfied with himself.

'And they mention that?' said Charlie. Montcada nodded. Charlie punched the air and let out a bizarre whooping sound.

Eddie was well and truly perplexed. 'What the hell are you two talking about?' he asked.

Charlie answered. 'Madam Gigi is notorious. She's this French bird in her sixties who was brought up in a convent, but ended up running brothels for the Krauts during the war. When they liberated Paris, she had to escape and moved down here. She knew Franco, I was told. Now she runs these regular, invite-only gatherings for the rich and famous in her villa up in the hills. Naked birds everywhere. They're dressed up as bunny girls, cops, nurses, nazis. It's all whips and chains, squirty cream, stuff like that. Not just girls, there's plenty of pretty boys too, for the guests who are into that. Anything goes. There're bowls of condoms, sex toys, tubes of lube everywhere. It's like one of them Roman orgies'.

'She has about fifty paying guests going to each event,' said Montcada. 'Politicians, businessmen. Captains of industry. Media barons. They pay a lot of money to attend'.

'Why is this is relevant?' said Eddie.

'Lucian Soparla has a relationship with one of the escort girls that works at these events,' said Montcada.

'She takes covert photos for him,' said Charlie. He twisted to face the lawyer. 'Have you asked him? Does he have pictures of McCallister?'

Montcada grinned again. 'Several. And they are most explicit'.

Charlie grabbed Montcada by both ears and kissed him on the lips. 'Willy, you're a goddamned fucking lifesaver. I'll make a call to Godfrey-fucking-McCallister tomorrow and let him know just what I have on him. He'll have no choice but to drop the charges on Bill'.

'Mr McNaughton will be released tomorrow. Mr Taylor should be able to leave the UK in a few days too, now. After that we wait and see what they do next. If you are right, and either of them was a part of a…conspiracy, perhaps their actions will betray them?'

'Like how?' said Eddie. 'What actions?'

'If it was me,' said Charlie, staring at the burning end of his cigar, 'I'd get the hell out of town. A secret like that won't last five minutes down here. And they'd know what would happen if I found out'.

'What if they don't want to get out of town? What if they come after you instead?' said Eddie.

Charlie pulled up his shirt to reveal a black, snub-nosed revolver tucked into his belt. He stared at Eddie, his eyes devoid of emotion.

'Well, let us hope that there is another explanation,' said Guillem. He placed his glass down on the white coffee table and rose to leave.

'Call me when you've dropped Mike back to his apartment,' said Charlie. Guillem nodded. 'And tell him to keep a low profile. Tell him what you said to us…about walking on eggshells'.

'As you say, Charlie' said Guillem. 'Good night, Eddie'. Eddie raised his glass to bid Guillem farewell before gulping down the remaining contents.

'Nightcap?' said Charlie.

Eddie shook his head. 'Nah,' he said as he stood up. 'I'm done in'.

Charlie patted him on the shoulder. 'Yeah, too much drama for one day, right?' He grinned. 'I'm locking up,' he said, as he started towards the front door, a set of keys in hand.

Eddie paused, watching his brother walking away.

'I think you're wrong, Charlie. About Mike and the others'.

Charlie kept walking. 'I guess we'll see'.

CHAPTER TWENTY-FIVE
DONE A BUNK

Three days later

Eddie woke early after a restless night. At least, he noted, the painful wartime nightmares seemed to have gone. He had not had one of those unwelcome intrusions for a few weeks.

Perhaps they were gone for good?

He drew the curtains. It was still dark, although the sun's imminent arrival was being telegraphed by the peachy-red hue on the horizon. He peeked towards the alarm clock by the side of the bed. It was 5:53am.

'Fuck it,' he thought. 'I'm going for a hike'.

Three hours later, Eddie sat perched upon a rocky outcrop on top of La Concha, the iconic mountain that dominates the horizon north of Marbella. His tee-shirt was drenched, and he was panting. He had driven up to the *refugio* - a rustic hotel for ramblers on the mountain's north-easterly haunches - in a black Ford Sierra XR4i that Roger had lent him a few days earlier. Eddie had parked the car before marching uphill at full pelt, not stopping for rest until he had arrived at the 1,200-metre-high peak. He pulled a foil-wrapped round of cheese sandwiches from his backpack and devoured them quickly before downing a can of what he decided was a bad, Spanish imitation of Vimto. Why had he not brought water instead? he thought. He loosened his boot laces, leaned back against a granite block and surveyed the landscape before him.

To the east, to the left of him, Eddie could see the sprawl of Malaga city and decided he should get his ass over to explore it sometime. Marbella town, Puerto Banus and the surrounding built-up areas lay a lot lower in front of him. Far off to his right, he could see the Rock of Gibraltar, and beyond that, the long peaked ridges of the Dif mountains over in Morocco. It was a majestic vista. Breathtaking. He lit up a Marlboro and closed his eyes, a fresh gust triggering an involuntary shiver of his bare, sweat-laden shoulders. This was bliss. He had not been this at ease for a very long time. The trials and tribulations of the last few weeks, the lingering guilty pain from having left his wife and daughter, and the brutal intrusive memories from the South Atlantic had evaporated.

Eddie could have sat there for hours, had a noisy group of north-European walkers not been approaching. He strapped up his backpack, re-tightened his laces and stood up and after taking one last glance at the beautiful scene and committing it to memory, he began the trek back down to the car five miles, and several hundred metres below.

Eddie arrived back at Charlie's villa at a little after eleven-thirty, planning to soak in a bath before rustling up a hearty meal. His plans were thwarted, however, when he found Roger, Kenny and Charlie in the middle of a heated discussion on the driveway.

Eddie dropped the backpack on the ground next to his brother. 'Problem?' he said, his tone failing to mask his weariness.

'Yeah,' said Charlie. 'We ain't seen Mike since he got released'. He shot Eddie a glance that said "I told you so".

'It's only been a couple of days,' said Roger. 'He'll turn up. He's probably gone on a bender. You know what he's like'.

'What if he ain't?' said Kenny. 'What if he's done a runner? He's even more broke than us, his businesses have been closed, and his bird's dumped him. Why wouldn't he just pack his stuff and fuck off, hey?'

Roger gave Kenny a threatening look. 'Is that what you'd do?' he asked.

Kenny paused, no doubt regretting his choice of words. 'Nah, course not,' he replied.

Eddie was still processing what Kenny had just said about Veronica leaving Mike. 'Veronica and Mike split up?' he interjected.

Charlie rolled his eyes and stabbed an index finger in his brother's sternum. 'You can put that thought right out of your head,' he whispered.

'He's done a bunk, I know he has,' said Kenny. 'We can kiss good bye to that poxy bail money'.

'Hang on a sec, didn't he buy some woman a flat?' said Eddie, feeling that he was the only person present with a clear head. 'Before we went to England?'

'Of course!' said Roger. 'In Estepona. He's got a Spanish bird there. Raquel, weren't it?'

'You're right. I'd forgotten about that,' said Charlie, shaking his head. He pointed at Kenny and Roger. 'The apartment he got her is down by the port, near that shitty Irish bar. What's it called?'

'The Randy Leprechaun?' said Roger.

'That's the one,' said Charlie who was now stomping towards the open front door to the villa. 'Me and Eddie will meet you there'.

'I just ran up a mountain,' said Eddie realising that chances of enjoying a long, hot bath were rapidly diminishing. 'I need a wash'.

'Shower later, you ponce. This is important'.

Eddie jogged towards the house to avoid the curtain of gravel that was being thrown in his direction by Kenny's silver Mercedes as it pulled away.

Charlie's Porsche pulled up on a service road above the port area in Estepona. The place was a hotspot for holidaymakers and was already full with groups of tourists milling around.

'Remind me to buy you some bleedin' deodorant before we head off,' said Charlie as he clambered out of the car.

'I said I needed a wash,' Eddie said, but his brother's attention was elsewhere. Charlie had spotted a commotion at the entrance to an apartment block across the street, and he was already rushing towards it.

Eddie peered through the crowds to see two women who appeared to be wrestling on the ground. One of them was a curvy woman with brown skin and long black hair. The other, Eddie realised, was Veronica.

He barged past a group of teenage kids and sprinted towards the melee. As he got there, he saw Mike exiting from the building, flanked by Kenny and Roger.

'Fuckin' hell,' said Mike upon seeing his two girlfriends locked in near mortal combat, no little amusement on his face.

Charlie lifted both women to their feet, placing himself between the warring parties. 'Enough,' he shouted. The Spanish woman took a step back to sit down on a small wall, whimpering. Veronica stood, her arms crossed, glaring past Charlie at her love rival.

'What the hell are you doin'?' said Mike to Veronica. His answer came in the form of a vicious slap across the face.

Eddie grabbed hold of her and manoeuvred her away. 'I thought you didn't care about him anymore?' he whispered.

'That ain't the point,' she replied, a line of phlegm emitting from her mouth.

'That bitch crazy,' said the Spanish woman. 'She hit me. In face. Look!' She touched the inside of her lip and held out her hand to Charlie to show the fresh blood.

Charlie reached for his wallet and extracted several notes, which he placed into the Spanish woman's hands. 'Go get yourself a drink, there's a good girl'. He lifted the woman up and directed her back into the apartment, before returning to face Roger and Kenny. 'You two get Veronica back to her car and make sure she gets home. Me and this dumb bastard are going to have words'. He was pointing at Mike.

Veronica stomped past Eddie towards her car, Roger and Kenny attempting to keep up. 'You okay?' he asked. She ignored him.

'Ed. C'mon,' shouted Charlie, who was now escorting Mike towards the open doors of The Randy Leprechaun pub.

The pub's interior was almost empty, its patrons preferring the sun-soaked seating outside. Charlie shoved Mike towards a wooden bench in the corner. 'Sit down, you fuckin' idiot,' Charlie ordered.

Mike, looking like a scorned puppy, did as he was told.

A waiter walked towards them and handed out food menus. 'Good afternoon, gentlemen. Can I tell you about our specials?'

'Fuck off,' said Charlie, still glaring at Mike. Eddie gestured at the startled man to leave, pulled up a stool and sat down next to Mike.

'Go on then,' said Charlie, arms folded. 'Tell me'.

'Tell you what?' Mike replied.

'Tell me what you were up to'.

'Nothing. Just wanted to see Raquel, didn't I?' said Mike. He folded his arms too, the pair of them looking like angry lovers.

Charlie kept glaring, saying nothing until Mike relented. 'Okay, fine. I spoke with the Moroccan geezer'.

Charlie almost exploded. 'I fuckin' knew it. You just can't do what you're told, can you?'

'What Moroccan geezer'?' asked Eddie, feeling somewhat out of the picture. Charlie responded.

'That dope dealer what I specifically told Mike not to talk to a few weeks ago and several times before that,' he said. 'Coz, that's the last fuckin' thing we need to get caught up in right now'.

'But Charlie, don't you see? It's our way out of this mess,' said Mike, still unwilling to toe the line. 'He's got a shedload of the stuff but nobody to move it. He needs us. It would be a bloody bargain. All we need -'.

Charlie leapt forward and pushed Mike back with both hands. 'What don't you understand, you stupid bastard?' Mike's shoulders dropped, and he swung away, exasperated. 'Guillem explained it to you. They're cracking down on us. All of us. They've agreed on the extradition treaty. You're putting us all at risk, Mikey. One more incident like this and…and we're fucked. Fucked, you get it? Do yer?' Mike nodded. 'I need your fuckin' word on this,' said Charlie, holding Mike by the collar.

Mike stared at Charlie, and through gritted teeth, said, 'Fine, I'll drop it'. Charlie held his gaze for a moment, searching for signs of deceit, before relaxing his grip and sitting back.

'I know you're just trying to fix the situation, Mike. But you gotta do things my way'.

Mike straightened his shirt. 'I always do, Charlie. And look where it's got us'. He shook his head, still smarting from the reprimand, and rose to leave.

'I need you back in Marbella,' said Charlie.

'What, so you and your baby brother can keep a watch on me?' said Mike.

'If that's what it takes'. Charlie stood up and tried to put an arm around Mike, but Mike pushed the peace offering away.

'I'm going back. But not coz you're ordering me to'. He shot Eddie a threatening glance. 'But coz, I am going to find out who told my Veronica about Raquel'. He pushed a chair aside, barged past Eddie - nearly sending him to the floor - and stomped away.

Eddie sat down next to his brother. 'What was that about?' he asked

'He's just pissed off I did that in front of you. Relax, this is good'.

'How is this good?'

'Because,' replied Charlie, 'If Mike was involved in cheating us on the diamonds, he wouldn't have been off trying to do some stupid fucking dope deal, would he?'

Eddie thought about it. It made sense. Mike had come to Estepona hoping to organise a deal to raise quick cash. It was not the behaviour of someone sitting on a trove of diamonds.

'I guess you're right,' he said. 'But I still got the feeling he has it in for me'. He glanced out the window to see Mike clambering into a grey Audi 80 rental car. An icy shiver ran through his spine. 'You don't reckon he knows about -'.

'You and Veronica?' said Charlie, already ahead of him. 'Let's hope not. But best you watch your back tonight'.

'What's happening tonight?' asked Eddie, unaware of any plans.

'We're hitting the beach club again'.

'The place where I had to pull Kenny out of the pool?' said Eddie, in disbelief.

'That's the one'. Charlie seemed surprised. 'What, didn't I tell you? Them photos of the posh toff at the sex party worked a treat. They released Bill. He's back from England later, and we're throwing him a party.'

CHAPTER TWENTY-SIX
GOING ALL IN

Charlie drove down to Marbella Beach Club. They pulled up outside the venue, next to a lengthy queue of waiting attendees, or 'plebs' as Charlie referred to them. He tossed the keys to one of the parking attendants and, as usual, a doorman recognised Charlie as he approached and beckoned the brothers towards the VIP entrance.

'Busy one tonight!' said Charlie while slapping several bills into the man's hand.

'Yes, Mr Lawson,' the doorman replied. He seemed a little nervous. 'Your group is at a corner table on the private patio this evening'.

'Hey? Why aren't we at our usual table near the pool?' The doorman leaned towards Charlie and lowered his voice.

'It's the new owner. He had explicit instructions'.

'New owner?' said Charlie.

'Yes, Señor Ortega'.

'Ortega?' said Charlie, his surprise and anger evident. 'Daniel Ortega?'

The doorman nodded and pointed to the growing queue at the door. 'I must go'. Charlie remained rooted to the spot, still processing the news.

'Who's Ortega?' asked Eddie.

'A pain in my fuckin' arse, bruv. That's who'. Charlie nudged Eddie on the elbow. 'C'mon, let's find the others'.

Eddie followed his brother towards the building and to where another security man waved them towards their table. It was hidden from the already-crowded pool area behind a four-foot-high, dark-tinted glass barrier, and underneath a series of dark wooden beams wrapped in grape-laden vines. Most people might consider it a pleasant spot, but Eddie knew that his brother had organised the evening to show the Marbella who's who, that it was business as usual; that the crew were still together, and relevant. Whoever this "Ortega" person was, they had scuppered his brother's plans.

Eddie spotted Bill excitedly talking with Roger and Kenny, each with a fat cigar in one hand and a cocktail glass in the other. Carol and Judy sat together holding extravagant cocktails, in full gossip exchange mode.

'So, did she take him back or what?' said Carol.

'Dunno,' replied Judy, too engrossed to notice Charlie and Eddie passing by. 'But Roger reckoned Mikey knows she had it off with Eddie and he -'.

Carol, finally realising that the brothers were standing within earshot, beckoned at her friend to shut up. It was too late. Eddie had heard.

'Evening Charlie,' said Carol, meekly. 'Hi Eddie'.

'Ladies,' said Charlie.

Eddie tapped on his brother's elbow to get his attention. 'Did you hear that?' he whispered.

'We'll deal with it,' said Charlie.

'Deal with it? How?' Eddie demanded, but Charlie was already giving Bill a bear hug.

'Cor blimey Bill, didn't they feed you when you was inside?' he said, pinching Bill's waist. Bill laughed.

'He didn't like the menu in the remand centre,' snorted Kenny. 'No paella'.

'Food was bleedin' awful, Charlie. Worse than when we was in the Borstal,' said Bill. 'First thing Gary did when I got out was to take me for a posh dinner uptown'. He offered Charlie a cigar. 'Cost a bleedin' fortune'.

'A fortune, hey?' said Charlie, shooting Eddie a suspicious glance. 'Well, it's good to have you back again. There's a lot we need to get you up to speed with, though'.

'So the lads said,' said Bill, somewhat solemnly. 'What d'yer reckon happened?'

'Not here, Bill. The walls have ears and all that'.

'Oh, yeah. Right-ho,' said Bill. 'And thanks for getting me out. To tell you the truth, I thought you'd all forgotten about me at one point'.

Charlie smiled and put his arm around Bill's shoulder and waved at the revelry all around them. 'Just enjoy the night, okay. We can talk business tomorrow'.

Kenny and Bill were nodding in agreement, but Roger was looking straight past them at something else. 'Charlie,' he said. 'It's Ortega'.

Eddie followed Roger's gaze to see a well-groomed Spaniard in a tailored suit who was mounting the marble steps to the building accompanied by an attractive brunette and several burly men. Eddie watched as Ortega held the wooden door open for his female companion. As he did so, the Spaniard looked straight across to where the British contingent were, and grinned. It was not an expression designed to offer warmth, thought Eddie. Rather, it was one that wreaked of confidence and control. It was deliberate, and it carried a threat. It said, *this is my patch, and you are not welcome.*

'Fuckin' dago thinks he owns the place,' said Kenny.

'He does,' Charlie replied. 'He bought it. The geezer on the door told me as we came in'.

Roger lowered himself down onto one of the padded chairs. 'So that's why they've hidden us away in this corner,' he said.

Kenny was still staring at the building into which Ortega

had entered. One of the Spaniard's minders stood outside, arms crossed. 'Reckon we should go in there? Tell that smarmy cunt where he can shove his fuckin' club?'

'Calm down, mate,' said Charlie. 'Remember what Guillem said. We can't afford no trouble right now'.

A disturbance in the crowd caught Eddie's attention. A well-built, middle-aged man in a suit stumbled from the dance floor like a combine harvester emerging from a field of mature corn. He was shoving dancers in every direction, ambivalent to their complaints.

'Is that Mike?' said Carol as he arced towards them, a beer bottle in one hand, the other grasped around Veronica's wrist, pulling her behind him. Eddie placed his drink down on a nearby table. His pulse had quickened, and he already had the familiar pre-fight feeling stirring in his gut. They watched as the pair walked towards them; Mike looking like an undefeated boxer approaching the ring, Veronica with her eyes to the floor like a prisoner of war. Mike released Veronica and pointed towards an empty seat.

'Sit down,' he commanded. Veronica stared up at Eddie and mouthed, 'He knows'. He spied a bruise on her arm.

Eddie's blood was boiling. 'Did you hit her?' he said, his fists curled ready for action. Mike ignored him and lifted the beer bottle to his lips to take an extended swig.

Charlie moved between them, putting a hand on his brother's chest. 'Eddie, not here -'.

Eddie, however, was not for placating. 'I said, did you fucking hit her?' he repeated.

Mike twisted towards Eddie. His face was grim, his pupils large and eyes bloodshot. 'Did you fuck her?' he drawled.

'Oh, Christ,' said Charlie under his breath. Eddie and Mike both pushed Charlie aside to stand toe to toe.

'She says you didn't,' said Mike. 'But I reckon she's lying. So? Did yer, soldier boy. Did you fuck my missus?'

Eddie held Mike's glare, saying nothing.

Roger attempted to intervene. 'C'mon lads -' he said, but Mike shoved him back.

'I want the truth. Did you fuck my missus?' he repeated.

'Last I heard,' said Eddie, 'She wasn't your missus no more'.

Mike smirked, before pushing Eddie full-force with both hands. Eddie was braced, but he was still sent backwards into a table. A beer glass fell onto the floor and shattered. He took a step to one side, steadied himself and adopted a combat stance.

Mike laughed. 'Try your luck, pretty boy'. Eddie could see that Mike was now wearing his brass knuckle-duster on his right hand.

'Stop it,' shouted Charlie, but it was to no avail. His brother's momentary interruption was all Eddie needed. He pushed himself off from his rear foot, blocked Mike's right arm with his left forearm and delivered an uppercut to Mike's chin with his right. It was a blow that would have ended most bar brawls, but his opponent was more robust than most opponents.

Mike rubbed his mouth with the back of his hand and spat blood to the floor. 'That all you got, you pansy?' He lurched towards Eddie, feigned with his right, and swivelled to deliver a blow towards Eddie's stomach with his left, but Eddie anticipated the move; hundreds of hours in the boxing ring and several years of close-quarters combat training in the army had armed him with a muscle memory that put him at a distinct advantage in any fistfight.

He twisted to his left, sucked in his stomach to allow Mike's fist to punch into thin air and, with Mike now unbalanced, hit him to the side of the jaw with a twisting clenched fist. Mike's face shuddered and his eyes closed, and he fell sideways onto a table, sending it and all of its contents to the floor in a crescendo of noise.

Two security guards ran towards them.

Charlie blocked their passage with outstretched arms and his patented charm. 'It's alright, fellas. Just a minor disagreement between friends. It's over. We'll pay for any damages, don't worry'. He reached for his wallet.

Eddie remained in a fighting stance, glaring over the now mumbling and bleeding Mike.

Roger and Bill reached down to lift Mike up from the broken glass and spilt drinks and placed him into an upright chair. 'He's in a right state,' said Roger to Charlie while dabbing blood from Mike's face with a hanky. 'We should get him home'.

'He was in a state before we got here,' said Veronica, still ensconced on her chair. 'He's been snorting coke all afternoon'.

'What?' said Charlie. 'Mate, that's not you. What were you thinking?' He curled his hand around Mike's head.

'Can't let the kids have all the fun, can I?' slurred Mike. 'So, you gonna tell me, Charlie?'

'Tell you what?'

Mike lifted a weary arm and pointed towards Eddie. 'What about her…and…and your brother?'

Charlie shook his head. 'Mate, no,' said Charlie. 'That night Veronica stayed over. She slept in my spare room'.

'I thought you left with that blonde tart?' said Mike, trying to reconstruct the events of that night several weeks earlier.

'Nah, turned out she had a husband back at home. I got a quick blowjob before she buggered off in a taxi. We all went back to my place. Veronica, me and Ed. She was trollied and went straight to bed. Eddie and me, we were up for hours talking. We both passed out on the sofas. Nothing happened, mate'.

'You promise me, Charlie?' said Mike.

'Get it into your thick skull, nothing happened'. Charlie patted Mike on his cheek. 'I promise'.

Mike lifted his head towards Veronica. 'I'm sorry, luv,' he said. 'I shouldn't have -'.

'It's just a bruise,' she said, faking a smile.

'C'mon, let's get you out of here,' said Roger. He glanced at Judy. 'Mike can sleep it off at ours'.

Judy sighed and put her drink down. 'Flipping hell, can't we have one bleedin' night out without someone having a punch up?' she asked, before picking up her jacket.

'Here, me and Bill will come with you,' said Carol.

'Call me in the morning,' said Charlie as he watched them leave. 'Let me know how he is'. He swung to his brother. 'You alright, bruv?' Eddie nodded. 'Good. Good,' said Charlie. 'After all that drama, I need a leak. Kenny, go get us a round in'. He headed towards the main building. Kenny rose as instructed and made towards the bar.

Eddie felt a gentle hand curl around his bicep.

'My hero'.

'Are you serious? My brother just stone-cold lied to his best friend for us'. He pried her fingers from his arm and thrust his hands into his jacket pocket.

'You think Charlie lied for us?' she said, dismissing Eddie's assertion with a sarcastic laugh. 'You don't know your brother at all'. Eddie wasn't listening, he was patting his trouser pockets. They were empty. He had lost Charlie's keys.

Shit.

'Lost something?' Veronica said in a childlike tone. Eddie was now scanning the floor.

'Keys,' he said while lifting a wooden chair to peer underneath. 'Charlie gave them to me to look after'. He dropped to his knees to look under a heavy wooden table.

'Charlie gave you keys? For what?'

'Just…keys. But they're important. I need to find them,' he said. He pointed towards an arrangement of plants in clay pots near where he had been standing when Mike and Veronica had arrived. 'See if they are over there'. Eddie lifted another table, then several more chairs. Nothing. 'Fuck,' he cursed. Veronica remained crouched over the plant pots, her back to him. 'Any luck?' he asked.

'Nothing here,' she said.

'Fuck,' he swore again. His head was spinning. How would he explain this to Charlie?

'What's so special about them?' she asked, still facing away from him.

Eddie did not have time to answer. Kenny returned, panting. 'We got more trouble,' he said, gasping for air. 'Charlie needs you'.

'Give us a sec, Ken. I've lost -'.

'Eddie. He needs us now!' The expression on Kenny's face told Eddie that whatever trouble Charlie was in, it was serious.

'Okay,' said Eddie. 'Veronica, keep looking. I need to find them'. Eddie started after the already departing Kenny.

Veronica watched until Eddie and Kenny had vanished into the crowd, before she unclasped her hand to reveal the set of keys.

One was smaller, tubular and made of steel. The other was larger, flat and made from brass. It was a double-sided, seven-lever mortice lock and bore the logo of the safe manufacturer, Schwab - a logo she had seen before, two years ago, in the secure room underneath Charlie's bar.

She dropped the keys into her handbag and pulled it over her shoulder.

Eddie followed Kenny out into the open area where Charlie stood waiting for them behind the trunk of a palm tree. There were several hundred people in the club now. It was loud, bright and chaotic.

'Kenny said we've got trouble?' Eddie asked.

'We do,' his brother replied and lifted an index finger towards a group of young men gathered around a table thirty feet away on the opposite side of the pool. They were loud, animated and, from their accents, most definitely from East London.

The beach club was located in a basin-shaped dip between two gentle slopes and with no breeze to speak of, the smoke from hundreds of cigarettes and joints hung low in an unnatural cloud making it hard to see.

Eddie squinted at what Charlie was pointing at. 'No fucking way,' he exclaimed upon recognising the first of the group. It was Bobby Pickering, and his entire crew accompanied him.

Eddie and Charlie glanced at each other. 'What the fuck?' said Eddie.

'I'm going over there,' said Charlie. 'Kenny, get Veronica out of here'. He reached into his pocket and took out the car park token. He held it out for his brother. 'Go get my car and be ready to get out of here'.

'Fuck that, I'm staying with you'.

'No, you're not,' his brother insisted. 'We can't antagonise them, and I want to know I can get out of here sharpish. Go and don't let them see you'.

Eddie sighed. He had no desire to abandon Charlie, but he had to agree with his brother's logic. 'Be careful. This ain't no coincidence'.

'I know that, Ed,' said Charlie. 'Go on, go'.

Eddie swivelled around and started making his way around the pool, masking his face with his left hand but still monitoring the East End crew. Charlie waited thirty seconds before walking towards them. Eddie saw Bobby Pickering push himself up from a sun lounger upon seeing Charlie. He held out his arms and the two men embraced, after which Charlie pulled up a chair and sat down. Eddie was well out of earshot, but he could imagine what conversation was about. He studied the group's body language. All seemed calm. Still, he thought, there could be no good reason for Pickering's crew being in Marbella and in this club in particular.

He was just about to head out to collect the Porsche when he spotted another face he recognised - Jeremy Crampton. A cameraman accompanied the overweight television reporter. They must know Charlie was in the club, he thought. Shit. He peered back at Charlie and the East Enders, who remained locked in conversation. Charlie was talking in an animated manner but seemed relaxed. There was no imminent danger there, he decided. Crampton, however, was clearly making his way towards Charlie and the East End crew.

Eddie put the parking token back in his trouser pocket and tailed Crampton through the crowd of dancers. He had to prevent Crampton getting that meeting on video, but there was no way Eddie could get to Charlie before the camera was in range. What to do? Cause a distraction somehow? But what? How?

Then he saw his opportunity.

Crampton was pushing through the crowd close to the pool edge. The cameraman was right behind him. Eddie darted between a man who resembled Simon Le Bon and a young woman who was the spitting image of Sheena Easton. The man swore at Eddie as he shot past. 'Simon' and 'Sheena' could get it on later, he thought as he reached the back of the cameraman. He hoisted the man upwards, stepped to his right and dropped him and his equipment into the pool.

The splash caught Crampton's attention, and he spun around to face Eddie. The sight of the cameraman - who, it quickly became apparent, could not swim - splashing around in the pool, caught the attention of most of the people in the club including Charlie, Bobby Pickering and his entire crew.

Eddie peered at his brother, who stood open-mouthed, staring straight back at him. Charlie started to shout. Eddie could not hear what his brother was saying, but he could lip-read well enough.

'What the fuck are you doing?' Eddie could do nothing to reply, except to shrug.

A lifeguard in tight black speedos dived into the pool to rescue the cameraman who was now bubbling underwater.

Eddie felt a hand grab his jacket. He twisted with an instinctive movement and blocked the unknown assailant with his left forearm and prepared to strike with his right fist only to realise it was only Crampton.

The reporter was incandescent with rage, saliva hanging from his top lip as he shouted. 'You arsehole,' he screamed.

'Sorry, mate. It was an accident,' Eddie said, unable to suppress a wry grin.

Crampton stepped towards him - so close, Eddie could smell his breath. The reporter had eaten fish not long ago. 'Fuck you,' Crampton screamed while stabbing at Eddie's chest with a stubby forefinger. 'And fuck that idiot brother of yours'.

'Blimey, someone's got a potty mouth when he's off-camera,' said Eddie.

'I'll get you,' said Crampton. 'Just you see. I'm doing a special show all about Charlie's crew. I'm going to burn them, and I'm going to burn you. You...you piece of shit, bastard son of a whore'.

Eddie grabbed Crampton's wrist and twisted it to force the reporter to his knees. 'Say that again, I dare you,' Eddie snarled.

'I know what you are, Edward Lawson. And I'm not frightened of you or your pretend brother'.

Eddie twisted Crampton's wrist another ten degrees, and the reporter yelped out in pain. 'You may not be frightened, but if I break your arm, it will still fucking hurt'.

'Eddie! Enough'. Eddie peered up to see Charlie, who grasped the back of Eddie's collar and pulled him up. 'They called the fuzz. We gotta go'.

Eddie released Crampton and followed after Charlie. 'Simon Le Bon' gawped at Eddie as he sprinted past.

Charlie pushed in front of the queue for the parking attendant. 'Gimme my keys,' Charlie demanded.

'Oi, there's a fucking queue,' the man at the front of the line shouted. He was tall and well built, but he still fell to the floor like a sack of potatoes when Charlie slugged him in the gut.

Eddie stepped towards the shocked attendant. 'My brother would really like his car keys now'. He held up the numbered token.

The man reached into the wooden box where the guest's keys were kept and found the Porsche's fob. 'Here you go, sir,' he said, his lip quivering. 'It's…it's over there'. The man pointed to the Porsche parked under a palm tree.

'Much obliged,' Eddie replied and handed Charlie the keys.

'If there's so much as a speck of bird shit on my car, I'm coming back for you,' Charlie said to the attendant as he strode away towards his car.

As they got into the car, Eddie asked, 'So? What's going on?'

Charlie twisted the key in the ignition, and the engine burst into life. He slammed the gear stick into first, and the Porsche pulled away with a squeal from the tyres. 'Well?' Eddie tried again.

'They had to leave England in a hurry. Police was on to 'em. They think someone ratted them out'.

'Fuck,' said Eddie. 'But why are they here?' Charlie ignored a set of red lights at a junction, drove straight out onto the main road across the traffic, threw the car into a tight left turn then floored the throttle. A police car sped past on the opposite carriageway a few seconds later.

'He said he'd tell us tomorrow morning,' he said. 'When we meet them at their place'.

CHAPTER TWENTY-SEVEN
FUCKING COCKNEYS

'I don't understand why we're doing this alone,' said Eddie.

It was the morning after the events at the Marbella Beach Club, and he was standing next to the silver Porsche in a secluded lay-by off the road to Istan.

Charlie stood nearby, urinating under a pine tree. They were about three hundred metres up, and overlooking the Embalse de la Concepción, the vast freshwater reservoir that supplies Marbella and much of the Costa.

Charlie zipped up his fly, wiped his hands on his jeans and walked back to the car. 'Pickering wanted it this way. Just me and you. They are sure that someone grassed on them. They think it was one of our crew'.

'That's bullshit,' said Eddie. 'We ain't got nothing to gain in them getting made'.

'I know, Ed. But someone ratted them out. They had to do a bunk overnight. Left everything behind. Pickering is fucking pissed, and he wants answers. More than that. He wants half the haul'.

'Didn't you tell him the diamonds were fake?'

'Course I did, but they read the papers. They think we made off with ten million quid's worth'.

Eddie sized up a large pine cone and aimed it at a spot between two saplings while picturing Keegan's goal against Argentina in 1980. His football skills let him down, however, and he sliced it against the Porsche's front wing. Charlie groaned. 'Sorry, bruv'. He rubbed the new blemish off the silver paint with his sleeve. So what now?'

'We wait. They'll be here soon. We follow them to wherever they're hiding away and, well, tell 'em how it is'. Charlie lit up a cigarette.

'And that's it?' said Eddie. 'What if they don't buy it?'

'Then we talk it out. We make things square, somehow. Nobody wants a war'.

'I'm not so sure. I've been around a lot of nutters in my time, and I'm tellin' you, Pickering's not right in the head'.

The sound of a car approaching interrupted the conversation. They watched as a grey Citroen emerged from behind a bank of shrubs from the main road. 'That's them,' said Charlie.

The Citroen pulled up alongside the Porsche, the engine still running. Eddie could see there were two men inside as Charlie approached the vehicle. Gerry Lannigan, Pickering's junior lieutenant, wound down the driver's window.

'How we doin' this then?' said Charlie. Lannigan stared at him without answering, a stony expression on his face. Eddie readied himself, expecting the young Londoner to produce a gun. 'Well?' Charlie tried again.

'Follow us. Don't get too close,' Lannigan replied, before starting to pull away.

'Right,' said Charlie. 'I guess we follow them'.

The Lawson brothers got back into the Porsche and followed the French saloon. After what Eddie guessed was about twenty minutes, they pulled off the tarmac road and onto a long dirt and gravel track that led into a dense pine forest. The trail ascended around small hillocks for about a mile. The Porsche was struggling with the undulations, and the Lawsons were being flung around inside the German coupe.

'Fuck,' shouted Charlie as the car hit yet another rock. 'This is killing my suspension'.

'That might be the least of your worries in a minute. Look,' said Eddie, pointing at a single-story stone building that had just emerged into view. Bobby Pickering stood outside, flanked by four other men. 'We're outnumbered seven to two if this goes south. I hope you know what you're doing, bruv'.

'It's gonna be fine. Trust me'.

They pulled up near the cottage and Charlie killed the engine. Pickering walked towards them. 'Enjoy the ride?' he said, grinning. 'C'mon, kettle's on'. He turned and walked back to the building's open front door.

Eddie looked at Charlie. 'All this for a cup of tea?' he whispered. Charlie shrugged and climbed out of the Porsche. Eddie followed his brother.

Three of the East End crew stood outside as sentries. One was carrying a pump-action shotgun, the other two had pistols stuffed into their waists. They scrutinised Eddie and Charlie as they entered the cottage.

Pickering was sitting at a wooden table upon which were three mugs of tea. He gestured towards two empty chairs. 'Ain't no sugar, sorry,' he said.

Eddie moved to a chair that offered the best view of the door. Charlie sat opposite Pickering. 'Okay, we came. So let's talk,' he said.

Pickering pulled a packet of cigarettes and a metal lighter from out of his shirt pocket. He extracted one cigarette, lit it and sat back, saying nothing.

'Bobby, what do you want?' said Eddie. Charlie shot him a look - let me do the talking!

Pickering took a long look at Eddie, then chuckled. 'Some of my boys out there think we should blow your brains out. They think you stitched us up. But I like you. Both of you'.

'I told you, Bobby,' said Charlie. 'We got scammed. Someone switched the diamonds on us. All we had was useless rocks -'.

'Quartz,' said Pickering. 'Yeah, you said that last night. Thing is, that's a bit hard for the boys to swallow. You get that, right?' He peered at Eddie again.

'You got paid for the job, didn't you?' said Eddie. 'We got fuck all, except now we've got TV reporters climbing up our arses, watching every move we make. I reckon you came out of it cushty'.

Charlie kicked him under the table. 'What my brother means, is that we did what we agreed. We paid you the seventy five grand after the job. It's us what's out of pocket'.

'Yet here you are, living peaceful lives in paradise, all safe and sound. You, your crew, your little brother here. Wives, girlfriends, enormous villas, posh apartments, gold Rolexes and fancy sports cars'.

'We had all that before, Bobby. We got nothing from this job,' said Charlie.

'I believe you. I reckon the entire job was a stitch-up from the start. My guess is your inside man was trying to take us all for a ride. Maybe the depot manager was in on it? Or your man Gary even? Who the fuck knows? But *we* got shafted. That I know'.

'If you believe that then why are we sitting here drinking shit tea halfway up a mountain?' said Eddie.

'Coz, me and my crew were almost nabbed. And you lot weren't,' Pickering snarled. 'I lost everything. My house, cars, all the dosh I had stashed away - what took me ten fucking years to build up. What I took a lot of fucking risks for. It all went when the filth raided my gaff. My boys here are in the same boat'.

'That's not on us,' said Eddie.

'Ain't it?' said Pickering.

Eddie began to reply, but Charlie put his hand across his

chest. 'Bobby,' he said. 'Why would we burn you? We ain't got no reason to do that. There's nothing to gain'.

'That's what I kept tellin' myself. It didn't make no sense to me, neither. But then it hit me. What if, and it was just me speculating at first, but what if the reason you boys all got it so good out here, is because you did a deal?'

'Deal? What deal?' said Charlie.

'I've heard the rumours - "Charlie Lawson has this ex-KGB spook spying on everybody. Politicians, businessmen, fellow Brits. Gathering shit on them. Blackmailing them to get his way, to get deals done"'.

Charlie sighed. 'It's not like that, Bobby. I don't do deals with the old bill,' he said.

'So you say, Charlie. So you say'. Picking fiddled with his cigarette for a moment, then looked at Eddie. 'But soldier boy here does,' he said.

'You what?' said Eddie.

'What the bleedin' hell are you talking about?' said Charlie. 'My brother ain't no snitch'.

'You sure about that?' Pickering looked over his shoulder and nodded towards Lannigan. 'Bring him in'. He twisted back around, picked up his mug and took a drink of the tea. 'Ugh. You weren't wrong. This tea really is shit'. He tossed the cup into the empty stone fireplace where it smashed.

Lannigan returned, accompanied by two more of the East End crew who were lugging a fourth man in through the door. His feet had been bound, and he had a bloodied sack over his head, but Eddie recognised the bright yellow shirt and sunburned, freckled arms. One of the crew kicked the back of the hooded man's knees and forced him to kneel in front of Charlie. Lannigan handed Pickering an expensive-looking Nikon SLR. Pickering examined the camera.

'What's going on?' said Charlie. Pickering reached towards the trembling man and pulled the hood off to reveal Philip

Metcalf, bloodied, bruised and with duct tape around his mouth. He was shuddering.

'DCI Philip Metcalf. But I gather you know him already. We caught him sniffing around the back of your bar, Charlie. Then we took a brief visit to his hotel room in Marbella. You can imagine our surprise when we found photos and recordings of you, your crew and Eddie here. Did you know your brother had a pleasant lunch with him at…what's the place called?'

'Marlon's,' said Lannigan, while handing Pickering a notepad.

'Marlon's, yeah. That's it'. Pickering held up the pad to show Metcalf's scribbled notes. 'Eddie and him had a really nice chat it seems'.

'It weren't like that,' said Eddie.

'It fucking looks that way to me'.

'You're barking up the wrong tree,' said Charlie. 'Metcalf's been on our case for months. Years, even. He tried to get us for a job we did in the seventies. He's not even a copper no more. They suspended him for going off-piste. He's just a sad, lonely old fuck with nothing else to do'.

'I don't see it that way,' said Pickering. 'What I see is you lot cavorting around in the sun without a care in the world with all your fancy things, living the life of Riley. Even when they nab one of you, you get off with it. Mikey getting released here in Spain, for instance. Bill getting off the hook back in Blighty. Yet they came for me and my boys. How's that happen, hey Charlie?'

'You got it all wrong, Bobby,' Charlie replied.

'Prove it to me'.

'How do we do that, Bobby? What do you want?' said Charlie. Pickering grinned. He stood up and pulled a revolver from his pocket.

Fuck, is this it? Thought Eddie.

'First, I want some cash. I like it down here. We might stick around. I figure two hundred grand will get us set up'. Pickering extracted four cartridges from the gun.

'And?' said Charlie.

'And I want Eddie here to end this mother fucking rozzer'. Pickering held out the revolver. 'You got two rounds. One in the heart, one in the head. We've already had him dig his own hole outside. You drove right past it. Gerry here will escort you both there and see it gets done'. Lannigan lifted up the pump-action shotgun and gestured at Eddie to get up. Pickering stepped in front of Eddie as he got up from the chair.

'If you try anything, your brother will find a nine-millimetre gap between his eyes. Are we clear?' Eddie glared at Pickering, hands curled ready to spring at the East Ender. Lannigan pointed the shotgun at Eddie. 'I said, are we fucking clear?'

'Pick up your fuckin' pig buddy,' said Lannigan.

Metcalf looked up at Eddie. He had an open gash above his left eye, and his nose was bloated and encrusted in dried blood. His eyes were full of desperation. Eddie looked to Charlie for support, but he averted his gaze.

'This is wrong,' he said.

Pickering tapped on his watch. 'The clock's ticking, Edward.

Lannigan cut the tape around Metcalf's feet. 'Run piggy, run,' he laughed.

Eddie put an arm around Metcalf's torso and gently lifted him from his crouching position. The former policeman tried to say something. He was, no doubt, pleading for his life, but the sound was muted by the duct tape.

The impromptu grave was by the side of the track, close to the parked cars. It had been well chosen, being hidden from view by the dense forest beyond. It was only a hundred yards from the cottage, but Metcalf had taken a severe beating from the East End gang and was limping.

'Get it done,' said Lannigan, pointing the shotgun at Eddie.

'You know there's a farmhouse just the other side of this hill, said Eddie. 'They'll hear the gunshots, for sure'.

The young East Ender shook his head. 'They'll just think it's hunters shooting pigs or something. Get on with it'.

'Boars,' said Eddie.

'What?'

'Wild boars. That's what they hunt in these parts. Not 'pigs'. It's an important part of their culture'.

The East Ender raised an eyebrow. 'I don't fuckin' care what the fucking dagos shoot. What I want is for you to kill this poxy cop.'

'But that's the thing,' Eddie replied. 'It ain't hunting season. Not for a few months. If anyone hears gunshots now, they'll be straight onto the Spanish cops, won't they?' The East Ender appeared confused. Loyal he was. Bright, he was not. 'But it's alright, Gerry. I got an idea. Keep your gun on the copper'. He started towards the Porsche.

'What the fuck are you doing?' Lannigan demanded. He lifted the shotgun to his arm and trained it at Eddie's torso.

'Getting the tire iron. We'll do it the old fashioned way. Much quieter…and a lot more fun'.

'Tire iron? Are you fuckin' mad?'

Eddie ignored the younger man. 'Here you are,' he said, holding up the glossy black lever. He swung it through the air like a mini baseball bat. 'That'll do the job. Don't you reckon?' Eddie looked at the shaking Metcalf and chuckled. 'C'mon, Gerry. You hold him'.

'You think he'll do it?' said Pickering. He sat observing Charlie, his pistol on the table next to him. 'Didn't look to me like he had the stomach for it'.

Charlie grimaced back at him. 'He's a soldier. It's what they do'. The sound of two muted pistol shots echoed out. Charlie breathed a sigh of relief, but his respite was short-lived. The sound of a shotgun blast followed. Then another.

Pickering rose to his feet. 'Something's wrong'. He pulled out his pistol and shoved it into Charlie's side.

'Get up,' he ordered. 'Outside'.

Pickering, Charlie and the other five East Enders stepped out of the stone building then fanned out, holding a variety of weaponry. The forest was deadly silent.

'Gerry?' one man called out.

A faint cry came from behind the cars. It sounded like Eddie. 'Over here,' he called. The group cautiously approached the front of the cars, then moved around the side towards the site of the makeshift grave. Lannigan lay face down in the dirt. The back of his head was missing, a patch of blood and brain matter next to the body. Eddie lay behind the Porsche, groaning and holding his side.

'What the fuck happened?' Pickering screamed. He pointed his pistol at Eddie. 'You killed Gerry'.

'No, no,' said Eddie, panting'. He lifted his hands to reveal a small hole in his now bloodied shirt. 'It was Metcalf. Your boy, Gerry, slipped over in the mud and dropped the shotgun. Metcalf tried to grab the revolver from me, twisted it towards my gut and shot me. Then he shot your boy in the head'.

'You're fucking lying,' screamed the East Ender.

'Had Gerry killed anyone before?' said Eddie. Pickering didn't answer. 'I thought not. He fucking froze'. Eddie moaned. 'Shit, I think the bastard got me in the spleen. I need a doctor'.

'Where's the fucking cop?' Pickering shouted, waving the Browning around like he was trying to swat mosquitos with it.

Eddie pointed to the back of the Porsche. 'I got him in the back as he tried to run'.

'Why's he in my fucking car?' said Charlie appearing to be more concerned about the state of his upholstery than the recent demise of two human beings.

'Coz, we need to dispose of the body. Properly. The geezer was a fucking cop. You don't want some nosy dog walker coming across the corpse in a few weeks time. We need to weigh the body down and sink it in the lake down there. Make fish food of it'. Eddie moaned again and looked at his wound. 'I think the bullet's still in there'. Pickering walked over to the back of the Porsche. Metcalf's crumpled body lay across the rear bucket seats. The back of his yellow shirt was peppered with buckshot, and crimson with blood. Pickering cocked his pistol and lifted the rear hatch.

'What are you doing?' shouted Eddie.

'Making sure that's what'.

'The flipping fuel tank is under the seats. You trying to kill us all?'

Pickering looked at Eddie, then back to the body, seemingly undecided. After a tense few seconds, he released the hammer back with his thumb and pushed the gun back into his waist. 'Some fucking soldier you are,' he said to Eddie then trudged towards Charlie. 'Take that useless brother of yours and that corpse and get the fuck out of here'.

Charlie walked to Eddie and helped him to his feet. 'You alright, bruv?'

'We need to get out of here,' Eddie whispered, staring intensely at his brother. 'Now'. Charlie helped Eddie to the passenger seat and closed the door, then made his way around to the driver's seat.

'Two hundred grand, Lawson,' shouted Pickering. 'You've got one week to pay, or we come after you. You and everyone you care about'.

Charlie started the ignition and swung the car around to face back down the track, then pulled away. 'I'm sorry, Ed. Sorry you got shot. And sorry you had to do…that'. He waved a thumb towards Metcalf's body. Eddie was staring into the side mirror. 'Did you hear me? I said I'm sorry'.

'Drive, Charlie. Just drive'.

Charlie drove the Porsche down the bridle path and back onto the tarmac road. Eddie glanced behind. 'Mother fucker,' Charlie shouted. 'What was I thinking?' He punched the steering wheel. 'Ain't no way we can pull two hundred grand together. Not in a week'.

'Charlie,' said Eddie.

'And what we gonna do with…that?' Charlie continued thumbing towards the rear of the car.

Eddie pointed towards a tourist viewing area overlooking the lake. 'Pull up over there,' he said.

'You can't dump a body there. It's too public'.

'Just pull over'.

'No, we gotta get lower down. Fill his trousers with rocks or something. Chuck him in the water, like you said -'.

'Stop the fucking car,' Eddie shouted.

Charlie pushed down hard on the brakes and slid the car onto the grassy verge. 'What? What is it?' he asked, checking the mirror.

Eddie waited until the car had come to a stop. 'We faked it'.

Charlie gawped at his younger brother, still not connecting the dots. 'Faked what? I don't understand'.

With perfect timing, former Metropolitan Police detective constable Philip Metcalf sat up in the rear seat, groaning.

Charlie jolted as if having just received an electric shock. 'Jeeeesus fuuuckin christ -'. He pulled the door lever and fell sideways out and onto the dirt, holding his chest as if trying to stop an impending heart attack.

Eddie reached to the back seat and released the silver tape from Metcalf's face. 'Are you okay?' Eddie asked him as he cut at the tape around the injured man's wrists with a pocket knife.

'I'll live,' said Metcalf.

Charlie lurched back towards the car, reached under his seat and pulled out his Colt 1911. He pulled back the slide to chamber the first round, then pointed it in Metcalf's direction.

DEN OF SNAKES

Eddie lifted his arms to shield the man in the rear seats. 'Nobody else is getting killed today, Charlie'.

'Are you fucking insane, Eddie? We can't let him go. Not now'.

'Yes, we can. Put the gun down'.

Charlie shifted to his side, trying to get an improved angle on Metcalf. 'Get out of the way, Ed'.

'You don't have to do this,' said Eddie. 'We can trust him'.

'What are you fucking on? Trust him. He's a bleedin' rozzer'. Charlie's hands were shaking, his face crimson.

'We're gonna let him go'.

Charlie did a double-take between Metcalf and Eddie. 'We can't. First thing he'll do is go straight to the Spanish police and then its all over. We're all be going to the slammer. You, me, Kenny, Roger, Mike - all of us. Bill and Gary, too. It will all be over.'

'Look at me,' said Eddie. Still holding his hands up, he manoeuvred himself out of the passenger's door and strode around the front of the vehicle towards Charlie. 'He made me a promise'.

Charlie turned his head towards Eddie, the gun still trained on the rear of the car. 'A promise? He's Old Bill, you can't trust him'.

Eddie stepped between the car and Charlie. 'Listen to me. I had to shoot that cockney wanker back there. I had no choice'.

'You should have just…shot him,' blurted Charlie, pointing at Metcalf.

'That's not who I am, Charlie. And it ain't you neither'. Charlie remained planted to the spot, his eyes alternating between Eddie and the rear of the Porsche. Eddie stepped towards the car. 'Mr Metcalf?' The former policeman grunted from deep down behind the seats. 'It's okay. Charlie ain't gonna shoot you'.

'You sure about that?' said the unconvinced Metcalf.

'Gimme the gun, bruv,' he said. Eddie slowly lifted his hand

and wrapped it around the Colt. Charlie hesitated for a moment, then surrendered the weapon. Eddie let out a sigh of relief. 'You can get out now,' he said towards the car.

Charlie stumbled away to the wooden fence that marked the boundary of the viewing area. The lake sat a few hundred feet below. He stuffed a cigarette into his mouth, hurried to light it, took an elongated draw and then another. 'Now what?' he said, as Metcalf got out of the car.

'Drop me back to town,' said the former policeman. 'I'll make myself scarce. Forget I saw or heard anything about…this'.

'I got your word on that?' said Eddie.

Metcalf nodded. 'You saved my life today, Edward Lawson. Twice. I'm in your debt'.

Charlie marched back towards Metcalf, index finger pointed at the man's brow. 'You go back on this, and I will make it my life's fucking mission to find you,' he said.

Metcalf stood up straight, wincing as he did. 'I do not like this any more than you do, Lawson'. He cleared his throat. 'But you both have my word'. They stood glaring eye to eye.

'Fine,' said Charlie. Get back in and stay out of sight. And don't go bleeding on my seats no more'. He stormed back around to the driver's door and sat down slowly.

Eddie lifted the passenger seat for Metcalf to clamber back in. 'A word of advice,' said Eddie. Get on the first bus out of Marbella. Those cockney bastards know your face.'

They dropped Metcalf off outside his hotel, a low-rent affair on the outskirts of Marbella, and watched as he limped towards the entrance.

'You honestly think we can trust him?' said Charlie.

'I saved his life. So, yeah', he said through gritted teeth, the pain in his side making it hard to talk.

'You alright? We can't go to a hospital, but I've got this dodgy quack who can clean you up'.

'That would be good'.

Charlie seemed perplexed. 'I still don't get it though,' he said.

'Get what?'

'Metcalf shoots you, and you want to help him. How the fuck did that scrawny streak of piss get the gun off you, anyway?'

'I shot myself,' said Eddie.

Charlie looked at him as if he was speaking a foreign language. 'Huh?'

'I shot the cockney in the head then used the second round on myself. It's just through the skin. Still fucking hurts though'.

'You shot yourself?'

'Its just a flesh wound. Then I used the shotgun on Metcalf's shirt and wiped it in the dead geezer's blood to make it look I'd shot him in the back as he ran away'.

'All that to save a copper'.

'Yeah'.

Charlie stared at his brother. 'You're fucking nuts'.

Eddie nodded.

'I suppose I am. But I made a promise to myself after the war. I ain't doing anyone else's killing never again'. Charlie sighed.

'This is all my fault,' said Charlie. 'Fuck. How did we get in such a mess? I just wanted to get the property deal done. Get out of this business. People are getting hurt. You were right, what you said back up the hill there. It's not who we are. Everything we did…it was just circumstances. But I don't know what to do now, bruv. I think I'm fucked'.

'You'll think of something. You always do. But can we get back to your place and get hold of that doctor friend of yours now? I did mention I got shot, yeah?

CHAPTER TWENTY-EIGHT
NOT ENOUGH DOUGH

As soon as they arrived back at the villa, Charlie started calling around the rest of the crew.

'I don't care what you're doing, Rog. Get your backside here, now,' he shouted into the receiver. 'Bring Judy too. This involves us all'. Charlie hung up the phone, downed his scotch and flopped down onto the brown leather couch in his office. Eddie was standing at the open door, and his brother beckoned at him to come in.

'That them all?' asked Eddie as he sat down at Charlie's desk.

Charlie nodded. 'They are on their way'. He pointed at Eddie's side - 'Did the quack do a good job?'

Eddie lifted his tee-shirt up to reveal his bandaged torso, 'He said he's seen quite a few bullet wounds in his time'. Charlie gave him a wry smile, behind which Eddie sensed there were secrets he would prefer not to know. 'So, what's your plan?'

'Raise two hundred grand, somehow,' Charlie answered, while pouring another whisky. 'What else can we do?'

The idea seemed impractical to Eddie. The job they'd pulled off in England a week earlier had been an act of desperation by an ageing crew down to their last funds. Now that the diamonds had turned out to be worthless quartz, their options were even more limited. 'How you going to manage that?' he asked. 'Seems to me everybody's tapped out. I reckon you need to consider different options'.

'Like what?' said Charlie. 'Go to war with Pickering's crew?'

'Nah, just the opposite'.

'Well go on, bruv. I'm all ears,' said Charlie, leaning forward. He seemed confident about what Eddie was going to say.

'I said it before. Maybe it's time for you to up sticks and start again somewhere new?' Charlie lowered his forehead into his hands and sighed. 'I mean it, bruv. Sell this place, and whatever other assets you've got, and get out'.

'You're saying I should give up?' said Charlie.

Eddie shrugged. 'Recognising when to retreat is as important as knowing when to fight. You can't win every battle'.

Charlie stood up, shaking his head. 'But I'm so close. Don't you see that?'

'Close to what? Getting arrested? Getting killed?' said Eddie.

'Getting what I deserve,' Charlie growled.

It was Eddie who was shaking his head now. 'There are people out there, a lot of them, who'd agree with you. Only their definition of "what you deserve" differs significantly from yours'.

'Fuck them'.

Eddie realised he was pushing his brother's buttons, but this might be his last chance of making the point, so he pushed harder. 'Who, Charlie? Fuck who? Pickering's crew? The local families? The politicians? The police?' Charlie was wagging a finger at him to stop, but he continued. 'What about your own crew?'

'What about them?' demanded Charlie.

'You don't trust them'.

'I will handle them,' said Charlie.

'This is high stakes stuff. You need to know who's on your side'.

'Yes, I do, little brother. And I'll find that out soon enough. We both will'.

A shrill beeping sound interrupted the exchange to announce the first arrival at the villa's gate.

Charlie walked away. 'Get yourself cleaned up,' he said, pointing at the dried blood on Eddie's hands. 'And nobody needs to know about Metcalf'.

Kenny arrived first, then Bill and Carol, followed by Roger and Judy. They each fixed themselves a drink and made themselves comfortable in the large living room to wait for Mike. The mood was tense.

'Do you know what's going on?' Bill asked Eddie quietly. 'The wife's got a right huff on and Charlie ain't saying nuffin yet. What happened with Pickering's crew?'

'They just talked,' Eddie replied.

Bill frowned, and he pointed at Eddie's side. There was a small bloodstain visible on his clean shirt. 'Sharp words was they?' he said.

A car pulled up outside. Roger peered out of the window. 'Mikey's here'.

'About bloody time,' said Kenny.

Charlie came back into the room, directing Mike to a sofa.

'No Veronica?' said Judy.

'She's here,' snapped Mike. He peered back towards the door. 'Powdering her nose, probably'.

'Right, I'll cut to the chase,' said Charlie. 'Me and Ed met Pickering this morning'.

'Why are they here in Spain?' Roger interrupted.

'If you let me fucking finish, Rog. You'll find out'. Roger sank back into the sofa, arms crossed. 'As I was saying, we met

Pickering and his crew. The good news is that Bobby believed me when I told him about the diamonds'.

'What's the bad news?' said Mike?

Charlie took a deep breath. 'They had to do a bunk and leave everything behind'.

'Yeah, so? It's what we did in seventy-nine,' said Bill.

'Yeah, but the thing is they figure we owe them'.

'How do we fucking owe them?' said Mike. 'They got fucking paid! We got nothing'.

Charlie shifted uncomfortably in his chair. 'They think we grassed on 'em'.

'Why would they think that?' asked Carol. You boys was all there with them in London'.

'Quiet girl,' Bill said in a hushed tone.

'Nah, Carol's right, Bill,' said Roger. 'Why would they think we fucked them over? It don't make no sense'.

Charlie reached forward to refill his glass from the bottle of Famous Grouse.

Mike answered. 'I know why,' he said. He stood leaning against the wall, cigarette in hand. 'Coz, they think we did some kind of deal to protect what we have here. Ain't that right, Charlie?'

Charlie stayed quiet.

'Shit. I knew it,' said Roger. 'I knew all that cloak and dagger stuff of yours would come back and bite us, Charlie'.

'All that "cloak and dagger stuff" has protected you for a long time,' Charlie snapped. 'It got both Bill and Mike out of the fucking slammer for a start'.

'What does he want?' asked Mike.

Charlie took a swig before answering. 'Two hundred large'.

'Two hundred grand?' said Judy. 'Where's that coming from, then?'

Roger had his head in his hands. 'She ain't wrong, Charlie. 'I've had to take money out of the dealership. I can't afford to buy any new stock until something comes up. Probably gonna have to close the site in Estepona for a start'.

'Same with my restaurant,' said Bill.

'And my cafe,' Carol chirped in.

Charlie stood up and ran his hands through his hair. 'We ain't got no choice. They know too much. We need to get them out of our hair'.

'We could take 'em out,' said Mike.

'We ain't doing that'.

'Why not?' asked Mike.

'Have I not made our situation abundantly fucking clear for you, Michael? One false move, one more fuck up, and they'll have us on the next available plane back to Blighty in handcuffs. Guillem made it crystal clear. "Walking on eggshells", remember? Look, gentleman…and ladies. I'll cut you all in on the Majestico deal if you help me sort out this problem with Pickering'.

'But your property project still needs funding, don't it?' asked Bill, confused.

'I got some emergency money to keep it ticking over'.

'From who?' asked Mike.

'That doesn't matter. All that matters is that we can stump up the money to get Pickering out of our hair and move forward. If we don't do that…we won't have nothing'. He pointed to an A4 writing pad on the coffee table. Several biros sat next to it. 'Take a sheet each. Make a list of what you can get your hands on inside a week. Cash you've got stashed away. Watches you can sell. Jewellery. Cars you can shift. Freezers of frozen meat, gym equipment, suits you ain't never worn, anything. Even that considerable shotgun collection of yours, Mike'.

Charlie ignored Mike's muffled complaints and tore off a sheet of paper for himself, picked up a pen and started writing.

Bill and Carol were having another private tiff.

'Me mum bought us that for our wedding,' she said. 'It's

bloody ugly, she's dead, and it's worth a couple of fuckin' grand. Put it on the list'.

'Fine,' Carol hissed and started scribbling on the paper. 'But you're selling all your bleedin' golf clubs'.

'Fine,' replied Bill.

'Pass them all here when you're done,' said Charlie. Eddie watched for a few minutes as the others scribbled away, then reached for a piece of paper for himself.

'Not you, bruv,' said Charlie.

'I want to help,' Eddie insisted. He wrote down a single item before topping up his glass and sitting back in the chair.

After a few more minutes, and seeing that the others had all finished, Charlie called a halt. He collected the paper and started to go through the assorted lists, jotting down numbers on a separate sheet as he did so.

Veronica slipped into the room, apparently unnoticed by all but Eddie. She was wearing tight stonewashed jeans and a blue Le Coq Sportif sweater that was several sizes too big for her slender frame. She wore barely any makeup - not that she needed it, thought Eddie - and her movement seemed impaired. She seemed drunk. Or high. She perched herself down at the stool by Charlie's Yamaha piano, seemingly lost in thought.

'I don't see your Omega on the list, Roger?'

'I ain't got it no more, Charlie. I lost it in a poker game'.

Judy slapped him on the arm. 'That watch cost me ten thousand quid!' she said.

'You really reckon that Merc's worth twenty grand, Ken?' said Charlie, ignoring Roger and Judy's disagreement. 'Got the logbook, have you?' Kenny shook his head. 'More like ten, then,' said Charlie who was now holding the last sheet of paper. He stared at it for a few seconds, then patted Eddie on the back, saying nothing.

Carol's inquisitiveness got the better of her, and she peeked at the item Eddie had written. 'Military Cross and bar,' she read out aloud. 'What's that?'

'It's his medal, ain't it? From the Falklands,' said Bill.

'You sure about that, son?' said Mike. He seemed surprised.

'I'm sure,' said Eddie.

Charlie had totted up the list. He frowned. 'Dammit,' he said.

'How short are we?' asked Roger.

'Eighty grand'.

'So what do we do?' asked Kenny. Mike placed his glass down firmly and sat forward on the couch.

'Can I propose something?' he said, looking at the others.

'Go on then,' said Bill.

'The Moroccan I met -'.

Charlie slammed a fist onto the coffee table. 'No,' he barked.

'It's easy money,' Mike replied tersely.

'What are you talking about?' said Judy, directing the question at Mike.

Charlie answered. 'He wants us to be drug dealers'.

'It ain't dealing. It's just transporting,' said Mike. 'We'd just be helping the Moroccans offload their gear, and selling it on at a very attractive profit to our Dutch friends'.

Charlie slammed the table again. 'Are you fucking deaf? I said no'.

Mike got up, slammed his glass down, splashing the contents onto the coffee table, and marched towards the door.

'You coming?' he said at Veronica, having already passed her and without waiting for a reply. Roger followed after Mike.

'Let the grumpy fucker go,' said Kenny.

Roger shot Kenny an angry look. 'And let him go do something stupid again? How will that help?' He jogged off to catch Mike.

'Here we go again,' said Judy and put her glass down before following her husband.

'So now what?' asked Kenny.

'We'll have to raise money on our properties,' said Charlie.

'That ain't a quick process,' said Bill.

'I'll talk to Pickering. Get us some more time'.

'You think he'll wait?' said Eddie, one hand clamped on the gunshot wound in his side.

'What else is he gonna do?' Charlie replied. 'If we ain't got the dough, we ain't got it'.

Kenny pushed himself up and shook Charlie's hand. 'Let me know what you need me to do'.

Charlie walked Kenny, Bill and Carol out of the room and to the front entrance.

Veronica was standing by the door watching the men leave, then wandered towards Eddie. She held out her hand to reveal the keys that Eddie had lost during the fracas with Mike at the beach club.

He plucked them out of her open palm and stared at them, a wave of relief sweeping through his body. 'Thank you,' he said. 'Where did you find them?'

'I went back to to the club to ask yesterday. One of the bar staff found them'.

'You have no idea how relieved I am to see these again,' he said. She stared at the key for a moment, her face portraying what seemed like a deep sadness. 'Are you okay?' he asked.

She shot him one of her contrived and debilitating smiles. 'Of course,' she said. 'See you around'. She spun around and strode away, leaving him alone.

He had gazed at her departing figure until she was out of view, then stared once more at the keys.

Thank fuck. That saves some explaining to Charlie.

Eddie thrust the keys into his pocket just as Charlie returned, flanked by Kenny and Mike. They all bore concerned faces.

'What's up?' asked Eddie.

'Trouble,' said Kenny. Charlie strode to his office desk, unlocked a drawer and pulled out a silver revolver which he slipped into the waist of his jeans.

'It's Charlie's bar,' said Mike. 'There's been a fire'.

The flames had been mostly extinguished by the time Charlie and Eddie arrived at what was now the former site of Charlie's Bar. The road was blocked off by a police car, so Charlie double-parked further up the hill, and the brothers ran down to the chaotic scene.

The fire crew were now sifting through the charred remains in search of the last vestiges of the blaze, giving an occasional burning ember a blast from their firehose as a precaution. The inferno had taken less than twenty minutes to turn the popular, ex-pat drinking hole into a pile of charred, wet timbers and soggy ash.

Charlie lifted the temporary plastic police barrier and walked slowly to the bottom of the steps, of which only a few now remained. He was speechless.

'I'm sorry, bruv,' said Eddie, trying to console his brother.

Barry, now a bar manager without a bar, was talking to the fire crew. He spotted Charlie and beckoned the Lawsons over. 'This is the fire chief,' he said. The man, a proud-looking individual who, Eddie guessed, was in his fifties, spoke in broken English.

'Is bad fire. Very bad. Destroy all of building'.

'I can see that,' said Charlie. 'What I want to know is how it started'.

The man shrugged his shoulders. 'Is impossible to say today. The council, they send engineer to see and make a report'.

'When?' snapped Charlie.

'I cannot say. Is not my department'.

'I have valuable things stored in the basement. I need to get back into the building'.

'Is not possible, Mr Lawson. There is much debris on the staircase from the roof. Metal and glass. Is dangerous. No persons are allowed until everything is cleared. Understand?'

DEN OF SNAKES

'Yeah, I understand,' said Charlie, growling. He pulled Barry away from the fire chief. 'Tell me what you know'.

'I turned up at midday to open up, just like I always do. The door was already open, but I thought nothing of it. Sometimes one of the girls arrives before me so I didn't clock it at first at went inside. That's when I smelled the smoke. I called the fire service straight away then tried the cellar door, but the smoke was too thick'.

'It started downstairs?' said Eddie. 'You're sure about that?'

'Hundred percent. As soon as I opened the door, I felt the heat'. The bar manager pointed to his face. 'Look, I lost half of my fucking eyebrows'.

'So someone broke in and set a fire in the basement?'

'I think so, Charlie. Yes', the barman said. 'It makes no sense, right?'

Charlie let the question hang. 'Get yourself home, Baz. I'll give you a bell when I need you'. The barman nodded and sauntered away.

Charlie lit a cigarette and gazed at the smouldering pile of black debris. 'The loan I took from Fernandez. I signed over the bar as collateral. Whoever set the fire must have known that. They're trying to destroy me. And they're succeeding'.

'You can't be sure of that,' said Eddie.

Two police officers and a fireman were erecting orange and white plastic barriers around the bar's perimeter. A mobile TV news van had parked up at the police barrier. The crew were endeavouring to position their camera and sound equipment.

'Time to go,' said Charlie. They started up the hill towards the Porsche.

'What now?' said Eddie as he got into the car.

'We got no choice, now,' said Charlie. 'Pickering's crew. We've got to kill 'em'.

CHAPTER TWENTY-NINE
CAUGHT WITH THEIR PANTS DOWN

It had not taken the Five Bullet Crew more than a few minutes to arrive at a consensus on whether they should wipe out their East End rivals. Criminals are rarely willing to surrender the proceeds of their risky trade, and the prospect of shelling out two hundred thousand pounds of their ill-gotten gains to Pickering's crew had been a bitter pill to swallow.

Now, with Charlie incandescent with rage at having seen the smouldering wreck of his cherished beach bar, and the likely prospect of their own business interests suffering a similar fate, it took less than ten minutes to drop five old bullet casings into the plastic cup with 'yes' scribbled on the side of it. It had been a foregone decision. Driving to Charlie's villa and dropping the quintet of brass cases into the cup had been a somewhat perfunctory process.

'How and when?' asked Bill.

'Strike while the iron's hot,' said Mike. He reached for a large canvas kit bag, unzipped it to reveal several shotguns and pistols. 'Who needs a heater?'

Eddie looked at the open bag with dread. He felt the marble floor go soft beneath his feet and the ghostly odour of damp gorse and cordite seeped into his brain.

'What about you, soldier boy?' muttered Mike, 'Ain't no military cross in this for you'. Eddie was uncertain if Mike was trying to wind him up again, or whether he was offering him a way out.

'Course he's fucking doing it,' said Kenny before Eddie could reply. 'He's one of us now'.

'I don't recollect him getting a bullet with his name on it,' said Mike.

Roger was examining an old Webley revolver that he had lifted out of Mike's bag. 'That one's quite a kicker, mate. Sure your arthritis can handle it?' said Mike.

'Very fuckin' funny,' Roger replied. He pointed the unloaded revolver at the shaven man and made a 'Bam!' sound.

'Careful, Rog,' said Bill. 'The last geezer what pointed a gun at Mikey ended up in a wheelchair for the rest of his life'.

It was clear that Roger did remember and offered the weapon back to Mike. 'I've got mine in my car,' he said.

Charlie stood to face to his brother and gave him a look that a disappointed schoolmaster might have made if his star pupil had just admitted he didn't do his homework. 'You've got my back on this, right?' he said.

Eddie pictured the moment their mother had made her deathbed request to his young self. *Look after your brother, Eddie. He's going to need you*.

'Ed?' Charlie asked.

'There's got to be another way,' Eddie said. 'If you do this… if *we* do this, there ain't no going back'.

Kenny stood looking at Eddie like he was a gatecrasher at a high society wedding, where he was the bride's wealthy father and Eddie some rag-wearing street oik. 'They fucking torched your brother's bar,' Kenny said in an incredulous tone. 'Ain't no "going back" already. Not for them'.

'How do we know the Cockneys did that?' said Eddie.

Kenny's eyes bulged in their sockets. 'It ain't bleedin' rocket science, is it? What do you want? Forensic bloody evidence? CCTV footage? Course it was fucking them'.

'Eddie. Me and the lads would feel a lot better with you on our side, mate,' said Roger.

'Six against six,' said Bill.

Charlie steered his brother away from the others. 'Ed, I know it's asking a lot. I know you ain't been with us very long, and this ain't what I promised you…but I need to know I can count on you, bruv. Can I? Can I count on you?' He looked into Eddie's eyes, and then he said it. 'The old girl did tell you to look after me, remember?'

Fucker.

'You think she meant this?' said Eddie, pointing at Mike who was looking down the twin barrels of a sawn-off shotgun. 'Coz, I don't think so, Charlie'.

'Ed, I'm worried. I -'.

'So don't do it. It's that simple'.

'They burned my bar down. They're threatening our livelihoods'.

'Build another bar,' said Eddie.

'And they made you shoot that kid in the face,' Charlie whispered.

Eddie pushed Charlie away. 'You think I don't fucking know that? You think I can't see his fucking head explode? You think I don't see them? All the faces of the people I killed?' His throat was dry, his pulse racing. He felt dizzy.

'It's alright, Charlie. We're gonna need a driver,' offered Mike. 'Eddie, just get us there and get us the fuck out again'.

Charlie shook his head. 'No. No, we need to outgun them,' he said.

'We've got surprise on our side,' Mike replied. 'It will be easy'. He looked at Eddie. 'The kid's done more than enough for this flipping crew already'.

Charlie lifted a clenched fist towards Mike then, having thought twice, turned around and stormed out the door.

Mike fixed Eddie with a respectful stare. 'You wanna walk away, then walk away. This ain't your fight'.

Before Eddie could reply, however, Charlie returned to the room. He was holding a Browning 9mm semi-automatic. He pulled back the slide to cock it, peered into the breech, then released the slide and dry-fired the gun. Satisfied that it was in working order, he offered it up to Eddie. 'You're the driver. But you're still packing. If it goes pear-shaped up there tonight, the boys here need to know they can count on you to help'. He grabbed Eddie's left hand and thrust the cold weapon into it, then held up three loaded magazines. 'Don't disappoint me, bruv'.

The crew decided to hit the old farm building that the East Londoners were using, at two o'clock in the morning, figuring that Pickering and his crew would be drunk, high, asleep or with any luck, all three.

They drove up in an old Range Rover, one of Roger's dwindling fleet, its tired old engine belching out clouds of smoke every time Roger had changed gear. Eventually they arrived at a clearing at the side of the road a little under a mile from where the Cockneys' woodland hideout.

'It'll be like shooting fish in a barrel, boys,' said Kenny as he checked his gun, a Colt snub-nosed revolver. 'They won't have time to put their pants on before we drop 'em,'

'Yeah? Just make sure you shoot them and not me, you old sod,' said Roger. Bill sniggered.

'Oi! This ain't fucking chimpanzee playtime,' growled Mike, as they shook their legs after getting out of the car.

The Five Bullet Crew was a group of hard bastards and good at their chosen profession, but a well-oiled strike team they were not. It would have been, Eddie thought, reminiscent of a slapstick scene from Dad's Army if several people were not about to get killed. 'This ain't going to go well,' he thought. He tapped his brother on the shoulder blade and whispered, 'I'm coming with you'.

Charlie shook his head. 'No, you made your choice. Me and my crew have got this. You just be ready to get us out of here'. Charlie signalled at the rest of the group to move towards the farmhouse.

'Stay low,' Eddie whispered. 'Watch your flanks'.

'What's that mean?' he heard Bill ask. 'Flanks?'

Mike groaned. 'Jesus fucking christ. Just keep your bleedin' eyes peeled,' he said.

Eddie stood at the open car door watching Charlie and the crew move off into the dense pine forest that lay on the lower slope behind the farm building. They would be hidden from view until they were less than twenty feet away from the stone building. Assuming they were undetected, then they would be in the dwelling and upon the unsuspecting men in seconds.

It was a tranquil night - almost silent, save for the occasional sound of leaves rustling in the light breeze. Eddie stood, leaning against the Range Rover, his senses operating at maximum sensitivity. Something did not feel right. His pulse quickened.

And then he heard something.

It sounded like a twig snapping. He orientated his head towards the source of the sound. Nothing. He pulled the Browning from the leather shoulder holster and slipped the safety catch off. Another sound. This time like a muffled sniff. Someone was watching him from the shadows.

He lifted the pistol before him and creeped towards the sounds but froze when he heard yet another sound, this time much closer and behind him. Then someone spoke.

'Do not move,' the voice ordered. It was Bobby Pickering. Eddie peered over his shoulder to see a standing figure obscured by a substantial tree trunk. The only illumination came from the moonlight, but it was sufficient for Eddie to see Pickering was pointing a machine pistol at him. 'You might have been a fucking para, but this is a fucking MAC 10. Drop that pea shooter and put your hands on your head'. Eddie was familiar with the weapon, which could empty a thirty-round clip in less than two seconds. He did as instructed. 'Good lad. Now back away from the gun, towards me'. Eddie took five slow strides backwards.

'I can call them off, Bobby. Let me try,' said Eddie.

'Why would I do that, Edward? We've been waiting here all night for them geriatrics to turn up. Keep coming. That's a good boy'.

Eddie took three more steps before the night turned to day and his head filled with what seemed like lightning. He fell to his feet, blinded by the agony. 'And that,' said Pickering, 'is what a good old fashioned blackjack feels like when it's wrapped around your head'.

Eddie curled up into a ball, trying to use his hands to protect himself from further blows, but found them being bound with tape. Two men pulled him to his feet, and he felt the cold, hard metal of the MAC 10 against the underside of his jaw.

'Why ain't we topping him here?' said a second, younger voice.

'Patience, Stevie. All will become clear'. The butt of the gun moved around to poke Eddie between the shoulder blades. 'Now walk. Slowly and quietly. We don't want to ruin the show'.

Oblivious to the trap he was walking his crew into, Charlie reached the stone wall of the farmhouse first, peered around the corner then waved at the others to come forward. Mike, Roger, Bill then Kenny stood there in a line. Inside the building, they could make out the sound of someone snoring.

'This is gonna be so fucking easy,' said Kenny, grinning. Charlie pointed at Bill to go first.

'Why me?' asked Bill.

'Coz, I bleedin' said so. That's why'. Bill murmured something under his breath but did as he was told. He crouched down - but not as low as a younger, fitter man could have - then tiptoed towards the front door. He looked back at Charlie who stood a few feet behind him seeking instructions.

'Try it,' whispered Charlie, while mimicking opening a door.

Bill grasped the door handle and twisted it. He smiled. 'It's open'.

'Go on then,' said Mike who was crouching next to Charlie, with Roger behind him. Bill pushed on the wooden door to open it. The snoring inside continued unabated. The crew readied their guns and prepared to scramble into the building.

'Go,' yelled Charlie.

Bill led the way, running into the living room only to find it empty, save for a dying log fire and a large wooden table upon which sat a mono tape player. The device was playing an audio recording of a snoring man.

'What the fuck?' said Bill.

Mike ran to the back of the structure and pointed his shotgun into the sleeping area and kitchenette. Both were empty. The rear door was secured with a sturdy iron padlock and chain. 'It's a trap,' he said. 'Get out. Shit. Back, go back'.

Charlie, Mike, Bill and Roger all ran back to the front door but as they burst from the door, they found themselves blinded by the lights from several vehicles thirty feet away. They held their hands to their eyes, trying to regain some vision.

Mike hit the deck. 'Get down,' he shouted. It was too late. Several bullets smacked into the surrounding timber, one hitting Bill in the arm. He dropped to the ground, wounded, but still pointing his pistol in the vague direction of the unseen enemy.

'Drop the guns,' shouted Pickering. 'I've got young Edward'. Kenny, who had remained standing and holding his small revolver, tried to run back to the corner of the building, but came to an immediate halt when another volley of automatic fire hit the rocky soil in front of him.

'Try that again and I'll fucking end you,' shouted one cockney.

'Drop them, or we drop you,' Pickering commanded.

'Do it,' Charlie said. He flung his pistol forward.

'Fuck's sake,' said Mike, then did likewise with his shotgun. Roger, Bill, and Kenny followed suit.

'On your fucking knees,' said Pickering as he emerged from out of the cover of the car lights. Four more of the East End crew approached behind him carrying a variety of machine pistols and assault rifles.

Pickering walked up to Charlie and pointed the MAC 10 at his head. 'Fucking amateurs. Did you really think you could sneak up on us like that?'

'Where's my brother?' said Charlie.

'He's alive. He's tied up over there nursing a right nasty headache'. He gestured at one of his crew to collect the weapons lying on the floor, then crouched down in front of Roger and grabbed his wounded arm. 'You'll live,' he said grinning, then stood up. 'Two days ago I came to you with a polite request. All I wanted was two hundred grand - compensation, if you will, for loss of earnings and costs incurred from our recent association with you gentlemen'.

Sounding like a "no win, no fee" solicitor, Pickering walked along the line of cowering bodies and stopped at Kenny. 'All I wanted was a little recompense. But you tried to stiff my lads and me. You came up here planning to shoot us in our beds. This is very…disappointing'. He walked back to where Charlie lay. 'The price just went up. It's five hundred grand now'.

'You're havin' a fucking laugh,' said Bill who received a sharp kick to his shin from the boot of one of the East Enders.

'Do I look like a fucking comedian?' said Pickering. He pressed the MAC 10 into the back of Bill's head, forcing his face into the dirt. 'Do I have to blow this moron's brains out so prove how fucking serious I am, Charlie?'

'No,' said Charlie. 'We believe you'.

Pickering stood up, smiling. 'Smashing,' he said. 'On your feet'. The Five Bullet Crew pushed themselves up and dusted themselves down. Bill clasped the gunshot wound to his arm. Pickering signalled at one of his men to bring Eddie over. 'Now, Charlie. I want to get one thing clear with you and your dumb buddies here. I don't give a fuck about you. Any of you. I don't give a fuck about your wives, your girlfriends, your drinking partners, your business partners or any of your fucking family back home'. Two of the cockneys pushed Eddie towards the rest of Charlie's crew. 'If I ain't got half a million quid sitting in a fuck-off big pile in front of me in five days, I'll kill you and every single person you care about. You got that Charlie bleedin' Lawson?'

Charlie nodded.

Pickering moved closer to Mike. 'What about you, big man? You got that?' Mike responded with the bare minimum of nods. Pickering stared at the men lying on the ground, then shook his head. 'Nah, I'm not convinced'. He signalled at one of his crew, and the man jogged towards one vehicle. 'Now, I didn't want to have to do this,' said Pickering, as his crew member returned a few seconds later pushing a gagged and bound man. The prisoner was wearing a suit, the shirt untucked. He was shoeless and whimpering.

'Guillem?' said Charlie.

'The very same,' said Pickering. 'He was so scared he pissed himself in the car after we nabbed him'.

'What are you doing, Bobby?' said Mike.

'Making my point,' Pickering pointed the machine pistol at Guillem. The lawyer moaned from inside his gagged throat, his eyes full of fear.

'Don't do this,' Charlie pleaded, but the East Ender was already squeezing the trigger. It was all over in an instant.

Guillem's torso seemed to dance like a convulsing drunkard, before collapsing to the ground. A pool of dark liquid grew from under his mangled corpse.

'You fucking bastard,' Charlie screamed. He tried to get up, but one of the East Enders kicked him in the belly.

'Have I made my point?' said Pickering. 'Are you going to pay us, or do I have to shoot someone else?'

One of the East Londoners sniggered.

'You'll get your fucking money,' said Charlie.

'Good,' said Pickering. Then that concludes our business for today'. He signalled at one of his crew, a shaven-headed man in his twenties who emerged from within the farm building holding a petrol can. 'Burn it,' he told him.

The man lit a match and flicked it into the building's interior, flames appearing almost immediately.

Pickering started towards one of the cars, his crew already doing likewise. 'Five days, Charlie. Five days'. The car engines started up, and doors slammed shut.

'What the fuck do we do now?' said Roger, transfixed by the sight of the burning building.

Mike watched the two cars drive away into the darkness, then glanced at Charlie. 'How about I call the Moroccans, now?'

CHAPTER THIRTY
GOING ALL IN

'Go over it again,' said Eddie as he lowered his aching body onto a chair at the head of the kitchen table in Carol's restaurant in Marbella old town.

Dawn was still over three hours away, and none of the crew had slept, but the men - tired as they were - were now in no doubt that they needed a plan to raise a lot of money. And quickly.

Mike sat to Eddie's left, Roger next to him - sporting a freshly applied bandage around his arm. Kenny stood near the door, fidgeting with his car keys. Bill sat perched on the edge of a brown vinyl couch accompanying the reclining Charlie, who lay there eyes closed, and rubbing his forehead. The air was thick with cigarette smoke.

'What didn't you get the first time?', said Mike. 'It's bleedin' simple'.

'That's what you said about knocking off half a dozen sleeping cockneys,' said Eddie. 'That didn't go so well, did it?'

'Alright, fucking hell', Mike relented. 'So, we rendezvous with the Moroccan's fishing trawler off the coast and take on a ton of dope. Then we bring it back, load it into a truck, drive it up north and meet up with my contact who will pay us the five hundred grand we need. Like I said, simple'. Mike looked at the rest of the old-timers for support.

Eddie sat still, running his finger around the rim of his coffee mug.

'Sounds like the solution to all our problems to me, Ed,' said Bill.

Eddie disagreed. The plan sounded like pure fantasy to him. Too good to be true; as thin as paper. 'Where's the boat going to come from?' he asked.

Kenny piped up. 'A neighbour of mine's got a thirty-foot yacht moored up in Puerto Banús. I've been out in a few times,' he said. 'He's in Florida for a month. I know where he keeps the keys'.

'And it will get us out there and back?' said Eddie.

'No worries. It's only a year old'.

'Okay'. Eddie directed the next question at Mike. 'Tell me how we get a ton of hash from one boat to another in the middle of the sea'.

Mike rubbed his eyes and leaned forward. 'The Moroccan geezer said that it's all wrapped up nice and tight in polythene in fifty-pound packages what float. They bung them overboard, strung together on a long rope. We just hook one end and pull it all on board. They do it all the time. No hassle'.

Eddie pictured the sight back in 1982 at Port San Carlos on East Falkland. The British forces had elected to come ashore there before mounting the assault to recapture the eastern island. Landing craft had collided, dinghies had capsized, men had fallen overboard while descending from the troop transporters and sizeable amounts of kits and supplies had sunk to the bottom or floated away into the Atlantic. He knew the sea was a challenging environment.

'How many packages are we talking about?' he said.

'Forty,' said Mike. 'Fifty tops. He said it takes about ten minutes'.

'Sounds risky', said Eddie, rubbing his chin. He leaned

forward to look at the map of the southern Spanish coast that lay on the table in front of him. 'And then? Where do we get it ashore?'

Roger stood up, winced, then leaned forward and pointed to a long sandy cove, east of Estepona. 'There. Casares Costa. Big long beach with multiple exits'.

Eddie examined the location. 'Looks like a residential area. Not very covert'.

'They're building a new estate of holiday homes there, but it's not finished. Shouldn't be nobody around at that time of night'.

'How far is it from the road to the water?' said Eddie. 'These packages will take some shifting'.

'No more than twenty yards,' said Roger, pointing to the east end of the bay. There's a small car park by the roundabout, you can't see it from the main road. We can park the truck there, no probs'.

'And what about the truck?' said Eddie. 'It's got to carry a ton and be in good condition. It must be, what, six hundred miles up to the French border?'

'More like seven,' said Bill.

'Okay. So where do we get the truck from?'

'Just rent it,' said Bill. Eddie gave him a sceptical stare.

'Using fake ID,' said Roger.

Eddie nodded. 'Whoever does that needs to wear a disguise, said Eddie. 'They can't be caught on security cameras'. He rubbed his chin again. 'What about comms?'

'CB radio sets?' suggested Bill.

Eddie shook his head. 'Every trucker in the area could pick us up with them. Charlie, would your man Soparla know where we can get hold of some VHF two-way sets?'

Charlie hadn't spoken since he had sat down and was exhibiting a thousand-yard stare, oblivious to the conversation taken place a few feet away.

'Any suggestions, bruv?' said Eddie, louder. Charlie remained lost in thought. Bill tapped him on the arm.

'Huh?' said Charlie, before realising that all eyes were on him.

'Ed's going through Mike's plan, Charlie' Bill said. 'So far, so good, but we'd need a set of radios. Can Lucian help with that?'

Charlie scratched at his stubble. 'I'll ask him'.

'Alright then,' said Eddie. 'So we know how we're picking the dope up and what equipment we need'. He turned back to Mike again. 'Just one more question'.

'Go on'.

'The buyer,' Eddie said. 'This Dutch guy'.

'Yeah?'

'Can we trust him?'

'I reckon'.

'You reckon?' said Eddie.

Mike nodded. 'Yeah'.

Eddie got the distinct impression that the rest of the crew were privy to more than he was at that precise moment. 'That doesn't exactly fill me with confidence, mate'. Mike stubbed his cigarette out into a beer can. 'How do you know him? Is he good for the cash?'

'He's good,' said Mike.

'He's good?'

'That's what I said, ain't it?' Mike snarled. He seemed frustrated and gestured at Charlie with a nod that said; "tell him already".

Eddie looked at his brother. 'Would you care to fill me in on whatever I'm missing, Charlie?'

His brother forced himself up off the sofa with a grunt, reached for and opened a can of lager. 'The dutchy owes me,' he said after taking a swig. 'Remember that ginger kid that was serving drinks at mine that first night you was here?'

'The one who's old man was serving time for gun-running

for the provos?' said Eddie. He sensed that the rest of the crew were waiting for Charlie to drop a bombshell.

'Yeah,' said Charlie, his gaze focussed on the table. 'Seamus, the kid's dad, was buying of guns from him'.

'From the dutchman?'

'Yeah,' said Charlie.

'And?' Eddie countered, wondering where this was going. Charlie looked pensive now.

'I made the introduction,' said Charlie.

'Between the Dutchman and the Irish guy?'

'Yeah'.

The realisation hit Eddie like a sucker punch to the head. 'You helped this fucker buy guns for the IRA? Guns they used on British soldiers, like me and my mates?'

Charlie nodded. 'I didn't know what they was gonna use 'em for, did I?' pleaded Charlie.

'Well they weren't going fucking duck-hunting was they?' said Eddie. His mind was in a spin. Images of his tours in Northern Ireland flashed past - police stations surrounded by watchtowers and razor wire, the cramped interiors of armoured personnel carriers, nationalist rioters screaming at him and his fellow soldiers, screaming curses and lugging stones their way. Petrol bombs, burned-out cars and blown-up bodies.

He lifted his shirt and pointed at a cluster of small scars on his side. 'That was a fucking IRA pipe bomb,' he said. He turned around to reveal another, more prominent streak of a scar on his lower back. 'That was a provo bullet, from an AK47 most likely. If I'd been moving even slightly slower, it would have killed me'. He placed his right leg onto a chair and pulled up his trouser leg. A sprawling burn mark clad his shin and calf. 'That was a Molotov cocktail. I was standing in a line between the Protestants and Catholics, stopping them from getting at each other. I was lucky. A nineteen-year-old kid took most of it. He'd only joined our unit a few days before. He didn't look too pretty after that'.

'I'm sorry, Ed'.

'You're sorry?' said Eddie. He had edged to within six inches of his brother, so close he could smell his breath.

'What more do you want me to say, bruv?' said Charlie.

'You can tell me why you did that? When you knew them guns would be used against me, your fucking brother. How about explaining that?' Kenny tried to intervene, but Eddie waved him away.

'Business, Ed. It was just business,' said Charlie. 'Ain't nuffin more complicated than that'.

Eddie grabbed Charlie by the throat, forcing him back down into the couch. He looked into his brother's eyes and saw a coldness looking back at him. As quick as it had materialised, Eddie's rage dissipated. It was clear to him now. He had known it all of his life but never been willing to admit it. Now he did.

'Just business? That's all it's ever been, ain't it?' he said. 'You never gave a fuck about anyone else. All you've ever cared about is yourself'.

Charlie responded with a simple, affirmative shrug. 'And you're different?'

'To you? Yeah, Charlie. I'm fucking different'.

'Bollocks,' his brother sneered. Before you got involved with us, you was on your way to Angola.' Charlie pushed Eddie backwards and forced himself up again. 'Why was that, hey? What selfless, higher purpose was you going to do that for? To give them democracy? For honour? For your country?' He poked Eddie in the chest and whispered, 'I'll tell you why. For money, Eddie. Blood-fucking-money'.

Eddie shook his head. 'You don't know what you're talking about,' he said.

'The fuck I don't,' said Charlie. 'It's all you know how to do, that's what you told me. And you needed the money'.

Charlie, now very much energised, pulled his cigarettes out from his shirt pocket and lit one. Then, through a cloud of fresh smoke, said, 'We might not be blood relatives, you and I. But don't kid yourself, Eddie. We're from the same stock. We are the same. Only difference is, I fucking know what I am and I always have. Whereas you have been deceiving yourself all your life'.

At that moment, Eddie's worldview collapsed.

Eddie leaned back against the wooden table. 'He's right,' he thought. *He's fucking right'*. There was no right to be wronged by being a mercenary. You weren't serving some higher calling. You were a hired gun - expendable cannon fodder serving at the beck and call of one faceless power broker trying to get one over another. His face betrayed his thoughts.

Charlie smirked. 'Penny dropped has it?' he snarled.

'Enough,' said Mike. 'Leave the kid alone. He don't owe you nothing. Or the rest of us'.

'He's right,' said Roger. 'This ain't your fight, Ed. No shame if you want to walk away'.

'I think you're all missing the fucking point,' said Charlie.

'What point is that?' said Roger.

'If we don't do this. If we don't pull off this score, it ain't just us what Pickering's gonna go after. It's the girls. It's Carol and Judy. It's our families back home'. Charlie shot Mike then Eddie the same furtive glance.' It's Veronica'.

The entire crew was looking at Eddie now.

He knew he should walk away and get the hell out of this accursed town, but Charlie was right. Again. Eddie had seen what Bobby Pickering and his crew were capable of. They were not 'old school' villains. They were of a new breed. The kind that was willing to do anything and hurt anyone that got in their way. Eddie had shot men in the army, and he had shot Gerry Lannigan. That made him a killer. Pickering, however, was a cold-blooded murderer and Eddie had no doubt that he was a threat to the women. Sending them back to England would make them no safer.

And if that was true, he thought. 'Then what's stopping the

bastard getting to Mary' He sat back down on his chair and downed the remains from his glass of scotch.

'I'll do this, but not for you or this fucking crew,' he said. 'I'm doing it for my daughter'.

'Good,' said Charlie. 'Set it up Mike'.

CHAPTER THIRTY-ONE
MOROCCANS

The decision made, and after several industrial-strength coffees, the Five Bullet Crew swung into action with all the efficiency of the old days.

Kenny drove back to his apartment block and promptly broke into his neighbour's flat to steal the absent man's boat keys. Bill, acting upon Eddie's advice to disguise himself, acquired a golden-blonde toupee and mirrored shades, then set off to a commercial vehicle rental shop in Malaga along with Roger, to hire a truck. Eddie purchased several maps of Spain from a local newsagent, then returned to the cafe where he set about planning the routes to and from Santander. Mike, as Charlie had instructed, accompanied Lucian to buy a set of Soviet military radios from an Israeli contact who operated out an industrial estate on the outskirts of Cádiz. Charlie drove to a chiringuito beach bar in Estepona to meet with the Moroccan's man in Spain and to conclude the drug deal.

Their tasks concluded, the Englishman all met back up later that afternoon to review their progress.

'So how'd it go with the Moroccan?' asked Mike.

'Seems like a straight-up geezer,' said Charlie. 'I met him in a mad beach bar in Estepona. You know it?'

DEN OF SNAKES

'Did you see the steel door at the back? I was told it goes underground to some old military bunker or something. Some local mafia boss owns it'.

'Yeah, the Moroccan told me that too,' Charlie replied. 'Anyway, it's on. And they only want seventy-five grand for the first shipment'.

'They must know it's worth a lot more than that?' said Eddie.

'He said his old man runs things over there and is keen to find a long-term partner who can handle all the logistics - getting it all into Spain, distribution across Europe. It's low risk for them that way. They just need to produce the stuff and get rich'.

Charlie put a briefcase onto the table and opened it. 'I've got forty-five grand here. Did you boys raise the rest?'

Bill reached into his jacket and Kenny into a backpack he had brought along. Together they put another twenty-five thousand pounds in.

'We're still five grand short,' said Charlie.

'I'm picking up eight grand from the pawnshop in the morning,' said Roger. 'It's for my sound system. It's worth twice that. Bastards are robbing me'.

'Buy another one when this shit's over,' said Charlie. 'Good, we've got the cash to buy the dope.

'How are we doing with the boat and truck?' asked Eddie.

'Truck's sorted,' said Bill. 'I got us a Volvo. It's in decent shape. It's parked up behind Roger's place in Estepona. It's an open-backed jobby, but we picked up a big tarpaulin to cover it over'.

'Good stuff, and the boat?'

'Piece of piss,' said Kenny and placed a large key fob onto the desk. The metal key ring was in the shape of three leaping dolphins.

'The radios are in the back of my car,' said Mike. 'They're Russian'.

'Russian? Are you sure they're okay?' asked Eddie. 'Did you try them out?'

'Soparla did. He said they're fine'.

'He better be right. Without radios, we'll never be able to coordinate the drop-off. We'll also be using them on the drive up to meet the buyer. One will be in the truck, the other in an escort car that will go a few miles in front to scout for any trouble'.

Eddie spread one map on the table and ran an index finger along the proposed route. 'We go from here to Granada, then up to Madrid. From there we go up this road, the E5, to Burgos. From there it's a straight line all the way to San Sebastian and on to where the exchange will take place, in a French village over the border, here in Hendaye'. He pointed to the ultimate destination. 'I've got alternative routes planned in case we run into the law along the way. It will be tight to get up there and back in time, Charlie. I don't like it. Can't this Dutch arsehole meet us a little nearer?'

'He won't cross the border. The Spanish police know what he looks like,' said Charlie. 'That's why he can't do the deal himself'.

'Sweet deal for him,' said Roger. 'We do all the work and take all the risks then he doubles his money'.

'Beggars can't be choosers,' said Bill.

Eddie clapped his hands to gain everyone's attention. 'Stealth is the order of the day here, gentleman. Stealth and vigilance. You all know what we're doing. Finish this, and we put this bleeding business with Pickering to bed. After that, you can focus on getting things back on track. Agreed?'

The crew nodded.

Eddie checked at his watch. It was just after six o'clock. 'Well, I suggest everyone grabs what kip they can. We've got a long day ahead of us tomorrow'.

They met up again that night at eleven o'clock outside Puerto Banus.

Kenny, Eddie, Mike and Charlie made their way down to the port before sneaking past the security booth - which turned out to be unmanned - and then along the gangway up to the yacht.

Bill and Roger loaded all the kit into the back of the truck, then started it up and headed off to the secluded car park on the western end of Casares Costa.

An hour later, as planned, the beach crew made the first radio call to the men on the boat which was ploughing its way out to sea. It was a cloudless night and the Spanish coastline soon became but a dark shape on the horizon. Kenny piloted the craft, with Eddie at his side perched on the second seat, scanning the horizon with a pair of binoculars. Mike and Charlie sat in two of the rear seats.

Bill's voice rang out from the two-way set. 'Mother Bear, this is Papa Bear over. You receiving, over?'

Mike looked at the device with disdain. 'Mother fucking Bear? What twat came up with that for fuck's sake?'

'It was Roger's idea,' said Kenny, chuckling. 'He said you'd hate it'.

Eddie lifted the radio's receiver and depressed the transmit button. 'This is Mother Bear. Picking you up loud and clear. Are you having fun at the beach party, over?'

'No gatecrashers to the party so far,' said Bill. 'Do you expect to arrive on time, over?' Eddie glanced at his wristwatch. 'Roger that, Papa Bear. We should be at the off-license in five minutes or so. If all goes well, we hope to join you at the party in under two hours, over'.

Charlie called out from behind him, 'Over there'. Eddie directed the binoculars to where his brother was pointing. 'Is that them?' he said.

'Looks like it,' Eddie replied, then peered again. 'Yes, I see the green signal light'. He picked up the radio receiver again. 'Papa Bear, we have located the off-license. Everything looking good, over'.

'Copy that. Call us when you are on your way, over and out'.

Kenny directed the boat towards the Moroccan's fishing trawler, and they pulled up alongside. Eddie counted half a dozen men on the deck of the elderly craft. One of them, a large black man called out. He seemed somewhat anxious to Eddie, who scanned the rest of the Moroccan crew for signs of an ambush.

'You are Charlie?'

'I am,' Charlie shouted back.

'You made it in very good time, English'. The man reacted and chortled.

'Nothing to this smuggling lark,' Charlie shouted back.

'Not when the sea is good to us like tonight,' the man said, flashing a set of remarkably white teeth. 'You have my money, yes?'

'We got it, my old mucker. Give us a sec'.

Charlie pointed at the tightly wrapped black package that contained their seventy-five thousand pounds. 'Get that over to them, boys'.

Eddie and Mike lifted the package which they had tied to a spherical buoy. They heaved the float overboard along with the bundle of money. The Moroccan produced a long pole with an iron hook at the end and fished around for the submerged rope. He located it in a few seconds and began tugging the package and the float up onto the fishing trawler.

Eddie put his hand to his waist and on the cold metal of the Browning pistol he had stuffed into it. 'This is where we find out if we can trust them,' he whispered.

The Moroccan with the bright teeth grabbed hold of the money package and dropped it to his deck. 'I check it. If it is okay, we give you the hashish'.

Charlie looked tense. Mike too. He had a shotgun ready at his feet, out of sight of the men on the other boat. Kenny was holding a silver revolver under the ship's wheel in one hand.

Eddie's heart was pounding. If the men on that boat had automatic weapons, they could overwhelm Charlie's crew in the blink of an eye.

'Is all good,' the Moroccan called out. He said something to his waiting crew.

'Be ready,' Eddie whispered his hand on the pistol butt. The safety catch was off, and he had a round chambered already. He need not have worried, however. Two of the Moroccans lifted another float, this one an empty oil drum, and pushed it over the side of the trawler. An orange nylon line followed it and then, one by one, rectangular packets, about the size of four shoe boxes, splashed down into the water.

'Help me get it hooked up, Mike. Eddie, you keep an eye out for unwanted visitors,' said Charlie.

Eddie picked up the binoculars and began scanning the horizon for other vessels. The moonlight was glimmering off the water. The yacht was a dark blue colour, but still all too visible, he thought. 'Hurry it up guys, we're sitting ducks here'.

'I got it,' said Mike. He heaved on the pole, pulling the float towards the side of the boat. Eddie heard the dull thud as it contacted the yacht's hull.

'Thats it,' said Charlie. 'Go on, pull it up'. Mike heaved on the pole once more until the float was level with the side of the boat, then Charlie grabbed it and yanked it on board. Both men then started heaving on the line.

'You have it?' the Moroccan called out.

'We got it,' shouted Mike, as he wrapped his hands around the first of the packages, then dropped it onto the wooden deck. 'Keep them coming'. Eddie put the glasses down to help.

Charlie chuckled. 'It's like a tug of war,' he said. Only each time we pull, ten grand lands at our feet'. Kenny left the cabin to push each of the damp packages to the rear of the vessel. It took fifteen minutes to get the entire load onboard.

'You have it all, English?' said the Moroccan.

'We do,' Charlie shouted in reply. 'Pleasure doing business

with you'. The Moroccan laughed as he saluted a brief farewell, then started barking orders at his crew. The trawler's engine, which had been lazily chugging away, increased in intensity and the water behind the vessel churned.

'Let's make like shepherds,' said Eddie to Kenny.

'Huh?'

'Get the flock outta here'.

Kenny pushed the boat's throttle lever forward, and the engine below them roared. 'Full steam ahead,' he shouted.

Eddie watched as the distance between the two boats increased. In a few minutes, he had lost sight of the Moroccan's. 'What a business,' he thought. They must be able to live like kings in Morocco, doing this. He sat back, leaning against a pile of the hashish packages, and looked up at the moon. The vista looking back towards the Spanish coast was serene, almost cartoon-like. He was struggling to keep his eyelids open. 'No harm in catching forty winks,' he told himself, but had closed his eyes for only a few seconds when Mike shouted out a warning.

'I hear another boat'.

Eddie grabbed the binoculars and sprung up. 'Where?' he said.

Mike had his hands cupped around both ears, trying to gauge the direction of the sound he had just heard. 'That way,' he said, pointing over to their left.

Eddie could make nothing out above the sound of their own boat engine at first, but then he heard it. The subdued roar of what could only be some kind of naval vessel. He bounded over to the cabin and hit the light switches. 'Kill the engine,' he barked at Kenny. 'Everyone, quiet!'

The boat's engine coughed to a stop, and they sat bobbing from side to side in the gentle swirling sea, the water lapping at the ladder at the craft's rear.

'I see it,' said Mike. 'Coastguard patrol boat'.

'Fuck,' Kenny said, voicing what the others no doubt also felt.

Eddie lifted the binoculars towards the sleek grey vessel. 'It's six or seven miles away, I reckon. Looks like it's heading south west'.

'Won't they pick us up on their radar?' said Kenny.

Eddie looked back in the direction they had just come. 'The Moroccan's boat will be a much bigger radar signature. The hull was metal. This thing's fibreglass and plastic'. He peered at the coastguard boat again and breathed a sigh of relief. 'I think we're okay'.

'We should get moving in case they change their minds,' said Charlie.

'Aye aye, skipper,' said Kenny, and he pushed the throttle forward to full power. Mike looked at his watch.

'How long will it take to get to the truck?' he asked.

Eddie checked the charts, peered at the mountainous coastline. 'About an hour, maybe less'.

'I'll let Pappa Bear know,' Kenny said, reaching for the radio receiver.

Mike shook his head. 'Next time, I pick the fuckin' call signs,' he muttered then slid down to the deck, resting this head on his forearm and shut his eyes.

They arrived, fifty minutes later, at the eastern end of Playa Ancha, the long sandy bay that stretches from the small fishing village of San Luis de Sabinillas to the rocky outcrop at Casares Costa which is dominated by the ruins of a sixteenth-century Moorish watchtower.

As Kenny had said, the new estates of holiday homes, or *urbanizacions* as the Spanish called them, remained very much under construction, and the beach appeared free from prying eyes.

Eddie and Mike jumped into the dark shallows and were greeted by the visibly relieved Bill and Roger, who bounded across the sand to help unload the hashish bales.

'Are we glad to see you lot,' said Roger, as Kenny released the anchor down into the water.

'How'd it go,' asked Bill. 'Any trouble?'

'Almost ran into the coastguard on the way back,' said Kenny. 'Other than that it went like a dream'.

'We could do this every week,' Mike declared as he dangled the first of the dope packages over the side. 'We'd pay for them apartment blocks of yours in no time'.

Charlie muttered something under his breath. 'Let's just get this job done, hey?' said Eddie, once again acutely aware of how vulnerable they were at that moment.

It took ten minutes to empty the boat of its illicit cargo, at which point Kenny clambered down the ladder at the back of the yacht and splashed his way out of the shallow waves. Behind him, a flickering orange glow was emanating from within the cabin.

'You didn't tell me you would burn the fucking thing,' Eddie hissed, his survival instincts now even more heightened.

'Don't wanna leave no evidence, do we?' said Mike as they ran back to the car park. The fire was taking hold quickly.

'Jesus fucking christ, move it before somebody sees it,' Eddie ordered.

They raced to the back of the truck, which was waiting in the darkness with the engine ticking over. Roger was at the wheel. 'All aboard that's coming aboard?' he shouted in a playful voice.

'Get a fuckin' move on,' shouted Eddie. The truck pulled away at an agonisingly slow pace, and he scanned the road for signs of traffic. It was approaching three o'clock in the morning on a weekday, he reasoned, and they were hardly in the middle of tourist central. 'Still,' he thought. 'I'll be glad when we're a few miles down the road'.

The lorry came to a halt in the empty yard behind Roger's car dealership on the industrial estate north of Marbella. It was just past four o'clock. It was deadly quiet aside from an occasional shrill call of a randy cicada, and a distant dog barking.

The weary crew disembarked from the truck's rear door and made their way into the single-story building via the back door, lugging their rucksacks. Once inside they each claimed a space on the floor and unpacked their bedding.

Eddie crawled into the same sleeping bag he had taken to London for the United Security robbery. That job had proven to be a failure on account of the haul of 'diamonds' turning out to be worthless quartz. It had, however, shown the crew at their most capable. Eddie drifted into sleep, hoping that the Five Bullet Crew would be just as professional over the coming twenty-four hours. He harboured a strong suspicion their days as a unit were numbered.

Little did he realise just how short their future together would be.

CHAPTER THIRTY-TWO
ROADTRIP

Eddie drifted back into consciousness at six o'clock the next morning. It took several seconds for him to establish where he was. It was dark, but he could sense someone moving in the room. He put his hand down to where he had left the Browning.

'Alright, bruv. Just me,' said Charlie. 'Wake the rest of 'em will you. I'll stick the kettle on'. Eddie did as he was told, then made his way to Roger's office, using the smell of fresh toast as a navigational aid.

'Get that down yer,' said Charlie as he entered the room, holding up a mug of coffee. The others arrived, equally weary.

'Eat up quick. We leave in fifteen,' Charlie commanded.

'What day is it?' asked Mike, sounding anxious.

'Wednesday. Innit?' said an unsure Kenny, yawning.

'It's Wednesday, yeah,' Bill said, his mouth full of half-chewed toast.

'Shit,' Mike cursed. 'I'm sorry, Charlie. I forgot'.

'Forgot what?'

'I'm supposed to report in at the cop shop, ain't I?'

'What are you talking about?' said Kenny.

'For fuck's sake,' Charlie cursed. 'That's today? What time?'

'Ten,' Mike replied.

Charlie buried his head in his hands.

'Is someone gonna tell me what you're talkin' about?' said Eddie, yet again feeling distinctly under-informed.

'Mikey has to show his face at the police station every week,' said Charlie.

'Part of the bail conditions, weren't it,' said Mike. 'Don't worry, Charlie. I'll fuck it off'.

Charlie shook his head. 'You can't. This…what we're doing here is exactly what they're on the lookout for. If you don't show your ugly mug, they'll come looking for us, too. Fucking hell'.

'Do we have time to wait for him?' asked Bill.

'Only if that truck of yours does a hundred and twenty,' said Eddie.

'So, what then?' asked Roger.

'It don't change nothing,' said Eddie. 'Bill, you and Roger go in the truck as planned. We'll be in radio contact. Me and Kenny will take the car. We'll be about five miles ahead, scouting for trouble'.

Mike sighed. 'You sure you don't need me?' he asked.

Eddie gulped down a mouthful of coffee and glanced at his watch. 'It's probably for the best. You can keep an eye on the girls while we're gone'.

'If nuffin else goes sodding wrong,' said Roger, frustrated by the enforced change of plan.

'We'll be fine. There's plenty of time to get up to the rendezvous for eleven tonight as planned. The exchange won't take ten minutes, but we'll need a few hours kip before we head back south. I reckon we can be back at around eight tomorrow evening'.

'Best we get moving,' said Bill. The crew guzzled the last of the coffee and gathered their kit.

'I'll clear up here,' Mike offered as they bid him farewell. He cut a forlorn figure, thought Eddie as he stepped outside.

Charlie, Roger and Bill clambered up into the truck's cabin and signalled at Kenny in the driver's side of a red Lancia HF Turbo, one of Roger's few remaining cars.

The radio in the car squawked into life. 'Testing, testing one, two, three,' Roger's voice said from the black box. 'This is Fat Boy, are you picking this up, Jack Rabbit, over?'

Kenny snorted. 'Ha, Mike would've loved that one'. He twisted the key in the ignition and the tuned engine burst into life.

Eddie grabbed the mic and responded. 'Getting you loud and clear…Fat Boy. See you at the first stop. Out'.

He hung the plastic device back on the radio.

'Right, let's get this show on the road'. Eddie peered up at Charlie, who was sitting in the right-most passenger seat in the truck cabin, and gave his brother a thumb's up. Charlie seemed not to notice. 'Lost in thought,' Eddie decided.

Kenny pulled the Lancia away and out onto the road. 'Not too fast,' said Eddie. 'Radio range is ten miles, tops. Less when we're up in the hills'. He looked in the wing mirror as the green and red truck pulled onto the road behind them.

'Did you know Mikey had to go to the cop shop?' asked Kenny. 'Nobody told me'. His tone had a distinctly deliberate note. He peered at Eddie, waiting for a response.

Eddie just shrugged. 'It is what it is'.

'I suppose so,' said Kenny. he did not sound convinced. He was fishing for something, Eddie could tell. 'Just a bit of a surprise though, innit? Him not remembering till this morning'.

'He's tired. We're all are, Eddie replied. He pointed at a road sign to indicate they were approaching the turning that will take them onto the coastal road towards Malaga. 'We're coming off here'.

'I just hope it don't go pear-shaped. Us being a man down now, coz of that dozy sod,' said Kenny.

'We'll be fine'. Eddie lit a cigarette and wound down the window.

The sky was clear, save for a few wisps of cloud around the upper reaches of the dark peaks on the horizon. He looked at his watch. It was 7.20am. They would pull over and make the first radio check-in at eight o'clock, while waiting for the truck behind to come into sight, then moving off ahead of it again. That would be the pattern for the entire day - drive, pull over, wait for Charlie, Bill and Roger to come teasingly close in the truck, then drive away once again - a perpetual game of vehicular kiss chase.

'Stick some music on,' Kenny said. He reached across and opened the glove box to reveal a heap of cassette tapes. 'I grabbed them from Roger's shop,' he said. 'Don't know what's there'.

Eddie spied a Thompson Twins album, pushed it into the car stereo and pressed play. "Doctor Doctor" played through the door speakers.

'What the bleedin' hell's this crap?' said Kenny.

Eddie just smiled, his arm resting on the open door window, and took a long drag on the cigarette. He could feel the lack of sleep already.

This will be a long day.

Fat Boy, the truck, and Jack Rabbit, the nippy hatchback, carving their way northwards through the Spanish countryside, their occupants taking it in turns behind their respective wheels and stopping only to refuel and to grab supplies of water, snacks and confectionery.

They reached the outskirts of San Sebastian ten minutes after nine o'clock and stopped at a Repsol garage close to the French border. They parked up at the edge of the expansive, gravel lorry park, away from other cars and commercial vehicles.

'I need a piss,' said Kenny, pushing the passenger door open. Eddie got out, his boots crunching in the gravel, and stretched his back, clicking it in several places.

'You sound worse than me,' said Bill who had climbed down from the truck, its hot engine ticking away'.

'All good?' Eddie asked while reaching down to touch his toes.

'Apart from Roger polluting the air as usual,' said Bill.

'I told you. I can't help it,' Roger complained. 'Doc said it was congenial'.

'Pretty sure he meant "congenital", mate,' Eddie said.

Charlie appeared from around the far side of the truck. His eyes were darting from side to side, surveying the space around them as he stuffed a fresh cigarette into his mouth. 'You alright, bruv?' said Eddie.

'Yeah, no worries,' said Charlie, without making eye contact. 'Keep an eye out. I'm gonna check on the kit'. He moved to the toolbox behind the cabin, opened it, then pulled out an object wrapped in an oily rag. He unravelled it to reveal a Sten gun and several magazines.

'Let's hope we don't need that,' said Eddie, as Charlie pulled back the weapon's bolt then dry fired it.

'I ain't taking no chances,' he said, before wrapping the gun back in the rag. 'Right, we all clear what we're doing?' The others assembled around him. 'You wanna go through it one more time, bruv?'

'Sure,' said Eddie, before clearing his throat. 'The rendezvous point is about eight miles over there,' he said, pointing towards the border with France.

It was almost night now, and they could see the lights of several boats out on the sea to their north.

'We're meeting in a car park on the western side of a small harbour,' Eddie continued. 'It's all industrial stuff around there, so it should be empty but Ken and I will go in first, check things out then radio for you boys to come and join us'. He looked at Kenny. 'You sure know what this Dutch fucker looks like?'

'I know him,' he replied, nodding.

'Good. Assuming they are here in good faith and ain't gonna try nothing, then we get this done as fast as we can, take the dough and get the fuck out of there as fast as possible. Bill, you're driving the truck. When you drive in, swing it around and stop with the back facing the sea. They can pull up next to us. That will stop prying eyes from seeing what we're unloading'.

'What if they want to try it on?' said Roger. 'I mean, we ain't had too much luck with being able to trust people of late, have we?'

'It'll be fine,' grumbled Charlie.

The men traded glances, each of them sharing the same familiar pre-event jitters. The coastal air was surprisingly chilly for the group who were dressed for the Costa del Sol, not the Bay of Biscay.

'Everyone checked their weapons?' asked Eddie.

'About a dozen times already,' said Kenny.

'C'mon,' said Bill. 'Let's get this over with'. He climbed up into the truck cabin and started the engine. Eddie started walking towards the red hatchback.

'Hold on,' Charlie called out. He shuffled towards Eddie, hands stuffed into his jeans pockets.

'What is it?' Eddie said. Charlie peered at him. He seemed to be struggling to summon the right words. 'Charlie. You're scaring me, mate. What is it?'

'I just…I just wanna -'. He paused.

'Yeah?' said Eddie. Charlie gazed out towards the dark horizon and to the intermittent, sparkling lights on the water far away.

'You coming up here with us. Doing what you've done already. Doing what you did the other night. Helping me…us, helping us to sort out this...this fuckin' mess with them East End bastards -'.

'It's okay, Charlie'.

'No. No, it's not. I mean, I got you involved in this whole shitty business. If it weren't for me, you'd be -'.

'Gettin' my arse shot off in Timbuctoo?' said Eddie.

Charlie forced a laugh. 'Whatever happens after this. No matter what goes down, I want you to know I'm sorry. Sorry for not keeping you out of it. Okay?'

Charlie's demeanour was worrying Eddie. Was his brother worried about meeting the Dutchman and his men? Was he scared? Or was it something else?

'Everything will be fine. One last hurdle and we're all in the clear again,' Eddie said.

Charlie nodded, his eyes still failing to hold Eddie's stare. He put his arm around Eddie's shoulder and hugged him. 'I know, but if it don't. If something goes wrong tomorrow, promise me you'll get the fuck out of this country. Get on the first train, plane or ferry you can and get away. Far away. And don't come back'.

'Charlie, are you sure you're okay?'

'I said promise me,' Charlie reiterated.

Eddie nodded. 'I promise'.

'Good'. Charlie released him and straightened up. His eyes were watering. 'I made mistakes, but I always did what I had to do'. With that, he turned back to the truck.

'Hurry the fuck up, will yer?' said Kenny, who was sitting in the passenger seat of the Lancia.

'I'm coming,' said Eddie, watching Charlie head back towards the truck. Something that his brother had just said was troubling him. What had he meant by, "If something goes wrong *tomorrow*"? His brother had meant *tonight*, hadn't he?

'Come on!' Kenny shouted.

Eddie walked to the red hatchback and sat down behind the wheel, then started the engine. Kenny sat next to him, his silver revolver between his legs. Bill was in the back, holding a sawn-off shotgun.

'Everything okay?' said Bill.

'Yeah, mate,' Eddie replied. He pulled the Browning from his waist and pulled the slide back to chamber a round. 'Let's fucking do this!'

Passing through the Spanish border into France had been easy. While there was still an official border between Spain and France, the former country's impending entry into the Common Market had led to a relaxing of the manning of the border crossings. Eddie had seen two Spanish policemen in a car at the checkpoint, but they had shown zero interest in the passing traffic.

The Lancia pulled up at the entrance to the car park at the French port at Hendaye. It was a sizeable area with the land side enclosed by a tall masonry wall about ten feet high. The interior was empty save for a few commercial vehicles, their drivers no doubt tucked up in a hotel bed close by.

Eddie killed the engine and lights, opened the driver's door and climbed out to scout the area. There was a cargo ship moored up at the far side, its powerful diesel engines throbbing away. Other than that, there was little sign of activity.

Eddie checked his watch. It was only ten-thirty. They were half an hour early. Charlie and Roger had parked the truck up at the side of the road a mile back, and would wait for the call on the radio from Eddie to bring it to the port.

'See anything?' said Bill.

'I don't think so,' Eddie replied, only then spotting figures moving in the shadows on the far side of the car park.

'What is it?' said Kenny.

'There's somebody there,' said Eddie. The dull yellow glow of a nearby sodium street light was hampering his night vision.

'Stay here,' he said, and took several steps forward, through the brick entrance.

'You're early, English,' a male voice said.

Eddie pointed the Browning in its direction, but his eyes had still not adjusted.

'Show yourself,' Eddie ordered. He heard Kenny getting out of the Lancia behind him, then saw the burning ember of a cigarette. 'I said, show yourself. Now!'

A man emerged from the shadows, hands up by his head, and stepped forward. He showed no fear of the weapon being directed at his midriff.

'No need for the weapon, my friend. We're only here to do business'. Eddie realised that the man was speaking in a Dutch accent. 'I am Jens,' said the man, holding out a hand. Eddie kept the pistol pointed at the approaching man.

'It's alright, Eddie,' said Kenny. 'That's our guy'. Kenny walked up to the man and shook the Dutchman's hand. Eddie lowered the pistol and moved back to the car. 'Good to see you again, Jens,' he heard Kenny say.

'And you, Kenny. It's been too long, yes?' He gestured behind him. 'Matthijs and Basti are here with me, in our van'. He looked back towards the red hatchback, an eyebrow raised. 'I am thinking you don't have my hash in that, no?'

'Nah, Charlie and Rog have it. They're in a truck parked up the road'. The Dutchman peered out of the entrance back up the street.

'Don't you guys trust me any more, Ken?'

'Course we trust you, mate. Can't be driving a truckload of dope in here without checking for the cops first though, can we?' Kenny turned back to face Eddie who was standing behind the car door. 'Give your bruv the all-clear, son'.

Eddie turned to face Bill, who was still sitting on the back seat. 'What the fuck's he playing at? There could be half a dozen blokes over there waiting to ambush us for all we know. What happened to scoping the place out first?'

Bill shrugged. 'Ken knows the geezer, they go back years. It'll be fine'.

'I hope you both know what you're doing,' said Eddie, he started up the Lancia and pulled it inside the vehicle park, behind the wall then reached for the radio's mic. 'Fat Boy, this is Jack Rabbit over'.

There was no answer, just a low-level white noise. Kenny and the Dutchman approached the car.

'Problem?' said the Dutchman, a fresh cigarette in hand.

Eddie ignored them and tried the radio again.'Fat Boy, this is Jack Rabbit, come in please'.

To Eddie's relief, Charlie's voice came back over the two-way. Kenny grinned and lit a cigarette for himself. He was far too relaxed for Eddie's liking.

'Jack Rabbit, this is Fat Boy. Are we good to proceed to the party, over?' Eddie looked over his shoulder at Kenny and the Dutchman, who could have been two friends catching up in the pub on a Friday night.

'It seems so,' said Eddie. 'We're with the host, over'.

'Copy that, Jack Rabbit. We'll be with you in two minutes, over and out'.

Eddie placed the mic back. 'Now what?' he said.

The Dutchman seemed amused. 'Now, you give me a shit load of drugs, and I give you a big bag of money. Come this way'. He turned and started strolling across the dimly lit car park, Kenny at his side.

'I don't fucking like this,' said Eddie. He started up the engine and flicked on the sidelights - just enough to give a better field of vision but not too bright to attract attention. The Dutchman pointed towards the white van where his two colleagues stood, arms crossed. Eddie felt for the reassuring bulk of the Browning in his belt as the Lanica crawled behind the walking Dutchman and Kenny.

The headlights of the lorry appeared in the rearview mirror, as it passed through the entrance into the port. 'Might as well announce our presence to the whole fucking world,' Eddie mumbled. He pulled up several spaces from the van, positioning the car for a speedy getaway and remained in his seat with the engine running. The truck pulled up next to the Dutch vehicle, and the two groups of men got to work.

The fifty bales of hash transferred from truck to van in under five minutes, then Jens handed Charlie a black duffel bag. Eddie watched as his brother peered inside to examine the contents. Satisfied, he shook the Dutchman's hand and signalled to the other Brits to depart.

'You let me know if you can get another shipment, okay?' said Jens as Charlie walked away.

Kenny climbed back into the passenger seat of the Lancia after letting Bill in the back. 'See. Nothing to worry about,' he said, as Eddie pulled away.

'Let's get out of here and back over the border before we count our chickens,' Eddie said. He fully expected an ambush as he exited through the brick gateway, but all was well, and he drove onto the road towards the Spanish border.

Only once they arrived back at the Repsol garage in Spain did he allow himself to relax. 'All had gone as planned for once', he thought. Or so it seemed.

They parked up in the secluded corner of the expansive lorry park and clambered out from the vehicles. Cigarettes were quickly placed in mouths and ignited.

'We did it,' said Bill. He was greeted with nods and relieved sighs, amid a cloud of smoke.

'This time tomorrow we'll have paid them cockney bastards off, and we can get back to what's important,' said Roger. He pulled a hip flask from his rucksack, took a swig, then passed it around. Charlie picked up his sleeping bag and shuffled to the truck door. 'Not want a nightcap, Charlie?'

'Nah, you're alright,' Charlie replied as he climbed back into the vehicle's cabin

'It's gonna kill me to see that money go to them wankers,' said Bill.

'Gotta do what we gotta do, Roger,' said Kenny, his tone morose.

Eddie checked his watch. It was half-past midnight. He pulled his sleeping bag from its stuff sack, leaned against the car and kicked off his trainers.

'We set off at six,' he said, yawning. 'Get some sleep. We're gonna need it'.

Eddie awoke to the electronic chirping of his wristwatch. The inside of the windscreen was misty with the moisture of his and Kenny's accumulated breath from the night just passed. He slid the sleeping bag down and poked Kenny into consciousness. The older man rubbed his eyes and groaned.

'I'll check on the others,' Eddie said, pushing the door open.

Bill and Roger were still asleep, but Charlie was awake already and stood smoking, peering through the chain-link fence at the seascape a few miles beyond. It was still dark, but the perimeter lighting provided sufficient illumination to see each other. A few vehicles were making their way along the main road close by, but it was otherwise a peaceful vista.

Charlie held out his cigarette packet, and Eddie took one while promising to himself that he would quit again, as soon as things returned to some kind of normality. 'Pretty, ain't it?' said Charlie.

Eddie nodded as he lit his smoke. 'You think it's all over, then?' he said. 'After we give Pickering that cash, I mean?'

'Let's see,' Charlie replied. It was hardly confidence-inspiring. 'Hopefully, that money gets the Cockneys off my back, but I've still gotta get everything going again'. Charlie sighed, still staring out towards the coastline. Behind them, Bill and Roger had escaped the confines of the truck cabin and were chatting. Kenny stood, arching his back nearby and grimacing.

'Don't lean too far, you old sod,' Roger teased. 'You might not make it back up again'. Kenny responded with a single middle digit.

'So, you're going for it still?' Eddie said to his sibling. 'In Spain, I mean?'

'Ain't no other way,' Charlie said. He seemed sad. Withdrawn. Broken, even.

'C'mon girls,' said Kenny. 'Can't stand here all fuckin' day'.

'Get ready, bruv. I need a quick word with Ken'. Charlie touched Eddie on the shoulder. 'Remember what I said. None of this was on you.' He tramped off back to the truck.

'I'm with Eddie,' said Bill.

'No, you and Roger are with me in the truck. Kenny's in the car'.

'C'mon, Charlie. I can't stand another day stuck in there with farty pants'.

'No,' Charlie repeated.

'Why not?'

'Coz, I fuckin' said so. Now shut up and get back in. We're behind schedule already'. He flicked the cigarette butt away and wandered over to talk to Kenny.

The years apart had not diminished Eddie's ability to detect that something was eating at his brother. He didn't know what it was, and Charlie was not in the most talkative of moods, but it had Eddie worried.

'See you in Marbella,' he shouted.

Charlie offered a faint smile in return. It seemed forced.

It was Kenny's turn to drive, so Eddie sat in the passenger seat. Kenny nodded towards the glove box full of music cassettes.

'Find something decent. Bit of Sabbath or something. None of that Boy George or "catchy koo koo" shit'.

'They're called "Kajagoogoo",' said Eddie.

'Whatever their fucking called. They're still shit'.

Eddie found a cassette on which someone had scrawled, "The Who - Who's Next".

'That old school enough for you?' he asked, holding the tape up for the older man to read the label.

'Fuck, yeah. Stick it in…said the nun to the vicar, haha'.

Eddie pushed the transparent cassette into the car stereo and turned it on. "Baba O'Riley" started playing from the speakers.

'I saw them a few times back in the late sixties,' said Kenny. His eyes had an energy in them that Eddie had not seen before. 'They used to play at the Railway Hotel in Harrow a lot'. He glanced at Eddie. 'You know it?'

'Yeah,' Eddie replied.

'Back when they were nobodies. Before they went off doing Woodstock and all that bollocks'.

Eddie sensed this was a chance to find out more about the side of his brother's past that he knew little about. He opened his cigarettes and offered one to Kenny.

'Yeah, cheers', Eddie held the lighter up for Kenny.

'I miss them days,' said Kenny. 'We had proper music back then. The Stones, Cream, Zepplin, Sabbath, Deep Purple. Proper fuckin' bands. Not like all this shit today'.

'Did Charlie like all that?' Eddie asked.

'Are you kidding? He was well into it'. Kenny chuckled as he took a draw on the cigarette. 'He had this black, leather biker's jacket what he nicked from a stall up Wembley market one Sunday'. He laughed again. 'Charlie took a bleedin' risk doing that, I'm telling you. The geezer what ran that stall was this huge nasty Irish fucker. Chased us halfway back up Wembley Way before we outran him'. Eddie hadn't seen Kenny like this before. The man seemed twenty years younger as he recounted his memories.

'When was this?' asked Eddie.

'Sixty-six. Sixty-seven, maybe. Anyway, Charlie loved that jacket he did. Wore it day in, day out for flipping years. We reckoned he slept in it. It ended up in a right scruffy state, but he still wore it every day'. The smile slipped away from Kenny's face. He seemed perplexed suddenly.

'Something up?' asked Eddie.

'Nah, I was just thinking I don't remember when he stopped wearing it'.

An ambulance car passed by on the opposite carriageway. Kenny pointed at the two-way radio. 'It's been a while. Best check in with the boys'.

They had been on the road for forty minutes. Eddie turned the volume down on Pete Townshend's wailing guitar and lifted the mic.

'This is Jack Rabbit, are you receiving us Fat Boy, over?' Roger responded a few seconds later.

'This is Fat Boy. We hear you loud and clear. What's your status, over?'

Eddie noted a nearby road sign. 'We just passed through a town called Talosa. Do we wait for you?'

Eddie heard his brother giving Roger instructions in the background.

'Not yet. Push ahead. We're about five miles behind. Let us know if you see any sign of bad weather, over'. "Bad Weather" was the crew's agreed term for the police and Guardia Civil.

Eddie smiled. 'Copy that. The *weather* looks good where we are. We'll check in again in thirty, over'.

'Thirty minutes,' said Roger. 'Copy that. Over and out'.

Eddie hung up the mic and turned the stereo's sound back up. He yawned. The lack of sleep over the last week was wearing him down. Still, he thought, things should calm down once they paid off the Cockneys.

'What's the time?' asked Kenny.

Eddie glanced at his watch. 'Just gone ten thirty'. Kenny seemed to be trying to formulate a question.

'Did you want to swap over yet?'

'Nah. We'll plough on for another hour then swap over. You

get some shut-eye'. Kenny seemed unusually alert, his eyes dancing around their sockets.

'You sure?' said Eddie.

'Yeah. I don't want you falling asleep when you're behind the wheel later'.

Eddie reclined his seat a few inches, relaxed his head and was asleep in seconds.

The rapid deceleration of the Lancia and the painful screech of its tyres thrust Eddie back into consciousness. It felt as if mere seconds had passed, but where before there had been craggy hills, Eddie saw only wide open plains. They were now stationary at the side of the road amid a cloud of tire smoke. Kenny was fighting with the radio mic.

'Fat boy, come in. Come in, god damn it'.

'What is it?' Eddie shouted.

Kenny didn't answer.

'Fat Boy. This is Jack Rabbit…Roger…what the fuck's going on?' The panic in Kenny's voice made it evident that whatever was occurring, it was bad.

'Kenny?' Eddie shouted.

'We gotta turn around,' he said. He glanced over his shoulder, plunged his foot to the floor and powered the hatchback straight across the road. They bounced over the gravel-laden central divider, and then onto the opposite carriageway. He worked through the gears like a madman.

'Kenny? What the fucking hell is happening?' said Eddie. The radio gave him his answer.

'I can't hold them off'. It was Charlie's voice, and he sounded desperate. 'They got Bill. Roger's hit too'. The sound of automatic gunfire cut across Charlie's voice.'

Eddie screamed into the microphone. 'Charlie. What the fuck's happening?'

'They forced us off the road. Bill was driving -'. More gunfire. 'Fucking bastards shot him in the face'.

'We're coming, Charlie. We're coming. Hold on'.

'You won't make it, bruv. They've pinned us down. I'm almost out of ammo'. Eddie heard more gun shots and the sound of smashing glass.

'Charlie!'

'Ed. Get out of here'. Another brief burst of automatic fire rang out.

'Give me a location, Charlie,' Eddie shouted.

'I'm out. I'm out. No more ammo'. Charlie's voice had morphed from urgent panic to utter resignation in the space of five seconds.

'Charlie -'.

'It was a setup, bruv. We both know who'.

'Charlie!'

'I'm sorry, Ed. I'm sorry. I'm so sorry'.

The line turned to pure static.

'Charlie?' Eddie started at the mic, awaiting a response. 'Charlie?' he shouted again. The car was slowing. Eddie slammed on the dashboard. 'What the fuck are you doing, keep going!' he bellowed.

'They're gone,' said Kenny. He pulled the Lancia onto the hard shoulder, and it lurched to a halt.

Eddie punched him in the arm, but Kenny barely reacted. 'We need to get to them,' he screamed. Still nothing from Kenny.

Eddie pushed the door open, sprinted around to the driver's door and pulled it open. 'Get out!' he yelled. He grabbed Kenny's arm, yanked him out of the car then pulled the seat forward. 'Get in the back'. He shoved Kenny in, jumped into the driver's seat, threw the gear stick into first and slammed this foot to the floor, leaving a twenty foot-long black mark on the tarmac behind him. 'Fuck,' he yelled, punching the steering wheel.

It didn't take long before Eddie caught sight of a plume of black smoke. He was still over a mile away, but he knew what it meant.

In less than a minute, the truck came into view. It had been driven into the concrete drainage gully at the side of the road and was now fully ablaze. Eddie slammed on the brakes, and the hatchback screamed to a halt. He leapt out, sprinted across the carriageway and then vaulted over the steel barrier between the north-bound and south-bound lanes.

Bill's body lay sprawled out at the side of the road. His teeshirt was dark crimson and half of his scalp was missing.

Eddie tried to get nearer to the truck, but the heat was unbearable and forced him back. Shielding his face with his hands, Eddie spotted Roger lying on his back, a pistol at his side and in a pool of his own blood.

'Charlie,' he shouted. 'Charlie'. Eddie moved around the front of the truck, getting as close as possible. The cabin had been punctured with dozens of bullet holes and Charlie's prize weapon, his Sten gun lay on the tarmac, an empty magazine beside it.

Eddie peered up towards the driver's door. The vehicle was a blazing inferno now, smoke bellowing out from the cabin. For a brief second he glimpsed a body slumped on the seat but the flames renewed in their intensity, soaring twenty feet up into the air and forcing Eddie to retreat.

He sunk to his knees, barely conscious of the sounds of police sirens approaching, and in that moment, Eddie knew that his brother was dead.

Time passed. Quite how much, Eddie could not tell. He sat slumped in the passenger seat of the red Lancia, as it hurtled along at over ninety miles an hour. Hazy memories of Kenny pulling him to his knees and back to the hatchback flashed by, but it was all a fuzzy montage of heat, smoke, tears and pain. His face stung as if it were severely sunburned. He peered into the mirror on the back of the sun visor. His skin was red and blotchy from the heat of the fire.

Eddie twisted around to look behind them, grunting as he did so. The road was empty - no sign of the burning truck or the plume of acrid smoke.

'You were out cold,' said Kenny. 'For ten minutes. Maybe more'. He thrust a bottle of water at Eddie. 'Wash your eyes out with that'.

'Where are we going?' said Eddie, coughing. His throat was sore from inhaling smoke.

'As far away from…there, as possible'.

'They were dead,' said Eddie, only now reconstructing what he had witnessed.

'I know, son,' said the older man.

Eddie poured a little water into his hand and splashed it into his eyes to rinse them. The discomfort brought back fleeting memories of being exposed to tear gas in Armagh, several years earlier. The water helped.

'He said it was an inside job,' Eddie said. Kenny nodded. 'He said we knew who it was'.

'Mike,' said Kenny. 'Has to be'.

'Why would he do that to us?' he asked, rubbing his eyes again.

'Because he's a selfish wanker, and because he's desperate'. Eddie looked at his watch, straining to focus. It was coming up to midday and would take another eight hours to get back to Marbella.

Eight hours to plan how he would make Michael McNaughton suffer.

CHAPTER THIRTY-THREE
THIS IS GONNA HURT. YOU

Kenny stood leaning against the Red Lancia Delta outside an apartment in Estepona's port. It was just approaching nine o'clock in the morning. Eddie, who had got out of the car further along the road before Kenny parked it, was now hidden in the shadows of a nearby restaurant's awnings. They were alone save for a team of rubbish collectors who were working their way up the street having just passed them.

Eddie peered up at the apartment on the first floor where Raquel, Mike's Spanish girlfriend, lived. Mike's car, the Audi A8 he had borrowed from Roger after his Ferrari had been confiscated, sat in the street behind the red hatchback.

Eddie nodded at Kenny to commence their pre-arranged plan. Kenny pressed on the doorbell several times in quick succession and stepped back into the street.

'Mike,' Kenny hollered. 'Mike, it's Kenny'. A light came on in the apartment. Kenny kept going. 'Mikey. I need to talk to you. It's Ken'. Eddie lifted the Browning High Power and pointed it towards the apartment entrance. The image of the burning truck was still foremost in his mind, and his blood was up. He wasn't at all sure if he would follow through on the plan, or whether he was just going to shoot Mike on the spot.

There was a ruffle of curtains at the window and the shadow of a figure moving around inside. Eddie heard a Spanish woman shouting, followed by the muted sound of a male voice. Eddie gestured at Kenny to keep going while monitoring the road for passersby. There were none.

'Mikey. Come on, mate. I need your help'. The light in the apartment came on. Eddie wondered if perhaps the woman had found herself a new sugar daddy, but a few seconds later the apartment block's front door opened and Mike appeared. He paused with the door open, alive to some kind of threat. Kenny remained leaning against the Lancia and was now feigning an injury. He had wrapped one arm around his belly and groaned.

'What is it?' Mike asked. He sounded suspicious. Kenny slid down the car door towards the pavement. Mike took a step forward but still had one hand on the door, ready to slam it shut at the slightest sign of danger - he and Kenny were not, after all, the best of friends. Not since the incident at the beach club when he had broken Kenny's cheekbone.

'Help me, Mike. Help me,' Kenny groaned. That did it. Mike started down the stairs towards Kenny who was turning his back on him, appearing to be struggling to clamber up from the ground.

'What is it? What happened?' said Mike. Eddie could see that Mike had a revolver stuffed into the back of his jeans.

As the big man approached Kenny, Eddie slipped out of his hiding spot and closed up behind him. 'Don't fucking move,' he said. Mike stiffened, realising straight away they had duped him. 'Go for that pistol, and I'll end you, right here. Right now'.

'What is this?' said Mike. Kenny rose up, snaked one of his freckled arms around Mike's waistline and extracted Mike's revolver. Eddie pointed the Browning at Mike's chest. 'I don't know what you think I've done -'. Kenny cracked him on the back of the head with the pistol butt. Mike's legs buckled, but he did not fall.

'Fucking traitor,' Kenny snarled. He shoved Mike, who now

had both hands on his head, towards the back of the car. 'Open it,' he said, pointing at the hatchback.

Mike glanced at Eddie. 'You're making a mistake, son'.

'It won't be the first,' Eddie said, his pistol still pointing at Mike's chest, his finger curled around the trigger. He nodded at Kenny, who took a length of electrical cable from his pocket and tied it around Mike's wrists.

Mike let out a resigned sigh, glanced at the apartment above - likely realising that he would not be returning to it again - and clambered into the back of the car.

Eddie moved forward, reached for the hatchback and slammed it shut. 'Move,' he shouted to Kenny who was still fetching the keys from his trouser pocket.

They drove to an industrial park on the northern outskirts of Estepona, pulling up to the roller shutter doors of a vehicle repair shop. A middle-aged man, with tattoos on both arms, beckoned them in as he lifted the steel curtain up. Kenny drove the Lancia into the darkened interior. After he closed the doors behind them, the man approached Kenny and Eddie and, speaking in a soft Liverpudlian accent, asked, 'It's all there. Just like you asked'. Kenny slipped the man a wad of banknotes. He checked the money before stuffing it into his back pocket.

'Don't come back today,' said Kenny. 'And not a fuckin' word. Not to nobody'. As if to underwrite the verbal warning, Kenny lifted his shirt to expose the silver revolver poking out of his waistline. The Scouser nodded, collected a jacket from a nearby table and ambled towards a door to the outside. As soon as the man had closed it behind him, Eddie reached for the release catch on the back of the Lancia's rear door. It lifted to reveal Mike laying in the foetal position, staring back up at him.

'Get up,' Eddie commanded, pointing his pistol at Mike who struggled to get out of the car's sunken boot with both hands bound behind his back, whereupon Kenny shoved him towards a wooden chair positioned between an old Peugeot van and a rusty, red MGB Sportster.

Mike shuffled forward, offering no resistance, and sat down, after which Kenny lashed his feet and arms to the chair with more electrical cable. Eddie strode around his prisoner, his gun held at the ready, until he was facing him. Mike seemed resigned to his plight - Eddie would have admired his calmness under different circumstances.

'Get on with it,' said Mike.

'Oh, I intend to,' said Eddie, his eyes fixed on Mike's. Eddie placed the heavy pistol down on the bonnet of the MG, strolled towards Mike, and hit him on the side of the face, full-force, with a left hook. 'Tell me why you did it,' he growled.

Mike blinked to regain his vision and spat out a mouthful of blood. He glared back at Eddie. 'I didn't do nothing, son,' he said. He twisted his head to face Kenny, who remained standing behind him. 'I ain't no rat'. Eddie hit him again, this time with a right uppercut. A pain shot down his forearm and he had to grit his teeth to hide it.

'They killed him. My brother. They shot him and left him to burn in that fucking truck'. Eddie struggled to contain his rage. He clenched his teeth and struck Mike once again with another right hook to the cheek. This time Mike could not hide his discomfort. He panted for a few seconds, eyes clenched shut as he fought the pain, and spat out more blood and with it, a molar. Kenny was grinning. He is enjoying it, Eddie thought. Too much.

Mike lifted his head back up and sighed. 'I know you ain't gonna believe me, Ed. I probably wouldn't neither. Not in your shoes'.

'You going to tell me you know nothing again?' said Eddie daring him, his fists clenched tight.

'You've had this coming for a long time, you wanker,' said

Kenny, his finger tapping on the revolver's trigger guard. Mike gave him a bloodied grin.

'What's so fucking funny?' Kenny demanded, his finger working its way onto the trigger and his grip on the pistol tightening.

'Feeling tough with a gun in your hand and me all tied up, huh?' Kenny lifted the pistol. 'Surprised you ain't cum in your pants already you snivelling little shit'.

'Keep calling me names. See what happens'. The pistol was now pointing at Mike's thigh.

'Now that's funny,' said Mike.

'Yeah, how's that?' said Kenny. Mike grinned, releasing a two-foot-long string of blood and saliva from the side of his mouth. It landed on the floor at his feet.

'It's funny,' said Mike, turning to look at Eddie. 'Coz, I always figured he'd stab me. In the back'. Something in Mike's eyes concerned Eddie. His bloodlust had diminished, being taken up instead by Kenny.

'You still want to tell us you're innocent?' Eddie persevered. 'That you had nothing to do with what happened to them?' Mike's head dropped a little lower. He rolled his lower jaw around, wincing as he did but offering no response.

'Just fucking shoot him,' said Kenny.

Eddie ignored him. He took a step nearer Mike and lowered himself down to his knees, then thrust out a hand to clamp Mike's throat. 'You betrayed your best friend, my brother. Say it'.

'Can't say what ain't true'.

'Shoot the fucking bastard,' Kenny snarled. Eddie tightened his grip, pressing his thumb and forefinger hard around Mike's larynx.

The older man coughed. 'Do what you gotta do,' he said, blood dribbling from his mouth. 'But I can't tell you what you want to hear, coz it ain't what happened'.

Eddie released his grip and stood up. He stood poised,

ready to deliver a volley of blows on the man's face, but his gut instinct was telling him that Mike was telling the truth. Could Mike be innocent? And if so, who was it that had betrayed them? He pushed the thought away and continued. 'You're the only one that knew the plan who weren't there with us. Only you, Mike. How stupid do you think we are?'

Kenny seemed agitated. Like his prize was slipping away. 'C'mon, Ed. He's the reason Charlie, Rog and Bill are dead. Fucking end it. Kill the bastard'. Kenny was egging Eddie on with the pistol in his hands, but Eddie would not be rushed.

'Gimme one good reason why I shouldn't put a bullet through your eye, Michael'. Mike simply shook his head once more and spat out more blood. 'You are the only one that knew about the truck, the route. The whole fucking plan. You told someone, didn't you? You sold us out? Why? What for? Money?' He punched Mike again, but less hard than before. 'At least have the decency to admit it before I shoot you'.

'There ain't nothing more I can tell you, son. It don't matter, it's all over now. It's all gone'.

Kenny pushed his revolver against the side of Mike's head. 'Let me fucking do it,' he said.

Eddie pushed the gun away. 'Admit it,' he shouted in Mike's face.

'Pull the trigger already. This is getting boring'.

'I agree,' said Kenny and raised his pistol again.

Eddie stepped in between them and grabbed the gun out of Kenny's hand.

Kenny gawped at Eddie with consternation. 'What the -'.

'I'll handle it,' said Eddie.

'Don't tell me you believe him?' said Kenny, shaking his head. 'He's lying. He fucking did it'. Eddie said nothing, but he was wavering and Kenny could see it. 'For Christ's sake, Eddie. Your face is still red from the heat of the fire. The fire that your brother fucking died in'.

Eddie pushed Kenny away. He shifted back to Mike. 'Who did you buy the radios from?' he said.

Mike seemed confused by the change of tack. 'Some Israeli geezer...in Cadiz. Soparla took me to see the bloke. Charlie organised it, remember?'

Kenny tried to interject once more. 'What the fuck does it matter where the radios came from?' Eddie ignored him.

'What did you tell the bloke?' asked Eddie.

'Nuffin'.

'You sure about that?'

'Yeah, well, no'.

'Yes or no? Which is it?'

'I didn't say nothing about the plan'. Mike was thinking hard now.

'But?' said Eddie.

'But we said they had to work at long distance. And at sea'.

'So this bloke. This dodgy, back street peddler of military kit knew that we were doing something "at sea" '.

'Yeah, but we could have just been going Pike fishing for all he knew'.

'Pike are freshwater fish, you moron,' said Eddie. Eddie's head was racing. Had Charlie told Soparla what the crew were planning? Was the Romanian behind what had happened to Charlie and the others?

Mike was not the sharpest tool in the box, but it was beginning to dawn on him he was not the only suspect now.

'You think maybe Soparla did this?'

Eddie lowered the pistol. 'Seems possibly, don't you think?'

'So what? We're not shooting him now?' said Kenny, his jaw quivering in disbelief.

'Nobody's shooting nobody,' said Eddie.

Kenny shook his head and pointed a boney finger towards Mike. 'You're making a mistake,' he said.

'So people keep telling me,' said Eddie as he untied Mike.

'Lucian wouldn't have sold us out,' said Kenny. 'He's our man'.

'Ain't everyone?' said Eddie. 'Until they're not'. He helped Mike to his feet. 'I thought it was you'.

Mike waved his apology away. 'I weren't there. I should have been'. He rubbed his jaw.

'It wouldn't have changed anything. Except you'd be dead too'. Eddie offered him a handkerchief. 'Are you alright?'

Mike snorted his derision at the question. 'You hit like a girl. Don't they teach you army blokes anything?'

Eddie laughed. 'Guess I'm rusty,' said Eddie. 'We could go again?'

Mike wiped the blood from his face. 'Thanks, but I'm off to find that bastard Soparla. You pussies coming?'

CHAPTER THIRTY-FOUR
CAN LUCIAN COME OUT TO PLAY?

Eddie pulled the Lancia up around the corner from the apartments where their new suspect, Lucian Soparla, lived.

'That's it,' said Mike, pointing up to the second floor as he got out of the passenger seat. 'There's a staircase at the side of the building'. He lifted the seat forward for Kenny to get out of the car.

'Let's see if the bastard's in,' said Eddie, striding forward. They clambered up the concrete staircase and approached the door to the Romanian's flat.

'It's open,' said Mike. Mike lifted his sawn-off shotgun and pushed the door open, Eddie covering his back with his pistol. The three men tip-toed inside. The living room was a mess, but whether it had been the scene of a recent brawl or whether its occupant just lived like that, Eddie could not tell.

'Fuck me, what's that smell?' said Kenny. Mike, who had opened the door to the flat's only bedroom, answered.

'I found Soparla'. His face was grim. He gestured at the others to look inside. Eddie prepared himself, moved to the door and peered in to see the Romanian's dead body. His hands were bound behind his back and his mouth gagged. He had a bullet hole between his eyes.

Eddie lowered his pistol. 'Guess we can rule him out then,' he said.

'Oh, Christ,' said Kenny, covering his nose and mouth with the back of hand. He pointed inside the small ensuite bathroom. There, crumpled up in the bathroom, was the naked body of a woman, her long blonde hair matted with blood.

'Looks like she was in the shower when the shooter arrived,' said Mike, shaking his head. He reached for a bathrobe and placed it gently over the woman's body.

'Who'd do this?' said Mike.

'Someone that wanted something,' said Kenny. 'Pickering's crew. Has to be'.

'I don't know' said Eddie. Kenny frowned.

'Who else could it be?' he asked. Eddie scanned the room. The front door showed no signs of damage - Soparla or his girlfriend might have willingly let the assailant in. The drawers and wardrobes were all still in place, the sheets remained on the bed and the furniture appeared unmoved. A suitcase sat on top of one wardrobe, still zipped shut.

'It ain't been searched,' he said. 'Looks to me like someone was tying up loose ends. Someone that knew what Lucian and his girlfriend did for Charlie, maybe. And the secrets they could tell'.

'That Spanish politician Charlie squeezed?' asked Mike. 'Sophia Valázquez? Fernandez maybe? Or Daniel-fucking-Ortega?'

'It could be any of them. Either way, we need to get out of here'. Kenny nodded, and they hurried outside, pulling the door behind them.

Mike tapped Eddie on the shoulder and lowered his voice. 'What if Charlie and Lucian were -'.

Kenny's panicked call from outside interrupted whatever it was Mike was about to ask.

'We got company,' Kenny said. He pointed to a red Fiat

DEN OF SNAKES

Panda on the street below from which were emerging several men.

Eddie recognised them instantly. 'It's Pickering. There's five of them'. He observed them for a few more seconds. 'They're coming up'.

'Fuck,' said Kenny in a panicked voice. 'Is there another way out of here?'

Eddie glanced back along the hallway. Lucian's apartment was the last one on that floor - there was no other way down. 'We're cornered. Find cover'. He ducked down behind a wall-mounted air conditioning unit and raised his gun towards the staircase twenty feet away. 'We're gonna have to shoot our way out of this'. He braced himself against the concrete column behind him. He could hear the Cockney's voices at the bottom of the staircase. He steeled himself - ready for the firefight to come - but then noticed Mike waving to catch his attention.

Eddie darted across to peer over the edge to see two sturdy-looking, cast iron drain pipes attached behind one of the building's concrete columns. There were sturdy-looking support brackets every two feet, making for a half-decent ladder. 'Get going,' he urged Mike, but the older man shook his head.

'You first. I'll cover you'. Mike strode away and pointed the shotgun towards the stairs. 'Go, now!'

Eddie shoved Kenny towards the edge. The short man did not need a second telling and flung a leg over the concrete wall, grabbed hold of one of the pipes, then started to climb down as fast as he could. 'Mike!' Eddie called out.

'Find out who did this, Ed,' Mike said, his eyes reddening. Pickering and his crew were almost upon them. Mike pushed Eddie towards the pipes. 'Get the fuck out of here. And make sure my Veronica is safe'. He spun on his heel and strode towards the stairs.

Eddie climbed over the edge, lowered a heel down onto one of the support brackets and grasped hold of a pipe. As he did so, his Browning slipped out from his belt and plummeted to the ground below. It landed on a patch of dirt and weeds right next to the startled Kenny. 'Shit'.

He looked back to see Mike raising the shotgun to his shoulder. The first of the East Enders appeared on the staircase. The man could not have had any idea what was about to happen to him. A lick of flame burst from Mike's gun, filling the unlucky man's leg with of a cloud of metal pellets. His blood splashed onto the whitewashed walls behind him, and he fell backwards down the stairs.

The other East Londoners were now taking evasive action. A second man attempted to raise a machine pistol towards Mike, who was still moving towards them, but a second blast caught the man in his shoulder and face, and he too crumpled to the floor.

Mike flung himself behind a column and attempted to reload the shotgun. He inserted two fresh cartridges from his pocket, cracked the gun closed again and stepped out into the hallway, but a bullet struck him in his side, stopping him in his tracks. Another shot hit him in his thigh. He dropped to one knee and tried to lift the shotgun up, but then a third round hit him in the right shoulder. The gun fell from his hand, and he let out an agonised roar.

Pickering strode forward, aiming his weapon at Mike's head. He kicked Mike's sawn-off away. 'Where's the others?' he demanded, but Mike was saying nothing. The East Londoner barked an order at his men. 'Search it. Careful. They're around somewhere'.

Eddie lowered himself out of the men's view, burying his head between the two pipes. The sensible thing to do would be to escape, but he had to bear witness to what was about to happen. For Mike's sake.

The two men, who had just kicked open the door to Soparla's flat, emerged back onto the walkway. One of them looked about ready to vomit.

'Anything?' said Pickering. The shorter of the two men shook his head.

'Someone else got here first. They're both dead. The geezer and his bird. Both shot'.

'Fresh?' asked Pickering.

The man shook his head. 'Nah. At least a day. Fucking stinks'.

'Check on the other two'. Pickering lowered himself down to his knees and glared at Mike who was panting, exhausted and spent. 'How are you, Micheal?'

'I've had…better days'.

Pickering waved his gun towards the apartment door. 'Know who did that?' he asked.

Mike lifted his head to look Pickering in the eyes. 'Figured you did'.

Pickering grinned. 'He ain't no use to me dead. Some Spanish geezer came to see me wanting to know what the Romanian knew. He was going to pay well. Very well'.

'Guess we're all…in the dark then,' said Mike, now struggling for breath.

'Seems that way'.

One of Pickering's men returned, having checked on their fallen colleague. 'Sam's okay. Just needs patching up. Keith's in a bad way though. Don't reckon he'll make it'.

'Get them to the car,' said Pickering, his voice assertive but calm. He shifted back to Mike. 'Any last words?'

'I wanna fuck your mum again,' said Mike.

Pickering snorted with laughter. 'She'd have enjoyed that, the old slag'. He thrust his pistol into Mike's chest and two shots rang out. Mike's body slumped to the floor as the East Ender spun away and marched back towards the stairs. Eddie could see the dead man's face. It displayed no sign of fear or suffering.

'Quite the opposite,' thought Eddie.

'Eddie,' Kenny called from below. 'Fucking hurry up'.

Eddie could hear police sirens in the distance and climbed down as fast as he dared. 'They shot him,' he said to Kenny as he reached the floor.

'Course they did'. Kenny's reply was emotionless. Matter of fact, even.

'Do you even give a shit?' said Eddie.

Kenny looked at him, offering no response, then jogged away towards an alleyway, without waiting to see if Eddie was following.

Eddie glanced back up the pipes down which he had just climbed, an escape that Mike had found for him but not taken himself. Eddie had started the day intending to kill the man. Mike, it had instead turned out, had saved his and Kenny's life. Eddie still did not know who was behind the deaths of his brother, Roger and Bill. Nor did he know what Pickering was planning, but as he started after Kenny, he promised himself that he would find out and that he would make them pay.

Eddie and Kenny watched from behind a wall as the East Enders drove away, before then hurrying to the Lancia. Eddie handed the keys to Kenny.

'Drop me off near Charlie's bar'.

'Why?'

'I want to check on something,' said Eddie. 'You find Judy and Carol. Tell them to pack a bag and get out of Marbella today'.

'They ain't gonna like that,' said Kenny.

'Fuck what they like,' Eddie barked. 'Whoever did this is cleaning up. They're in danger too'.

'And then what?' asked Kenny.

Eddie looked at his watch. It was approaching two o'clock in the afternoon. 'Gimme your phone number. I'll call you when I have something'. He found a biro in the car's glove box, ripped off the lid from his cigarette packet and scribbled Kenny's phone number on it, then inserted it into his wallet.

He pointed at a bus stop just ahead of them. 'Let me out

here'. Kenny pulled the car over and Eddie got out. 'Hang on,' he said, then went to the rear of the car and opened the rear hatchback. He picked up a tire iron, a hammer and a torch and placed them into a sports bag before closing the hatch and returning to the driver's side.

'I'll call you this evening'.

'Be careful, kid,' said Kenny.

'You too'.

CHAPTER THIRTY-FIVE
SEX, LIES & VIDEOTAPES

Eddie made his way through the backstreets that led down to the beachfront and to the blackened ruins of his brother's bar.

Little survived of the upper structure except the concrete columns, several twisted metal beams and some masonry walls. The local council had erected sections of temporary, interlocking steel sheet fencing, and black and yellow tape marked, *"Policía. No entrar"* surrounded the entire area.

After surveilling the scene for several minutes and certain there were no police present, Eddie crossed the road, taking care to hide his face with his hand. He slipped between a gap in the fencing and darted up the remains of the stairs that lead into the bar's former entrance.

The concrete beams and columns remained in place, albeit blackened, but the ceiling was no more; its charred remains and shattered glass littering the floor. Taking care to avoid the dangers underfoot, Eddie made his way towards the cellar entrance, thankful that he was wearing combat boots and not some pair of flimsy trainers.

The aluminium door to the beer cellar was now a molten mass on the concrete floor, and the concrete staircase and brick wall beyond was pitch black. He pulled the torch out of the bag, switched it on and directed it down into the abyss below. The air was damp and thick with the fumes of combusted materials.

He edged down, checking the integrity of the stairs with each step until he reached the bottom, at which point he stepped into a shallow pool of water. It was several inches deep and seeped into his boots. He made his way along the corridor, pushing between the warped remains of a dozen beer barrels and other detritus. The atmosphere was dank and acrid. Eddie shielded his mouth and nose with a handkerchief while attempting to avoid tripping over the unseen obstacles under the water.

Eddie reached the steel door that once prevented entry to Charlie's secret room. It was ajar. He pointed the torch at the wall above the door and examined the seared brickwork and plaster. He had been around enough fire-damaged buildings to read the pattern of scorch marks and realised that the room was the source of the inferno. The realisation came as no surprise.

He tried to yank the door open, but it was wedged firm, so he thrust the crowbar into the gap and tugged with all his might. The door gave way with a groan, and he pulled it open wide enough to slip inside. He directed the beam around the room and saw little remaining of the workbenches and lockers. There was, however, a potent smell of gasoline.

He swung the light towards the old electrical cabinet behind which Charlie's safe was hidden. The panel door was wide open, as was the safe inside, which was empty. Whoever started the fire must have known what was inside, and they had burned the building to cover their tracks. Eddie examined the steel door. It was blackened and somewhat warped, but the lock mechanism was intact.

With nothing more to learn, Eddie made his way back along the dank passageway, up the stairs and out of the ravaged building. He strode up the hill away from the bar, leaving a trail of wet footprints behind him, and racking his brain for answers.

How could anyone have defeated that steel door and its

hefty, seven-lever mortice lock? It would have been almost impossible to pick.

And then it dawned on him.

He stopped in his tracks, and an icy shiver ran down his neck.

He knew how they had done it, and he knew who. Now he had to find out why.

Eddie flagged down a taxi and told the driver to take him to Charlie's villa, but as the car drew close, he spotted two police cars parked outside. 'Keep going,' he shouted.

The villa gate was wide open, and he could see two more police cars and an ambulance on the drive. At least a dozen police officers were milling around the gardens.

Fuck.

'Where you want to go, hombre?' the Spanish driver said.

'Banús. Take me down to the port'.

The driver pulled a u-turn and headed back the way he had just driven, with Eddie sinking low in his seat as they passed the villa again. He told the driver to stop close to the apartment block where Mike had lived with Veronica, paid the man and got out.

He had walked scarcely thirty yards before spotting another police car. It sat straddling the edge of a pedestrian crossing, its two occupants scrutinising passersby. Eddie slipped into a bar and sat down at a table with a view out onto the road and the apartment block above it. He sat there for over three hours pretending to read a newspaper before darkness arrived and, he guessed, having worked his way through a dozen drinks.

The first police officers got relieved by two colleagues at eight o'clock, but the replacement officers were no less vigilant. Eddie would find no entry with them present. He looked up at to the upper floor to the apartment where Veronica lived. He could see lights on inside. Someone was home, but who? He had to get up there somehow to find out. The apartment building was an independent structure, but the neighbouring building stood less than two feet apart and was of a similar height. If he could get up to the roof level of that building, perhaps he could jump across to Veronica's apartment block and climb down onto her balcony?

Eddie paid the waitress - who had eyed him with suspicion over an hour earlier - smiling at her and leaving a generous tip, then left the bar and crossed over the road.

The building that neighboured with Veronica's comprised several apartments on each of its five floors. They all shared a common staircase and elevator with uninhibited access from the ground level hallway. After ensuring that he was not being watched, Eddie ascended the stairs, making his way to the very top where he encountered a grey door that barred his access to the roof outside. He removed the crowbar from the sports bag, and thrust into the doorjamb, splintering the wood and forcing the door open in an instant.

He stepped out onto the roof. It was dusk now, and the sounds of music and revelry from the bars and restaurants below masked his footsteps on the gravelled roof surface. As Eddie approached the edge of the structure, it became apparent that it was a little closer to Veronica's building than he had thought, but was about ten feet higher. He composed himself, took a few steps back, then ran forward and propelled himself across the gap before landing with the skills gained from having completed several dozen parachute jumps.

He made his way to the side of the building, below which was the balcony to Veronica's apartment, and listened for voices. After hearing nothing, he climbed over and lowered himself down. His efforts to remain stealthy were foiled, however, when he knocked over a porcelain plant pot which smashed onto the floor. The apartment had French windows. There was nowhere to hide.

Another light came on from inside, and Veronica emerged from the kitchen. She was holding a carving knife. Her surprise at seeing someone standing on her balcony evaporated as she recognised Eddie. She placed the blade down onto a table and approached the glass door. She stood looking at him for a few seconds as if trying to gain some composure, then turned the key in the door and pulled it open.

'Well, if it isn't the Black Magic man,' she scoffed. 'The police are looking for you'. She reached out to touch him as he entered, but he brushed her away.

'Are you alone?' he whispered.

'Yes, just me and Mr Smirnoff, she replied. He walked to the apartment door and checked the lock. Veronica strolled towards one of two white sofas and lay down, bringing her legs up and tucking them underneath her. She beckoned at him to sit down.

'I'm sorry about Mike,' Eddie said. Her eyes fell to the floor.

'Were you there?'

Eddie nodded. 'He saved my life'.

He noticed a flicker of a smile as she reached for her cigarettes, but it dissolved as quickly as it had appeared. 'Did you hear about Debbie?'

'The barmaid Charlie was knocking about with?'

She glanced at him. 'They found her floating in Charlie's pool this morning with her wrists cut. The police are saying it was self-inflicted. Weren't no fucking suicide though, was it?'

Eddie's heart sank. How many more people are going to suffer? 'Maybe she was at the villa when someone broke in?' he said.

'Or maybe she knew too much?' Veronica swallowed. 'I'm scared, Eddie. What's happening? Who's doing this?'

'I don't know, but whoever it was also got to Soparla before we did. They killed his girlfriend too'.

Veronica wiped tears from her eyes with the sleeve of her blouse. She remained quiet for a while, staring at a point on the floor, lost in thought. After what seemed like an age, she whispered, 'They're after Charlie's secrets'.

'They are,' Eddie replied. 'And they're killing anyone connected to them, or to Charlie. It's like whoever is doing this is cleaning up, removing all traces of him and his time here'. He moved across and sat on the coffee table close to her, reached out and held her hand. 'If you know anything, Veronica. Anything -'.

'Why would you think I know anything?' she snapped.

'I went to Charlie's bar today,' he said. He saw a reaction in her eyes. It was only brief, but it was a reaction for sure. 'I went inside. Downstairs'.

He was scrutinising her now. Her eyes broke away from his stare and she reached for her glass and caressed it.

'Charlie had a room down there,' he continued. 'It was a workshop, of sorts. It's also where he hid all the files, pictures, audio and video recordings that he and Lucian collected'.

Veronica lifted the glass to her lips, but she was still avoiding any eye contact.

'But I think maybe you knew that already,' he said.

She downed the contents of the glass and stood up. For a moment, their eyes locked, but then she walked over to the French windows and gazed outside. 'Nothing surprises me anymore, Eddie. People come here to party. All they see is the sun, beaches and bars. The all-night parties, and the flash cars and villas'.

She placed a hand on the glass and pressed her forehead against it to look down onto the street.

'But when you've been here long enough, it sucks you in. It changes you'. She looked back to face him. 'I fell out of love with Mike a long time ago. He treated me like shit at times, but it wasn't always like that. He used to be a charmer. He used to be…kind'.

She swivelled around, her back to the glass, and her eyes fell on the kitchen knife that she had placed there when Eddie first arrived.

'Too many years hiding out down here,' she said. 'The parties, the booze, the hangers-on and the drugs...the things it makes you do. It changed him. It changed Charlie. It changed us all'.

Eddie stood up and strolled towards her, placing himself between her and the knife. 'I thought it was Mike that ratted on us and got Charlie and the others killed,' he said. 'I was going to kill him. Truth is, I nearly did. But I was wrong about him. He told me to look out for you'.

'He really said that?'

'Those were his last words to me'.

'Why didn't you save him?' Veronica said, her voice laden with accusation.

'I couldn't reach him, and I'd lost my gun. But I can help you'. He reached for her hand, but she moved away, back to the drinks cabinet.

'I'm too late for saving, Eddie,' she said as she poured a large measure of vodka into two glasses, opened the small fridge nearby and placed two cubes of ice into each.

'Do you have somewhere you can go?' he asked. 'Back in England, I mean'.

She paused for a moment, thinking. 'My aunt,' she replied. 'She has a house in Surrey. I could stay with her for a bit, I guess'.

'No other family?' Eddie said.

She shook her head. 'Mum died when I was seventeen. She was an alcoholic. I never had a dad,' she took a swig from the vodka and moved back to the sofa, placing a glass down for Eddie. 'I'm the product of a dirty, one-night stand she had in Southend with some mod lad. She was sixteen when she had me'.

'That's rough'.

'Would you come back to England with me?' she asked.

Despite his deep suspicion that she knew more than she was letting on, he yearned to say yes. She was as alluring as the day he had first set eyes on her. Part-kitten but also part-wolf, he reminded himself. 'I have to find out who killed Charlie and the others,' he replied.

She looked away, tears in her eyes. 'If you keep digging, you will find things you don't like'.

Eddie shrugged. 'You might be right'. He looked at his watch. 'I should go,' he said, rising to his feet. He started towards the door.

'Wait,' Veronica said, her voice pregnant with guilt. I need to tell you something'.

'I think I know already,' he said.

'You don't, Eddie. You really don't'.

'Charlie's secret little den. I think you -'.

What she said next hit him like a cricket bat in the gut. 'That mercenary job in Angola,' she said. 'They didn't call it off'.

He gawped at her, replaying what he had just heard. 'What did you say?'

'It was me that called you,' she said. Tears were running down her face now.

'I don't...I don't understand'.

She answered him, but this time in a Scottish accent. 'The colonel...the colonel said to inform you...that the mission you signed up for is no longer going ahead'.

Stunned, he tried to answer, but words were failing him.

'I told you I was good at accents,' she said, returning to her own voice.

'Why...why would you do that?' he said, struggling to quell the black anger boiling up inside him.

'It was Charlie,' she said. 'He made me. He didn't want you to leave. He wanted to keep you here'.

Eddie stormed towards her, grabbed her arms and thrust her up against the wall, sending a framed photo of her and Mike to the floor. 'How could he make you?'

'It's the truth, Eddie. I had no choice'.

'Lies. More fucking lies. You just wanted to keep me here. Your new toy to play fucking mind games on. Do you know what you've done? All this shit. Everything that happened? Everything I'm caught up in now. You did that'. He was shaking her.

She cried out loud, trying to break free. 'He had a tape. In that case'.

'What tape?'

She broke free of his grip and fell back onto the sofa.

'What tape?' he demanded again.

She was sobbing uncontrollably. 'I wanted to go back to England. To be an actress again. I told him one evening. Your brother...I told him about two years ago. Before I knew what he was like. I told him I was leaving Mike and going back to England. He said he wouldn't allow it. He said he would destroy my chances of ever acting again'.

'How could he do that?'

'He had the Romanian look into my past when I first got together with Mikey. He had a tape of me, from before I got my first acting roles'.

'What...fucking...tape?' he snarled.

She reached for her cigarettes, but Eddie smacked them away. He stood glaring at her, his heart thumping hard inside his ribcage.

She stood up. 'I was young, desperate. I needed money. Mum was already in treatment centres. We'd lost the house'.

'What fucking tape?'

She took a deep breath, composed herself, stood up and then shuffled over to a large wooden closet. She opened the door to reveal a dented, metal box - Charlie's case packed full of his illicit secrets.

'I saw the keys. At the club. When you and Mike were fighting. I picked them up, and I kept them. I'd seen them before, Eddie - when Charlie first showed me the tape. When I saw them, I knew he had given them to you. He told you the combinations too, didn't he?'

Eddie was stunned. 'How did you -'.

'The combinations. What are they?' she said.

Eddie found himself again unable to speak. It was as if a tornado had been unleashed inside his skull. Everything was spinning.

Veronica pulled the case out of the closet, and it fell loudly onto the hard tiled floor. 'Open it. Then you'll understand'.

Eddie stared at the case, a growing sense that everything he thought he knew was about to be re-written.

'Open it,' she pleaded. He lowered himself down to kneel in front of the metal box, then thumbed each of the combinations, one wheel at a time.

2-4-0-4

1-2-0-6

Eddie pressed the two round buttons, and the metal latches snapped open in unison. He lifted the lid, then sat back.

Veronica kneeled down next to him and rummaged through the packed contents. There were wads of photos wrapped in elastic bands. A myriad of documents, audio cassettes and videotapes, each with hand-written labels. She sat back, one VHS tape in her hand, then held it out to Eddie.

He took it from her and looked at the white sticker on it.

Dirty Schoolgirls - *Veronica Peters, audition, 18th May 1977.*

'I was seventeen, Eddie. I didn't know what I was getting myself into. They got me drunk. Gave me pills. They made me do things'. She took the cassette from him and slid her nails into the little groove that gave access to the black magnetic tape inside.

'Charlie was blackmailing you?' said Eddie, incredulous.

Veronica was removing the black tape now, tugging at it until there was an enormous pile on the floor next to her.

'He paid two thousand pounds for it, just so he could control me. I'd have gone home two years ago otherwise. I had offers to audition, good offers. Television and films, but I couldn't go. He told me if I left Mikey, he'd send copies to the media. To my agent. He said he'd destroy me'.

She stood up, collected the bundle of tape and deposited it into the fireplace, then reached for a matchbox on the shelf above.

'I told you, Eddie. If you go digging, you won't like the answers. This town is a den of snakes. Get out while you still can'.

Veronica struck a match and dropped it onto the tape, which ignited in an instant. She stared as it burned, her eyes red and tears streaming down her face. 'I know you want to fix everything,' she said. 'But you can't. Go home and forget about all of this. Forget about Charlie. Forget about me'.

She handed him a set of car keys. 'It's a blue Mini Metro. On the second car park level'.

She turned her back on him and ambled towards the bedroom. But there was one more thing Eddie needed to know.

'Why did you burn the bar?' he said. 'I'd never have known it was you if you hadn't done that'.

Veronica stopped, her hand on the door knob. 'I wasn't going to. It wasn't why I went there. But when I found myself down in that room, it all came flooding back. What he did to me. What he made me do. How he hurt me'. She peered back over her shoulder, tears trickling down her cheek. 'And I knew that for the first time I could hurt Charlie too. So I did. I burned down his bloody bar'. She opened the door. 'Do what you want with that case. It's your responsibility now'.

Eddie took the lift down to the subterranean car park beneath the apartment block, found the car and placed the big case in the back.

The exit was around the corner from the entrance at the front of the building where the two policemen sat in their patrol car. The automatic gates opened, and he drove away with the two uniformed officers clueless to his presence.

Under different circumstanced it would have been a moment that would have amused him, but Eddie was in no mood for laughter.

He was on a mission now.

CHAPTER THIRTY-SIX
ALL IS NOT WHAT IT SEEMS

Eddie found a cheap hotel and booked himself in for two nights. Other, more discerning travellers may have questioned how the establishment had secured its second star, such was the grim state of the room and common areas, but Eddie cared not. It had a cheap grocery store next door in which he purchased some basic food and a bottle of questionable Scotch.

Back in his room, Eddie gobbled down an entire baguette and a slab of smoked cheese, and filled a plastic tumbler with the amber liquor, then sat staring at Charlie's case. It was the size of a medium suitcase but fashioned from aluminium. The steel hinges and lock mechanisms were of an industrial nature. It must have weighed over eighty pounds with its load of illicit contents. He supposed its original purpose was for the transportation of valuable electronic equipment to destinations of uncertain security. He downed his drink, then knelt in front of the case and entered the two number combinations.

Quite what he was searching for, he was not sure - something that might shed light on who had ambushed the lorry and killed Charlie, Bill and Roger? Maybe. Information that might shine a light on what malevolent entity was pulling the strings that had led to the deaths of Mike, Debbie, and

Soparla and his girlfriend, perhaps? He sifted through the multi-coloured files, manilla envelopes, plastic wallets, cassette tapes, and wads of photos, barely noting the contents as if he would sense what was relevant, and what was not.

Eddie sat back after twenty minutes, surrounded by the various paraphernalia and stared at it all, none the wiser. He forced himself to his feet, stretched his aching back and poured a fourth serving of the dubious whiskey.

'What the fuck am I doing,' he thought.

He kicked at the case out of frustration and lifted his tumbler to his mouth. At that moment, something, which had been propped up inside the case, fell over. It was an A5-sized black and red notebook. He reached down and thumbed through it. The book was half-full, and contained summarised, hand-written notes of what seemed to be phone calls. The date of the most recent conversation was just a week earlier, a call between Charlie and some planning official at the council. He leafed back through the pages, one by one, until another note stood out at him.

July 17th, 1985.
13:22
Eddie called HAWKWOOD. UK number. Confirmed travel Kinshasa.

Eddie stared at the date. It was the week he had first arrived in Marbella and was a shorthand note of his call to Colonel Hawkwood, the owner of the mercenary company and Eddie's former commanding officer in the Paras. Charlie, or maybe Lucian, had been listening in on the call.

Eddie's head, fuelled on cheap forty percent proof liquor,

reeled at the possibilities. Had Charlie been playing him since he had first arrived in Marbella? He felt a heavy, nauseating sensation in the pit of his stomach. Everything that had happened since - the parties, Veronica, the United Security robbery, the arguments and fights, the boat journey to the middle of the Mediterranean, the torturous drive north to the French border, the deaths, all of it. Had it all happened because his half-brother had been manipulating him just as he did to so many others? Had Eddie been just another puppet to Charlie all this time? Veronica had claimed Charlie had forced her to deceive Eddie, but maybe she was in on it too? What about Kenny?

Eddie fumbled for the bottle of liquor, filled the tumbler and gulped at the contents. He hadn't felt this lost and directionless since being kicked out of the army. Back then, in 1983, he had been to visit a psychiatrist several times. It had been a condition imposed upon him by the sympathetic judge who had shown Eddie considerable leniency, after the police arrested him for his part in a bar brawl in Sheffield. The shrink had prescribed Eddie some "special pills" to help him get through the darker moments. He had not taken one for over a year, but boy did he crave one now.

He refilled the plastic container again and again, and drunk himself into a stupor, then collapsed on the floor surrounded by the contents of Charlie's case of secrets.

Eddie came to again the next day, gasping for water and with the mother of all hangovers. Once he was able to open his eyes and to focus sufficiently to read the time on his watch, he established that he had been asleep for around thirteen hours. His body had evidently shut down after the cumulative stresses and strains of the previous days and weeks. He pushed himself up only then to realise that he had been laying in a puddle of his own urine. Luckily, given he had no spare clothing with him, his drunken self had possessed the sense to remove his jeans before letting loose. A voice screamed at him from the deepest recesses of his head.

Get a fucking grip, soldier.

It was the voice of his drill instructor from basic training. Eddie had hated the old bastard when, as a snotty raw recruit, he had first encountered the man, but had come to respect him in the months that had followed. His bellowing, commanding voice had stuck with Eddie and frequently made itself known in his subconscious.

He stood up, rubbed his eyes and went to the bathroom where he then took a long, cold shower then downed several glasses of water. He wrapped a towel around his midriff then sat back on the bed. He was not yet willing to give in to the temptation of despair and self-pity. He picked up his wallet and removed the business card of Col. John J Hawkwood (*retired*), the reached for the hotel phone and dialled the number. It took nearly ten seconds for the line to connect to the office in London, but it was answered after a single ring.

'Hawkwood International,' said a woman. Eddie cleared his throat.

'Hi, my name is Eddie Lawson. I'm a friend of the Colonel'.

'Mr Lawson? Oh, yes. We tried to contact you a few weeks ago. You had been expected for a placement overseas, but we hadn't heard from you. The colonel was quite concerned'.

'Yeah, I'm sorry. There was some…miscommunication here, on my end. I'm very sorry. Would it be possible to speak to the colonel about it? I'd like to explain'.

'He is out of the country at present, but I can get a message to him if you would like?'

Eddie could feel the relief surging through him. He felt sure that the colonel would understand what had taken place if only Eddie could talk to him. 'That would be -'.

He halted mid-sentence. At his feet was a brown A4 folder

from which a batch of black and white photos were protruding. He could only see a small portion of one of the images, but it was instantly recognisable and made his blood run cold. He squatted down and opened the folder to reveal a series of covertly surveillance photos of a woman and a young girl - Eddie's former wife, Hayley, and their young daughter, Mary.

'What the fuck?' he said.

'Excuse me?' the woman on the end of the line exclaimed. Eddie placed the receiver back down onto the phone and thumbed through the photos.

They had been snapped in several locations on different days. Each was dated, the most recent being in January of that year - five months before Eddie has turned up at Charlie's Bar seeking his brother's help.

'Motherfucker,' he snarled. He immediately picked up the phone again and dialled a number from memory. He felt a nervous apprehension in his chest as the phone rang for an agonisingly long time before, finally, a voice answered.

'Hellooooo,' said his daughter.

'Mary? Honey. It's me. It's Daddy'.

'Daddy? Where are you?' she answered, all matter of fact. A wave of painful emotions seeped over him.

'I'm in Spain, baby. How are you? How's mummy. Are you all okay?' He did not get an answer but could hear her mother speaking in the background. Mary, it was clear, was not supposed to be answering telephones.

'Hello, who is this?' his ex-wife said, curtly.

'It's me'.

'Eddie?' she said in a hushed voice.

'How are you? How's Mary?'

'We're doing…fine, Eddie. All things considered. Why are you calling? I suppose you're drunk again?'

'No. No, it's not like that,' he said. 'It's just…I wanted to make sure you were okay'.

'We're fine. Listen, I'm sorry, but I can't -'.

'Wait, it's not like that. I'm in Spain'.

'Spain?'

'I came out here a month ago. To see Charlie'.

'Your *brother* Charlie?'

'Yeah,' said Eddie.

'What's that selfish bastard up to these days?' she said. Eddie looked at the photos in his left hand.

'Not much. Listen, I got myself into a mess. A real bad one'.

'Oh, Eddie. When are you going to learn? What is it this time? Another fight? Drugs again? Look, I've moved on. I can't get dragged into -'.

'That's not why I'm calling'.

'Then what?' she said. 'Why are you calling?'

He paused. *Why am I calling her*? 'It's just -'.

'What?' she asked.

'It's just…it's…I don't know what to do'.

Eddie heard her let out a tired sigh.

'I'm not your counsellor, Eddie. You left us, remember?'

'I know, but you always had the answers, Hayley. I just thought…forget it. I'm sorry. I'll let you be'.

'Wait,' she said. 'Whatever this problem is, and I don't want to know what it is, just…just do the right thing'.

'How do I know what that is?' he asked. There was silence on the end of the line. 'How do I know?'

'You're a good man, Eddie. You'll know. I'm sure of it. I've got to go'.

'I'm sorry. Sorry for everything I put you through. All that shit'.

'I know you are,' she said sympathetically. 'I know'.

'Tell Mary I love her,' he said.

'Take care of yourself, soldier'. She hung up.

It was all Eddie could do to hold back the tears.

Toughen up, Soldier.

He took another look at the black and white photographs in his hand then put them back into the folder. At that moment,

Eddie knew that he could not leave Marbella. Not until it was all over. Not until he had finished what Charlie had started. Whatever it took.

Felix Suarez, the desk manager at the Hotel Fuerte, stood surveying the brightly lit entrance lobby, smiling. He was having an excellent day. All of his team had turned up for work for once, and everything was running smoothly. There had been not a single complaint from any of the over three hundred guests.

Felix liked days like this one. It meant he wouldn't be on the receiving end of an angry tirade from one of the hotel's tight-arsed owners at the end of his shift, and that was beneficial for both his angina and his blood pressure.

'Felix,' a voice called. It was one of the receptionists. She was holding a phone receiver in one hand and waving it at him.

'Who is it?' he asked as he strolled towards her, still smiling.

'He said his name is Lawson,' the receptionist said. The smile slipped away from Felix's face.

He took the phone, turned away from his colleague and lowered his voice. 'Hello?'

'Is that Felix Suarez?' the voice on the end of the line asked.

'Who is this, please?'

'My name is Eddie Lawson. Charlie's brother. We met a few weeks ago if you remember?'

'Mr Lawson, of course. I heard about Charlie. I am so very sorry, señor. If there is anything I can do for you, please let me know'.

'As it happens,' said Eddie. 'There is'.

CHAPTER THIRTY-SEVEN
A MAN WITH A PLAN

The offices of Sinmorales Aseguró Partners, Marbella.

Carola Rosario-Herrera worked for Sinmorales Aseguró Partners in Marbella. Her official job title was *Paralegal*, but in reality, she was a glorified dogsbody. It fell on her to open the office up first thing in the morning and to have everything ready for when the partners, solicitors and other staff arrived for their day's work.

Some of the other, actual, paralegals treated her with disdain.

'How on earth did she get that job?' she had overheard one of her female colleagues exclaiming just the previous week. Carola did not care what the others thought of her. She knew things they did not; stuff you pick up when you happen to be sleeping with one of the senior partners.

Carola had only just unlocked the front door and disabled the alarm before the telephone rang. She looked at the gold Cartier watch on her wrist - it was one of many gifts she had received from her benefactor, Señor Belmonte. It was not yet eight o'clock.

'Who on earth calls at this time?' she thought. 'Don't they know the office hours are nine to four-thirty?' She placed her prized Gucci handbag down on her desk - leaned over her desk and reached across to lift the receiver.

'Sinmorales Aseguró Partners, how may I help you?' she said in Spanish in a disgruntled tone.

'Take a message,' the male caller said in English.

'Excuse me?' said Carola, somewhat taken aback.

'I said, take a message'. The voice was commanding, so she did as she was told. 'Tell me when you are ready'.

Carola reached for a legal pad and pen. 'Go ahead,' she said and started scribbling as the caller spoke. 'Okay, yes I got it,' she said.

'Read it back to me,' the man said. 'I need to know you got everything'.

Carola picked up the paper pad. 'It is a message for Señor Belmonte. You say you have information relating to three of our clients - Señor Daniel Ortega, Doña Sophia Valáquez and Señor Juan Fernandez. This information was previously in the possession of a British citizen, Mr Charles Lawson, now deceased. You will make this information available for sale to the highest bidder. Our firm is to expect another call from you at eleven-thirty, at which point you will provide us with the location at which an auction shall take place here, in Marbella, at midday. Prospective buyers should bring with them significant funds in cash which must be in US dollars or British pounds, but not Spanish pesetas'. Carola took a breath. 'Was that everything?' she asked.

'That's everything,' the man said.

'And who should I say called?' She waited for an answer, but the line went dead and she placed the handset down.

Fucking English.

DEN OF SNAKES

Eddie placed the receiver down onto the phone. The first part of his plan was now in motion.

Now for part two.

He sat on the side of his bed in his hotel room. Charlie's metal case lay on the floor in front of him, its contents packed away inside. He stubbed out a cigarette on the top of an empty beer can, then picked up the phone again. He glanced at a handwritten number on the inside of the cigarette box, then started dialling.

'It's me,' he said.

'Hey, kid,' said Kenny. What's up?'

'I need your help'.

'Of course, what do you need?'

'I'm staying at *Hotel El Pachucho*. D'ya know it?'

'I can find it,' said Kenny.

'Good. Can you be here at ten-thirty?'

'Sure. What are we gonna be doing?'

'Catching a killer,' said Eddie.

Thirty minutes later, Eddie was sitting inside a small cafe around the corner from his hotel. He was donning three newly acquired items; a yellow tee-shirt that bore the words, "La Vida de Marbella" in pink writing on the front, a red baseball cap, and a pair of reflective, silver shades. The metal case sat on the floor to his side, between his table and the wall.

A duck shell-blue Renault 4 pulled up outside, and Veronica stepped out. She peered into the shaded interior of the cafe, seemingly uncertain whether to enter.

Eddie removed the sunglasses and beckoned at her to come inside. 'Where did you get the car from?' he said.

'I borrowed it from my elderly neighbour. I told her mine was being serviced, and that I needed to take my friend to the doctors'. She gestured towards his tee-shirt. 'New look?' she said.

He gave her an apologetic grin and offered her a chair. 'Figured I'd blend in,' he said, gesturing at the similarly attired tourists sitting at the surrounding tables. 'You sure you're up to this?'

Her reply was instant. 'It's the only way to finish it'.

'Okay, then,' Eddie said. He stood up, placed some coins on the table, then reached for the case and accompanied Veronica to the Renault. She opened the rear door so that Eddie could load the metal case inside. 'Now remember, get to that payphone and wait for my call. Do not come to the hotel until I call you. Not under any circumstances. Tell me you understand'.

'I understand'. Veronica reached for his hand. 'Eddie...do you think you can forgive me?'

'Let's talk about that another time,' he said. 'If we live past today'.

She nodded, then pulled open the driver's door and lowered herself in.

'Twelve-thirty,' Eddie said.

'I'll be there,' she replied. She started the car up, gave Eddie a sorrowful smile, then pulled away.

Eddie watched as the light blue car disappeared out of view. 'That's the third, and final, part of the plan underway,' he thought. Everything was in motion now, there was no going back.

It wouldn't be long before he would find out who he could and could not trust.

Kenny pulled up outside the front of Eddie's hotel in his silver Mercedes, a little after half past ten.

Eddie was already waiting for him outside. He flicked a

cigarette into the road and hurried to climb in. 'Sure you weren't followed?' he asked as he sat down and belted himself in.

'I'm sure,' said Kenny. 'You gonna let me in on this plan of yours?'

'Sure. In ninety minutes, I will inform several influential people where they can find me and Charlie's stash of nasty secrets'.

Kenny's eyes narrowed. 'You've got Charlie's case?' he said.

'I do,' said Eddie. 'And I told them I will sell it to the highest bidder'.

'You serious?' said Kenny.

Eddie nodded. 'That I am'.

'How the fucking hell did you get it?'

'Long story. All that matters is I have it. Now, can we get moving?'

'Where to?' Kenny asked.

'Hotel Fuerte'.

'Hotel Fuerte?'

'Yeah, seemed appropriate. What is this? Twenty bleedin' questions?'

Kenny sat back, pushed the gearstick into first and pulled away. 'What do you hope to achieve?'

'To flush out who killed Charlie and the others'. Kenny flicked on the car's indicator and prepared to make a left turn. 'What are you doing? It's straight on,' said Eddie.

'I'm nipping back to my flat. After what you just said, I need a shooter'.

'There ain't time. Besides, it's just me that's gonna face these people. I want you to stay put out of sight'.

Kenny stopped the indicator and scratched his chin. 'I hope you know what you're doing, Eddie' he said.

Eddie gazed out of the car window. 'I do, Ken. For the first time in a long time, I do'.

CHAPTER THIRTY-EIGHT
THE PRICE IS RIGHT

Hotel Fuerte, Marbella. 11:18 a.m.

Eddie approached the Hotel Fuerte, having left Kenny safe in his car and out of sight in the hotel's underground car park. He was gripping a black plastic bag under his arm. As he stepped into the lobby, he noticed the desk manager approach him. They shook hands.

'Everything is ready, Mr Lawson. Just as you asked. Come, I'll take you up'. The Spaniard directed Eddie towards the stairs and handed him a piece of paper with a handwritten note on it. 'A lady called for you. She said she is waiting for you on this telephone number, "to deliver the package" '.

'Thank you for doing this, Felix,' said Eddie. 'I'm so sorry, I can't pay you anything'.

'No need. Your brother was very good to my family and me. I do this for him'. The man noticed that Eddie was looking at the several CCTV cameras in the lobby and stairwell. 'I can disable the cameras?'

'No,' Eddie said. 'I want this all on tape'.

They made their way to a large, double-door on the first

floor. Felix unlocked it, opened the door and handed Eddie the key. 'The telephone is over there,' said Felix, pointing at a table to their right.

'Best you make yourself scarce now,' said Eddie.

They shook hands once more, and the Spaniard departed, closing the doors behind him.

Eddie glanced at his watch. It was 11:27 a.m. He sat down at the table, lifted the phone receiver and dialled a number.

'Sinmorales Aseguró Partners, how can I help?' It was the same woman Eddie had spoken to earlier that morning. She sounded nervous.

'I called earlier. Will your clients be attending the auction?'

'They will, Mr Lawson'.

So, he thought, they know who I am already. 'All of them?'

'Yes, all of them. You said midday, yes?'

'That is correct,' said Eddie

'And the location?' the woman asked.

Eddie could make out muffled male voices close to the woman and could imagine the scene - her sitting at the reception surrounded by the law firm's senior partners, and some very nervous clients. He hesitated for a moment, looking up to the ornate plaster mouldings of the ceiling above him.

'Mr Lawson?' The location of the meeting, if you will?'

'Hotel Fuerte. The first floor conference room,' he said, then placed the receiver down. He took a cigarette from the packet and put it in his mouth.

No going back now.

He remained still for a while, tipping ash into a nearby plant pot, until the cigarette burned down to the filter, before standing up and wandering to the centre of the enormous room. There, as instructed, Felix had arranged several tables - one for Eddie, with three more evenly fanned out in front of it. The tables were located in the centre of the conference room, which appeared to be in the latter stages of a refurbishment. Dozens more tables and towers of stacked chairs sat nearby, draped under dust covers.

Eddie pulled a chair out from under the table, placed the plastic bag on the surface and sat down, readying himself for what was to come. He removed the Browning semi-automatic from inside his belt, placed it down on the chair next to him and pulled the table cloth over it. He lit another cigarette and sat watching the door, whistling "Hungry Like A Wolf", by Duran Duran. He closed his eyes, leaned back on the chair and thought about the events of the previous several weeks.

It all seemed so unreal. Eddie had travelled to the south of Spain to find Charlie, to borrow the money he needed to travel to Angola. But there were other ways to get money. Had he come to Charlie for some other reason? He had, and he now understood why - a desire to heal his relationship with his adopted sibling. But that was not all - he had also wanted to try to 'fix' Charlie. They may not have been blood brothers, but Mr and Mrs Lawson had raised them as such in that pokey old terrace house in South Harrow all those years ago. There had been only a few years when he and Charlie had been genuinely close - how actual brothers can be - but Eddie still cherished those memories.

If I hadn't come to Spain, Charlie and the others might still be alive.

He shook his head to eradicate the guilty sentiment, and lit yet another cigarette, but at the moment the flame ignited the cigarette, came the sound of shuffling feet outside the door.

This is it.

The door opened and a burly man wearing a grey suit peered inside, holding a revolver at his side. He spotted Eddie, scanned the rest of the room for a moment, and muttered something to whoever was behind him. Daniel Ortega followed after him, along with another bodyguard and a stout gentleman in a black suit who, Eddie guessed, was one of the law firm's senior partners.

DEN OF SNAKES

As they approached, Eddie stood and directed them towards a table. 'Señor Ortega. Have a seat, please,' he said.

Ortega observed Eddie for a moment. 'I hope you know what you are doing, Mr Lawson'.

'So do I,' thought Eddie, hoping that his self-doubt was not apparent.

The two bodyguards standing behind Ortega turned towards the sound of the door opening behind them. Two uniformed police officers entered and studied the environment, as Ortega's man had done a moment earlier. They too were armed, but their pistols remained in their holsters. Another man entered behind them - it was the bodyguard Eddie had encountered in the bar in Mijas, when Charlie had met and blackmailed the corrupt female politician. On queue, Doña Sophia Velásquez entered and advanced towards the centre of the room, the policemen struggling to keep pace with her.

'What is the meaning of this?' she demanded.

'We will, it seems, find out in a few minutes,' said Ortega.

Eddie gestured towards one of the two remaining tables. 'Please, Señora. Have a seat,' he said. 'I will explain when our third guest arrives'. Velásquez muttered something in Spanish, whipped around, and sat down, glaring at Eddie. Eddie peered back at Ortega, who sat supporting his chin with one hand, the fingers of the other tapping rhythmically on the table before him.

Several minutes later, the group were joined by the final invitee, the businessman Juan Fernandez. He strode towards the tables, accompanied by his own entourage of three large men and another lawyer. He took note of Ortega and Velásquez, and sat down at the last remaining table, saying nothing.

Eddie cleared his throat and stood up. 'Thank you for coming. I apologise for the cloak and dagger antics but, as I am sure you will agree, this situation calls for discretion'. The three guests and their various bodyguards, legal professionals and police officers exchanged furtive glances. Eddie continued. 'I have in my possession, certain valuables which I am certain you will all have an interest in acquiring. I propose to give these today to whoever agrees to my terms'.

Ortega interrupted him. 'And what, may I ask, are these "valuables" to which you refer?'

'If you do not know that, Daniel,' said Fernandez, 'you would not be here'.

'Still, said Ortega. 'I would like for Mr Lawson here to tell us, for clarity, so to speak. If that is acceptable to you, Señor Fernandez'.

Fernandez crossed his arms.

'I do not have time for this shit,' said Sophia Velásquez. 'Tell us what you have, or I will leave now'.

Eddie pushed himself up straight and took a deep breath. 'What I have is a large metal case full of all kinds of sensational information that could embarrass or even incriminate hundreds of prominent individuals here in Spain and elsewhere'. He paused, taking in the reactions of the three 'guests'.

Ortega chuckled. 'So it is true. Your brother was blackmailing people. How interesting'. He turned to look at the other two Spaniards. Fernandez scratched at his moustache. Velásquez had her eyes fixed on Eddie, her hands interlocked before her.

'You have this case here?' said Fernandez. He nudged one of his henchmen, who angled his head to peer under the table behind Eddie. The man's hand was inside his jacket where, no doubt, he had a weapon concealed.

'The case is nearby. Somewhere safe,' said Eddie.

'We cannot see it?' said Fernandez, shrugging. 'How do we know this is not some absurd charade?'

'I have some samples,' said Eddie, reaching for the black plastic bag. He pulled out two brown envelopes, stood up, strolled forward to hand one of the packages to Fernandez, and gave the second to Doña Velásquez.

Both Spaniards took furtive looks inside their respective packets, before closing them again.

'Is that sufficient evidence, Señor Fernandez?' The Spaniard said nothing. He did not need to - his expression said it all. Eddie peered towards Ortega. 'It seems Charlie didn't have anything on you, Daniel. Which leads me to wonder, why are you here?'

'I am here, because if that case falls into the wrong hands…it will cause problems in my town. I would prefer to avoid that'. Ortega glanced towards Fernandez and Velásquez.

The creaking of a door opening once more caught everybody's attention. A blonde, fair-skinned man and a slim woman in a short black dress had stumbled into the room, locked in a passionate embrace.

One of Velásquez's police guards reached for a pistol. As a reaction, both Fernadez's and Ortegas's henchman did likewise. The blonde man removed his hands from his female companion. 'Shit. I'm sorry,' he said as he and his female companion backed out of the door. The various police officers and bodyguards waited for the door to close before lowering their weapons.

Doña Velásquez stood up. 'Enough. Put this ridiculous affair to an end. What is your price, Mr Lawson?'

Eddie grinned. This was going as he hoped. 'I'm a simple man with simple tastes. I don't need a big villa, designer clothing or a Ferrari on my driveway'.

Fernandez banged his fist on the table. 'Then what do you want?'

'I want whoever killed my brother to face justice'.

'Justice? How interesting,' said Ortega. He swivelled on his chair and looked at Fernandez and Velásquez.

Eddie continued. 'If one of you can deliver the person responsible for these crimes, Charlie's case is yours, and you can do whatever the fuck you want with it'.

Fernandez loosened his collar. Velásquez whispered to one of her men.

'What if one of us was responsible, Eddie?' said Ortega.

'Then,' said Eddie. 'I guess it's up to the other two to resolve the matter'. He sat down on his table.

'This is preposterous. I have nothing to do with any murders,' said Fernandez.

'So why are you here, amigo?' said Ortega.

Fernandez glared at him. 'I am here to ensure that my reputation remains untarnished'.

Ortega snorted in derision. 'Come, come now, Juan. I think in this situation, we can all drop the pretence. We both know what you get up to behind that cloak of civic respectability. Just as we both know what Señora Velásquez has done to get where she is today'.

'You need to be quiet, Ortega,' the woman said. Her bodyguards were glaring at their fellow Spaniard.

'Actually, I think Daniel has a point,' said Fernandez. 'Perhaps you are worried that Charles Lawson's secrets might be your undoing. Perhaps you had him killed?'

Velásquez waved the accusation away. 'And what of the five hundred thousand pounds you lent to Charlie? Money he sunk into that construction project of his, a project which I also know you were keen to take over. Many would consider that motive to enough'. She shifted back to address Eddie. 'I despised your brother, Mr Lawson,' she said. 'However, Charlie was a shrewd man who understood the power of the information he gained, and he used it extremely well. I did not have him killed'. She said something to her lawyer again, and he picked up his briefcase from the floor and placed it on the table in front of him, awaiting further instructions. Velásquez continued. 'I'm not here to help solve murders. I'm here to buy Charlie's case'.

The lawyer opened the case to reveal multiple bundles of British banknotes. 'One hundred thousand pounds. Take it or leave it,' he said.

'Maybe, you didn't hear me earlier when I said I don't want your money?' said Eddie.

'The *íngles* is trying to divide us,' said Fernandez.

'Perhaps he is succeeding,' said Ortega, chuckling.

'Enough,' Fernandez shouted. 'Whatever our differences, Señora Velásquez, the Ortega family and I have done business together for many years'. He looked to his left and right. Both of his fellow Spaniards nodded their agreement. 'Did you really think we would turn on each other?'

Velásquez eyed Eddie like a lioness stalking its quarry. 'Indeed. Was this your only plan?' she said. 'To break a pact that has lasted years? And for you, some petty criminal?' She covered her mouth and whispered something to Fernandez, who nodded, and gave one of his bodyguards an instruction. The man gestured towards his partner, and the pair began to manoeuvre around the three tables, eyes locked on Eddie.

'It seems you have overplayed your hand,' Ortega said as Fernandez's bodyguards drew closer.

'Maybe, maybe not,' said Eddie as he backed towards the chair where he had left his pistol. 'But by my reckoning, someone wants Charlie's case. And if he or she thinks I am here trying to sell it to you, then -'.

Eddie stopped mid-sentence as the conference door flung open and five men burst in. It was Pickering's crew, and they were armed with shotguns and sub-machine guns. The two police officers and five bodyguards pulled out their weapons and aimed them at the new arrivals.

'Nobody fucking move,' one of the East Enders shouted. He had his shotgun aimed at the head of one of Velásquez's men.

'Who the fuck are you?' Fernandez demanded as the East Enders approached.

'We're who you wanna be negotiating with,' another voice said. It was Bobby Pickering. He stood in the doorway holding Veronica by her hair, Charlie's case on the floor at his side. The

East Ender kicked the door shut, and pushed Veronica forward, dragging the heavy case behind him.

Eddie's heart sank. How had they found Veronica? He had told her to wait with Charlie's case at a payphone a mile away, and to wait his call.

Pickering pushed Veronica to the floor in front of Eddie, who now found himself surrounded by British gangsters, Spanish bodyguards and corrupt policemen, all of whom were pointing their weapons at one another.

'I'm sorry, Eddie,' Veronica said. 'They must have followed me'.

Pickering picked up the case and laid it down on the table at which Eddie has been sitting. Eddie edged backwards, trying to get within reach of his pistol, but one of the Cockneys stopped him in his tracks, striking him in the stomach with the butt of his shotgun. He fell to the floor, gasping for air.

'Gentlemen and ladies,' said Pickering. 'We don't want no trouble, but if trouble is what you want, my boys here are ready to dispense it'.

One of the East End gang pulled back the bolt on his MAC10 to emphasise his leader's threat.

'Now, I gather you are all here for this'. He pointed at the case. 'So let's get straight to business. What are your opening offers? Do I hear two hundred grand?'

'One hundred thousand. Not a penny more,' said Velásquez.

Pickering glared at her, gnashing his yellow teeth together. 'Not fuckin' good enough. I'm not leaving here without at least double that. And the longer this takes, the higher my price goes'. He pointed his pistol at Fernandez. 'What about you, pops?' You gonna give me two hundred grand for it?'

Eddie scanned the room. There were now thirteen men holding guns on each other. He made eye contact with Ortega who, he could see, also recognised their plight.

Ortega rose to his feet, his arms raised in submission. 'Are we to understand that it was you that killed Charlie Lawson and his associates?'

Pickering laughed. 'Nah,' he replied, slowly walking towards Ortega. 'We didn't do that. Oh, except for one of them'. Pickering glanced at Eddie. 'I did shoot Mike. But that was self-defence that was'.

'Didn't look like self-defence from where I was watching,' said Eddie.

Pickering pointed a boney index finger at Eddie, a look of delight on his face. 'I knew you was there. Hiding in a cupboard was yer? Like a fucking coward?' He strode to where Eddie lay prostrate on the parquet floor and bent down to whisper in his ear. 'If I had wanted Charlie or any of you boys dead, it would have happened already. I told you, I'm a businessman. All I want is what's rightfully ours. Now, on that note…'. He stood up. 'Which of you dagos is going to pay me my fucking money?' he hollered, his saliva spraying Velásquez who reeled back in disgust.

Eddie shifted towards Veronica who was sitting on the floor, swaying. 'When I say run, you run,' he whispered.

Pickering was pointing a gun at Juan Fernandez now. Eddie peeked at his pistol on the chair underneath the table a few yards away. The East Enders who was guarding him was still pointing his shotgun in Eddie's direction, but the man's attention was elsewhere. Maybe they could make a break for it?

As it happened, they did not need to.

The doors burst open again and a gangly man appeared holding a TV camera, followed by another, shorter individual with a mobile lighting unit, and then a third who was carrying with a fluffy microphone. Jeremy Crampton stormed in behind them, howling at his crew to get out of his way. All four halted, realising they had walked into a veritable powder keg.

'Shit,' the cameraman said.

'Get that camera,' Velásquez screamed at one of her men. The police officer backed away from the rest of the armed men, and dashed over to the TV crew. Sensing that things were about to turn for the worse, Eddie scanned the room for an exit. It was at that moment that he spotted Kenny peering at him through the glass of a fire escape door, some thirty feet away.

Eddie tapped Veronica on her shoulder and pointed at the grey door. 'Kenny's over there. Get ready to run'. She nodded her acknowledgement.

Meanwhile, Velásquez's henchman was arguing with the TV crew. 'Give me the camera,' he snarled, but Crampton stepped forward and pushed the astonished gunmen backwards.

'You can't have it,' he shouted, but the Spaniard sprung forward and pistol-whipped Crampton across the jaw. The plump British reporter fell backwards like a sack of potatoes.

'Move it,' the policeman shouted, waving his gun at the TV crew. He kicked Crampton in the gut. 'Get up. Get over there'. The officer moved to shut the double doors once again, his semi-automatic pistol in his hand, but as he closed it someone shoved it from the other side. It was now the policeman who fell to the floor as five Guardia Civil officers in green uniforms burst through the open doors, brandishing their weapons. One of them trained his shotgun on Velásquez's man on the floor, who was pointing his pistol back at the Civil Guard officer. They shouted at each other in Spanish as the remaining officers advanced into the room.

'Everybody drop their guns,' their officer shouted. 'You are all under arrest'.

Ortega, Fernandez and Velásquez's men pointed their weapons at the new arrivals as they edged forward, then back at each other, uncertain where the most significant peril came from.

Pickering pointed his pistol at the leading Civil Guard officer, gripping it with both hands.

Velásquez lowered herself to the floor along with her lawyer. A violent firefight was only seconds away, and Eddie knew it.

'Go,' he whispered to Veronica. She crawled out from under

DEN OF SNAKES

the table, took a quick glance at the scene playing out behind her, before moving towards the fire escape door, staying low. Kenny stood, beckoning at her and Eddie to come.

The man Señora Velásquez had ordered to recover the TV camera, was now struggling to get to his feet while being shouted at by the Civil Guard officer holding the shotgun.

Nearby, one of the East End crew had his submachine gun trained on one of Velásquez's police officers, who pointed his Beretta pistol back at him. The policeman was shouting in his mother tongue, the Londoner roaring back in a thick cockney accent. As the man backed away, he bumped into Juan Fernandez who was attempting to take cover under his table.

The policeman toppled to the floor, knocking a glass of water over on the table.

The glass fell onto its side, and rolled slowly towards the edge of the table before falling off and smashing onto the floor.

And then the shooting started.

Eddie did not stop to see who had fired the first shots. He bent down, grabbed the handle on the metal case, yanked on it with all his strength, and bolted towards the fire door. Behind him, a cacophony of small arms fire, yelling and tortured screaming erupted. He sensed bullets flying close by, and saw holes appearing in the wall ahead of him near the fire escape. Veronica was almost through it already. Kenny was squatting in the open door waving at her and Eddie to come. Fragments of plaster and wood were landing on the floor in front of them.

Eddie darted left and right to evade the gunfire coming his way, with the weight of the metal case hindering his movements. A bullet flew past his ear, so close he felt the wave of hot air. He flung the case through the door and dived into the hallway beyond. A series of holes punched through the door a second later, covering him in splintered wood and broken glass.

'Get a fucking move on,' Kenny screamed from down the corridor, his arm around Veronica.

Eddie could see who had shot at him. It was Pickering. The

Cockney was scrambling to reload his pistol with a fresh magazine and Eddie froze as the leader of the East End crew lifted the gun towards him and took aim. But Pickering did not get the chance to shoot.

Sophia Velásquez stood behind him holding a police carbine and shot the East Ender in the back. As Pickering dropped to the floor, blood spraying from his body with each bullet, Eddie heard Velásquez shout, 'Nobody calls me a fucking dago!' Seconds later Velásquez fell victim to a burst to her stomach from the East Ender with the MAC10.

Some table cloths were burning, and the room was filling with smoke. A chandelier crashed to the tile floor in a crescendo of light and noise, but even that was eclipsed by the blast of what could only have been a concussion grenade. The room went black, but the barrage of gun fire and screaming continued.

Eddie lay on his back, open-mouthed. Nothing he had seen in Northern Ireland or the Falklands could compare to this madness.

'Are you fuckin' coming or what?' shouted Kenny.

Eddie shook his head to divorce himself from the scenes of intensifying carnage playing out in the conference room. He grabbed hold of the case and forced himself to his feet. There was blood on his trousers, he had no idea if it was his.

He lifted the case and started running as fast as his feet would carry him.

CHAPTER THIRTY-NINE
THE DEVIL YOU KNOW

'You've got everything in that case, right?' said Kenny as they approached the door to the Hotel Fuerte's underground car park. Kenny held the door open and ushered Eddie and Veronica through.

'Most of it, yeah,' Eddie answered. Eddie scanned the car park but could not see Kenny's Mercedes. 'Where's your motor?' he said, panting from the exertion of running while holding the case down two flights of stairs and along several corridors.

Kenny did not answer, but it was at that point that Eddie noticed that the older man was holding a silver revolver. Random memories were returning to him and connecting as his blood replenished with fresh oxygen. Kenny had not had his gun when he had collected Eddie earlier. 'Where d'you pick up the shooter?' Eddie asked.

Kenny backed away, his finger tapping on the trigger. A voice answered from behind Eddie, and in that instant everything became clear. It was a voice he had known since his early childhood. Veronica raised her hands to her face. She looked shocked.

Or was it fear?

'I gave it to him, bruv'.

Eddie swivelled around to see his brother ambling towards him, holding a semi-automatic pistol. Eddie was dumbstruck. A wave of nausea swept over him. Charlie stopped ten feet from his brother and pointed at the case. 'I'll be taking that'.

Eddie's fingers tightened around the handle, and he moved backwards.

Charlie pointed the gun at his brother's chest. 'Don't be fucking stupid. Gimme the case then you and her get to walk away'. He gestured at Kenny to take the case. 'I got them covered, Ken'.

Kenny stuffed his pistol into the back of his belt and approached Eddie. Eddie glared at him.

'Why?' said Eddie.

'It was always gonna end this way. Once the money dried up'.

'They were your friends,' said Eddie, incredulous.

'Villains don't have friends,' Kenny answered, a dirty grin on his face. 'And the money from the drug deal goes a lot further when there's only two of yer'.

'It goes even further when there's only one,' said Charlie.

Kenny froze, the sudden realisation of his staggering error writ raw across his face. He slowly lifted his hands and turned back towards Charlie. 'But, Charlie. We -'.

Charlie shot him twice in the sternum, the blood from the exit wounds in his back splattering across Eddie's face. Veronica screamed as Kenny's body went limp, then fell backwards like an toppled Spruce tree. He laid there on his back, his limbs twitching and with blood frothing in his open mouth as his life-force seeped away. Veronica fell to her knees, sobbing.

'This ain't how I wanted it,' said Charlie. 'That's the honest truth'.

'What did you want then?' said Eddie, edging backwards, putting his body between Veronica and his brother's smoking pistol.

Charlie took a step forward, training the gun on Eddie once more. 'You know what. For us to be a team again. The Lawson brothers - back together, like the old times'. Charlie's eyes betrayed the rose-tinted memories to which he was referring.

Eddie could hear the wailing of distant sirens approaching. 'We were never together,' he said, still shuffling back towards the car park door.

'What are you talking about, bruv?' said Charlie. His surprise seemed genuine.

'Brother? You weren't no brother to me,' said Eddie. 'You never gave a fuck about me'.

'That ain't true'.

'You never gave a fuck about mum and dad, neither'.

Charlie's finger tightened around the trigger. His face twitched with anger. 'They weren't *your* parents,' he said. 'Now, if you want to make me really angry, you keep shooting your mouth off, and we'll find out how far brotherly love goes'.

'Give him what he wants, Eddie,' Veronica pleaded.

Charlie glanced at her, then back at Eddie. 'She's a smart one, her. Knows what it takes to survive'. He grinned. 'Does what she has to. Does *who* she has to'. He laughed. 'Now, gimme that case, and you and your slut can walk away. I promise'.

Eddie had no leverage, and he knew it. He lowered the case to the concrete floor and backed away, taking Veronica's hand and directing her back towards the car park door.

'Clever boy,' said Charlie as he squatted down beside the case and thumbed at the small metal wheels on the first of the combination locks, still holding the pistol in the other hand.

'Go to the door,' Eddie whispered to Veronica. She remained rooted to the spot, her eyes fixed on Charlie's gun. He pushed her hard as the first lock clicked open. 'We're going,' said Eddie, he turned around and started walking.

The door was just a few feet away when Charlie called out. 'Wait'.

Eddie froze, his body braced, expecting the corkscrew-like impact of a bullet at any moment.

'They always knew you were the better one. Mum, for sure. Dad too, though he might never have said it'. Charlie's eyes were full of sadness. 'Go. Fuck off'.

Eddie did not need telling twice - he knew what was about to happen. He grabbed Veronica's arm, pulled the door open and pushed her through, closing it behind him. 'Run,' he said. 'Fucking run'. They hurried back along the corridor they had traversed only a few minutes earlier with the now-deceased Kenny. The hotel's fire alarms were clanging as they approached the door to the stairwell that led back upstairs.

'What's happening?' Veronica shouted as Eddie kicked it open.

'I took everything out of the case'.

'What?' she said.

'I filled it up with telephone directories and free newspapers,' said Eddie, pushing the door shut behind them. As he moved towards the stairs, they heard two loud cracks. Splinters of wood appeared in the door behind them, and holes punched into the cinderblock wall opposite it, spitting grey dust into the air. 'And Charlie just found out'.

They sprinted as fast as they could back up to the fire door to the ground level reception area. Eddie opened it just enough to peek inside, but spied a Guardia Civil officer standing on the other side, his radio crackling with activity. Two more stood guarding the lobby entrance, assault rifles at the ready. Eddie glanced at his shirt, which was splattered with Kenny's blood. They were not getting out that way. He eased the door shut. 'Up another flight,' he whispered.

They charged up another two flights of stairs, back to the door that led into the corridor that went to the conference room that had been the scene of the mammoth firefight ten minutes earlier.

'You didn't trust me,' said Veronica as they pounded up the stairs.

'What?'

'You gave me the case to look after,' she said.

Eddie peered down the staircase to see Charlie emerging from the car park at the bottom of the stairs. 'How could I know who to trust? Everyone was using me. You used me'. He peered through the glass door into the conference room. The sprinkler system had engaged and was dousing the flames that still rose from the stacks of furniture that had caught alight. Bloodied corpses lay strewn around the floor in pools of maroon, a variety of weaponry surrounding them. Seeing no signs of life, he yanked the door open and, after one more check for any movement, entered. He pointed to the secondary entrance on the opposite side of the room. 'There,' he said to Veronica. 'Go. Look straight ahead and go'. He pushed her forward, then grabbed a wooden chair and rammed it under the door handle. That should block Charlie's path, he thought.

He followed Veronica, covering his mouth to protect himself from the acrid smoke. She had slowed, trying to pick her way through the dead henchman, cockney gang members and corrupt policemen. He saw the crumpled, bloody bodies of Pickering, Fernandez and Doña Valáquez as he grabbed her hand and pulled her across the slippery surface towards a set of oak doors beyond. The intense smoke stung his eyes. 'Stay low,' he shouted above the din of the fire alarms.

They were almost at the wooden doors when they sprung open and Charlie stumbled into the room, panting. He had somehow found an alternative route and outflanked them. He lifted the gun towards Eddie, wiped sweat from his eyes with his sleeve, and marched towards them.

'Where the fuck is it?'

'It's safe,' said Eddie, knowing that he and Veronica were as good as dead if his brother believed anything else.

Charlie stepped over the intermingled limbs of legs of

several bodies. So intent was he on getting to his brother, he failed to notice that one of the men was still breathing.

'Charlie,' Eddie called out as the man, one of the East Enders, pushed himself up and reached for a submachine gun at his side.

Unsure if this was some attempt at diversion, Charlie kept his pistol pointing at Eddie but risked a quick glance behind him. The wounded man was inserting a fresh magazine into his gun. Charlie swivelled around just as the Londoner pulled the trigger. A healthy individual would have mown all three of them down in seconds, but the man had a head wound and with blood trickling into his eyes, his aim was wayward. Fire spat forth from his gun, one of which grazed Charlie's leg, but Lawson senior dispatched the wounded assailant with three rounds to the chest, and the Cockney slumped back down. Charlie spun back around, his gun pointing once more at his younger brother.

'Eddie just saved your life,' said Veronica.

'And I'll return the favour. If he gives me what I want'.

'Look around, Charlie,' said Eddie. 'It's over'. The brothers stood five yards apart, eyes locked on each other, saying nothing. Searching for a tell. Charlie lowered the gun, as if steeling himself for the task ahead.

'Too many people have died,' said Veronica. 'You need to stop this'. Charlie cast his eyes towards her. They were stone cold. Remorseless.

'And that,' he said. 'Is why I can't stop'. He lifted the gun towards Veronica and shot her in the thigh. She screamed and fell to the floor, clutching at her left leg.

'No,' Eddie yelled. He hurtled at his brother. Charlie got another shot off, grazing Eddie in the forearm, but it failed to stop him and the pair smashed into each other like a pair of opposing prop forwards.

Eddie grabbed Charlie's hand that held the pistol and forced it towards the floor. Another shot rang out, the bullet heading off across the length of the vast room. Eddie landed a blow on his brother's cheek, but it lacked the power needed to do any damage and Charlie slammed Eddie in the ear with a fist, turning his world dark for a moment.

They grappled on the wet floor, each failing to land meaningful blows, all the time trying to gain control of the black pistol. Eddie scrambled on top of Charlie for a moment, but received a jarring knee to his groin. He winced, one hand still clamped onto Charlie's wrist, and brought his open palm down onto his brother's nose. Charlie groaned, and his hold on the gun failed. It slid across the water-soaked parquet floor. Eddie made a move to seize it but Charlie, showing a nimbleness that belied his physique, grabbed Eddie by the throat, his fingers digging deep, pushing his brother back away from the gun.

They twisted away from it, Charlie on top of Eddie with two hands on his brother's neck.

'Charlie -', Eddie pleaded, now struggling for air.

'We could have done grand things,' said Charlie. He had his knee on Eddie's chest, directing all of his excess bulk upon his younger brother while squeezing his throat with all his strength.

Eddie fought to dig his fingers into his brother's tight grasp, but the lack of oxygen diminished his energy. He poked at Charlie's face with one hand, scratching his cheeks, but Charlie lifted himself higher, out of Eddie's reach. Eddie started to blackout and would have done so had a wooden chair not then crashed across Charlie's head.

Veronica stood shaking at Eddie's side, her left leg drenched in blood before she collapsed back to the hard floor. Eddie gasped for breath. Charlie was on all fours to his left, clutching the back of his head. The blow of the chair had knocked the wind out of his brother, but he would quickly recover.

The gun was close by him.

Eddie rolled towards a broken Perrier bottle, reached for it, pushed himself to his knees, and up on his feet. Still dazed, he wiped the blood and blackened water from his eyes and took a step towards Charlie, but he was too late - his brother had recovered the pistol.

Veronica lay moaning a few yards away to Eddie's left. She was trying to drag herself away, leaving a trail of blood on the wooden floor. Eddie stumbled towards her but then heard the pistol being cocked. He twisted to face Charlie, who stood motionless, observing Veronica's struggles.

'Dad was right about you. You were too soft'. He lifted the gun towards Veronica. 'Did she tell you about that porno she was in?' said Charlie. 'I made her recreate it. Just for me'.

'Please don't do this, bruv'.

'Bruv?' said Charlie, still aiming the gun towards Veronica. 'But that's the thing, Eddie. It's just like you said. We ain't really brothers, are we?' He glanced back at Veronica, pure malice in his eyes.

'Please don't,' Eddie begged, but his pleas fell on deaf ears as Charlie took aim and shot Veronica in the chest. She screamed and dropped flat to the floor. Eddie yelled. He started towards his brother, but the gun was trained back on Eddie. Charlie backed away, spitting blood to the floor.

'I need what was in that case. I told you, I ain't never going back to the slammer'. Veronica was still alive but was struggling to breathe. Eddie put his hand into his trouser pocket and pulled out his hotel key. He held it up for Charlie to see.

'*Hotel El Pachucho*. Room 44. It's under the bed'.

'Toss it over,' said Charlie, training the pistol on his brother. Eddie did as he was told and Charlie caught the key. He examined it for a second, verifying it was real. 'It weren't supposed to end like this,' he said. He took aim at Eddie, his finger curling around the trigger. 'But if you ain't my brother, then you're a loose end'.

Eddie stared at the dark inner barrel of the gun, waiting for the explosion. A peculiar thought occurred to him - would he see the bullet that killed him? He closed his eyes.

He felt the pain in his shoulder before he heard the gunshot. The bullet's kinetic energy spun him around, and he stumbled backwards. He grasped at the wound and sank to his knees, expecting the second shot any moment.

But no *coup de grâce* was to follow.

Charlie howled in agony and Eddie opened his eyes to see his brother grasping at a knife jammed into his calf, the hilt of the blade embedded in one side, the point protruding from the other.

Daniel Ortega lay a few feet away, his white shirt stained red with blood. Despite the gunshot wound to his hip, the Spaniard was slithering away from Charlie, one leg trailing limp under the other. Charlie raised his pistol and fired twice, the first missing by an inch, the second catching Ortega in the heel of one foot. The Spaniard cried out but kept pushing forward.

'You…fucking…dago…bastard,' said Charlie, phlegm dripping from his open mouth. He reached down, grasped the knife and yanked it out, letting loose an agonised roar. He dropped the blade at his feet and stumbled towards Ortega. Despite the gaping wound in his leg, which was now oozing blood, Charlie caught up with the Spaniard and kicked him in the ribs. 'Turn over', he yelled. 'Look at me, you piece of shit'.

Ortega stopped crawling, paused for a moment, then rolled over to lay flat on his back, looking up at Charlie, smirking. 'I know you, Lawson. I always knew you. I saw what you really were'.

Charlie spat a ball of red saliva at the Spaniard and leaned over him. 'Yeah, and what did you see?' he said, the gun pointing at Ortega's head, a look of delicious expectancy on his face.

Ortega lifted his head towards the gun, his eyes locked on the Englishman's. 'I look at you, Charlie Lawson,' he said, through gritted teeth. 'And I see nothing'.

Charlie pointed the gun at Ortega's shoulder and fired. The Spaniard grimaced, but did not cry out. Charlie pushed the barrel to Ortega's forehead. 'What do you see now?' he said.

They were to be Charlie Lawson's last words.

Eddie, having picked up the knife that Charlie had pulled from his leg, had rammed it forward with all his might through his brother's rib cage and straight into his heart.

The gun fell from Charlie's hand, and he sank to the floor, pulling his brother down to his knees. He grabbed for Eddie's hand and glared at his adopted sibling for a few seconds, blood trickling from his open mouth, then crashed to the floor. A pool of dark red grew out from underneath him, diluting with the water from the sprinklers.

'Eddie,' Veronica called. Her voice weak.

Eddie backed away from his brother's lifeless corpse and crawled over to where she lay on her back, one leg folded under the other. Her breathing was laboured now - like a series of rapid, lethargic hiccups. Eddie tried as best as he could to lift her, his body shaking from its own trauma.

She somehow mustered the effort to raise a hand to his cheek. It was cold. He looked deep into her eyes. 'We would have been good together, Eddie Lawson,' she whispered.

He wrapped his arms around her. Her blouse now sodden with the blood from the wound in her chest, her eyes closed, and she fell limp in his arms. The pain in his side from the bullet wound was excruciating, but he continued to hold her. Tears ran down his cheeks. He would have remained there, holding her surrounded by bloodied bodies, discarded firearms and damp smouldering furniture until the police had arrived if it had not been for a gentle hand on his shoulder.

'She's gone,' said the man who had crept up behind him. Eddie looked up to see the sympathetic face of former Detective Constable Philip Metcalf. 'We need to get you out of here'.

CHAPTER FORTY
FAMILY COME FIRST

Two weeks later

Eddie stood under a bus shelter shielding from the incessant drizzle, the collar of his donkey jacket turned up to block out the autumnal chill. He peered at one of the grey, pebble-dashed terraced maisonettes across the street.

A postman ambled past, thumbing through a bundle of letters, and shot Eddie a suspicious glance.

'Morning,' said Eddie before taking a drag from his cigarette.

The front door of one dwelling opened and a girl with long blonde hair emerged from within, holding a satchel in one hand and a metal lunch box in the other. Eddie leaned back behind the scratched glass of the shelter. The girl wore a dark green skirt and school blazer. 'Hurry, mummy,' she shouted. 'We'll be late'.

A woman's voice answered from within. 'We've got ten minutes, Mary. It's fine'. The woman, a slender brunette in white jeans and a black woollen coat, stepped from the door and pulled it shut behind her. She opened an umbrella and reached for her daughter's hand. 'Come on, then'.

Eddie observed from his vantage spot as his ex-wife and their daughter wandered away. Once they were out of view, he flicked the cigarette butt into the gutter, and cut across the road towards the front door. He reached into his pocket and removed a sealed white envelope, about the size of a paperback, and glanced at the message he had scribbled on it.

> *This should cover the rent for a few months.*
> *I'll send more when I can.*
> *Tell Mary I love her. Ed.*

He thrust the packet through the metal letterbox, then strolled away.

CHAPTER FORTY-ONE
THE CROWN JEWELS

Chelsea Bridge, London.

Eddie stood gazing out onto the dirty brown waters of the Thames as a rubbish barge throbbed by underneath, belching black smoke into the cold, grey London sky. A District line train trundled across the railway bridge a hundred yards to the east, heading towards the smog-stained hulking mass of Battersea power station. He watched, with a certain amount of satisfaction, the passing commuters as they strode past, oblivious to his presence, and he wondered if there could ever have been a different reality in which he could have been one of them.

'Edward Lawson,' a man's voice called out. It was Jeremy Crampton. 'I would have thought you would be more careful,' he said. 'What if I had been a policeman?'

Eddie smirked. He had been well aware of the overweight TV reporter approaching for several minutes. Crampton, whose face still bore the evidence of his tribulations in Spain over the previous weeks, was lugging a Slazenger sports holdall over one shoulder, the exertion getting the better of him. The reporter wiped the sweat from his forehead with a handkerchief, nodding towards the battered beige suitcase at Eddie's feet. 'Is that it?' Eddie nodded.

'You got the money?' he said.

'I do,' Crampton replied and dropped the holdall to his feet. He wiped his face again, knelt down and unzipped the orange bag to reveal several bundles of banknotes. 'Thirty thousand. Small denominations. Used notes, just like you said'. He pushed himself back up to his feet with a wince. 'Now, show me what you've got for me'.

Eddie nodded and reached down to lift the suitcase onto the stone wall at the side of the bridge. He flipped the latches and opened it. Crampton's eyes lit up, and he took a deep intake of air at the sight of the myriad documents, notepads, wads of photos, videotapes and audio cassettes.

'Is that everything?'

'Pretty much,' said Eddie. Crampton raised a hand towards the case, but Eddie seized it and fixed the reporter a firm stare. 'You could do a lot of damage with this,' he said. 'All these people. Businessmen, bankers, celebrities, sports stars, pop stars, politicians, police officers. Other journalists. So much dirt. I reckon you could make television shows for ten years with all this'.

'You have no idea,' said Crampton, unable to hide his glee at the treasure trove in front of him.

'It doesn't bother you about the lives you would destroy?' Eddie said.

Crampton let out a disbelieving snort. 'Like you give a shit,' he said. 'I brought you the money, give me what I came for'.

'I don't reckon I will'.

'What?' said Crampton in disbelief, only then noticing the gun stuffed into Eddie's trouser belt. It was the deactivated, silver-plated Luger that his brother had given him. It was incapable of firing, but Crampton was not to know that and he froze. 'We had a deal'.

'I'm a fucking villain,' said Eddie, grinning. 'I lied. Now, smile for the camera'. He pointed towards the roadside to where a parked black cab sat parked on a double yellow line. The driver was holding a compact camera and took a series of quick photographs.

'What is this?' blurted Crampton.

'This,' said Eddie. 'Is me putting an end to this whole fucking shit show'.

'Now, wait a minute, Lawson. If you think I'm -'.

Crampton paused mid-sentence as Eddie heaved at the open suitcase and pushed it over the edge of the bridge. It plunged into the murky water below, followed by a cloud of multicoloured paper. Eddie stepped aside as the TV reporter leapt forward in a pathetic attempt to stop it. 'No!' he screamed, spinning back to where Eddie has been standing only Eddie was no longer there.

Eddie was already closing the passenger door of the taxi behind him, waving. 'Thanks for the dosh,' he shouted through the open window as the black cab pulled away. Crampton lurched after it in a fruitless attempt to get to the open window, but he could never have made it. Eddie chuckled as the TV reporter dropped to his knees at the side of the road behind him.

'Enjoy that, did we, Edward?' said the driver. It was Philip Metcalf. He glanced at Eddie in the rearview mirror.

'You have no idea,' said Eddie as he opened the holdall and examined the banknotes. 'He will have a hell of a time explaining that to his bosses at ITV'.

'That he will,' said Metcalf.

'Half of this is yours'.

The former detective laughed. 'That's terribly kind of you,' he said. 'But I think I'll draw the line at driving a wanted felon to the ferry port if it's all the same to you'. He gave Eddie a fatherly look in the mirror. 'Just make sure you put it to good use'.

'That I will'. Eddie sat back, retrieved a packet of Benson and Hedges from his pocket and flipped the golden carton lid open. He stared at the cigarettes inside for a moment, but closed the lid and flung the packet out the window.

Metcalf raised an eyebrow in the mirror.

'Figured it's about time I quit', said Eddie. He placed his hands behind his head and yawned. 'How's the new career suiting you?' he asked.

Metcalf grinned. 'Extremely well, as it happens. And it's certainly a lot safer'.

It began to rain, and Metcalf switched on the windscreen wipers.

'What about you, young man? What does the future hold for you now?'

Eddie looked at the grey cityscape outside. 'Well,' he said. 'I've only been back in this bloody country two weeks, and I've already had enough of the weather. And besides, there's a gipsy waitress in Salamanca I owe a meal to'.

THE END

PLEASE POST AN AMAZON REVIEW

Thank you for reading this story. I sincerely hope that you enjoyed it and I would very much appreciate your support.

Reader reviews are the lifeblood for most authors. Without reviews, it is very hard for readers to find a book. It would therefore mean a lot to me if you would take 5 minutes to provide an honest review and let others know what you thought.

Search for *'Den of Snakes Action Thriller'* or 'Damian Vargas' on Amazon.

ALSO BY DAMIAN VARGAS

Six Hard Days In Andalusia

An Action Thriller

A worn-out gangster who seeks redemption before he meets his maker. The prodigal daughter who has fallen from grace. A corrupt mayor bent on building a criminal empire, and who has the local police and politicians in his pocket. A bitter ex-pat who comes across the scene of a drug deal gone wrong. And an unfortunate English tourist who gets caught up in the middle of the whole bloody mess.

Head to damianvargasfiction.com for more information, or simply search for the book title on your preferred Amazon store.

The Dark Place

A Suspense Thriller (coming June 2021)

They escaped justice in 1945, but vengeance has found them.

La Mesita Blanca, Costa del Sol, 1970. When Inspector Jesus Garcia is awoken by a call from the chief of police, he realises that this will be a day like no other. A fifteen-year-old boy – the son of one of the most influential members of his town's secretive community of German nationals – has gone missing.

In the week he was due to retire, Garcia is told in no uncertain terms that he has one day to find the boy and to catch the culprit. Should he fail, it will be more than his retirement that is at risk.

Garcia, who had survived the brutality of the Spanish civil war and the three decades that followed by steering clear of situations such as this one, must now confront not only his own past, but the legacy of his nation's troubled history if he is to save the boy. With the secret police on their way, Garcia finds himself embroiled in the murky world of fugitive war criminals, vengeful Nazi hunters and the Machiavellian intent of multiple state actors.

An innocent life is at stake, but as Garcia quickly discovers, there are secrets that must be kept, a history that cannot be told, and that monsters hide in dark places.

Head to my web site and sign-up for my author mailing list to get advance warning of when it will be released (save money on the Amazon pre-order).

damianvargasfiction.com

ABOUT THE AUTHOR

Damian Vargas is an emerging author of action thrillers with a dark vein of humour.

Damian is a self-exiled Brit, living and working in Spain on the Costa del Sol. A child of the 1970s and 1980s, he was brought up on an entertainment diet of intrepid adventure novels, gritty crime dramas, epic war stories and low-budget British science fiction television.

Experiencing everyday life in southern Spain opened Damian's eyes to the dark underworld that occurs (mostly) beyond the view of the annual influx of British and other holidaymakers. These regular criminal goings-ons, coupled with the rich tapestry of life and stunning locations on 'The Costa del Crime', sparked a deep desire to write fast-paced action and thriller stories. ***Six Hard Days in Andalusia*** was the first of these and was followed by the prequel, ***Den Of Snakes***, both of which are available on Amazon. Several more books are planned, including ***The Dark Place*** (due for release June 2021), the plot of which revolves around a secretive community of German nationals living in a secluded mountain village in the south of Spain, and an British WW2 veteran who arrives to expose their terrible wartime crimes.

His motto is "Wisdom Comes To Those Who Stray", he has a love for indie/punk rock in dank seedy venues, a fascination with the number 27, and harbours an intense dislike of spiders.

He once met Mark Zuckerberg, but couldn't think of anything intelligent to say, and David Hasselfhoff, while dressed up as Ron Burgundy.

- amazon.com/author/damianvargasfiction
- facebook.com/damianvargasfiction
- instagram.com/vargas_fiction
- pinterest.com/vargasfiction

THANK YOU

It means the world to me that you read this.

If you have not already done so, please consider signing up for my mailing list. You can get free eBooks, be part of my advanced reader teams and get to hear when new books are being released before anyone else. I won't spam you and I will never share your contact details with anyone else.

Since I was a child I have entertained myself by constructing stories. I do it on planes and trains, in cars, on beaches, in dull meetings and, frequently, to get to sleep. Making up stories has always been enjoyable for me. That is why I write.

Damian Vargas.

DamianVargasFiction.com
damian@damianvargasfiction.com

SOCIAL MEDIA

More stories coming soon! You can get free short stories, find out when my next books are coming out and grab special offers on my web site. Sign up for my newsletter from the link below:
- www.damianvargasfiction.com

Follow Damian Vargas on social media:
- Pinterest (*character, location and other research*)
- Instagram (*location scouting*)
- Facebook page (*author community*)
- Twitter (*book news & ramblings*)

Get in touch by email:
- info@sbfiction.com

Printed in Great Britain
by Amazon

74398643R00260